DEDICATION

For my husband who is my best friend, my greatest fan and supporter, my expert grillmaster and sous-chef, and my only love of 52 years and counting!
Thank you for everything you are, my sweetie!

WILD LILY

THOSE NOTORIOUS AMERICANS, BOOK 1

CERISE DELAND

ISBN for Digital: 978-1-953878-11-3

ISBN for Print: 978-1-953878-12-0

Photographic credit: Period Images

Cover Art: Wicked Smart Designs

❀ Created with Vellum

WILD LILY, BOOK 1, THOSE
NOTORIOUS AMERICANS

Money can buy anything, can't it? Those brash Americans--their dollars and charms work wonders. Until they learn that money can buy anything...but love.

An American heiress with brains, a fortune—and no desire to wed to gain a drafty castle and an indifferent husband.

A marquess with a disastrous view of marriage, tumbledown estate, debts—and a conscience that won't let him wed for money.

Can he allow himself to admit he loves her for herself?

Can she surrender to a man who fears the high price of love?

Lily Hanniford is an American heiress with beauty, wits— and the unique desire to wed for more than a drafty castle and a loveless marriage.

The Marquess of Chelton needs money. A lot of it. Not an affair. Especially not with the delightful American who believes wedded bliss should include such ridiculous ideas as laughter—and love.

But they both desire what they should not want—each

other. Too bad, passion has prices. And both Lily and Chelton are caught.

Is the cost of love too high a price to pay for Chelton?

And is the cost of surrender too dear a price to pay for Lily?

WILD LILY, BOOK 1
DARING WIDOW, BOOK 2
SWEET SIREN, BOOK 3
SCANDALOUS HEIRESS, Book 4
RAVISHING CAMILLE, Book 5
IF YOU WERE THE ONLY GIRL IN THE WORLD, Book 6
LET ME CALL YOU SWEETHEART, Book 7

CHAPTER 1

September 12, 1877
Boulevard Haussmann
Paris, France

"$\mathcal{B}$e quiet as a mouse," Lily whispered to her cousin Marianne as they took the first step down the central staircase toward the foyer. "Papa arrived home a few minutes ago. I bet he's in his study and maybe he hasn't seen that scandal sheet."

"And never does," said Marianne, holding her hat on her head as she ran. "Hopefully, the comtesse should be here for our appointment."

"So we might get past Papa's study easily if—"

"Oh, no." Marianne halted mid-stride. "Foster."

The Hanniford family butler here in Paris appeared at the bottom of the stairs. His wispy white hair fell was combed back in perfection and he focused on Lily and Marianne with droopy eyes like a sad bloodhound. He'd unlocked the front

1

door to them both at midnight with his usual silence. Lily had asked him not to mention to her father what time they arrived home, but she was certain the man, referred to tycoon Killian Hanniford by another American millionaire, would not withhold such information if asked.

She descended the steps, her hope of concealing last night's escapade from her father, fleeing on a sigh.

"Miss Hanniford," he said, directing his gaze at her, "and Mrs. Roland, please follow me."

"Foster," Lily said, wishing for a clue as she tried to keep pace with the servant's crisp walk. "Does he know?"

The man turned his head and considered her, dare she say, with pity. "He does, Miss. The tabloid is in his possession."

Marianne clutched her arm. "I thought the footman said the one he brought to us this morning was the only copy on the doorstep?"

Lily's heart skipped a beat. "He did."

"Mr. Hanniford," said Foster, "brought home his own copy when he arrived minutes ago."

"Oh, dear." Lily might have guessed her father, who prided himself on up-to-the-minute knowledge of any importance to his family or his businesses, would learn of her and Marianne's escape to Montmartre last night. "Not good."

"Precisely," said the butler as he knocked on the door to his employer's study and opened it for the two women. "Sir, Miss Hanniford and Mrs. Roland."

Lily and Marianne advanced on the carpet in front of the forty-four-year-old millionaire whom many in America feared, envied and even admired. He stood tall and imperious, hands clasped behind his back, still in his evening clothes. The sleek black wool was a match for his thick hair and his large ebony eyes, while the ivory scarf and shirt, the gold waistcoat, were rich counterbalances to his ruddy complexion and the commanding demeanor that beguiled women and intimidated adversaries. In his hand was a copy of the broadsheet that the family footman had given to Lily's maid this morning.

This interview would not be pleasant. Lily girded herself for the coming storm.

"I understand from Foster and Thomas, the downstairs footman, that you've already seen this."

Lily nodded.

He leaned toward her. "What's that?"

"Yes, sir. I have."

"Perhaps you'd like to learn too that I sent Thomas out and he has returned, confirming that local Parisian kiosks have hundreds of copies for sale on every corner."

Oh, a disaster. She clasped her hands together, even as she understood that one did not show weakness in front of a man like her father. "I am sorry for this, Papa."

"Sorry," he said as if he considered one who had spilled tea on the expensive Aubusson rug. "Intriguing word."

She winced.

"Wouldn't you like to choose another?"

"Sir?"

"Such as 'appalled'?"

"Regret. That's a better word."

"It is. But it does not match my sentiment."

"No, sir." She was certain it didn't.

He stared at her. "I won't debate this with you any longer, Lily." Her father threw the scandal sheet on top of his desk and peered at her over his wire-rimmed glasses. "I want only a good marriage for you. Last week it was riding in the Bois de Boulougne without an escort. The week before, trying a bicycle on the sidewalk. Now this. Why must you fight me with these escapades?"

Yes, she'd gone to the Montmartre café and watched those women throw up their skirts in the *cancan*. Shocking as that was, her night had been thrilling. But she did have two defenses. "I didn't go to embarrass you, Papa."

"You did anyway."

Still. What was she? His to dispense with? Order about? She was his daughter, almost of age. Almost. And she countered him with her other weapon. "No business dealing of yours depends on my behavior."

He arched a black brow. "You are not so naïve as that."

She wasn't. But she'd gone for another reason. One her father repeatedly refused to accept. "I don't want a husband—"

"Eventually, every young woman has one," he countered. "And I have the money to ensure you—"

"Get one. *Any* one!" She flourished a hand.

"Not true. I would not marry you off to any man unworthy of you."

"I hope not."

"I take that as an insult, my girl."

"I don't mean to be ungrateful."

"You are, sadly. But in the meantime," he said and punched a finger into the paper, "your antics will not endear you to any man, rich or poor."

Lily Hanniford held her ground. She had twenty years of practice standing up to her sire, a wizard of finance and a ruthless shipping magnate whose wealth stunned many on both sides of the Atlantic. But how could she predict that a Parisian artist might find it amusing to caricature an American girl visiting a cabaret? "I wanted simply to *see* the *cancan*, Papa. Not *do* it."

He set his jaw and glared first at her and then her cousin by her side. "I hold you responsible, Marianne. You are older and should be wiser. I told you to be prudent. Keep Lily in hand."

"It's not Marianne's fault." Lily sent a consoling look at her pretty blonde cousin who always withstood Black Killian Hanniford's outbursts more stoically than she. "I said she could remain home if she preferred."

"Ah." Hanniford focused on his niece. "So will you tell me you went to this *cabaret*, an innocent to the slaughter?"

Marianne tipped her head to and fro, the look on her face whimsical amusement. She was older than Lily by nine years, a widow, worldly and witness to the savagery of a civil war that had sent her husband to his grave. Because of or perhaps in spite of that, Marianne had a zest for living and a ripe sense of humor. "I may have shown some enthusiasm for the adventure."

"*Some?*" Hanniford snorted. "You probably wanted to learn the dance yourself."

"Hmm. Yes. It is rather difficult," Marianne proclaimed.

Lily suppressed her laugh.

But her father was not amused. No.

Hands on his hips, he glared at Lily. "Who escorted you inside this—this Café de Abbesses?"

Lily winced.

"Tell me, please, you did not go without a man in attendance."

"He was kind." A fellow who had a fancy for her, Lord Pinkhurst, was a sweet man, rich in his own right and therefore without reason to fear Killian Hanniford.

"Kind! Who. Was. He?"

"A gentleman of our acquaintance."

"One of *my* acquaintance?"

Lily shifted from one foot to the other. "Yes."

Hanniford cursed mightily. "His name?"

Lily hated to admit it. "I will not tell you."

"If you fail to reveal his identity, I guarantee you it will go worse for him."

She would not have Pinkie pay prices for his kindness to her. He wanted to marry her, she was certain of it. And perhaps he'd agreed to escort her and Marianne to the *guinguette* to compel her to become his bride, but she wouldn't do it. "If you ask about, if you discover who he is, if you hurt him, Papa, I shall leave for America the first chance I get."

He blinked. "You threaten me?"

She did not flinch. "No, sir. I would not be so unkind."

"I could lock you in your room and throw away the key."

"You could." But won't. "How then to get a groom?"

"Dear heaven. How can this get worse?" He peered up at the ceiling.

Marianne stepped toward his desk. "Uncle Killian, please. We had a wonderful time. The music was gay and charming. The dancers were—"

"Naked?" He glared at her.

Marianne pulled back. "Partially."

He ran a hand over his mouth. "You try me, both of you. Did you dance with your escort?"

Lily shook her head. "No, sir."

"Drink?"

"Oh, yes," Lily said, recalling the wine with a bitter bite, "but it was terrible *vin rouge*."

He snorted. Then he turned to Marianne. "Did you sing?"

Marianne nodded. "Only with the patrons."

"That's some reprieve, I suppose. Why wouldn't you give them your best soprano, Marianne?"

Her emerald eyes sparkled, even as she lifted a shoulder in sheepish delight. "I didn't know the French lyrics."

"And your gentleman saw you both safely home?"

"He did." Lily was happy to tell him that. "In his carriage. We stayed only for a few songs."

"And do you think that brevity lessens the damage you have done to your reputation?"

Lily had no response for that. "Could I hope a man would value a woman with a bit of courage?"

"Or foolhardiness."

There was that. "I agreed to sail to Europe with you for your benefit more than mine."

"Did you now? How kind of you."

"Papa, I—"

"Enough! This," he thundered as he put his fist down on the newspaper, "is not to occur again. Do you hear me?"

"Yes, sir."

"Marianne?"

Her cousin bowed her head. "Yes, Uncle Killian."

"My order is to use this time in Paris wisely. Go to the shops. Buy clothes, perfect your French and make a name for yourselves as the refined beauties you are, not as ladies of the night!"

"Oh, Papa, we wouldn't," Lily rushed to add.

"You think it's fine to drink and dine with artists and riff raff?"

"Oh, sir," Marianne said, "they are poor but happy."

"And very polite," Lily added.

"Dear God." Her father sank to the chair behind him.

Lily kneaded her hands. When her father reached the end of his patience, he would become quiet. Terribly so. Then burst forth with an ultimatum that would end all hope of compromise. "I didn't like the cartoon, either, Papa."

"Oh, really?" He stared at her. "Offended you, did it, that he portrayed you holding up your skirts to show your ankles?"

She nibbled her lower lip. She hated to admit her vulnerable pride. "I hated that he drew me with dollars spilling from my skirt pockets."

Killian Hanniford's swarthy complexion turned livid. "And I suppose we must be grateful he didn't show you lifting your skirts higher like those dancers?"

"Quite so."

He ground his teeth. "Nonetheless, this is not acceptable by you two, the cartoonist or his publisher. For this artist's miscalculation to make fun of my daughter, I have sent for the owner of this rag."

"To come here?" Lily felt as if the air had left her like a pricked balloon.

"Where else?"

"Already?"

He arched a dark disdainful brow. "Would you have me dally?"

"No. No, of course not." She was gratified he'd act to quell the insult to her. But he was known to overreact. "I'd like the artist reprimanded. Warned, you see."

"Not the publication set to ruin?" Hanniford was smiling ruefully, his electric temper masked by his self-deprecating humor.

Lily didn't like people destroyed for their follies. She preferred them scolded. Shown some mercy. Some hope of redemption. "Exactly."

"I'll deal as I see fit."

Oh, my. The publisher might lose his paper. At the very least, the cartoonist would be turned out on the street. Cartoonists in Baltimore and New York had toyed with Black Killian Hanniford's image and paid the ultimate price for their aggression against the man who'd first come to public fame as Baltimore's Black Irish Blockade Runner. Her father had even bought up half share in one of the newspapers who lambasted his actions, silencing any controversy over him.

"Please, Papa. Be kind."

He eyed her. "You mean that?"

"I do." She hated vindictiveness. "I really do."

"What's it worth to you?"

"Sir?"

He considered her with the gaze he trained on adversaries.

She fought to suppress a shiver.

"You heard me. What will you promise me for the courtesy to deal lightly with these men?"

Lily knew enough of her sire to understand that she held few advantages in bargaining with him. She had only one card to play. And she'd already dealt it.

"Well? What say you?"

Lily lifted her chin and stared him in the eye. She had obligations to Marianne who had eagerly anticipated living in Paris, going to the opera and art galleries while she perfected her French. Lily had also made a promise to her younger sister, Ava, who finished her schooling in Manhattan and would arrive in London next June along with their older brother, Pierce. "I promise to be polite, act properly and cause no more scandals."

He barked in laughter. "That's what you were supposed to do anyway. What's in this for me, for what I want?"

She stiffened her spine. "I'll do this for you and Marianne. I'll do it for Ava and Pierce to smooth their way in society. I'll do the Season in London, curtsy and simper and—"

He put up a hand. "Stop. Get to your wager."

If this were any lesser issue, she would have smiled that her father knew her so well. "I will stay for one year."

"One year?" he asked with skepticism.

"To the day."

"And during that time?"

She stood on the precipice of her freedom. "I will entertain any man you deem fit for me to consider as my husband. I'll keep an open mind and an open heart." She swallowed hard and fought to speak the words of her next condition.

He waggled his fingers at her. "Yes, yes, come on. The rest of it."

"But you will not influence me to one man over another. You will not meddle. And you will not buy me a husband."

"And if I refrain, what then?"

"If I find a man I can love, I will tell you and you will approve. No matter who he is, his wealth or lack thereof, or his connections."

He cleared his throat. "I see. And your threat, should I not abide by your condition?"

She had pin money she'd saved. Frugal all her life, she had accumulated more than five thousand dollars of her own. Before she'd left Baltimore, she'd arranged with a bank to extend her a line of credit in Paris and London, should she ever need it. If the banker had ever told her father of this, she didn't know.

But she was ready to reveal the depth of her commitment to directing her own destiny. "I will return home on the first ship I can book passage."

He flexed his square jaw. "And do you think to return to your status as my daughter in my home?"

She had always known how hard Black Killian Hanniford played to achieve his own ends. In business, he was ruthless, driven. But not merciless to his children. His forgiveness of Pierce's folly years ago was her best proof that his love for his family was his Achilles heel. Lily had seen how to hinder him by attacking him there.

She shook back her long dark ringlets over her shoulders. "I would return not to Baltimore but to Texas. Open the ranch that my mother left to me, rebuild the house and live there."

"Alone?"

She considered her clasped hands. "I'd hire a foreman and *vaqueros*. Take my maid. Raise longhorns and quarter horses."

"You wouldn't return to Corpus Christi to marry that doctor you both worked for?"

Marianne and she had volunteered in a small hospital in the small town on the Gulf of Mexico and nursed poor workers afflicted with cholera and all sorts of infections. But their tenure had been short-lived when Hanniford learned of their actions and demanded they come with him to Baltimore and on to Europe.

"No, sir," Lily told him. She didn't love the man.

"Or you?" He turned to Marianne.

It was her cousin who favored nursing and who had mourned the injunction not to aid the doctor and his patients, even as she seized the opportunity to move to Baltimore and live with the Hannifords in style and comfort.

Marianne shook her head in resignation. "I won't return, sir."

And Lily understood that. Marianne was many things. A widow of thirty, a genteel lady of education and breeding, a former mistress of a four-hundred-acre farm near Spotsylvania, a caring nurse of Confederate soldiers wounded on her land, she was all that. But Marianne was also a woman who wanted to laugh again, a lady who yearned to forget the wounded and dying whom she'd tended, and a very accomplished artist who longed to sketch and paint far away from the turmoil of war and pestilence. She did not like conflict of any kind. And she appreciated that her maternal uncle had welcomed her into his family and into his home when she was without hope or hearth. He had granted her a yearly income of fifteen thousand dollars for the rest of her life, in honor of her mother, the dead sister whom he'd loved dearly. Banking the money, she spent little of it and could count herself wealthy in her own right. She owed her Uncle Killian her own allegiance and cooperation and would not risk his disfavor.

"Thank you for that," he said.

Her cousin nodded.

He was silent for a long moment while he examined them. "Very well. We have a deal. One year for you, Lily. And for you, Marianne, my largesse, for as long as you behave discreetly."

His lips spread in a strained smile. "Now go. I understand from Foster you have a fitting at Worth's."

Lily breathed in relief. "We do."

"Well, then spend my money. Buy everything you love. Buy some of what you hate. I told Worth's assistant weeks ago that the sky was no limit. You're both to have everything you need for the Season." He nodded toward the door. "I have an appointment in an hour. I must prepare. So the two of you must get out."

"Thank you, Papa." Lily beamed at him, giddy at the reprieve, delighted she hadn't had to use her father's own indiscretion here in Paris against him to win her case.

"I am grateful, sir," said Marianne.

"Good. Go." He waved them off. "And prove it to me."

They hastened to leave him.

"We must have our coats. Our hats. Where is the comtesse?" Lily was rattling on, nerves jumping inside her as she surveyed the hall. "She should be here by now to accompany us to Worth's."

The Comtesse de Chaumont was an impoverished comely widow whom her father paid handsomely to introduce them to Paris customs and the cream of French society.

But the vast foyer was empty, save for Foster who awaited them with a frown.

Lily's heart was pounding like a mad thing. She'd survived. Bargained. Won! The prize far off, but nonetheless a victory. But soon they'd go to London where men by the droves would dance upon her and kiss her hand. Aside from her sizable dowry, she hated to think why they'd bother. She was passably good looking with ink-black hair, a firm figure and pale blue eyes with rather thick lashes, but she'd seen much lovelier girls. More stunning women.

Yet other aspects of her life had preceded her appearance in any London drawing room. Those were not flattering. 'The Blockade Runner's Daughter with a Dowry Fit for a King' declared one English gossip sheet, describing 'Black' Hanniford's business interests in the City. Another called her 'The Millionaire Cowgirl' and ran a sketch of her riding a bull, her hand in the air as if she were busting a bronco. She was no porcelain doll to pour their tea and smile like a simpleton in their parlors. She had intelligence and health and a desire to spend her days doing something useful. That might not be nursing, but it definitely was not acting like an aimless, spoiled creature with feathers for brains.

"I can't believe he agreed to my condition," she said to her cousin as Foster fetched their coats and parasols from the hall closet. "I know you think I'm mad, but I had to try again."

"And you won!" Marianne smiled at her with twinkling green eyes. "Amazing."

"I always feared I'd walk down the aisle with a bouquet comprised of my newly beloved's tailor's bills." The smile on Lily's face disappeared as she leaned over to whisper. "Now I bet the publisher will not dare put in a cartoon of Papa with his French mistress."

Marianne smoothed the skirts of her day dress. "How right you are."

Foster approached. The butler's long face was a cipher. He'd been recommended to them by the Jeromes, whose daughter Jennie had married the second son of the duke of the Marlborough a few years ago. Mister Jerome had said that Benjamin Foster excelled at smoothing the path for American families in Europe. The servant understood the challenges of etiquette, but he was also discreet, a vital asset to those attempting legitimacy among the old aristocracies.

Marianne turned toward the mirror and checked her hat and her long platinum curls dangling from her elaborate coiffure. "I plan on telling anyone who'll listen how he earned his money."

Lily fingered a ribbon hanging from her red velvet toque. "It's not the kind of story they're used to."

"Definitely not," Marianne said, her forest-green eyes wide with pride. "They're for those who claim supremacy by an accident of birth. Men who rise to power by packing others off to the guillotine. They don't understand men who rise from poverty to wield a fortune. Isn't that right, Foster?"

"Yes, ma'am."

Lily sighed. "Nor do they understand women who don't want to be the doyennes of high society."

"Quite so," said Marianne with a tip of her head. "I personally prefer to become an expert in chocolate macarons."

"And increase the width of your corsets," Lily teased.

"Precisely. Speaking of clothes, where is the comtesse anyway?"

"She would harp at us for a moment's delay for our show-ing," Lily complained. Clemence Bernier, the countess of Chaumont, was never late for a fitting, claiming it the height of incivility. "Foster, do we not have any messages from her?"

"I'm afraid not, Miss." He held up Lily's coat. "This is unlike her."

Lily sniffed. "Very."

"Might she regret and apologize?" Marianne asked with a wry smile.

Lily lifted a finger in imitation of their tutor. "'*Regard!* It is forbidden to be late for your appointments with your designer, your milliner or your jeweler. However, enter a ball an hour later than the invitation. And for the opera, arrive at midnight.'"

Marianne chuckled. "'And two hours late for a rendezvous with your lover.'"

Lily made a face at Marianne. "As if you and I shall ever have lovers."

"Oh, I don't know," Marianne said as she let Foster help her on with her coat.

"You wouldn't!" Lily was laughing.

Marianne met her gaze with serious eyes. "I can dream, can't I?"

"No. You can't. Papa would have you for breakfast."

"Foster," Marianne said to the servant, "you are listening to none of this."

"No, madam. I am quite deaf," he said, but his mouth twitched with a rare smile.

"Shall we go on without the comtesse?" Marianne asked Lily.

"Let's." She considered her cousin's quick change of subject. Marianne had become a widow when her husband had died on the battlefield at Gettysburg more than thirteen years ago. Never, to Lily's knowledge, had she been attracted to another man. Beautiful as she was with a wealth of shining white-blonde hair and eyes green as a glade, Marianne could attract any man she wished. But she had never received anyone in Galveston or Baltimore. None in Paris, either. Yet. "I'm certain she'll meet us there."

Lily allowed Foster to assist her with her coat. "She

wouldn't want to miss the ability to gossip about us to her friends."

"Oh, you have a dastardly view of our dear poor Chaumont."

"Don't you?"

Marianne lifted a shoulder. "She's so eager to please. A little like a pampered hound. When she's not barking orders at you, she reaches for approval."

Marianne stared at herself in the mirror. "I would bet she has a lover."

"Whom she supports on Papa's money."

"Oh, you are bad," Marianne reprimanded her with a grin.

"Foster, do you know any of this? Is our comtesse enamored with a gentleman?"

"Miss, even if I knew, I could not say."

She took her gloves and parasol from him. "I long to hear her explanation. And in the meantime, we can sip Monsieur Worth's white wine and eat his marvelous French cheese."

"The better to grow fat."

"And spill over our corsets." Marianne hooked her arm through Lily's. "All the better to lounge in our morning gowns in flagrant dishabille."

"Outrageous, Madam Roland." Lily had never heard Marianne desire anything. She seemed content living with the Hannifords without a home, husband, or children of her own. So this outré declaration was so deliciously flamboyant of her. Lily chuckled as Foster opened the front door and their coachman doffed his hat. "It's time to order the most expensive silk and satin Papa's money can buy."

CHAPTER 2

"*R*emy, I say. I cannot go on." Julian Ash, the Marquess of Chelton tugged at his linen cuffs as his friend's town coach sped up the Rue de la Paix. "I must sleep. It's two in the afternoon! I'm dead as a rat in a trap."

"If we nap now, we'll never awaken and miss supper with Vicomtesse du Valerie and opening night of the opera." Julian's friend gave him a searing look. With a flourish of a large hand, Andrè Claude Marceau, the Duc de Remy, drew aside the coach's elaborate damask window hangings. "Regard. The day is young."

"And bright." Flinching, Julian jerked away.

"We're dressed for it,," Remy said as he picked at the lapel of his evening coat, his sky-blue eyes merry.

"*Oui?*" Julian shook his head in derision. "Might I point out, however, no one would appreciate our attire?"

The big Frenchman laughed as he always did, deep in his throat, enjoying life to the fullest. "At Mimi's, they don't care how you look."

"Perhaps not. But they will care how we smell." Julian lifted his arm to inhale the aromas wafting up from the sleeve of his own black wool evening coat. The acrid odors of smoke, whiskey and very cheap perfume made his eyes water. "I need a hot bath."

"Come to my house. I'll have Pierre draw one for you."

"Your valet has odd tastes, Remy. Last week when I flopped at your house, the bath he prepared reeked of camellias." Julian fixed a wary eye on his huge Norman friend. "I went to the Rothschilds' ball and smelled like a debutante."

Remy shrugged. "The ladies flocked to you, did they not?"

Julian scowled. "Chickens and hens. A damn silly gaggle."

"All after your title."

"And after you for your mystery."

"That's called charm, old boy." Remy winked and smoothed a nonexistent moustache.

Julian burst out laughing. He shrugged into his coat, but a flash of pain in his head cut his haste. "I must go home. I'm up to nothing but sleep."

The two of them had spent the evening in the card room of the Marquis de Tourelane where every vice was on offer from the finest Sancerre and the purest opium to the prettiest Solange. After such a night, Remy's tawny hair stood askew and his large blue eyes sagged with the night's indulgences. Uncharacteristically disheveled, he looked like a horse had run over him. Julian wagered he himself appeared no better. Flexing his shoulders, he winced. Had a herd of beasts trampled him as he had played cards?

Screams and shouts cut the air. The normal sounds of the boulevard filled with the finest carriages and smartest horses carrying their passengers to and from the extravagant shops along the Rue de la Paix were gone. Chaos reigned and in a rising crescendo, too.

"What's the problem?" Julian asked Remy who had shifted to take up the full of the window. "A riot?"

"A crowd."

"Someone's crying."

Julian pulled back the window shade. The throng along the pavement, mostly well-dressed ladies in walking suits and lavish hats, buzzed among themselves and craned their necks to see above those in front of them. One woman grabbed another's arm and urged her inside a shop. "I don't see any *gendarmes*."

Remy opened the overhead hatch to his coachman's box. In rapid French, he asked if the man could see the problem.

He responded but both Remy and Julian looked at each other and shrugged, unable to discern his words in the rising din.

"Stop, Valmont. Stop!" Remy rapped on the coachman's box. "Shall we?"

"Let's." Julian was out his side and Remy out his in the same moment.

The two of them ran up the middle of the broad avenue, darting hither and yon among the melee.

"A cab." Julian spied a black hackney and pointed.

He and Remy swung around a cluster of ladies, one wringing her hands, another standing still, tears sliding down her cheeks.

"Overturned?" Remy craned his neck above the melee.

"Not yet. But the horse is out of control. Come on."

The two broke into a run at the same time, weaving and darting among the shocked pedestrians.

"Let us through," Julian shouted, skirting bystanders.

"Pardon. Pardon." Remy grabbed one lady's shoulders, picked her up and put her aside.

Confronted by chaos, Julian and Remy halted in their tracks. The small black hackney swished back and forth along the cobbled street as the horse charged this way and that among the throng. Atop the swaying perch sat the driver, wide-eyed and yelling at the animal. He struggled to keep the reins from slipping from his hands.

A doleful cry came from inside.

"A woman's in there!" Remy shouted.

"The horse," Julian yelled, as he ripped off his coat and ran toward the animal. He was a sturdy Breton, his chestnut coat dull, his flaxen mane gray, his long teeth bared in abject fright.

Julian understood spooked horses. He'd calmed many who'd been scared by lightning, an errant cat or the sudden snap of a broken harness.

"All of you, get back. Go in the shops," he said in English and began in French when Remy barked at them to do as he said.

The crowd parted. Cleared.

Julian saw Remy had managed to climb up on the box. His extra weight slowed the animal. The horse whinnied, changed direction and headed into the alley between two buildings.

Julian ran alongside him, pleased when he realized the alley was blind. This horse had corned himself.

"All right, all right, old man." He soothed the animal, one hand out to ward him off in case he'd take an idea to rear up in the air. The alley was narrow and if the animal decided to attack him, he'd not survive. "You've nowhere to go. Honestly. Nowhere. Look what you did here. Made a scene. What will all the lovely mademoiselles think of you, eh? And your master here, what will he do without you? You must settle. Must settle."

As he spoke, the horse snorted and thrashed his head to and fro. But he gave up the crazed prancing and slowed.

Julian shrugged out of his coat, spread it between his hands, then glanced at the box.

Remy who sat beside the driver had somehow caught up

the second rein. Squashed together on the tiny perch, the cabby and the burly Frenchmen were a sight. One tiny, one huge. One blubbering, one tranquil.

"Come here, my boy," Julian cooed to the fine French workhorse. "I'm here to help you. Feed you. I'll find something from these merchants, don't worry. For now, let's get acquainted." Continuing in a low voice, he appealed to the animal with his tone and casual demeanor. The horse looked about, stomped a bit and stopped. Julian nodded to him to approach. "That's right. No need to run like a bedlamite."

A few minutes more while the horse snorted—and he stood, unhappy and unbowed. But peaceful.

Julian ventured to touch his nose. Pet him. Stroke him. "You are capable of this. I know it. And when you are quite calm, we'll see if we can find a carrot or an apple. Something wonderful. A reward."

Remy chuckled from his seat. "Talk to him like a lover and you'll have a new friend to follow you home."

Julian stroked the animal's nose. "I have too many high-tempered creatures at my house already. I'm sure monsieur has a better idea for him."

Remy arched a brow. "You'd better give the withers a good look before you make assumptions."

Julian turned to the side and saw the marks. The lash of a whip never did look good on any creature, man or animal. "Ask him what happened in the street."

The two bantered back and forth. Remy at first inquisitive. The cabby, defensive. Then Remy annoyed, angry. The cabby, blustering.

"A dog ran between the hooves," Remy told him.

"What the hell is a dog doing in the Rue de la Paix? It's fine, boy. Fine." Julian grabbed the horse's straps. "I'm mad, but not at you."

"The pet of a grand duchesse, he says." Remy jumped down from the box.

"Well, she should've tethered him."

"He escaped her," Remy said as he headed for the door of the hackney and pulled it wide. "Mademoiselle? Ah, ah. Madame le Comtesse. Are you well? Can you move?"

Julian peered around to catch sight of Remy reaching inside the cab to offer his hand.

"Can you walk?" he asked her in French. "Shall I assist you?"

"*Oui, oui, merci.* Oh, Monsieur le Duc, it is you. An honor to have you help me. An honor," the lady ran on in French, her tone that of a frightened bird. Julian recognized her as the Comtesse de Chaumont, a young impoverished widow who befriended rich Americans to pay her way in Parisian society.

She put one long gloved hand in Remy's and stepped gingerly from the interior, her chestnut hair hanging in clumps in total disarray, her elaborate gown torn at the hem, a hank of lace dangling from her generous bosom.

"Madame! Oh, my dear lady!" One woman ran toward Chaumont.

"Madame!" called another.

Two ladies—one blonde, one dark—sailed down the alley toward them. Both held on to their hats and lifted their skirts well above the dirty cobbles as they approached.

"*Merci,* Monsieur le Duc," the Countess de Chaumont said with a watery smile at Remy. "I fear I am quite weak."

Remy offered his arm. "Lean on me, madame."

"I will." She took a step and crumbled.

Remy caught her up just in time and led her to rest against the side of the carriage.

"Are you in pain?" the young woman with ink-black hair

asked the injured Frenchwoman. "If she's hurt her neck or back, she must not stand."

Her voice struck Julian, a low contralto, seductive as good, warm scotch. As he beheld her, two long waves of hair escaped her little red hat. And he killed the urge to reach out and rub the strands beneath his fingers.

"Do you have pain, madame?" Remy asked Chaumont.

"Pain?" The comtesse offered a small smile to the lady, a hand going to the crown of her head. She patted her lank curls, her eyes dazed. "I-I don't think so. My hat? My hat is gone. My hair's a fright. We will be late for our appointment. We mustn't. Monsieur Worth will be angry." She went on into laments in French.

"Do not worry, madame," the dark-haired girl told her, focusing on the older woman with fierce concern. As she spoke to the comtesse, she took the woman's hand, wrapped her fingers around her wrist, her lips moving and counting. Meanwhile, her companion bent to lift the comtesse's skirts above her ankles.

Shaking off his fascination with the brunette, Julian marveled that rarely had he seen ladies jump to another's aide with such concern. Never had he seen such efficiency among nobility for the health of another. Not even when his father had suffered a stroke in his club had any but the butler come to his side.

Like ministering angels, the two fluttered over the countess, gently soothing. The dark one looked into the comtesse's eyes, widened each in turn to murmur about the size of her pupils. Then she crooned sweet words while the blonde tested the fragility of the lady's ankles and shins.

"Your pulse is rapid," said the one whose voice wrapped around him like the red velvet ribbons of her tiny toque. "We should take you inside Worth's. We'll get a chair. A brandy."

"Can you stand?" asked the blonde.

The comtesse moaned and shook her head.

Julian found his wits. "She should not walk, Remy."

The two women glanced at him with such sharp surprise, he wondered if they'd noticed him restraining the horse.

"My friend is right," Remy said. "Madame le Comtesse is weak."

"But we must go inside for our appointment," Chaumont said.

"Worth can wait," Julian said.

The dark one locked her gaze on his.

He was pinned in place, struck by her frank search…and the crystalline blue of her eyes. First the voice, then the hair, now the eyes. He definitely needed coffee, sleep and a bath. Not usually given to raptures over feminine attributes, he smiled and reverted to politeness and some sanity. "Monsieur Worth has a sitting room, chairs, brandy and tea. Madame needs every one."

The dark-haired beauty agreed and turned to Chaumont. "Can you point your toes, madame?"

"*Oui*, you see?"

"Wonderful. Nothing's broken. But I'm not certain if she's turned her ankle."

The blonde directed her attention to Remy. "Can you carry her?"

Remy peered down at her with an intense sensual regard Julian recognized from years of accompanying his friend on midnight pleasures. "*Certainment.* Shall we adjourn, *Madame*? Hmm?"

"*Oui*," said the comtesse with obvious joy at the invitation.

"I'll see to the driver," Julian announced to the assembly with some envy that Remy would accompany the ladies and learn their names.

As the dark-haired one began to follow Remy, the comtesse high in his arms, she smiled at Julian—and the glory of it struck him like a ray of sunlight. "Thank you, sir. I saw what you did. You were quite gallant and I know many in the street are grateful for your service. My cousin and I are."

He inclined his head. "My pleasure, madame."

"Miss," she corrected him and offered her hand to shake. "Lily Hanniford."

He nodded in deference, his one hand tight to the horse's reins, the other taking hers. Her name flashed through his brain like fire. Hanniford. *She was Black Killian's daughter?*

He forced a smile and let convention and decades of training take him. She had flaunted etiquette and introduced herself, but the situation was unique. He could've laughed, but found her naturalness refreshing. Even her accent had a captivating wistfulness about it. He'd match it. "An American, I gather?"

"Right you are, sir."

"Perhaps I may present myself?" Despite the harried nature of their meeting, some propriety was in order.

"Of course." She tipped her head. Her complexion was as spotless as a camellia, her cheeks pink roses and her blue eyes danced in merriment.

Panic washed over him. Uncharacteristic as that was, he pushed away the need to analyze the emotion now. He wanted to bolt but recounted her assets instead. After all, he appreciated beauty. He applauded spontaneity. She possessed both. And something more. He liked her readiness to help her friend. Her skills at it. All that he reluctantly added to the marvelous smoke of her voice, her flat American pronunciation and her heavenly azure eyes. God, he loved her eyes. "The Marquess of Chelton, at your service."

Her lashes fluttered. So she might not observe the finer points of etiquette when meeting a strange man, but she understood what was required of her when meeting a titled gentleman. And no, her manner indicated she did not recognize his title. He had the advantage for now, and he exhaled, in odd and silly relief.

She dipped into a small curtsy. "Lord Chelton, am pleased to meet you."

"The pleasure is mine, Miss Hanniford. Please do attend Countess Chaumont and your friend."

"The lady with me is my cousin."

"I see. Well. Let me deal with the business here. The driver, the horse, the damage. Do please go inside."

"You'll join us?" she asked with a polite regard that he could have sworn held a winsome note of hope.

Such anticipation usually repelled him. Proper young ladies found him and his title alluring, even if he rarely returned the sentiment. But Miss Hanniford raised her brows in appeal and for the life of him, he had no idea why he could not disappoint. "I will indeed."

She lingered, taking in his features with a subtle caress of those incredible eyes. "Very well. I'll tell them."

He nodded. "Of course."

Minutes later, he'd sorted the business of the damaged hackney. Paying the driver for the Countess de Chaumont's journey, he added twenty extra francs for the wheel and frame of the conveyance. Julian also promised the man he'd look for the owner of the dog who had caused such disaster. Then he strode back to the main boulevard and entered the foyer of the establishment of the couturier Charles Worth.

Inside, a slim young man approached him and Julian asked for the countess's party. The receptionist was tut-tutting about the accident as Julian followed him down the marbled hall and up the winding staircase. In one of the private viewing rooms on the next floor, upon a plush red velvet chaise longue, the countess sat with her feet up, shoes off. Wiggling her bare toes at the request of Miss Hanniford's cousin, she appeared happy and quite well.

"I can move my toes but I'm less confident of my ability to walk." She took a sip of Monsieur Worth's dark brandy from a cut glass and made a pitiful pout at Remy. "You were so helpful to me, Monsieur le Duc. Might you assist me home? Ah, here you are, Lord Chelton. What news of the driver and his carriage?"

Interested in her own predicament, Chaumont did not do her duty to introduce him to Miss Hanniford's companion. From what he gathered, the lady must have already acquainted the others with each other. He would have liked a formal introduction to Lily Hanniford, even if it meant she might learn his family name—and seek to run from the man who was thwarting her father in a business deal.

At the moment, he could best surrender manners and secrecy to sharing information with Chaumont about her carriage. "The driver has asked a boy to fetch him a stable hand. One wagon wheel is precariously balanced. One side of his cab is caved in. He'll need quite a bit of repair on that hack, I'm sorry to say."

"Oh, what damage! Will he charge me for it?" Chaumont ran a hand through her brown hair, now totally loose of its pins. "I don't know if I can afford to pay such a bill."

Julian went to stand beside Remy. At this vantage, he could look directly down at Miss Hanniford and into those arresting blue eyes. "The driver claims a pet dog ran into the street. Tangled up in the horse's legs. The person who should pay for the repairs of that hack should be the lady who owns that dog. Don't you think?"

"I agree," Remy said.

"Ah, Miss Hanniford, Mrs. Roland, *bon jour*." A tall, slim woman in severely cut black serge sailed into the room, her hands clasped in distress. She must be the *vendeuse* assigned to the two women. "Ah, such a *catastrophe.* My apologies for my delay. I have heard of your terrible accident in the streets. It is so horrible. I cannot imagine. But I see that Henri has given you brandy. May I offer it to the rest of your party?"

"He did already, Mademoiselle Gerard," Miss Hanniford said.

"Not for me, Mademoiselle," Remy replied.

"Nor me. However, you can tell us," Julian said, "if you have a patron in the house at the moment who owns a small dog."

The *vendeuse*'s eyes went wide. Worth's sales girls did not speak of other clientele. "Ah...er...Monsieur—?"

"Lord Chelton," he informed her. "Is there such a customer here in house now?"

"It would be indiscreet of me, my lord, to reveal—"

"Gerard, let me be clear. There was a serious accident in the boulevard." He felt no compunction about addressing her simply by her last name. She was not worthy of niceties if she did not understand the import of his question and the problem created by her careless client. Besides, he had no patience with those who did not see the implications of their actions. "It could have cost Madame le Comtesse her life. Others fled in fear of theirs. A horse was terrified. A driver, too. His carriage damaged. If a runaway dog caused this— and we have statements that this did occur—then the lady who owns the animal must pay the bill."

"But of course. I understand." Deferential, eyes cast to the floor, Gerard bowed her way backward. "If you will but wait a few moments, I will inquire."

"Do that."

Silence reigned for a tortuous minute.

"Splendid, my lord Chelton." Chaumont giggled, lifting her glass in honor of Julian and draining the brandy.

Remy chuckled. "Chelton can intimidate the devil. I say

you got Gerard's attention."

"Indeed. She'll return with a criminal," said Miss Hanniford with a grin.

All five of them laughed.

Chaumont pushed herself up amid the cushions. "I am remiss in my duties. Permit me to introduce to you to the ladies, Lord Chelton."

Julian expected that she had already introduced Remy properly. As Chaumont spoke, he noted how Miss Hanniford settled more comfortably into her chair, not objecting nor revealing that they had already made their own acquaintance outside. Chaumont went on and he was soon appraised that the blonde lady was Lily Hanniford's cousin. A married lady, it seemed by her manner of address.

"That settled," said Remy and turned to the two Americans. "Tell me if you will stay for your fitting? I offer my carriage to escort you home."

"Thank you, Monsieur le Duc," Lily said, "but no. We must remain. My father expects it. No accident of rain, sleet or frightened dog amid the carriage wheels should prevent it."

Her cousin quite agreed. "Uncle Killian is a taskmaster."

Remy was not deterred. "I have my carriage close by, farther down the street and I'm sure my coachman is attempting to pull forward amid the crowd. I'd be quite happy to offer to take you home. All of you."

"*Merci beaucoup*, Remy." Chaumont was quick to accept. She leaned back, regarding him with hazel eyes misty from her consumption of alcohol. "I must not desert my duties. I am charged with escorting Miss Hanniford and Mrs. Roland through the rigors of a Paris *entre*."

"No, madame." Lily had other ideas. "Thank you, for your kindness. If you wish to return home, certainly, do go with the kind man."

"*Et vous?*" she asked her young American charge and Julian could see the desire in Chaumont's eyes that a moment with the fabled Remy was what she desired. "You also need assistance, *oui?*"

"Madame, please. We can proceed with our selection of fabrics and styles. Our carriage is scheduled to return for us in two hours. In the meantime, we would be very reassured that you are on the road to recovery if you were in your own home resting."

Julian fought a smile. He could detect from Chaumont's dreamy expression that the wily widow hoped to return to Remy's home to engage in a particular type of recovery. Injured ankle, be damned.

"Please do not trouble yourself," Mrs. Roland assured Chaumont with a pat of her hand. "We can finish ourselves."

"If you think it possible." Chaumont postured prettily.

"I do," Mrs. Roland said.

"I insist," said Lily.

The *vendeuse* strode in. Her attention focused on Julian. "Pardon."

"Well?" asked Julian.

She bit her lips. "I have found the lady you seek, my lord."

"Who is it?" Julian asked her.

"The Grand Duchess of Volenska."

Remy frowned at Julian. "Anna Drobova."

"Trouble?"

Remy rolled his eyes. "No angel."

"It matters not." Julian inclined his head to Chaumont, Mrs. Roland and finally to Miss Hanniford. "I will leave you and discuss certain financial matters with the grand duchess. It was my pleasure to see you again, Madame le Comtesse. And a pleasure to meet both of you, Mrs. Roland and Miss Hanniford. Remy, I leave you to assist madame. When your carriage arrives, I'll have the doorman summon you to come down. Good day."

Both ladies bid him goodbye, but the one whose words lingered in his ears were those of the alluring Miss Hanniford. As he turned on his heel and followed Gerard down the hall toward another private room where Volenska waited, Julian experienced a distinct feeling of loss that he had not learned much about the American girl with the bewitching blue eyes. Nor had he any idea when he might see her again.

It shouldn't matter. He didn't like the odd experience of being entranced by a woman. It unsettled him, set his teeth on edge. Such feelings were rare. Once. Twice, perhaps he'd succumbed to a pretty face as an adult. He preferred the physical compulsion. The urge to mate. The erotic indulgence. The draining satisfaction. Resulting in freedom.

He could forget the American. Easily.

Minutes later, having dealt with the not-so-grand duchess, he waited in Remy's carriage at the entrance to the House of Worth. His irritation at the Russian woman, fierce as it had been, was gone. And in his ennui, his desire to gaze into Miss Hanniford's superb blue eyes loomed. He could find a woman comparable. Readily.

After all, she was American. Her diction, odd. Her self-confidence, prominent. Her spontaneity, genuine. She was rich, too. Obviously. Else what would she be doing employing the countess and attending fittings at the House of Worth? More than that, she was lovely. *Charming Lily*. Tall, graceful, elegant. But strong enough to deal with a tragedy in the streets and bodily danger to her friend. A flower who did not wilt. And in the bargain, luscious. With that pile of midnight hair and a ripe mouth that begged for plundering. A voice that echoed low in his brain with murmurs of whispery summer nights and silken sheets.

Worst of all, delicious Lily was that bastard's daughter,

Black Killian Hanniford. Of all the women in the world, he had to become enchanted with the beautiful blue-eyed child of the devil. No good would come of his desire to lose himself in her gaze. Her father had already attempted to get what he wanted and get it cheap. Their share in the shipping company for a pittance was enough of an insult. But to buy their country home in Kent for a song? Julian would not give away his dignity, his home or his family name in trade for a sales agreement. He hoped to God his father didn't.

As if lack of funds and the need to sell the family jewels weren't enough degradation to the ancestral line of the dukedom of Seton. He could not, would not become enchanted with a woman who came encumbered with such a rogue in her family.

He rubbed his eyes.

The coachman pulled open Remy's door and in climbed Madame le Comtesse. And as the conveyance rumbled across town and the three of them made polite conversation, Julian refused to ask about the creature who had so captivated him with one look. But Chaumont was a witch, uncanny in her perception that though he voiced not a word, not a question, he cared to know details about the lovely dark American.

By the time he stepped down from Remy's coach and his butler opened the door to his townhouse, he'd learned more about Miss Lily Hanniford. She was abroad husband hunting, and her father was providing a handsome dowry for his oldest daughter. Perhaps even for her companion, her cousin, the war widow, Mrs. Roland.

He must not care.

He was exhausted. He needed sleep. A sharp mind.

He'd seen blue eyes before. Beautiful ones. And what lay behind them was not always attractive.

Miss Hanniford was not different.

Therefore, she was not irresistible.

CHAPTER 3

"*T*he one who saved Chaumont was Lord Chelton?" Lily's father chuckled as they finished their light supper.

Lily put down her fork, alarmed how he was thrilled over the man's name. "Yes, sir. Along with this Frenchman named Remy."

Her father beamed. "You have the luck, the two of you."

"How so?" Lily went still as she gazed at her father at the head of the dining room table.

"The Duke of Seton, my dear, is Chelton's father." He sipped his port, laughing.

And here she had liked him. His ink-black hair, his chocolate-brown eyes. His sleek handsomeness and his quiet air of confidence. No priggish tone of the privileged Englishman about him.

"I couldn't have planned that better if I'd asked you to find him. Or asked poor Chaumont to suffer an accident in her cab. The Duke of Seton is one of the directors of the Cardiff Shipping Line."

Lily was riveted to her chair. "And you want to buy his

shares." Lily had heard nothing but this for weeks from her father. This Cardiff company was failing. Nigh unto bankrupt. Poorly managed since it had not made a profit during the American Civil War, the company was dying due to the directors had not repaired their fleet and half their ships remained in dock, rotting.

"I do. And it's who holds the keys to the kingdom more than old Seton."

"I don't understand." Marianne frowned at him. "If the sons of the aristocracy hold no power over investments or land or purse, why does this one?"

"Learned your lessons well about the English have, haven't you?" He smiled, his satisfaction with the news apparent in a wolfish gleam. "That Scotsman I hired to teach you the rigors of the social order did a wonderful job."

Lily scolded herself for her folly to become interested in the man. She mustn't care for him. Marquess or no. Kind or not. Handsome like the devil. None of it mattered if her father saw him as his opponent. She had always made a point never to take a position or an opinion on her father's business dealings. She wouldn't start now.

Marianne glanced at her and rushed to fill the silence. "What is it about that's different from others?"

"His father Seton is a gambler through and through. And piss poor at it. And while his son is the day to his papa's night and has a skill at winning hands, the boy also has a finer understanding of money than his sire. This is well known." He raised a finger to the air. "Chelton is a scoundrel, but not as big a one as his father."

Lily stared down at her empty plate. This news of Chelton's reputation was not welcome. She'd thought better of him. His readiness to help Chaumont. His obvious good-natured friendship with Remy. His perfect classical looks.

"Oh, I see." Her father peered at her over the rims of his glasses. "You liked him?"

Simply because Chelton and her father were business rivals, she would steer clear of him forevermore. "I did."

"Why?"

She pursed her lips. Chafing at her father's probe, she dare not reveal all the details about him that had aroused her in ways she'd never experienced. Chelton was an elegant creature, finely chiseled, much like a sculpture of a Greek god. Blessed with a sensuous mouth and large umber eyes, he had the mien of a man who should be obeyed and revered. She had presumed him to be a gentleman in the purest sense. Now she heard he was a gambler and as vice ran to vice, much else. In addition, he was her father's opponent in a business negotiation. How naïve of her to jump to the conclusion she could admire him. "He was quick to the rescue."

"I thought you said this Frenchman was the first one who got to Chaumont's driver."

"He did," Marianne said. "But it was Chelton who tamed the horse. Without him, they'd all be hurt or dead."

"I see. Good for him. And did he introduce himself to you?"

"He did," Lily said. "It was all properly done, despite the circumstances."

Her father sat, his eyes narrowing in consideration. "Fine. What we need."

Lily's eyes locked on Marianne's with hope of escape. "We should change."

"I detect you are running off," her father said to them, his light eyes dancing partially in jest, partially in warning.

"We are," Marianne said.

Lily rose, diverting her gaze lest her father see more than

she intended. "We don't want to be late for the Vicomtesse de Bourg's reception."

"We are expected to be late. This is not Knickerbocker Manhattan. Besides," he said, pinning her with hot intent, "shouldn't I hear more about this meeting of Chelton and you, Lily?"

"No, sir. You should not." She gave him a blithe look.

"And what of the Frenchman, Marianne? Was he so handsome you must flee without explanation, too?"

"Yes, sir. He was. But you mustn't worry, Uncle Killian."

"No? Why not?"

"He is too—" She paused, unusually stumped for words, one hand dancing in the air.

"Well? What?"

"Overwhelming. He is huge. A giant of a man."

"And? So?" her father urged.

Marianne blinked, her gaze suddenly dreamy. "His blond hair hangs to his shoulders and his hands are callused and scarred."

"Chelton has a friend who's a laborer? Yet he offered you his own carriage?" He arched his brows high. "Damned intriguing."

"No, sir," Marianne objected.

Lily caught her eye and shook her head in warning.

But Marianne missed her cue. "He's a duke."

Oh, lord.

"That is intriguing," Hanniford replied with gusto.

Lily rolled her eyes at Marianne who had not been intrigued with Remy, the Frenchman. No, not by a long shot. If there were a word for Marianne's reaction to Remy, it was mesmerized.

Marianne, flustered, shot from her chair at once, then came around the table and hooked her arm in Lily's. "Escape with me."

"Tell him no more," Lily pleaded as the two of them hurried from the dining room.

"I heard that!" he called out, but they took the circular staircase up to their suites. "I need details."

"We've no time, Uncle."

"We don't want to be late, Papa," Lily called down.

"We don't want to change the fashion." He came to the foot of the stairs.

Lily took hold of the hall banister and peered over the side. "Not on your life. It's de Bourg's small soirée. Then the opera, dear Father. And for that, you've paid good money."

"I have not paid a penny. We're guests!"

"All the more reason. Get dressed yourself," she told him, sailing off to shut the door to Marianne's sitting room.

She faced her cousin, shaking a finger at her. "You realize that now he knows Remy is a duke, Papa will investigate his family all the way back to the dark ages."

"He can do what he wants," she said. "I'll not have another husband, ever."

Marianne's vehemence about the subject of taking a husband was a mystery that no amount of cajoling could influence her to reveal. But Lily had seen her cousin's interest in the impressive French nobleman. Never before had Marianne shown any attraction to a man. And her recent declarations that she would consider taking a lover sparked the possibility that, given a chance, this Remy might fill that need for her.

Her cousin strode to her dressing room, turning her back on Lily and thereby hiding her expression. "Besides, I most likely won't see him again."

"And if you do?" Lily was quick to ask.

"It won't matter. Your father cannot persuade me to receive him."

"Or buy him for you?"

Marianne whirled to face her, her brows knit. "No. Not at any price."

~

"Remy is late." Julian's mother dropped her lorgnette on its gold chain to her chest and peered at him as if it were his fault Remy had not appeared on time. To irritate him, she always criticized the Frenchman over any trifle. A stickler for rules, she might be. But she hid behind them, as she did most strictures, for her own devices. This she used to needle him with his choice of his very unconventional friend. "We cannot wait longer or we shall miss my favorite aria."

Julian glanced about at those chatting in the rotunda of the new Paris Garnier Opera house. These were the season's ticketholders, men clad in tuxedoes and top hats, the ladies wrapped in diamonds, feathers and silks. He had greeted those he knew, and those whose financial interests were similar to his. "I'll escort you up to our box, if you wish, Mama."

"I do."

Julian was in no mood to argue with her. His head still clanged from his outing last night and this morning's accident. The surprise of his preoccupation with the Hanniford girl added to his discomfort. No amount of rest had rid him of the obsession with her pale blue eyes. Plus, the brief but bitter meeting this afternoon with his French partner in Cardiff Shipping had certainly not improved his attitude toward her or her father. Tonight, he'd agreed to attend this opera only because his sister wished his escort. God knew, he did not favor an evening in his mother's company. He had quite enough of her at home. But he wished to please his young sister who adored the dramatic doings of operas. He offered one arm to his mother and the other to Elanna. "Shall we?"

Elanna put her hand to his sleeve. Her hazel eyes twinkled in the light from the huge cut glass chandeliers. Dressed in a glistening gown of pink chiffon, she sparkled against the gold and rose of the marble walls. "You are good. I know you prefer Remy's company."

"Well, now." Julian smiled at her. She was such a good-natured girl, pretty with an abundance of rosewood-brown hair and porcelain skin, all of nineteen, finished with her first Season and without a suitor in sight. That pleased him. She was too sweet to shackle at so young an age. If he could continue to win sizably at the tables—or better yet find a suitable investor for the shipping firm—he'd help her remain single for years to come. No respectable but pitiless union for her if he could help it. "I like yours."

"Of course he does, Elanna." His mother had to have her say. "He prefers yours to many a girls'. I wish he could say he adored other feminine companions less."

"Now, Mama," Elanna scolded their mother as they walked up the gilded side steps of the cavernous Garnier headed for the huge rose marble staircase. "Don't quarrel with Chelton again. I won't attract a man if I'm scowling at you both."

"You could peer at a fellow with a dagger in your hand," he jested, "and the poor chap would hasten to offer for your hand."

"That would be remarkable," she conceded with a chuckle. "But still unworthy if he can't recite Romeo's speech without faltering."

Julian shook his head. Aside from her pleasant nature, his darling sister loved books, plays and poetry. She was articulate and funny. Aside from being very popular with young men.

Just that afternoon upon his return home, his feisty little sister had shown proof she could attract one man too many. A scoundrel had applied to his mother just that morning for the honor of courting Elanna. Wisely, the duchess had demurred and told the man she must consult with her son and her husband before approving. And as Julian expected, his mother favored the cad. The resulting row he and his mother had had set drums clanging in his ears, an unwelcome addition to his earlier headache. She had advocated a quick engagement for Elanna to the man, a baron of ancient English blood and little repute. Julian had flatly refused to recommend the scamp to his father. When she had told him they needed Elanna out of the house, on someone else's dole, Julian had fumed at her. He refused to sell his sister to the first bidder, or even the highest, let alone the most scandalous. Elanna had rushed in to the drawing room, calling for quiet deliberation. She tolerated their mother's shallow maternal instincts. He recoiled from them.

"You've no need for a man just yet." As they climbed the massive steps, Julian shot his mother a look of reproof and settled on Elanna with a benevolent smile. "Besides, I tell you, darling girl, you must add to your enviable talents for negotiation."

"You'll teach me how to play dice and win each time?"

"I think it better if I take you up to my gymnasium for boxing lessons."

"Oh, ho!" Elanna giggled over that as they took the red-carpeted stairs at a steady pace. "I imagine how that will charm my suitors."

"Boxing? And give me heart palpitations?" his mother asked. "I forbid it. I absolutely—"

"We know, Mama," he told her as they continued along the circular corridor toward their private box. "Do not fret,

Elanna. We'll find you a man who loves the sport. Then you can marry him and have at each other every day."

"I hope the 'having' would be more pleasant than that," she said with a wink.

His mother snapped open her fan. "Really. You encourage her. I disapprove."

Elanna sighed, casting about to admire the well-dressed throng of Parisians eager for a night of opulent music. "Doesn't everyone look marvelous? And don't you adore this building? Who decorated the interior? Do you know, Chelton?"

"No idea." The Paris Garnier overwhelmed him. The heavy limestone, the omni-present gilt, the wealth of dangling crystal chandeliers, the thick blood red carpet, the gargantuan size of the place took his breath. Sucked it right out him. Like a monster. He always hurried to his seat. Once in a box, surrounded by more ordinary dimensions of the red velvet privacy walls and appointed chairs, he found air and space and peace.

He patted Elanna's hand. "You love its grandeur. I understand that. Even if I don't appreciate it."

Elanna adored expansive buildings, bustling city thoroughfares and garrulous people. She was effusive, alluring in her ready acceptance of the universe. That included her embrace of avante-garde music, impressionist painting and all sorts of unconventional people. Men flocked to her, finding her exuberance enchanting. Last spring in London, two had seen her as fair prey. Julian had discouraged them easily, describing Elanna's depleted dowry and sending them packing. His parents never knew. He prided himself on a few scruples, yet for his sister, he wished to find a man with hundreds. Refreshing to be with, Elanna was a treasure Julian intended to guard. No roué nor chap with debts long as his arm would darken her path if he could help it. He'd welcome a rich man, but finding one of those in these dire financial times for a poor duke's only daughter would be a miracle.

"Your Grace! Lord Chelton!" A tall, hawkish gentleman approached them along the gallery. "Lady Elanna. How wonderful to see all of you here."

"Lord Carbury." His mother inclined her head as the earl strolled up to them. "We're delighted to see friends from home."

The man lived in the adjoining estate in Kent and their families had mingled and intermarried off and on for centuries. Carbury was a decade or more older than Julian and bore the signs of age in his lined forehead and thinning gray hair.

"Good evening, Carbury," his mother addressed him. "Are you in town for the running of the races?"

"I am. Cannot resist the lure." He took the duchess's hand to bow over it and then took up Elanna's to offer the same homage. "Here for another few weeks, then back to the lair. Winter comes. Must do the accounting. Hideous task. What of you? Here for the winter?"

"We return home next week." Julian had to smile at the way Carbury could not seem to take his eyes off Elanna. The widower was too old, too much of a fuddy-duddy for his virginal sister, but Elanna enjoyed his company when he came to call. And he had called often last spring and summer. He'd made no overture to Elanna. Made no offer for her hand. Yet the fact that he was here in Paris at the same time seemed a bit of a coincidence and Julian wondered if Elanna or his mother had told the middle-aged duke of their travel plans.

"I return for my scheduled instructions in landscape painting," Elanna told Carbury with a grin.

"Ah, yes, your efforts to exceed Mr. Turner," he joked. "I do recall."

Elanna lifted a shoulder. "I mustn't disappoint Monsieur de la Bran with my lack of advancement."

"You have determination," he said with assurance. "You will succeed."

A tall, dark, figure strolled abreast of their party. Waiting politely for an opening, he had turned to the two ladies who accompanied him. Julian's skin prickled with a sensation of being watched. And he stepped to one side.

When he looked into their faces, he had jolt. Beside Killian Hanniford stood the two women whom he'd met this afternoon in the midst of the accident. And like a magnet, he focused on the startling blue eyes of Miss Lily Hanniford.

"Good evening, my lord," the American millionaire said to Carbury in his leisurely American accent. "Forgive us for our tardiness."

"I am most delighted to see you. All of you," Carbury said, shaking hands with the gentleman and bowing to the ladies. "You are not late at all. We are reminiscing. Allow me to present my friends. My neighbors, too, they are."

Carbury did the honors most prettily, so well in fact that Julian could greet Killian Hanniford with equanimity. He'd met with the infamous American blockade runner three times in the past two weeks and known him to be blunt, forceful but polite. As a scrapper from the docks of Baltimore, Hanniford had acquired polish with his fortune. Here as in his offices, the man was tailored, barbered to a far thee well and his manners were impeccable. So fine in fact that Julian's mother, whether or not she knew of Hanniford's proposed raid of Cardiff Shipping, accepted the introduction with a smug look of satisfaction. A rare thing.

So when the moment came for Carbury to introduce Julian to the luscious Miss Hanniford, he easily grasped her hand and bowed over her soft leather glove. "I had the honor to meet Miss Hanniford this afternoon. And Mrs. Roland as well. Good evening, ladies. I trust you have recovered from the upset of the afternoon."

"We did. Thank you, Lord Chelton," Lily told him with a cool politesse that surprised and distressed him.

"You were very helpful, my lord," Mrs. Roland added with more graciousness than Julian perceived in Lily's greeting. "You saved us from disaster. Especially Madame le Comtesse."

"What is this?" his mother asked. "You told me nothing of a disaster."

Julian inclined his head. "It was a runaway horse and a frightened hack, Mama. Remy and I dealt with them both."

"And I, Lord Chelton," said Killian Hanniford with earnest thanks, "am the one most grateful for your intervention. Lily and Marianne told me all the details and I'm in awe of your quick thinking and your skill."

His mother cocked a haughty brow. "Chelton has always made a habit of walking into danger."

Thank you, Mama. Such a dubious commendation is so unwelcome.

"No wonder he did well today," Lily Hanniford said with smooth flattery that warmed him and made his mother turn to glass.

Julian did not know what to say to that. It was not often someone could take his mother's words and turn them into a compliment. Amusement curled his mouth. Appreciation made him grin.

"Here's Remy," his mother said and smiled at the man who bowed graciously to them all.

"*Bon soir.* Forgive me my tardiness," Remy said, his twinkling eyes traveling the party and pausing for a second on the widow Roland. "Another accident along the Rue de la Paix tonight. I fear we have a contagion on our hands."

His mother rushed to introduce Remy to the ladies, Hanniford and Carbury as if she wished him gone. But the chimes sounded for an intermission between acts and Carbury bent over Elanna, eager as a puppy and smiling at her.

He extended his hand toward the door to a nearby box. "I hope all of you will join me here. The Hannifords are my guests and the four of you would turn us into a very grand party."

Elanna pressed back against Julian's arm.

Remy grinned, his attention to Mrs. Roland flagrantly apparent.

And for himself, desire to be near charming Lily was raw. Better judgment screamed he should refuse.

But his mother was quick to agree.

"Let us go in, then." Carbury offered his arm to Elanna.

Not to be impolite, she nodded and hooked her hand in the crook of his elbow.

Julian's mother cast them a sideways glance, and at once, Julian's skin prickled. Was this his mother's ploy to push Elanna and Carbury together? It might very well be. The woman preferred her own company. Unless it benefited her to be social.

He set his teeth.

But as the party reshuffled to allow the pair to pass, Lily was suddenly by his side. His duty as a gentleman was to offer her his own arm.

"Thank you," she said in that voice that melted his rational mind and she placed her warm palm on his sleeve.

"Do you like Offenbach?" he asked out of the blue.

"I've never heard his works before."

"Ah," he said like a dolt, his brain utterly, ridiculously blank.

As all eight of them filed in to the box's anteroom where they could remove their wraps, instinct and manners drove him forward. He stood like a statue as Lily turned her back to him to help with removing her cape. Her fox fur-lined sateen was a deep shade of sapphire, darkly complementary to her flawless skin. His fingers brushed her bare shoulder as he slid the garment off her, only to make him catch his breath at the sky-blue silk gown that sluiced over her slim form. She looked like a shimmering ice goddess. She smelled like faint roses of summer. He was entranced. Silly him. She was quite exquisite, her skin as perfect as a pearl, her throat and the swells of her breasts, gloriously pristine.

What was wrong with him? For God's sake.

He never ogled a lady. Not since he'd been a randy twelve-year-old.

Still, he stepped to one side in the box so that Lily had a choice to sit next to him or insult him and walk to the other side where the only other seat was open. She surreptitiously checked his gaze, quickly glancing away as if their eyes had never met. But she sat beside him.

He let out his breath, relieved. The others took up the gilded red damask chairs and he settled in his own, congratulating himself like a lovesick fool that he could bask in the glow of the lovely American. She had more than beauty, too. He crossed one leg over the other, suppressing his satisfaction. She had wits enough to turn his mother's insult to a compliment.

Then Lily faced him.

He locked on to those remarkable blue eyes. She searched as if she rummaged for some lost treasure. He wished he knew what it was. He'd give it her in a second if only she'd remain forged to him. "Can I get you champagne from the Glacier?"

"No, thank you. Perhaps later."

Very well. What else might we discuss? "Did your fitting with Monsieur Worth go well?"

"It did."

If she were any other woman, she'd be heaping him with details of fabrics and colors, shoes and bonnets. But she gave him silence. How was he to get on?

But she raised her face. Dear God. Her perfect oval face and the eyes that spoke of banked blue fires. *Was that interest in him? Or not?*

He despaired of ever learning.

Frustrated, he removed his gloves. Her gaze fell to his hands, drifted away and returned. She seemed troubled, flexing her fingers. "How was Madame le Comtesse when you took her home? Better?"

"Remy did the honors. But when I left the carriage, she seemed quite…bubbly."

Lily's tension collapsed and she wore a grin. "She loves champagne."

"Shouldn't we all."

"You don't?"

"It depends on my mood."

"So. When you are happy, what do you drink?" she asked, playing with him now.

He arched a brow. "A burgundy with beef. A white from the Loire with scallops. A Scots whiskey when I am happy."

"And when you're sad?"

"A Scots whiskey."

She let out a laugh.

Had they overcome the tension? "And what do you like when you're happy?"

"Beer."

He guffawed and others in the box shot him a look.

She leaned close and he inhaled her alluring scent. "Do you?"

"Like beer?" He loved the look on her face, open and accepting, full of humor. "I like to drink it with good friends."

"Me, too."

Oh, he was undone. By her naturalness. By her lack of guile. "Then you and I must become friends and enjoy fine beer."

She turned away, swallowed hard and opened her fan. Whipping the thing so that the air around them grew crisp with tension, she raised the hope that he might have unnerved her as she did him.

Good.

The others spoke, conversed. Remy was fully engaged with Mrs. Roland. Carbury with Elanna. His mother chatted with Killian Hanniford and damn, if she wasn't smiling, unabashedly cooing to the American.

And Julian felt like a dimwit. Here he sat, silent. Undone. By the beauty of an American. A girl. Young and effervescent.

So much so, he had to admit to his great dismay, that he had lied to himself. Greatly. She was not forgettable. Not in looks or manner.

True, he liked all he saw. The elegant line from her ear to her shoulder. The delicate tendons along her nape. The way wisps of her hair fell, one by one, while she moved her head in tiny increments to or fro. The way she tipped her head when the orchestra struck up a chord that roused her. The unblemished expanse of her appealing décolleté.

He tore his gaze away, musing that he examined her like an artist memorizing his model. Remy, the true artist, would laugh at him.

He shook his head. Hot, bothered, he dug the program from his inner coat pocket. With blind eyes, he perused it.

But he thrust it aside. He did not care a whit who sang. Or what. Or when. He lived only for the view. How she sat, her long arms swathed in formal white gloves. Her hands resting, cupped in each other. Her back arching, her shoulders rising, her derriere flexing.

He shifted in his own chair.

He was besotted. He sat in a crowded opera house with nearly two thousand others, lusting for a woman to whom he'd spoken ten words.

He breathed deeply, casting about to find some other enchantment. What he saw were two gentlemen examining her, too. One man with a pair of binoculars in the box opposite them. Another man in the audience looking up in pure intoxication. Julian had no idea who they were. They had good taste. But no chance with Lily Hanniford. Not tonight. He was here to shield her from adventurers and charlatans. To throw a mantel of English correctness over the upstart Americans. To bestow on her, by his very proximity, a legitimacy and a value to Parisian society.

He crossed his arms and stared the two men down. *Oh, yes.* Nothing like the medieval glory of the Seton duchy to assure acceptance whether here or in London.

Whatever possessed him, he had no idea. But he reached over and took one of her hands to place on his knee.

She went to stone.

He smiled in irony. He'd been hard as a rock for the last hour.

She focused on her hand in his and in a deliberate move, pulled it away even as she leaned over to him. "My lord." Her voice was a whisper. "Please don't stare at me."

That she would mention his absorption in her was a faux pas no English lady of any breeding would ever commit. They'd take it as the compliment it was. Treasure it in silence and hope the man would come to call.

He could not respond. Would not. There was no discreet way. He had no alluring words. No apology, either.

Throughout the intermission when Remy adjourned briefly with Mrs. Roland to the Glacier and then through the next act Julian complied with Lily's wish. He grew testy trying to fulfill her wishes. To his supreme irritation, he surveyed the boxes repeatedly. He counted the numerous men who peered up at her. But then he'd glance at her and excuse their captivation. He understood their fascination and he was undone by his own.

When the lights came up, with the rest of their party, the two of them rose and conversed, mingled and laughed.

Remy rubbed his hands together. "Shall we adjourn to a café for refreshments?"

Lily was first to respond. "Forgive me, I've enjoyed this tremendously, but I fear I must return home. It's been a very long day. Excuse me, please. But, Papa, if you wish to continue the evening, do."

Hanniford made his own excuses and Mrs. Roland in turn. They would leave.

The party reclaimed their coats and made their way down the massive staircase, into the rotunda and on to the portiere where the private coaches lined up.

Julian was careful, bidding all good evening with polite enthusiasm. And he stood beside Remy, watching the Hanniford carriage depart.

"Care to join me for a bit of fun?" Remy asked, an arched brow indicating his interest in quite another topic.

"Thanks, no." He inclined his head toward his own conveyance far down the line. "I'll join the family for home."

"I need a drink. Conversation, too. Don't you?"

Julian recognized the light in his eye. Only a few women did that to Remy. "The comely widow interests you?"

"She does. I wish she didn't."

"I understand." He clapped a hand on Remy's broad shoulder. "Go home. Think better of it in the morning."

"One would hope so."

"*Au revoir*. Tomorrow then?"

Julian left him to climb into his coach and sink against the squabs. His mother chatted on about Carbury, all his marvelous assets, financial included. Thank God Elanna seemed immune. She sat back into the shadows and nodded at their mother's words of praise. At length, without response from Elanna, their mother grew silent. Only the rhythmic clopping of the horses' hooves on the cobbles pervaded the night air—and Julian was free to mull his dilemma.

Lily had warned him away from. *Good of her. Wise, too*.

He'd not mix business with pleasure. Never had. Wouldn't start now.

Devil of it was that he wanted her more than before. He ached with it. Swearing silently, he paused, struck with the clarity of his problem. And hers.

She enjoyed him, but she didn't want his attentions.

That was precisely how he himself wished to relate to women. Enjoy them. Admire them. Seduce them.

But not this one. Never delectable Lily Hanniford.

His conclusion was a dreadful one. He must not ever see her again. Let alone spend an entire evening watching her every breath. And getting lost in her blue, blue eyes.

CHAPTER 4

March 1878
No. 110 Piccadilly

"*O*ur latest invitations!" Marianne sailed into the drawing room, flourishing aloft the latest crop of large envelopes in her hand. She lifted one to her nose and, closing her eyes, inhaled.

"How many?" Lily stopped her pacing, grateful for the diversion from her worries over the imminent arrival of their first guests for tea.

"Three. Smelling marvelous, too," she said with the charm of a conspirator as she tore open one and plunked in the wing chair opposite Lily.

So many had arrived in that past few days that Lily had had to make a master list of all the details. What to wear was the least of their worries. Papa's expenditure of more than forty thousand dollars on both her and Marianne's wardrobes meant they could appear anywhere and be appreciated, even envied. But who their hosts were, what their rank was, who else might attend, who got the deeper curtsy, all were murderously delicate points that could kill their social acceptability. And acceptable, they must be, declared her father.

Dizzy with the complexity of who had invited her and her cousin to an array of luncheons, teas and musicales, she and Marianne had reassured each other their studies of such niceties had been superb. Their knowledge of etiquette finite. But the crush was great. Into the London Season only a week, they were exhausted and not rising before ten. Today was their first at-home tea and they'd been nervous as cats all morning.

"Oh, dear," Lily said beneath her breath. "I don't like the look on your face. Is it from someone on Papa's 'Awful List'?"

Writing down names of undesirable contacts from his business dealings, her father had dubbed his list 'The Unsuitables.' These were men or entire families whose presence was not welcome to the Hannifords' home. He'd made it clear they were not to be accepted under any circumstances, even if their lineage in Debrett's Peerage did go back to William the Conqueror. Among them, the names of the Duke and Duchess of Seton, their son, the marquess of Chelton, and their daughter, Lady Elanna, did not appear—and Lily was delighted. But feared none of them would ever call.

"No. Very nice." She put down a large card on the table beside her and went to work on the next one.

"Who? Do tell."

"A dinner party at the home of the Earl and Countess of Ely a week Wednesday."

"Ely? Doesn't he have a son who is a widower?" Lily recalled her father saying something like that. Meanwhile, Marianne tore open another envelope like a child opening birthday gifts.

"Mmm. Yes. And an ancient keep in need of a new roof. But this—" Marianne covered her mouth with two fingers. "Oh, my."

"What?"

"We're to go to a house party." Her dark green gaze locked on Lily's.

"Whose? How many days?" Could anyone keep up polite appearances for days, especially if, as Papa said, many of the married couples switched bed partners at night?

"Five days. Kent." She let the card drop to her lap, her vision glassy.

"Who?"

"Carbury."

The name rang a bell but Lily couldn't place— "Oh, no."

Marianne slowly nodded. "The Earl of Carbury. From the night at the Paris Opera."

Julian Ash, in all his impeccable glory, swam up like a genie before her eyes. Graceful, ruthlessly correct, every black hair in place. Julian of the intense looks. Julian of the warm hand. Julian.

Lily swallowed. "Carbury and he are neighbors."

"Yes. Chelton will be certain to attend."

Lily shifted in her chair, swinging around to stare into the fire. Since that night by his side, she had not mentioned the illustrious, unforgettable lord. He of the heroism in the Rue de la Paix. He of the opera box. He of the inscrutable lure to her senses.

Foster's voice intruded on her reverie.

"Miss Hanniford, Mrs. Roland, the Countess de Chaumont."

The French lady sailed into the drawing room in her newest finery, a bright mandarin silk tea gown that she'd purchased from Worth with the compensation she'd received for her services to the Hanniford women.

"The orange is very becoming." Relieved at the interruption, Lily rose from the sofa to greet her. Over the past few months, she thought of Chaumont more as a friend than an employee. "I'm so glad you decided to treat yourself."

"The generosity of your father is magnificent, Miss Hanniford. I shall praise him ever more. His employment comes to me at a time of desperate need."

"He is very grateful," Marianne told her as she walked around her to inspect her attire. "And this is superb."

"Only if I live," Chaumont joked and put a hand to her midriff.

"I understand." Lily put a hand beneath her breast and made a desperate face at the other two. "I am so corseted, I can barely breathe. And I'm so excited, I hope I don't spill the tea."

"You will do well." Chaumont squeezed her hand. "Do not think of it. Converse. Smile. Enjoy yourself and it will come to you."

"And if I make a mistake?"

"Never stop. Make the change when next you have the same task to perform."

"Yes, of course. I will do this well." Lily closed her eyes. Her father expected it of her. The three of them had traveled from Paris three weeks ago and upon their arrival had taken up residence in this house in Piccadilly. Beginning with a skeleton staff headed by Foster, the butler, they'd got on well enough while he hired a housekeeper, four more maids and three footmen. Chaumont had joined them from Paris last week and taken a small house near Hanover Square. With her, she brought two more trunks of clothes for Lily plus another two for Marianne. All had been diligently tailored to the precise measurements of each lady, crafted by those at the House of Worth.

Dressing the ladies in grand style was Killian's priority, closely seconded by furnishing the London house.

"No expense will be too great," Killian had often repeated.

He wanted a showpiece and had rented the house from an elderly earl frantic to pay his bills. As a backdrop for his business dealings and a venue to exhibit his wealth and his family, Killian reveled in his skill to wrest it from the desperate Englishman. The house sat on one major thoroughfare in London, a few doors away from Number One, the home of the Dukes of Wellington. A few houses in one direction, the Duke of Devonshire lived. The Rothschilds lived in the other direction. An American bachelor from Montana who had made millions from mining silver had recently rented the house next door. Across the street was The Ritz, where Killian dined often or had terrines de frois gras sent over for his lunch. This afternoon, he'd insisted that the chef send over *amuse-bouche* for the tea party Lily and Marianne hosted. Their first event at home in London, he wanted every detail to be the finest.

Chaumont surveyed the art in the drawing room. Pausing in front of an oil over the mantel, she looked at Marianne. "*Mon Dieu*, I am overcome. Is that painting by Monsieur Delacroix?"

"*Oui,* madame," Marianne said, walking toward the portrait of pianist Frédéric Chopin. "Marvelous for its delicacy, is it not?"

"Is this the one that some fool cut in half? The one with his lover, George Sand?"

"It is. Monsieur Hanniford likes Chopin's etudes and he decided he must have it."

"Even if," added Lily, "the piano in the picture seems unfinished and his lover, Miss Sand, is missing."

"No matter." Marianne chuckled. "Monsieur Hanniford likes it."

"And even though it cost more than all our wardrobes from Worth combined," Lily said with amusement, "he had to own it."

Marianne had found it in an auction house on the Champs-Élysées and had told her uncle about it. "He comes in here to view it each morning after his breakfast."

"Astonishing," said Chaumont, bending forward to examine the brushwork. "When we were in Paris, I knew he liked to visit the galleries, but I did not know he wished to buy pieces."

"He wishes he could draw or paint," Lily said as she led them to sit near the fire. "Marianne does both and knows a brilliant work when she sees it."

Chaumont put a hand to her throat, in her eyes stood awe. "I am enthralled. I did not know this about you, Madame Roland. I would like to see your work."

"Thank you. But no, I will not show any of it."

"She's very good," said Lily. "She won't tell you that, but I can."

"Oh, but you must let me see! I insist." Chaumont touched her hand to Marianne's wrist.

Lily answered for her cousin. "She refuses to show her works to anyone other than us at home."

"Today, after all your guests leave," Chaumont pleaded with Marianne.

"No, thank you. I do what thrills me. My work is not classical."

"All the better," Chaumont said. "In Paris, there is new interest in art. It spreads, I think, here too. We have—how shall we say?—new interpretations. Painters, sculptors. You met one of them a few months ago. He has created sensations with his women."

Lily could recall having met no artists. "Who is this?"

Marianne glanced away.

"Who?" Lily asked of Chaumont.

"The Duc de Remy."

"You did not tell me he is a painter," Lily said to Marianne.

"A sculptor," Marianne said quietly and strolled to the window.

Did she not wish to speak about Remy? "Does he have talent, Madame Chaumont?"

"Indeed." The comtesse inclined her head. "He has recently acquired a new commission for the City of Paris."

"How wonderful for him." Lily raised her brows at Chaumont, puzzled by Marianne's silence.

In answer, Chaumont lifted her shoulders. "He works in marble. Bronze, too."

"I understand he has a mistress." Marianne fingered the edge of the draperies. "Is that true?"

Chaumont gave a sharp laugh. "I understand he has sent her away."

"Really?" Within the word was hope.

"Truly, madame. My friends say he was bored."

"How can that be? She was lovely."

Lily cocked her head. How would Marianne know if Remy's lover were beautiful?

"Lovely or not, she has departed. The story goes that he gave her money to retire to the country. Gossips say he is… how you say in English. Pining."

Marianne whirled to face Chaumont. "Pining?"

"For a new woman."

"Oh." She struggled to smile. "What you would expect from an artist, *oui?*"

Lily had never seen Marianne so secretive. Indeed she was a very bad actress, feigning disinterest in Remy.

Marianne grew nervous, her fingers clutched together so

hard her flesh turned white. "He needs a new model, I expect. One who will pose for him in the nude."

How would Marianne know that women posed for him without their clothes?

"Does he," asked Lily, "need models who do that?"

"He does," Chaumont confirmed.

"How else could he impart realism, eh?" Marianne asked. "I saw two of his pieces. A man, tortured, which he named *Samson*. He was spectacular. *Diana* was another form and she was breath-taking."

Lily gazed at her cousin, marveling in surprise. "You've seen his works?"

"I went one day to a private showing. You'd gone to the book store along the Seine and I knew you would be hours."

Lily recalled the day, a cold one, when Marianne had left her to her own devices in the book store and gone off for an hour or more. Lily suppressed a grin, but was eager to tease her cousin. "I thought you'd gone in search of a new hat."

Marianne demurred with a small smile. "Perhaps, at first. But I'd seen a billboard outside the Louvre advertising Remy's exhibition and since I had met the man, I was curious."

Chaumont leaned toward her. "What did you think of his work?"

Marianne flourished a hand. "I liked the *Samson*, not the *Diana*."

"Rumor has it he sold the *Samson*," said Chaumont. "For many thousands of francs, too. Enough to make his bankers smile."

"I hope enough to feed him and a new mistress." Marianne's gaiety did not hide her jealousy.

"Oui, many artists earn a living." Chaumont said with a sigh. "People can afford to buy art now that we are done with

empires and wars and revolutions. All the more reason to cultivate your own talents, Madame Roland."

"I am not accomplished. And I was never trained. The war took my land and home. There was no money for frivolities like art instruction."

"But talent may not need instruction. You know I have many friends in Paris. You could bring your work and we could call on Remy—"

"Oh, no, *merci*, madame."

Was Marianne too quick to refuse?

Lily made a note of it.

"I do not wish to trouble them."

Chaumont muttered something about small *damage*, shrugging off Marianne's objection. "But they are quite friendly, eager to meet others who struggle with their art. When next we return, I will introduce you. We'll go up to Pigalle—"

Marianne laughed politely and took a chair opposite Lily and Chaumont. "No, no. I've heard of that crowd up on the hill in Montmarte. They are radicals."

"Remy is one of them," Chaumont said with nonchalance. "But no *revolutionaire*. You saw him. A normal man but with talent. He encourages the others, too. In truth, they are becoming the mode. Trust me. They live and breathe and eat and make love just like the rest of us. But if they render the rest of us in lines that are startling and new, is that to be condemned? Or ignored?"

Marianne gazed at her hands in her lap. "You put me to shame, Madame Chaumont."

"I do not mean to. If you are inclined to sketch or paint or sculpt or write or compose, is it not your life's work to perfect your vision and give it to the world?"

Those were probably the most profound words Chaumont had ever spoken to them. Lily gazed from the French woman to Marianne who raised her face to consider the countess, respect upon her features.

"You have a point, madame. I shall attempt to change how I regard my art."

"Do." She smiled broadly, her smile a genuinely benevolent one. "Now, we must think of our tea. Who has been invited? Refresh my memory."

Lily brushed the silk of her skirts, ready to recite the list they'd worked so diligently to perfect. For their first afternoon at home, Marianne and she had endeavored to make the party lively. Yet because their acquaintances were so new and limited, they invited other Americans they knew as well as the English they had met in the past few weeks. "Lord and Lady Templeton have accepted and they bring their son, Charles. Lord Pinkhurst. Lord Hardesty and his sister, Lady Rose. The Manchesters from Boston."

Chaumont tapped a finger against her lips. "Pinkhurst is a rogue. Not rich, but his charm makes up for the lack. And the Manchesters? Who are they?"

Lily was tickled to see Pinkie again. She hadn't since Paris and their escapade to the cabaret in Montmarte. "Bankers. My father has accounts there."

"And what of the Duchess of Landon? Did you invite her?" Chaumont had pressed heartily for the elderly lady to be added to the invitations. She was a doyenne who influenced society mightily. She'd led the town to accept newcomers like the Jeromes from New York and the Kings from Georgia. Hopefully, she'd shepherd the Hannifords from Baltimore, too.

"I did, but—" Lily shook her head. "She declined due to a prior engagement. But she begged to be remembered for our next tea."

"Excellent." Chaumont cocked her head. "What of Lord Chelton?"

Lily caught sight of the footman approaching with the tea tray. "I did not send a card."

"No?" Chaumont looked from Lily to Marianne and back again. "But he showed such interest in you in Paris."

Too much. Too quickly. That night at the opera, so close for so very long, his focus on her electrified her. His intensity stole her breath. His proximity set her afire. His hand on hers burned and branded. She admired his grace, she applauded his demeanor, she envied his *savoir faire*. But near him, she felt rough, uncut. Too buoyant. Close to him, she compared herself to any English girl. She was not sedate, not always serene. At home in America such contrasts never occurred to her. There she was in her element. Here, with him, she doubted she could ever be. "Really I think it best he not come."

"But he was most enchanted with you. I am certain. I saw it." Chaumont was triumphant in her declaration.

"I did not encourage him, madame."

Chaumont fell back in her seat. "Why ever not? He is most handsome and of a proper lineage."

Lily beseeched Marianne with a look. "You won't help me here?"

Her cousin laughed. "You're digging a big enough hole for yourself."

"Ah, thank you."

"Lord Chelton is heir to a very fine title, lands that are extensive and a few houses, one here in town."

Clutching her hands together, Lily vowed to close this topic. "His father and mine are in a dispute over a business dealing. I know few details, but from what I gather it is bitter."

"However, you told me their name is not on your father's list. Therefore, *viola!*"

"I tell you, madame, their dispute won't end amicably. I

know my father." She shot from her chair. "It's bad enough I came here appearing the pitiful supplicant with dollars in her hand shopping for a husband. But I will not entertain any man who thinks ill of me or my father. I agree to look at those gentlemen who appear before me, and I refuse to mix my father's aspirations for my future with his intentions for his own."

"As you wish, *Mademoiselle*. I will speak no more of him."

"Thank you, Clemence," Lily said, using the countess's given name for the first time and employing one of her father's techniques to endear an adversary to his cause. She needed the woman for many reasons, not the least of which was to smooth the path for her to meet men, many men, many English men of some means or much or none. Lily really did not care how many were set before her. How many she danced with or ate with or curtsied to. She cared only that none of them be an opponent of her father's. And no one bear the carriage or the beauty or the name of Julian Ash, the Marquess of Chelton.

Foster appeared in the doorway.

"Yes? What is it?"

"Miss Hanniford, the first guests have arrived."

"Wonderful." She could get on with this little tea party and end this useless argument. "Do show them in. We're ready for them, aren't we?"

Marianne tossed her a grin.

Chaumont nodded.

The procession began. The Templetons were an older couple, graying and doddering. Assisting them to their chairs was their son, Charles, also gray but very sprightly, talkative and nervous. Charles, his parents were quick to tell the ladies, was a bachelor. He deftly changed the subject to the weather.

In the midst of that, Lord Hardesty and his sister, Lady Rose, arrived.

"They rented a house near mine in Troyes last summer," said Chaumont as the two took their seats and were introduced all around. "Lady Rose is a talented pianist. I thrilled to hear her play each evening, the notes waltzing on the night breezes to my little house."

Lady Rose, a pale blonde with small plain features, inclined her head in polite acceptance of the praise. "You are more than kind, madame. I play only to amuse myself and my brother. Do either of you play? I notice you have a portrait of Chopin."

So on the conversation went among them all at a pleasant pace when Foster once more appeared to announce a new set of arrivals.

"Superb, Foster," Lily said, glowing that this reception was going along so very well with lively discussion and great harmony among them all. She rose to her feet.

But froze in her tracks.

Behind Mr. and Mrs. William Manchester and their daughter, Dahlia, stood the very man who had not been invited. He was imperious, tall and dark and faultlessly attired in a black suit, fine linen shirt and bronze waistcoat that set golden fires in his dark brown eyes. He smiled politely, his gaze finding hers, friendly and cool for teatime ambiance. Gratefully, she discovered her manners did not desert her and introduced them all in turn. He was appropriately apologetic for having intruded on the invitation. But Manchester came to his defense sighting a meeting between them that had gone on too long and the hope to bring him along, knowing the Hannifords wished to make new acquaintances here in London.

"We're delighted to have you, Lord Chelton," Lily lied through her teeth.

"Thank you, Miss Hanniford. I assured Mr. Manchester we had met before and you approve of me."

Approve? You rogue. You know I do no such thing. "We did meet in Paris when Madame le Comtesse's coach was waylaid by a dog running in the streets."

Lily moved, a hand out indicating he should sit beside her on the sofa. It was no particular honor as it was the only seat vacant. Settling into a quietude, she let the others complete the tale of the afternoon when Remy performed his valiant service in the Rue de la Paix. Taking his tea from her, Julian sat back to enjoy his proximity.

Manchester was an acquaintance of his father's. Well known in the financial streets, the American banker was hale and hearty, a fellow most got on with, especially indebted English aristocracy. Like his father.

Like me.

He'd known of the Hannifords move from Paris to Piccadilly. Following the details in the gossip sheets was easy. Too much so. His fascination with the Americans' comings and goings, their house, their furniture, their art purchases, had devolved into a habit. One he hated. One he could not seem to break. And he had tried. Repeatedly.

Lily Hanniford had rejected his advances at the opera.

He should move onward. Forget her.

The eyes, though.

They were the lure that drew him back.

The fact that she had told him to go hang was the other bit that hooked him.

Galled him.

Intrigued him.

Damn her.

He watched her. Poised, energetic, she lost herself in the

conversation. Forgetting about him? Had she? The consummate hostess, she appeared. Was she that well trained? He'd have to acknowledge the skills of an American finishing school and concede the possibility that she had learned very well. Such was possible. He had done the same. Spending years at his governess's knee, with his tutors, at Eton and Cambridge, he'd developed the art of banter, the challenge of the drawing room to remain pertinent and witty.

Whatever he contributed to the topic now was polite drivel. He knew it, didn't change it. Perhaps it was no more or less unimportant than what the others had to offer.

And in the meantime, he had the distinct pleasure of watching Lily Hanniford laugh and gesture and comment. She was, as before, natural, correct but uncomplicated. Exactly as he had remembered her, she shone above the other ladies. But he suppressed the compliment. It did him no good to think so well of her. He had come with one clear purpose to rid himself of the irritating curiosity that her eyes were not sheer blue. But navy. Or black. Or even red.

Red because she was a veritable witch to obsess him so.

And he'd come here, determined to exorcise her.

And he was a man of his word. Keeping promises, above all, to himself.

The afternoon passed. His tea grew cool. His goal grew colder.

Her eyes, he had copious occasion to note, were various colors. Resembling a summer's sky. A blue opal. A rare blue diamond.

Her brows, dark as her lustrous hair, were a perfect long arch.

Her cheekbones prominent.

And her lips….

He focused on them much too often.

Her mouth made a perfect full bow. Laughing, smiling,

grinning, speaking in glowing terms about their experiences in Paris and their move into this house.

The hour waned. The time for tea had passed.

The Hardestys and the Templetons made their farewells. The Manchesters rose to leave.

He must, as well.

As they stood in the foyer and the butler collected the guests coats and umbrellas, Mrs. Manchester told the Hanniford ladies that she hoped they would meet again soon.

"We're to present our Dahlia in society," Mrs. Manchester said with a frisson of delight. "Just like you, Miss Hanniford."

Dahlia Manchester pressed her lips together, blushing red as a radish. "Mama, please."

"You understand, I'm sure," the lady said by way of apology for her forwardness. "We're eager to get on with showing her about. Will all of you attend the Earl of Darforth's supper?" She took on the air of a conspirator.

Marianne shifted uncomfortably. Chaumont froze, her face made of ice, at the lady's gauche mention of another's invitation.

Julian set his teeth at the woman's breech of etiquette.

Lily smiled sweetly, ignoring the lack of protocol. "We will."

"Marvelous. And the Carbury house party?"

Marianne cast a stern eye at the butler to continue his task of assisting all with their coats.

Lily grinned, all grace. "That, too."

"Oh, wonderful." Mrs. Manchester clasped her hands before her in joy.

Dahlia secured the buttons on her coat. "Mama, we must go. Thank you so much for a lovely afternoon."

"The Carbury party will be our first in the country." The lady was not to be diverted. "Lord Chelton, I understand you are invited, too. So we will be a lovely intimate group."

His guts twitching at the possibility, Julian wished to show some restraint lest he wag his tail, eager as a puppy to see Lily again. "I'm afraid I have not yet replied."

Chaumont gave him the drollest look. "But your lands adjoin, do they not, Monsieur le Marquis? I would say you would be the first to attend, *oui*?"

"I have another pending engagement and may not be able to attend."

"A pity," said Mrs. Manchester.

And when Lily Hanniford's gaze met his, Julian stilled. Disappointment lingered in those blue depths. Longing, quickly covered by a fluttering of lashes.

So. She was conflicted as well.

Dare he deny the hunger he'd glimpsed in her eyes?

He'd be a fool to call it nil. An idiot to go. A cretin to refrain.

He bowed over each lady's hand and lingered before Lily. "I bid you good day. Until we meet again."

CHAPTER 5

"Good afternoon, Burton," Julian greeted the aging butler whom his father had brought with him from Shanghai three decades ago when their merchant house had gone bankrupt. "Is His Grace arrived in the library?"

His father had sent a note to his bachelor quarters earlier this morning. The man had been testy of late and Julian would rather face the fire than fan it by not attending his so-called 'urgent meeting'.

Besides, Julian adored the grand house. On Green Park, the family home of the Dukes of Seton backed to the flowing lawn near the old St. James's Palace. Not as grand as Spencer House farther up the green, nonetheless, the London residence was as renowned for its Palladian splendor. Maintained year-round by a regular staff of butler, two maids and two footmen, the white stone beauty rose three stories. Drafty as it could be in winter, it was refreshing in spring when the breezes from the park flowed into the jade Peacock salon and washed the wood-paneled library in sparkling sunlight.

"Yes, my lord. He awaits you there."

Unusual for the old man to summon him with any urgency. What was amiss? The mills? The workers? Julian divested himself of his walking stick, gloves, hat and coat. Tugging on his cuffs, he smiled at the taciturn servant whose good will he always was careful to cultivate. "Excellent. I shall go. Is my sister at home from her calls?"

"Lady Elanna arrived a few minutes ago, my lord. She and Her Grace also await you."

"Ah." A family meeting. Rare, those. And not a sign of a topic meant to bring a smile to his lips. Rather it importuned a row. "Thank you. I'll go up."

When he opened the door and strode through, Julian breathed in the abject silence—and the anxiety. His father glared at him. His mother took note of his presence and sniffed, her usual sign of impatience. His sister pressed her lips together, her eyes round and intense, pleading with him to save her from whatever evil had befallen her already.

"Good you're here. Come, come." His father waved him into his smoke-filled study. Standing before the fire, the old man hooked both hands behind his back and tipped his head toward the only remaining vacant chair. "Have a seat."

Julian took it, but couldn't take his gaze from his father. The man was pale. His skin an uncharacteristic color of gray. Whatever today's topic, it was worse than ever before.

His mother inhaled, her eyes floating along the alabaster mantel. "Now, Seton. Do get on with it, will you?"

"Have a dinner engagement, dearest?" his father chided his mother. "Why should I have to ask?"

"I must change. I hope this will not turn into one of your lectures about the foibles of your ancestors." Her snipe at him was an old one, centered on the poor traits he'd inherited from his forebears. Like ridiculing his wife.

"Have no time for the recitation, do you, pet?" He turned

to face the fire, but the sneer was one Julian heard. Had heard for most of his life.

The duchess was not to be intimidated. "No, none. These meetings of yours are tedious, Seton. I fear you are becoming infirm in your mind."

His father spun on his heel. At sixty-two, the man might be portly, he might have a shock of silver hair, but he had the black eye of a warlock and the disposition of one, given bait. At that, Julian's mother was quite expert. "I am not so infirm, as you put it, girlie, as you are at forgetting my orders."

His mother tsked, rapping her fan softly against her open palm. "You cannot incite me, George. Do be quick."

"We're in the shitter!"

She gasped. Her fan fluttered upward to her throat. "There is no need for vulgarity."

"Oh, there is need." He strode forward to face her and bend low, his nose nearly touching her own. His nostrils flared. "An urgent one."

Elanna swallowed loudly.

Julian inhaled, girding for the storm.

"Do you go to Lady Tottingham's this evening, by any odd chance?" His father was luring his mother with bitter words. "Do you?"

His mother turned her face to one side, her fan to her cheek, separating her from her husband's breath. "You've been drinking."

"Of course I have!" he bellowed. "I have cause. Just cause. You, my dear gel, give me cause."

She shot to her feet.

"Sit down."

"I will not listen—"

"Oh, you will, madam. In fact, you will do a great deal more than that."

She stared at him, her body swaying to and fro.

Julian hoped to God she'd sit soon or they'd be here all damn night.

She regained her chair.

Elanna closed her eyes.

Julian let out a breath.

"Now then. Affairs at Broadmore are in turmoil. Wilson has taken to his bed." Their bailiff for the estate had always been sickly, getting worse each year. "He's got a bad case of pleurisy."

"Or nerves," his mother added under her breath.

His father quelled her with fury in his black gaze. He dug a handkerchief from his trouser pocket and wiped his mouth. "Most—Most ungracious of you."

She rolled her shoulders.

Julian shook his head. She and Wilson had never gotten on.

Broadmore in west Sussex was the original land grant estate from the Crown to the first Duke of Seton two centuries ago. Nearly fifteen-thousand acres of prime land yielded the bulk of the crops that fed the two-hundred plus tenants and the coffers of the ducal family. Until the past few years. With poor weather, little investment in new plows and wagons, the lack of cash to purchase seed, the tenants who faithfully farmed the land were growing poorer. Unable to pay their rents in full. The skills of his father's bailiff there, Robert Wilson, were of little use. If the land did not yield, the tenants could not sell their grain or fatten their animals. They not only could not pay their rents, they sickened.

"Wilson is the best man in all Sussex. I don't doubt he's worn himself to the bone and I don't begrudge him a rest." This graciousness, this compliment was a new phenomenon his father had begun to exhibit as the profitability of their estate had diminished.

"He needs no rest, but replacement," his mother said.

"Absolutely not," his father disagreed. "Wilson insisted to rise from his bed and rallied to show me the estate books. We tallied the rents to date. Also balanced the sales of the grain against the expense of the seed for this spring."

Julian folded his hands, knowing what was coming. He'd known each year for the past three. Each spring the estate books had not balanced. Each spring, the Duchy of Seton sank deeper into the mire caused by the combination of abundant, cheap American grain imports and terrible weather. Rain, ice, snow had flooded their fields at Broadmore since last October and to a lesser extent at their smaller estate, his own, of Willowreach in Kent.

"We have enough money to run this house for two months. Pay the servants and the annual taxes. Then we must either sell it or let the house to any rich American who wants a fancy residence for his chicks."

"No," his mother said beneath her breath. "This is not so."

"Not? So?" Quentin George Makefield Ash, the seventh duke, barked in laughter. Then he advanced on his wife of thirty-six years with fire in his eyes. "Who are you, madam, to nay say me? I told you over and over these past few years. Now we are well and truly cooked as a Christmas goose. At Christmas, I told you that you must no longer visit your seamstress. You must do with last year's hats. I would not pay your marks. And worse…"

She lifted her face to stare at him, her mouth pinched, her skin drained of color.

"I refused to pay any of your chits to cover your debts at cards."

"They are not much."

He gave a sharp laugh. "They are not paid, either."

"But, but… George, you must. I cannot continue—"

"Precisely. I warned you years ago. You went on your

merry way. Even if, madam, we had means, your addiction to the tables has ruined us."

"Only my addiction?" She fixed him with slitted eyes. "What of yours?"

The old man's nostrils flared wider.

Elanna pressed back into her chair. Julian fought not to do the same.

His father sagged. "My amusements have long since ceased, Charlotte."

She raised her fan, the snap of the sticks the sign of her outrage. "Do not insult me with lies."

Elanna pressed her lips together. If she understood the implications of the *amusements* their mother indicated, his sister did not flinch.

"My interests in such pastimes ended last year. I could not afford them then, either in coin or affection."

"Last year's fancy has not given way to a new one?" his mother pressed, while she whipped up the air with her fan.

"No. If you took time away from the card tables long enough, you might have learned that from your so-called friends."

"I doubt it."

"What? You think they'd tell you any tidbit that might paint me in a good light?"

"As if you could stand in any good light."

Children. They were such frightful children.

"I will ignore that, dear gel. We have much to decide. Now…" He strolled to his desk and picked up a sheaf of papers. Thin rag. Invoices, they were.

"These," he said, holding aloft a few, "are yours, Madam. I will pay what I can of them from your monthly allowance."

"George!" She gained her feet. "I—I need that money."

He stared at her with sad eyes that offered only pity. Then

he picked up another stack, thinner, but still, quite a few. "These, dear Elanna, are yours."

"For gowns," said his mother, "for the Season. She must have them, George. Must!"

"Have them. Wear them. These I will endeavor to cover completely. But know, my sweet child, that they are to get you a man who can pay for any future frocks."

Julian ached for his sister.

She looked at her hands in her lap and nodded. "Sir, thank you. I understand."

"Well, sadly, girl, that is not all. We are in such a state that if you do not snare a suitor by June's end and marry by July, you must retire to Broadmore."

"Papa!"

"Permanently."

Julian hated to picture Elanna with a man who would not cherish her. Obviously, she hadn't either. But time was short for her to find a mate.

"Seton," his mother was atwitter, "this is outrageous. She'll be a laughing stock. People will think she's on the shelf or that there's something hideously wrong with her. And you know what they'll say..." Her eyes widened with suggestions of impropriety.

"What, dear Charlotte? What will they say? That she's committed a *faux pas*? Hmm?"

"Worse. Well you know it."

"Oh, yes. That some man assumed too many liberties with her."

"Stop that."

"That she had her chance and she chose once, chose badly, chose too quickly. That we'd hide her away for—"

"Enough, Seton." His mother fretted with the edge of her fan, now dormant in her lap. Her lips quivered, a sign of the onset of tears. "You torment me."

"The way you did me?"

"You know I hate discussion of money." She fished a lace handkerchief from her sleeve and dabbed at her eyes.

"Would that you would hate pissing it away as well," his father mourned.

"Oh, you are a cruel man. Cruel," she said, sniveling, real tears in her china-blue eyes.

Julian groaned.

This old argument between them was infuriating. They never openly stated their grievances in front of Julian and Elanna, but they could wheedle and cajole, criticize and affront with careful precision. The gist of it, which Julian had learned bit by agonizing bit, was some indiscretion that the two of them had committed when they first met. Each held the other responsible for the fault. Yet to hear them tell it, in the beginning each had loved the other with a searing passion. For more than a decade, they had turned to each other and burned with a sensuality that conceived his own life as well as Elanna's. Then, at once, the flames had died. In the ruins, they tore at each other's dignity. He in company with disreputable women, she in company with feckless gamblers. Why and how they could not lay down their arms, escaped Julian. Their feud taught Elanna and him a marital lesson to befriend others with caution. Intimacy was a folly meant for fools.

Julian had had enough of their bickering for today. "If you two can insult each other more profoundly, please do it quickly."

"You presume to order me, boy?" The old man pointed at him with a shaky hand.

Concern for his father's health coiled inside him. "Never. But this serves no purpose, Father. I've heard this tirade for decades and I'm quite tired of it. Tell us rather more about the finances, please."

"Very well. I have cut the staff. At Broadmore, two of the maids, one of the footmen. Here, I'll relieve the seasonal staff at the end of June. Four of them. Two upstairs maids, the second scullery maid and the new footman."

His mother caught a handkerchief to her eyes. "Disgraceful. The house will be a shambles. How will we manage?"

The old man shook his head. "You could pick up a feather duster."

"You're mad," she seethed.

"Right you are. So then! No more monthly shipments of wine. No refurbishment of the upholstery in the drawing room."

"Absurd!" his mother objected. "I cannot imagine. How can we attract a proper match for Elanna?"

Julian winced. Leave it to his mother to use Elanna as an excuse to get what she wanted. The woman had no scruples. Few motherly instincts, either.

"Ba!" His father put a hand on his hip. "She turned down two men last year. Old Wayland's whelp who has a bit of money."

"He's not yet out of dresses," the duchess objected.

He prefers men. Julian shifted. "He's not right for our girl."

"And Lord Canfield was—is a rogue," Elanna added. "With bad breath."

Julian stifled a laugh. "Marriage is too important to demand that Elanna take whatever comes her way."

"Like Carbury?" their mother said with the arch of one long brow and a pointed gaze at Elanna. "Why not? He's eager. Likes her. He's not bound himself up with debts, and he's out of mourning."

Elanna shifted. "He's very nice. But I dare say I cannot find it in my heart to—"

"Not for you, is he?" the duke asked. "Well then. Would

you be able to find it in your heart to take a position as governess?"

"*What?*" His mother gaped.

Elanna fell back in her chair.

Julian cringed.

"Or teach in a girl's school?"

"Surely, Seton," said the duchess, waving her handkerchief in a frantic beat, "you jest. You do. The girl will not, I say will not lower herself to turn to anyone's employ. Surely, surely —" She was on her feet, pacing the window, back to face her husband before his desk. "You cannot make her do that. It'd ruin us. Utterly."

The old man simply crossed his arms and studied her.

"What will people say, good sir?" she beseeched him.

"I applaud your social instincts, my girl. Thought you'd lost them. Sent them out to roost with all our money."

"Stop." She hung her head and stomped her foot. "Do. Stop."

"I cannot. As for doings here, there are enough funds for the ordinary teas, a few dinner parties, a musicale, if you wish. But no balls." His tone turned maudlin, almost apologetic. So very unlike his normal boisterous self. "I'm sorry, Elanna, but you'll have to dance at other people's invitation."

"What of the sale of Cardiff Shipping?" his mother asked, her handkerchief to her temple. "Will you do it? That could save us."

"Save us? You think so? Oh, if only that were so. Last winter, we had two offers. Neither of them was worth a prayer on Sunday. The better of the two came from the American. Hanniford." His father turned to him with a tilt of his head.

"I haven't seen him since Paris last autumn. And he has not contacted me." Julian hadn't wished to open that relationship again. Instead, he'd called upon their London lawyer and estate agent Phillip Leland last week in the City. On official business for himself to monitor his own investment in railroad expansion in the Cotswolds, he'd taken the occasion to ask if any news had come from Killian Hanniford lately. None had and Julian was happy for it. He did not wish to be reminded of Hanniford's beguiling daughter.

Julian brushed the wool of his trousers. "Leland believes if we hold out for another six months or until the new year, we would receive a better price for the company than is the current offer."

"How much better?" his father asked.

"Twenty percent more."

"Healthy." His father arched his brows. "And why would that be?"

"Leland courts two buyers. One wants the company to expand his own reach. The other wants it to gut it."

"And the twenty-percent advantage would come from stalling?"

"Exactly. Selling it to the first man who will see over time that the second man would not be favored. Not for his objective."

The duchess fretted. "Are there no other answers?"

"Certainly, there is only one other asset." His father arched a sardonic brow at his wife.

"My—my diamonds," she whispered, touching the base of her throat where her most precious necklace of all her jewels would adorn her on many an occasion. "But King Charles gave them to my great grandmama. I must not, nay cannot part with them."

"But will."

Her eyes popped wide. "If…if things are this bad—"

"Never doubt it, madam."

"No. Would you sell them? I won't allow it."

"You have no choice," his father said to her.

"But I'd have nothing to wear."

His father scoffed. "However, the sale alone could keep us until—oh, shall we say? January. At most."

"Oh, George." Her tears spilled over her lids.

"We are, despite your tears, in dire straits. I have done what I could for the time being. You will abide by my orders to trim your expenses, all of you. Anything else you wish to cut, do. There is no other solution. And know too that what I have done will not be the end of it. I cannot change the weather. I cannot improve the crops, not by much in any case. Elanna, you will find a husband. Madame, you will give me your diamonds. Come to think of it, your pearls, too."

Once more his mother put her hand to her throat. Her eyes wide, she looked as if her husband wished to cut her throat. "George. They were your wedding gift."

"What a sorry investment that was, eh?"

Tears cascaded down her cheeks. She struggled up from her chair. With a turn of her heel and a swish of her skirts, she raced from the room.

Silence reigned.

Elanna rose to her feet. "I will do my duty by you, Papa. I will help. I swear to it. I'll choose a husband. One you will like."

His gaze was for once paternal and held pity for his only daughter. "Elanna, do me and yourself a favor. Search diligently. But like him for yourself."

Julian witnessed Elanna thank her father and, for the first time in many years, she rushed to kiss him on the cheek. Then she hurried away, a hand cupping her mouth.

"Help her, can you?" The duke asked him as he watched her leave the room.

"Find a man? Such arrangements are not easily done."

"Well I know it. When you're young, the blood runs hot.

Too hot to show one's true nature. And deception does not build sound unions."

Julian shifted in his chair. This was his father's old story about the failure of all marriages, a metaphor for the nightmare that was his union. So he had loved his duchess when first they'd married and then what had gone wrong? From what Julian could ascertain, they had destroyed whatever respect they had, each for the other, with lies and flirtations, excessive gambling and drinking. Julian and Elanna had witnessed the results—and learned from them. He understood marriage to be a prison of mutual love and hate. Elanna, poor girl, thought their parents' relationship to be unique.

'The world,' she'd once told Julian, 'is not like that.'

Julian had looked for evidence to prove her right. He'd discovered one woman he'd thought worthy of marriage. But he'd valued her more than she him and so he'd put marriage from his mind. He'd marry to get an heir, but not for love.

"Some couples construct a congenial bond," the duke said, morose.

"Not many."

"I count four. Four. But they are not exempt from problems. A failed career, a malformed baby, a debilitating disease."

The sudden tragedies that racked one. "Sad."

"Carbury's the only one of my acquaintance who had a complete dash of success with a woman. And what do you know, she up and died. What the hell is that for justice? I'm shocked he's eager to marry again."

"Elanna is in his sights. But he would expect a dowry and marriage settlement from us." Julian had never asked what marriage portion his father had set aside for Elanna. But he had an idea of the amount. If his father wanted him to help her secure a husband, he'd have to know something of the details.

The duke rounded his desk. He sank to his chair, all the bluster of the argument out of him, deflated, diminished. He sat, running his fingers over the edges of his large ledger book—and his fingers shook. *Did he have a palsy?* "I have preserved some of her dowry."

"Some?" Anger warmed Julian's blood. "How much?"

The duke pursed his lips. "It may yield one thousand a year. Perhaps."

A pitiful sum. And why? There was only one answer. Julian smarted at the thought. "You borrowed against it?"

The old man inhaled, firming his jaw. "I had to do it. We had to eat."

And gamble. And whore. "I understood it to be five thousand pounds a year."

"It was. Your grandfather Downey gave your mother such a magnificent marriage portion that I was able to invest it for any daughters soon after we married. It was in South American products."

Julian made a fist. "Such as?"

His father smiled like a devil, ear to ear. "Bird shit."

"I'm sorry," Julian bit off. "Say that again."

"In the fifties, soon after the marriage, I invested it with speculators. Men who wanted to buy bird guano from Peru and ship it here to spread as fertilizer over the soil."

Julian knew of it, had met a few men who owned stock in import companies that shipped it in to England and Europe. In the tired soils of Britain and the Continent, the addition had improved yields double, sometimes triple, the norm. "I understood it was lucrative. I wanted to buy some myself but the stocks were closed accounts."

"They are. Worse, the money is bound in trust and will be granted to her husband to manage after the ceremony. Even then, he may take only ten percent of the total each year for her welfare."

"Have you told her?"

"I thought it best she never know. Not the terms. Not the sum."

"And Mama?"

"Does not know either."

"And you won't tell her," Julian said with certainty.

"Never. She'd harangued me to change the terms, the law be damned. She'd want it. At first it would be a portion. Then more. She'd risk it at cards or dice, lose it, lose it all. She's a pitiful gambler, boy. You know as well as I. She'd fritter it away and then what would Elanna have?" His father sighed. "I won't tell your mother on pain of full war in this house. You won't tell her either. And you know, it's for the best."

Dear Elanna, without any candidates. "She's seen the current lot. Danced with them all. Found no one who appealed."

"There must be someone. An Irishman? A baron, a knight. Or a Frenchman with enough land left to feed himself? What of your friend, the prince, Remy?"

"Elanna likes him. Nothing more."

"He must have cousins."

"No one I'd recommend to her," Julian told him. "But then—"

"What?"

"I have funds. Savings."

"*What?*" His father scoffed. "Twenty thousand?"

Julian was shocked his father came so near the mark. "Twenty-two. How do you know?"

"Shall we say, my friends are useful?"

"And unethical to chat about a fellow's worth."

"To your father? Not so. I hear what you win at the tables. I also know what you spend at your tailors. I had to find out when I saw no bills for you. And yes, I know you've often declared that you'd save Elanna from the marriage mart with your winnings. Good of you. But she must stand on her own. Time is nigh. She must marry."

"And you won't give out the sum of her dowry. Say you will not."

"And kill her chances? I'd lie and declare the sum is grand."

Julian was aghast. "No! She'll have every roué from here to Vienna at our door."

"If she can find a man whom she admires, who's worthy of her esteem, I'll gladly hand her to him. Money, title or not."

Once more, Julian was amazed at his father. If the man had a foul temper, if he berated his wife with joyous vengeance, if he liked his brandy, if he was a feckless manager of the estates, if he had no ingenious methods to improve the crops, he did love his daughter. He did wish her happiness. If when all was said and done, he did not see the error in lying about her wealth to protect her from fortune hunters or charlatans.

"Which means we come to you," the man said matter-of-factly, drumming his fingers on the desk.

Julian blinked, the change in topic a shock. He took a moment to guard himself.

Of course, the old man would come round to him.

"I wish to discuss your own marriage prospects."

"I have none."

"You must."

Julian took a deep breath. "I've told you before I will not be pressed."

"You were always difficult," his father muttered.

"On this issue, especially."

"I don't see why. You've always known you must marry."

84

"Do the begetting, eh?"

"If you find a comely gel, the experience of begetting is not ghastly. And if rumor serves up truth about your prowess, well you know it, too."

I won't marry for money. "I won't marry for advantage."

"I did."

"It's demeaning."

"But accepted."

"Among your set, yes." Julian gave him that.

"Yours too. Look at Marlborough's boy. At Waldron's heir. It is done,."

"But I won't," Julian spat. "They may care for those girls now, but later?" He scoffed.

"Live by pride alone and you will starve," his father warned.

Pride was not the problem. Fear of a shrew in his house. Irrational, demanding. One who turned on him or worse, turned on their children like Medea. No, he'd not take a woman unless she was malleable. "I'd like to solve my own problems."

"Good intentions?" his father asked with a strained smile. "Noble. But you cannot eat them. Nor pay our taxes or your mother's gambling debts."

"I keep trying." *But my skills at the table are just as bad as my mother's.*

His father shook his head. "I tell you, I married for love. A tender bit, but it passes."

Julian quelled the urge to laugh. That was how the man explained his and his mother's screaming matches, the crockery that flew, the insinuations that shook the rafters. "Passes, oh yes. Falls into—what did you term your relationship with Mama—disrepair?"

"No matter," the old man said and flung out a hand. "You tilt at windmills. Meanwhile we are soon to become known debtors. And there are options for you. Bright, comely options."

Julian stared at him. "Let me guess. You have suggestions."

"One in particular. The American Lily."

The American Lily, yes. That's how she'd come to be known in London. The tall, graceful girl with the perfectly oval face, the pile of midnight curls and those uncanny blue eyes that bore right through a man. She'd been photographed, her pictures copied and redrawn, *The American Beauty*, once maligned by cartoonists, now glorified by anyone who could catch a glimpse of her.

And Julian had tried not to follow suit. But yesterday, he'd succumbed and gone to tea at the house in Piccadilly.

"Well?" his father asked. "I understand you've met her."

His stomach churned. Julian didn't want an arranged marriage for himself and he would not wish one on a young woman he liked. Or this one who favored him one minute and not the next. "I won't marry her."

"Does she have warts on her nose? No. On the contrary, I understand she is quite lovely. And you like her."

Who had told him that? Elanna knew his reaction to her. His mother, too, had witnessed the scene at the opera in Paris. He'd been careless to allow anyone to see it. But he'd been entranced.

"You like her quite a bit."

"And I would predict you have more than one reason to suggest her," Julian said with bitterness filling his throat.

"She has thousands of reasons to commend her. More than that Van de Putte girl."

Julian had met the American, Priscilla Van de Putte, last spring and had spent the next few months escaping her clutches. Selfish, spoiled, Priscilla was the epitome of a woman he would never take to his arms, let alone to the altar. "I've avoided marriage so far. I intend to extend my run."

He rose from his chair and headed for the hall.

As he reached for the door, his father called to him.

He paused. "Yes?"

"I must tell you Killian Hanniford sent a request around yesterday to meet with me."

That spelled trouble. His father had no head for negotiating. "And?"

"He still wishes to buy shares of Cardiff Shipping."

"I see." Julian had refused to continue talks with Lily's father in Paris. He'd informed his father of it as soon as he returned to England.

"I must try because you couldn't get a decent price out of him."

And neither can you. "The company is decrepit. It needs new ships, repair of the old ones and new management. It's nigh unto bankrupt. Give over, sir. I wish to hear no more about it."

"But his daughter is worth so much more."

More than you know. Julian ground his teeth. "Sell your shares, sir, if you wish. But do not think you can barter away my marriage bed in the bargain."

CHAPTER 6

$\mathcal{L}$ ily and Marianne took the stairs down to main floor of Carbury Manor.

"I hope there's tea," Lily whispered.

"With fat cucumber sandwiches," Marianne said.

"Frankly, I could do with a shot of brandy." She hated being caged with a dozen people she did not know for four solid days. Worse, the Duchess of Seton was here and her greeting to them had not been warm. "Especially when facing a certain gauntlet."

Lily and Marianne had arrived minutes behind the lady and her daughter, pretty Lady Elanna. All four had politely recalled their meeting at the opera in Paris. When Marianne, bless her for her ingenuity, had inquired about the health of Lord Chelton, his mother was quick to add how well he was and that all could soon see for themselves, as he would be along soon. Lily feigned serenity at that news, while her stomach did a little flippity-flop. Thankfully, Lord Carbury kept the introductions brief and summoned the housekeeper to show the ladies to their bedrooms.

"How long does tea last?" Lily asked Marianne.

"Forever," Marianne said, as she took the last step into the marbled foyer.

Lily stifled a groan as Carbury's butler appeared from the service entrance.

With an officious nod, he showed them into the drawing room.

The party had already assembled and they alternately stood or sat, sipping tea and nibbling biscuits, looking as jovial as if they'd been stuffed for mounting. Carbury shot to his feet, offering his chair to Marianne and showing Lily to the sofa beside Lady Elanna. Carbury began the introductions.

"Her Grace met you earlier," he said and they exchanged polite nods. He went on to bring them to the three older ladies sitting like finely dressed little dolls in three separate wing chairs.

"Lady Struthers. Lady Summersfell. And Lady Fielding. I wish to present Mrs. Marianne Roland and her cousin, Miss Lily Hanniford."

The three ranged in age from sprightly to doddering to snoozing.

"What? What?" said the last one when she heard her named repeatedly invoked. "Yes. Yes, I see you." She struggled to loop her glasses over her right ear. "Pretty things. American, aren't you?"

"We are, my lady," Lily said, smiling at the woman's delicate skin, pale as parchment and just as pure. "We're delighted to meet you."

"Don't be silly, girl. If Carbury has his way, we three will take to our beds for four days."

"Now, madam," Carbury began, flustered.

"Tut tut, Gruffyd. We've known you too long."

"These ladies," he said as color rose to stain his cheeks, "are my great aunts."

"We love him," proclaimed Lady Struthers.

"He needs a wife," announced Lady Summersfell.

"And he's unlucky in love," mourned Lady Fielding with a shake of her head. "But you could do."

Lily smiled broadly. "Thank you for the compliment, madam."

"Aunt, *please*, do not press the young lady."

"Nonsense, Gruffyd. Thought you said you wanted a wife. Is this not the one?"

Lily swallowed the urge to laugh. But from the corner of her eye, she saw Elanna freeze, her teacup midway to her mouth.

Lord Carbury cleared his throat. "Aunt—"

"Tell me which is the one, Gruffyd. I must know so I can give her my dancing slippers. A gift from the Prince Regent, they were. Magic slippers." Her thin white brows shot high as she rolled her eyes back and forth in a merry beat.

"Madam." Marianne leaned over to take the woman's tiny wrinkled hand. "You must keep your slippers."

"Oh? Why?

"They fit you best. No one could mark the steps as you do in those shoes."

"Hmm. That was so. Brought me my William, they did."

"William was your husband?"

"Oh, no." She leaned closer to Marianne and cackled. "My lover."

Carbury cleared his throat. "Well, now, let me introduce the rest of our party—"

On he prattled, introducing three ladies, all young, one painfully so. That last was a blonde English girl with the chiseled features of a classical goddess. Mary Northridge was a distant cousin of Carbury's and meek as a mouse. The other two were Americans, older than Mary by one or two years and with the self assurance of old Knickerbocker New

York. Hilda Berghoff, quiet and flirtatious, was a brown-haired sylph with the slit-eyed look of a rodent. Her father, a Manhattan banker, was an associate of her own father's and Lily knew his reputation to be as mean as a rattle snake. Priscilla Van de Putte was a plump redhead with a hearty laugh. She was making a spectacle of herself and Lily surmised her parents had given her specific instructions to find a lord and make him hers. Quickly.

There was no mistake that the three men in the party were the three young ladies' quarry. Lord Pinkhurst, who'd escorted Marianne and her to the Montmarte cabaret, was in attendance, delighting all with his banter. Tall and rakishly tow-headed, he cut a fine figure of athletic build. That his dancing eyes retuned to Lily time and again was a compliment, but rather embarrassing. Priscilla Van De Putte was particularly put out by his attentions toward Lily. Though she tried to divert him, he seemed content to storm her defenses.

As for the other two men—Lords Torrington and Godophin—Lily questioned their abilities to court any lady. They were clumsy and nervous. Swarthy and intense, cousins, too, they grasped Lily's hand, each in turn, with unreserved enthusiasm. Their one talent was in the art of trivial conversation. That drew Hilda Berghoff toward Torrington like a fly to honey. Godolphin focused his comical smiles on Priscilla Van De Putte. Alas, that lady cared only for Pinkie.

Lily commiserated with the man. He must have felt her sympathy because he made his way to her side. "Have pity on me, will you?"

She bit her lip.

"I can see you hide your giggles." His mouth thinned. "I do the same."

"I bet that she's really quite nice when she isn't...um..."

"Stalking? That's the word you want, isn't it?"

"Hush, Pinkie."

"It's you I want. I could be out of my misery, if you'd only accept me."

He'd proposed marriage to her last week after tea. Complimented, she'd been flabbergasted and put him off. Indefinitely. "We have our understanding, do we not?"

"We do. I don't like it."

"I understand," she said on a whisper. Accepting her tea from the footman, she looked up as the butler appeared in the doorway.

"Lord Chelton, my lord," the man announced.

And in the tranquil room, cheerful in its yellow Chinoserie draperies and ivory appointments with its company of old and young, infirm and vibrant, seeking and sought after, the air changed. Fascination lent a fragrance to the atmosphere. She forgot Pinkie.

Who wouldn't?

Lord Chelton, Julian Ash in all his glory stood tall and smartly attired for the afternoon, each fold of his cravat in elegant perfection, his pin in place, his buttons done up, his trousers finely creased, his smile for each in turn, lazy and genuine. His eyes rested in hers, and with the greeting there, despite Lily's admonition to ignore him, bubbles of delight rose from her toes to her head.

Julian pushed aside the drapery and opened the casement window in his room. Dawn broke. Would that it might improve his sour mood. He gazed out upon Carbury's stable yard and the path to his block. One of the best in the county for good horseflesh. Unable to sleep, he'd decided to take advantage of it and ordered his valet to put out his riding clothes.

The Carbury house party had begun with tea two days ago. Julian's mother was in attendance and stayed well away from the younger set along with three other older ladies. They served as chaperones for the rest of the fifteen guests, plus their very solicitous host Lord Carbury. Among the chatty throng, he'd had not a moment with Lily. The lack made him testy, restless.

"Your coat, sir." His valet Richards offered it to him.

Julian shrugged into it, eager to be gone and out the door before any others. If ever he needed to exercise his mind, it was now. The guest list consisted of five young ladies, including his sister Elanna, Lily and her cousin Marianne, and, aside from him, three young men. All he had met previously, the ladies from social circles in London and the men from school. The men were as eligible as he and as financially wanting. Carbury had planned the numbers to his own advantage, making perfectly matched sets. That permitted the man to track Elanna like a hunting dog after a fox.

Julian could barely hide his tension watching his sister ward off the earl's interest. Consumed with ensuring Elanna could escape Carbury whenever she wished, Julian had not played well his role as guest. He'd done his duty to be polite to any of the young ladies' conversations. But his efforts were muddled, all due to his uncontrollable focus on Lily Hanniford. Still, he hadn't even had the opportunity to sit next to her. Though Lord Pinkhurst had—and she appeared to enjoy his attentions. *Curse the man.*

"I should count myself lucky," he muttered, buttoning his coat.

"Pardon, sir?" His man paused from brushing any lint from his shoulders.

"Nothing. Sorry, Pendley. Talking to myself."

"Yes, sir. I think you've a good morning for it, sir."

"Talking?"

"Riding, sir. The ground will be firm from the sun yesterday."

"That it will." He took his gloves from the valet's hands. "See you later."

He took the main stairs to the foyer and strode toward the back of the house and down the servants' stairs. At this hour, only they would be awake and working.

"Oh, my lord, I say!" Carbury's butler pushed from the long wooden table in the servants' hall. "You're up early. I'll send up a footman with breakfast."

"Please don't. Adams, is it?"

The butler nodded.

"I'm in no rush."

"But…tea? Before you ride, sir?"

"Thank you, no."

"Forgive me, my lord, but is this a new habit before riding?"

"I don't know what you mean."

"Miss Hanniford left a few minutes ago as well. No tea for her, either."

"Is that so?" Under those circumstances, Julian definitely didn't want anything to delay him. "I'll dine when I return."

"Very good, sir. With Miss Hanniford, perhaps?"

"Well, Adams, I cannot say. That depends on the lady. I think these American girls do as they wish."

"You've got that right, you do. She left alone, my lord."

"Did she?" He glanced toward the window, alarmed. "No maid?"

"Nor her cousin, either, sir."

"I see. Well, thank you. All the more reason why I should hurry in case she should flush out a fox or break a leg."

"Right you are. I will have the footman lay out the full service, say, in an hour?"

Julian agreed and turned for the stable block.

Carbury had a fine selection of horses and when Julian rode on succeeding days, he'd take more time to choose the best one. For income, he'd recently sold his own best stallion. This morning, he cared not a fig for the biggest or fastest. Two grooms obliged him, saddling up one large black beast, and pointing him in the direction of the lady who'd ridden off minutes ago.

She ridden east toward a forest glen he knew well because it abutted his own land of Willowreach. The budding branches rustled, dappled by the rays of the rising sun. The path through the thick growth was well-traveled and he was out only half a mile when the stallion he rode came up hard behind her.

She must've heard him approach because she looked back, and slowed her mount to a walk. He soon caught up.

"Good morning," he said, doffing his hat. Sitting side-saddle, she looked like a queen. An uncomfortable one. "You're up early."

"As are you." She nodded and he could not tell if she were happy to see him or not.

"Do you always ride this early?" He would keep this light and friendly.

"When I can." Her clear sky-blue eyes met his and beneath the navy velvet veil of her hat, she appeared fresh as the dew on the grass, not a hint of rouge or powder to her cheeks nor black to her incredibly long dark lashes.

His body tightened with interest. What a rebuke of his intentions to remain neutral toward her.

"Do you?" she asked.

"Do I what?"

"Ride this early always?"

"No."

"Are you escaping, too?" she asked, smiling as if they shared a secret.

He chuckled. Perhaps it was so early in the morning, she'd not acquired all her ability to stand off. "Indeed I am. I'm doing my social duty, but I find it…"

"Tedious?"

Frustrating.

She tipped her chin, the light of teasing in her eyes. "I would imagine you attend many engagements like this."

"Not if I can help it," he told her truthfully. "Shall we walk on?"

"Of course." She led her mount to his side and they headed down the lane. "I've enjoyed visiting with your sister."

"Elanna's a dear." He was grateful for the new topic. "Everyone likes her."

"She tells me she must marry soon."

"Does she? Well, it's so."

Lily gazed at him with curiosity. "Do I detect you're shielding her from Lord Carbury?"

"Obvious, am I?" Had Lily also perceived how intrigued he was with her?

She shrugged. "No. Forgive me if I—"

"You noticed my attention to him. That's fine."

She searched his eyes as if to see he spoke the truth, then glanced away. "Carbury seems intent on courting her."

"He is." Julian had been fretting about it for days. Now at Lily's mention of it, his worry doubled. "Too much so."

"Is there some reason why he does not suit?"

"Yes."

In the morning light, her exquisite counterpoint of her dark hair and her lustrous pale blue eyes struck him like glorious moonlight. She glanced away. "I'm sorry. I seem to have lost my sense of discretion."

"No. You haven't. And you asked. Lord Carbury is a fine gentleman. He's many years older than our Elanna but he has a solid income, a fairly old title and a sizable estate. He's respected in parliament and known for his prudence in his investments. He doesn't gamble, drink or..."

She tossed her head and her glorious eyes gleamed. "Dally where he shouldn't?"

"Exactly."

"Still you hesitate to approve of him. Why?"

Lily Hanniford was forthright. So unlike English girls. So unlike those who hankered after a title for its own sake and money for the spending. *God*, he liked that. *Her.* "He does not excite her."

"According to many, that's not a requirement for a good marriage."

"No, but it helps to put one on the path to a congenial union."

She grinned broadly. "For children, you mean."

And sport. "Men need heirs and spares. Daughters, too."

A frown lined her forehead as she looked down at her gloved hands on the reins. "It's true then that love is not a requirement for a proper match between an English lord and a lady?"

"Prudence has its benefits. Passion can turn bitter. Here in Britain, we've not been able to afford such a luxury for centuries." *Not now, either.*

Shifting in her saddle, she seemed perturbed. "So love is irrelevant?"

"Hopefully it comes later." He shrugged. His own parents' bitter relationship was his poor model.

"But does it?" She seemed to ask a rhetorical question.

Had her parents married for love? Was she as skeptical as he of the possibility of such unions? "We have a few instances where love came first and no good came of it."

"Ah, yes." She nodded once. "I've heard of the most famous one. Anne Boleyn."

He laughed. "There is that."

"And yet you advocate for a love match for your sister. How is that?"

"It's not easy. Not favored by my father, either. Elanna's sweet, charming. To her, the world is a treasure to be explored. I don't wish to see her disillusioned by a pragmatic match. All she needs is time to find the right man."

"Or the wrong one if she mistakes passion for love."

"I believe she's level-headed. Besides, I'd like to buy her that time."

"Can you?"

He shook his head. Why not be totally honest with her? "Not much. Only to the end of this season."

Her mouth dropped open.

They rode in silence for a bit.

Then very quietly she said, "So she'll have to search diligently to put off Lord Carbury. Does she know this?"

Julian squinted into a brilliant ray piercing the treetops. "She does. And she accepts it. Although she hopes for a reprieve—"

"It's not likely, is it?" she asked with some compassion.

"I'm afraid not. She's had her debut. No men she's met have appealed to her as husband material, sad to say. She's had suitors but turned them down."

"And now she's being pursued by a man she does not want and must accept." She sighed. "I hate to think of all the women who experience the same challenge."

Are you one of them?

He scowled at the mere idea she'd belong to a man who did not value those eyes, those lips, the spark of rebellion in her. That blithe quality he so admired could lead him down a perilous path.

But he yearned to follow the trail. And he felt compelled to inject some memorable element into this or she'd return to the house concluding he was an utterly dry piece of toast. To her, he wished, against all that was logical, to be at least memorable, if not irresistible. How to free himself of his fascination for her? "At home in Baltimore and Texas, how do you spend your days?"

She cocked her head. "Baltimore society is very much like this. Sedate, closed."

"Interesting?"

She tipped her head to and fro. "If you like discussing ships in dock and the art of raising thoroughbreds."

That surprised and pleased him. She was no faint miss without a thought in her head save ribbons and silks. "I wager you do?"

"I do."

He was surprisingly gratified by that. Could he predict that dinner conversation with her would never consist of a litany of the latest gossip about society's scoundrels and ne'er-do-wells? "And what of your days in Texas?"

"I didn't ever do needlepoint."

"Terrible at it?" he asked with delight tickling him.

"Hideous."

"Instead, you did what?"

She pursed her lips as she considered the trail ahead.

He wished he could commission a portrait of her in silhouette as she pondered a problem. In this, as in much else, she was exquisite. A beauty whose hair might gray, and whose eyes might dim, but whose dynamism would sparkle through. "Tell me. I don't bite."

"Hmm. You're sure?"

"I might have been too forward at the opera, but I have learned my lesson."

She turned the most distressing face to him. All large sad eyes, lax mouth, and miserable longing.

Dear God. Had she valued his advance? Even though she warned him away? Why?

What to do now?

He had no idea what to say. *Apologize? Repeat himself?*

The woman confounded him.

"Lily—" He watched her swallow hard on embarrassment and turn forward. "Lily." *Dear woman.* "Tell me, what you did at home."

Her mouth worked at words. "I—I herded cattle. Trained the sheep dogs, too. And when I got cleaned up and shed my trousers, I'd ride into town with Marianne to help nurse the sick who live along the docks."

He was aghast.

She waved a hand, gleeful, chuckling. "I know. You're astonished. No lady does that. No lady needs to do that."

"Dear me," he said, considering the sterling luster of her character. "We pale beside you."

"Don't make fun of me."

"I'm not. I'm stunned. You and Marianne nurse the poor?"

"She more than I. And she's much more knowledgeable than I. During our war between the States, she nursed Confederate wounded. What she knows about gun shots and diseases, no woman or man should ever have to learn."

"This must seem so mundane to both of you. The teas. The balls. This house party. Do you like any of it?"

She bit her lip and considered him beneath her lashes.

He chuckled. "All right. Just tell me."

"I appreciate good conversation. I enjoy tea and I love to dance."

"All good to know."

"But—"

"Yes?"

She rolled a shoulder. "I don't like being pursued."

Her bluntness delighted him. The fact that other men paid attendance to her did not. "I understand."

"Do you? Have you ever been? Pursued, that is?"

"Oh, I have. Last Season."

Eyes wide, she looked appalled. "Oh, come now. You cannot stop there. Who pursued you? Why? I must know the details. It's so rarely that a man is courted."

"I was not courted. I was *hunted*."

She rocked in her saddle with laughter. "But—but you escaped!"

He gave in to the admission with a grin. "I did. Don't ask me how."

"Oh, I know how. I see it in you. I have seen you do it here. Hilda Berghoff has an interest in you. And Priscilla Van de Putte."

"You are observant." *She had been watching him? Intriguing.*

"You have a mask. An expression of polite indifference."

"Do I?" *I'm not indifferent to you.*

Their mounts stopped at the edge of a shallow ravine, their hooves stomping the earth.

Her blue gaze locked on his. "I don't see it now."

"No, you don't." This close, he couldn't hide his interest in her. She was too perceptive, in any case. Little good it would do her. Or him, for that matter. He wouldn't marry any woman solely for her money. He certainly had never even considered marrying Killian Hanniford's girl for her wealth. His pride was too great to take a woman to his home and not want her physically, at the least. But his desire for Lily gnawed at him with growing hunger. He shifted in his saddle. Was his pride too big to bow to his father's wish to marry someone soon? Could he rid himself of his enjoyment of Lily's company? If he kept his distance, might he control his longing to possess her?

He spurred his horse to walk on.

She fell in beside him. The sun rose higher and she closed her eyes, her face to the sky. "I'm glad spring has arrived. I've been cold."

The weather. He could discuss it without danger to his heart. "Do you like it here in England?"

"I'm used to warmer weather in Texas and Maryland. Even Paris seemed less forbidding."

"Yet you'll consider staying here, living here, despite the temperature?"

"If I'm given good reason, yes."

"A husband?"

She fiddled with the scarf around her throat. "My father would like that, yes."

"Have you found any man you favor?" *Torrington, perhaps? Pinkhurst, God forbid?*

She smiled weakly. "You want me to be blunt again?"

"I'm hoping for an honest answer."

She examined him intricately. "All right. I haven't been here long enough to appreciate any one man's character."

"Does that mean you don't believe in hasty passions?"

"I've never experienced one, so I have no way to judge if I believe or not." She pushed aside a branch. "One thing I do know is that I will not stay in England solely to please my father."

"Good for you."

"I will remain only as long as…"

He didn't like the way she'd paused. "As long as what?"

"I'm amused or intrigued or…or I begin to believe in hasty passion."

He sent her a smile. "Smart. Is your father the kind of man who will allow his daughter to choose her own path?"

"Given good argument, yes."

He looked askance. "That sounds ominous."

"Not really. He promises not to force me to wed any one."

Good to know. "An interesting man."

"Thoroughly American," she said.

"So then you're here to enjoy yourself. The house parties? The rounds of calls? The balls?"

"All of it." She indicated the scenery as she patted the neck of her mount. "But, actually, that's a lie."

"Why?"

"I don't enjoy it all."

"No?"

"I hate riding side-saddle."

He gave her a rueful grin. A memory of the London cartoon of her on horseback flashed through his mind. "You don't look uncomfortable." *You look delicious in that midnight-blue riding coat and white stock.*

"I prefer my western saddle. How does a woman ever ride to hounds like this? She'd be hanging over the side like a ham in a smokehouse."

"I cannot tell you," he said, her humor tickling him. "I've never done it."

"Men should. They'd have more compassion for the weaker sex."

"You're not weak," he said with conviction.

She eyed him for a long moment then faced forward. "I'm getting stronger every day."

"Bravo. I think you should ride as you wish."

That brought her around to him, surprise and delight curving her lovely lips. "Here?"

"Why not?"

She snorted. "I'd be a scandal."

"You'd be a woman to reckon with."

"One to avoid."

"Try it."

"I can't. You know I can't. There's no place. Not in London in the middle of Rotten Row in broad daylight."

She'd look splendid in moonlight. "Ride at night."

"That's not—"

"Possible?" he objected. "Of course, it is."

"Oh, no. I can't take the chance. Not here. Carbury's stable boys would talk. Or his butler. I'd be the brunt of more cartoons. I hated that. So, no, thank you."

"Ride with me then."

She frowned at him so deeply he was sure she questioned his sanity.

"My estate is through those trees." He inclined his head toward the east. "My stable, too. And I have a stable hand who would never breathe a word about a lady's riding habits."

She shook her head. "You're serious?"

"Quite."

She bit her lower lip. "Why?"

Because I long to see you with stars in your eyes, your hair down around your shoulders, naked. He inhaled. She should spur that horse to a gallop. Run far away quickly. "I'd like to please you. Make you smile."

For a fraction of a second, her blue eyes softened. But she blinked. "If I were discovered, I'd be ruined."

"I'd guard against that."

"Your intentions would be—"

"Honorable? Of course, they would." He shifted in his saddle, his animal intentions totally shameful. He had only to look at her and he was entranced by her eyes. He had only to speak with her and he applauded her forthrightness. Her spontaneity, her humor undid him. The closer he got to her, the more she refreshed him.

"How do I know? What assurances would I have?"

"That I not touch you?" *How could I not?*

"That you wouldn't spread rumors about me."

"Why would I?" *When I want you for myself.* "I'd suffer no gain if I'd be known to have hurt you."

"So we'd be house guests who ride together?"

"Friends who ride together," he corrected her.

"Conspirators," she breathed, her face alight with devilry. "Oh, superb. How could we do this?"

CHAPTER 7

*W*ould the afternoon and evening never end?

Lily sighed, accepting a glass of sherry from a footman as they awaited the bells to go into dinner. Pinkie stood beside her, having maneuvered his way to her to discuss horses.

She liked him, tall and blond and full of life. Gay, too. But becoming a bit of a bore now that she had a chance to enjoy Julian's company.

"I should like to invite you to view my Arabian," he said in his clipped British accent. He had a habit to speak so rapidly that she had to concentrate to understand him. "A house party."

"House party?" she asked, like a loon.

"You'd like his looks."

"Whose?" She was searching for Julian. Where was he?

"My prize horse."

"Horse. Arabian. Right. I know cutting horses, my lord. You'd have to tell me what to appreciate in him."

"I would educate you, never fear. I say, are you well? You're squinting at me."

Oh, blast your rapid fire, sir. "Very well. Fine. Perfectly. Thank you. Do go on."

She spotted Julian enter across the room, his dark eyes sadder than a wet hound dog's as Hilda Berghoff presented herself at his elbow. Stifling a laugh, Lily focused on Pinkie who rambled on about his "superb creature" who would win him races and purses.

Lily could care less. She preferred to dream of riding with Julian. The dangers were many and could be disastrous, even enduring. Still she yearned for the excitement of it. More minutes with him. Alone. And to ride freely. Of course.

But the crux of her anticipation was that she trusted him to keep their secret—and she had no evidence she should. He'd been so casual about the offer, it shocked her. Would he offer such an escapade to an English lady? Or was she ripe for tricking? Mocking? He was a man of his class with all its foibles, and as such, he could flagrantly disregard society's rules and live to tell about it. Could she trust her instinct that with her, he might be honorable?

Julian's gaze met hers and the small smile curving his lips had her pulse beating faster. He'd been quick to name the arrangements for their ride. One hour after everyone had retired, he would meet her at the far end of Carbury's stables. Julian would escort her to his own stable block where he would have instructed his groom to saddle two horses for them. And hers would bear a man's saddle.

With a resounding thrill singing through her veins, she found herself staring like a loon into the eyes of Elanna Ash who had approached her and Pinkie. By her side was a doting Carbury.

"Horses?" said their host. "Don't care to know much of them. You, Elanna?"

"No, my lord. I prefer tamer pleasures. Art, for one." She

faced Lily. "Have you visited the South Kensington Museum since you've been here, Miss Hanniford?"

The young lady's words held notes of desperation in them and Lily feared she knew what caused them. "I'm sorry to say I have not. Do you enjoy it?"

"I do very much." Elanna trained her gaze on her with hot intensity as if to hold Lily's interest by force of will.

Lord Carbury stood, frowning into his wine. He'd acquired a pettishness whenever Elanna gave her attentions to someone else.

Had Elanna been too much pursued by Lord Carbury?

Lily was happy to offer diversion. "I like museums. Please tell me about the exhibits."

Elanna went on about the collection of furniture of recent periods. "Textiles from all over the world are displayed. I adore the Chinese silks, embroidered in threads of vibrant shades."

"That sounds wonderful."

Marianne smiled at her. "Perhaps after we return to town, we could all visit the museum together?"

"I'd like that very much," Elanna said and turned to Julian who had entered their circle. "What do you say? Would you attend us?"

"I'd be delighted to offer my escort."

Elanna leaned toward Lily. "Chelton is modest. He knows more about the Chinese silks than I, and he's always eager to share his knowledge."

And there it was, another reason to be in Lord Chelton's company. An offer that sent a ripple of glee through Lily. She was becoming quite a goose about how well she liked the man.

She caught his eye. "How is it you have an understanding of Chinese fabric?"

"For more than three decades, our family traded in

Shanghai. Our principle export was silk fabric and silk worms to England and France until recent peasant revolts near the ports cut off our supply and our factories were burned."

From the corner of her eye, Lily saw Lord Carbury lean toward Elanna. "My dear, would you care for more wine? The footman stands ready to—"

Elanna grew flustered by Carbury's intrusion into the conversation. She stared at him, then at his footman and found her voice. "No. Thank you. I wish no more."

The butler appeared at the doorway and announced the service.

"We should go in," Carbury said to her in a low voice that brooked no argument. "Would you lead the way?"

"My lord," Lily heard Elanna whisper to him, "it is not my place."

His lips thinned. Anger glistened in his eyes. "It could be."

"As the ranking woman here, my mother should have your arm, sir," she responded.

He glared at her.

A tingle of foreboding electrified Lily. What was the man about? The glint in his eye—of possession—was fiery. One that set Elanna back on her heels. One that had Lily fretting.

Carbury excused himself and went for the duchess. Throughout dinner, the man said barely a word. If others noticed, no one seemed to let the conversation lag.

At last, the six courses were ended and the women departed to the drawing room for tea, while the men remained for their brandy and cigars. That too, was short as the duchess and Elanna made their excuses to retire early.

Eager to escape upstairs and change her clothes, Lily grinned at Marianne as they hooked arms and made their way up the staircase.

"You're chipper," Marianne said. "Had a good time gazing

down the table at a certain gentleman, did you?"

"Shhh." Lily made big eyes at her.

"No one hears," whispered Marianne, "except the footmen who are supposed to be deaf. Blind, too, I hear. So tell me. What's going on between our host and lovely Lady E, hmmm?"

"Unrequited feelings?"

"I'll say."

"I didn't detect a mean streak in him when we met him," Marianne said.

"No. Still." Lily worried. "He does intend to ask for her."

"Fool's errand that will be. She won't be accepting him," Marianne whispered.

"Or maybe she will." Lily had to tell Julian. He'd want to know that Carbury might not be the perfect gentleman.

As they reached Lily's door, Marianne stopped. "Tired? Come to my room?"

"No. I can't."

Marianne tipped her head in question.

Lily hoped no sign of her coming escapade played in her expression. "I'm done in."

"All right," she said with some misgiving in her voice. "Good night, then."

"Sleep well."

The night air was brisk, the wind sharp as it rustled through the treetops and cut into the wool of Lily's riding jacket. She'd escaped the house easily, shooing her maid off to bed. She'd dressed haphazardly, tucking her hair up in a net under her pert little hat and then running down the back servants' stairs and out into the yard. She'd donned her trousers that she'd brought with her from Texas. The ones she usually wore on the ranch in south Texas fit her like a second skin, the wool expressly tailored to her curves by her seamstress in Corpus Christi. She was far from fashionable but only Julian would see her. Somehow, she didn't mind that. Despite the fact he was so high born, he seemed accepting of her American idiosyncrasies.

She strode across the pebbled yard toward the stables, pleased that the moon was bright enough to pick her way easily.

No one, thank goodness, was about. The lights from the house were few. Most of the guests had gone to their beds and she hoped that Marianne was among them. Lily had no desire to meet her cousin in the hall upon her return. She welcomed the secrecy of her rendezvous, treasured it even.

The stable was swathed in pale light and she heard only the flutterings of small creatures in the tall grasses beyond. There at the far corner of the stable was an irregular shadow.

Before she could speculate what it might be, a man stepped from the wall and into a beam of moonlight. No mistaking his well-cut silhouette anywhere. Dressed in a dark riding habit that fit his firm thighs and strong chest to perfection, he was quite stunning. Her breath stopped. She was meeting a man in the moonlight for the first time and she relished the adventure.

She grinned at her own boldness—and prayed it would not be her downfall. After all, found out, she'd never do this again. She'd be…oh, she didn't want to think about the possibility that her father would send her home. Or make her marry some man whom she did not know and could not want the way she was beginning to want this one.

The joy of it all was too grand not to wish the experience to be repeated. With Julian.

"I'm so sorry to be late," she said. "The ladies wanted to talk all night."

"The men as well," he said, his white teeth flashing in a wicked smile. He fell in at her side and offered his arm. "Allow me. Through the woods, you see. I don't want you to trip."

"Terrible. They'd ask how it happened."

"And you couldn't say you'd fallen in your bedroom."

She feigned horror. "I tripped over the rug?"

"How could you be so clumsy?" he asked.

"So indelicate. My, my."

The forest was thick but the path he led her on had been cleared of branches. They trod on a thick carpet of leaves, their footfalls subtle as whispers. They strode on for a while, their quiet companionable and comfortable for two people who'd known each other so briefly.

"You've come this way before, I bet?" she asked him.

"Often as a boy. I had a friend who was the estate manager's son and we played together, traipsing through the forest, running like ruffians, pretending we were Robin Hood and his merry men."

"Stealing from the rich?" she asked him, catching a glimpse of his far-off expression and smiling at his fond remembrance.

"Bringing justice to the peasants."

"Defying the sheriff."

"A noble calling." He grinned and patted her hand.

The clearing opened and she halted at the sight of a two-story house of white stone glimmering in the starlight. To one side stood the gray Seton stable block.

The folly of what she was about to do made her pause. She'd never been a hare-brained girl, taking chances, breaking social rules. But being with him felt not so much risky as audacious. She'd always envied women who could be. Women who said no to marriage, like Marianne. Women who did as they wished no matter the warning from men.

Like her mother. What was it then to ride at midnight alone with an eligible man? In a man's saddle. In britches.

"I hope you're not having second thoughts," he said and she glanced up to see concern wrinkle his dark brows.

"It's not wise."

"But you're with me. If you wait all your life to seize the fun of being alive, look what you've wasted."

"You're a philosopher?" she quipped, accepting his reasoning.

"Tonight, I am." He squeezed her hand. "Come ride. You'll be so proud you were brave. Mischief is worth the risk. Besides, I bet you'd do it at home."

"Oh, but there no one would know."

"No one will know here, either."

"At home in Texas, no one would blink an eye. Out on the range, women do ride like men and herd cattle too. But here, Chaumont and others have warned that the whole family could be subjected to ridicule if Marianne and I stepped out of line. What if you have a servant who's out and about, he could tell others—"

"He wouldn't.

She flung back her head to gaze up at him. "Oh, Julian. I can call you Julian, can't I?"

He searched her expression as if he met her for the first time. "I would think you must under the circumstances."

"I couldn't bear it if I were in the newspapers again. That cartoon of me on horseback was hideous."

He swung toward her and looped an arm around her waist. "If he saw you now, he'd cry bitter tears that his talents were so shallow."

"Your compliment is kind." *Exciting.* "But if word gets out…"

"It won't. I know that artist. Trust me, he wouldn't dare it again."

"How could you stop him?"

A mischievous light crossed his eyes. "Shoot him at dawn."

"You wouldn't dare."

"Oh, I don't know. Isn't that what they do in Texas?

She laughed. "Sometimes. Before the sheriff arrives.

"We have a sheriff who's just as slow.

She giggled.

He put a hand to her cheek. His touch calmed her, the heat of his skin on hers an endearment she hadn't expected. "I'd gladly shoot him for you."

"I'd hate to be the cause of you hanging."

"I'd hate to see you insulted." He stroked her cheek with his thumb. His lips parted and he drifted closer. "Lily. I may call you Lily, can't I?"

Her heart in her throat she could only nod.

"Lovely Lily. Have you kissed a man before?"

She shook her head. Gulped hard. "Have you?"

He considered the sky and hooted in laughter. "No."

Realizing her mistake, she laughed and rested her forehead against his chest. He stepped against her and the planes of his body were warm, solid temptation. He was aroused, mightily. She was flattered that he could be attracted to her… and she wrapped her arms around his waist and nestled closer to him.

"My lord?" A young lad's voice interrupted them.

She pushed away. Where was her brain? Her sense of decorum?

Julian cleared his throat. "Yes, Colin. Good of you to do this for me."

"And for me, Colin." Lily smiled at the gangly young man who stood before them and pulled his forelock. "We're grateful you came out so late at night."

"Not a thought you should give it, milady."

"Oh, I'm—"

"The lady," Julian told him, "is honored you've done her and me the favor."

"I'm pleased to do it, milord. Your horses are ready."

"We won't be long, Colin. Thank you."

They mounted and urged the horses to a walk along a country lane. They spoke little, a quiet camaraderie Lily relished. The sounds of the wind rustling the trees was their only accompaniment.

"It smells like rain. Do you think it might?" Lily asked him.

"Perhaps. We're not far from where I wanted to take you. Follow me. We may still have time before it starts."

He spurred his horse to a trot and she followed him down the lane. At once, he stopped, turned and waited for her to catch up.

"There," he pointed toward a flat plain before them. "If you'd like to try your hand at racing Polly, here's your chance."

She surveyed the terrain, rising in her saddle and smiling. "It seems to be more than three acres."

"Four. You cannot see it well in the dark, but it's a lovely clear expanse where you can enjoy yourself. Trust me when I say that Polly will too."

Lily patted the mare on the neck. "She's very responsive."

"Knows her manners, that one."

"Will you ride with me?"

"Better yet. Shall I race you?" he offered.

"Why not? You know Polly's speed better than I, especially against that fine beast you've got here."

"Horatio knows when to let a lady win."

"That's not very sporting," she challenged him with a tip

of her chin. "You assume I'm no match for you."

Horatio snorted.

Julian chuckled. "He knows Polly and you."

"Doubtful, sir," she teased him.

He arched a disdainful brow. "We'll race. Straight to the stone barrier. You'll know it when you see it. Four feet high, pale stone. No jumping it, mind you. Turn. Then back to this marker. Here under this tree."

"And the winner gets to name her own prize."

"Ha! What did you have in mind?"

"Another run tomorrow night?" she asked with giddy hope.

"Incorrigible, you are."

"A deal?"

"Of course."

She beamed at him. "Ready?"

Off they went, she in the lead and intent on winning, he at her heels and fast closing the distance.

Polly was a speedy lady and Horatio had met his match. It tickled Lily to bend low in her saddle, feel the power of the animal beneath her and admit that the surge of excitement flowing through her had nothing to do with the horse, the ride or the moonlight.

The freedom of it, that Julian had arranged it for her, raised her laughter and her appreciation of him. She liked him, much more than she'd anticipated, more than she'd predicted when they met in Paris. There, she'd been struck by his classic handsomeness, his form. There, she'd thought him imperial, so far above her socially that she'd been aghast at his attentiveness. Now that she knew him, she could acknowledge he was generous, kind and so attractive that she could not, would not ignore him.

At the turn, she stopped and hailed Julian with a grin of delight.

He playfully scowled at her.

"I'll beat you if you keep doing that," he shouted.

She dug in her spurs and Polly responded with speed.

But Julian gave a good race, digging in only inches behind her.

At the final mark, she rejoiced in the win, proud that she'd risked exposure, grateful to him for the opportunity.

"We won!" She whipped her hat from her shoulder where it had fallen and dangled by its pins.

"By a nose!" He was laughing as he permitted Horatio to prance around her and Polly.

"Polly deserves a bucket of oats. And I'd like a firm promise of tomorrow night."

Julian laughed heartily. "You love the taste of risqué business, eh?"

"I won't deny it."

"I'll risk it with you."

Drops of rain hit her face. She pushed curls from her cheeks and dragged off her net caul. The wealth of her hair fell to her shoulders, hanging in long curls over her jacket.

His dark gaze shot to it and back to her eyes, where he lingered. His consideration heated her blood, making her shift in her saddle, noting the tension in her belly was new, welcome and unwise.

In the distance, the crackle of thunder rent the night air.

"We should return quickly. Come on," he said and headed back toward the stables at a trot.

But the heavens opened in a steady downpour, the rain seeping into her jacket. Julian and she trotted straight into the open doors.

Julian was off his mount in a thrice and strode over to help her down. "You're soaked straight through."

"You, too." She felt the wet wool of his jacket as she braced herself on his shoulders and slid to the earthen floor.

Colin appeared from the back of the barn, rubbing sleep from his eyes as he took the reins of Horatio and Polly.

"Thank you, Colin," Julian said and then her turned to her.

"We must get you home before you catch a chill." He glanced around the dim interior, then reached over to a line of tack hanging on the wall. He whipped off a horse blanket and stepped to her. "Here, let's put this around you. I'll go up to the house and get a coat for you. You can't go back to Carbury's in the pouring rain. Not wet as you are. I should have thought of this."

"You cannot predict the weather."

"Foolhardy of me, anyway. I should have taken better care of you."

"I'm fine."

"Now, you are. But if you take sick—"

"I've never been ill a day in my life."

"Bloody well good for you."

At his rough words, she threw him a smile.

"Sorry. But you need a change of clothes, a shot of whiskey and a good warm bed."

"Hopefully, this downpour will end soon."

He was rubbing her shoulders and securing the blanket around her throat tightly. "Only servants are in residence at the house. I'll run up. My mother's winter coat would fit you. Elanna's would be too short."

"So why don't we both go? You need dry clothes, too."

He tipped his head. "If we're caught—"

"By whom? If no one in your family is there? Where is your father?"

"London."

"So then."

"Stay here."

"Not on your life!"

118

hey ran like children along the stone path up to
the servants back door. It was unlocked and Julian
thrust it open easily, pulling her inside.

"Come. Here's the kitchen. No fire, but it's warm and dry.
Sit there." He looked her over. "You're drenched. Hell."

He took four huge strides, disappearing into another
room and clanging about. If he kept up that racket, the whole
house would soon be awake.

She rubbed her arms, grateful to be out of the storm, but
wary of servants who might have been roused.

When he returned, he had his hands full of toweling.

Grateful to be rid of the blanket that smelled of horse, she
shrugged it off and folded it. He hurried to wrap a large
towel over her head.

She giggled. "You could wake the dead the way you
scoured that room."

"My housekeeper is quite deaf."

"You're kidding."

"Not at all. She's never been quick to any sound." He
scrubbed her head with too much dedication.

"Ooof." She picked up a corner of the towel to glare at him.

"Sorry. You need to dry your hair." He rubbed her scalp furiously.

"If you don't stop, sir, I'll be bald!"

"Sorry." He bent to peer at her. "Take off your jacket."

She balked. She had removed her corset for this adventure and if she took off her jacket, it would most definitely be apparent that she was a rather loose woman. In more ways than one. "Ah. I don't wish to. Unless... Do you have anything to replace it?"

"Not yet. I will." He dropped another towel around her neck.

"Splendid. I'll wait."

"No. You will not." He began to pick at the buttons on her coat.

She slapped his hands away. "Stop that."

"You do it then. I'll not have you die of cold at the risk of a layer of clothing."

She clutched her stock to her throat. And true, it was wet, but she had few choices here. "It's not just any layer."

Confusion over took his brow. "What?"

"Can you please find me another coat?"

"I will if you promise to begin to unbutton that now."

She tsked. "Hard bargainer."

He stood. "I'll be back with brandy and when I do, you'll have that jacket off."

"Fine, fine." Fretting over that, she undid her last two buttons. Beneath it, the cold cotton of her blouse was damp. Under that, her skin was ablaze with the delicious nature of her predicament. But what Julian didn't know was a good thing. "Hurry, please."

He left her, ran up the steps and away. In the silent house, she marveled that no one had yet heard them. How many servants did he have? And were they all deaf?

She shrugged out of her jacket, covering her wet blouse and her beading nipples with the ends of a towel. Shivering in the damp cotton and trying to focus on how soon she'd be warm didn't work.

Julian returned within minutes, a large coat in one hand and a man's shirt—*his?*—in the other.

"I can't wear that." She had admired his form, his broad chest, his muscular build. He was fit, firm, a marvelous example of manhood, but she was more than adequately endowed. And his shirt, tailored as it was, would not adequately cover her attributes.

"Why not?" He held it up. "Perfectly fine linen. Clean."

She ground her teeth. "It won't fit."

"Of course, it will." He quirked a brow. "Oh. Um. Won't it?"

He had this odd expression on his face which slowly, slowly turned to recognition and then, he laughed.

She tapped her foot on the stone floor. "You're not helping, dear sir."

Still chuckling, he stepped toward her and put his hands around her waist to draw her to her feet. "I see that. I am sorry."

She couldn't help but cuff him. "Take me back."

"Wet?"

"As I am, yes! Now." She took his hand and marched them both toward the window.

But lightning streaked the sky and a loud boom shook the house.

She lurched backward.

Against his all too solid chest.

He embraced her, one hand in her hair, one cupped her nape and the lure of his warmth was irresistible. She sank against him, reveling in his support. He was assurance and beneath his riding pants, he was aroused.

She didn't want to move or even breathe. Could he find her attractive? Still? Even though she'd told him at the opera to ignore her? He certainly did find her company appealing. Much as she'd always declared she'd never tolerate a man as demanding as her father, she liked a man with a mind of his own. This man.

"I like you," she told him astonishing herself for saying what she felt for him.

He trailed his fingers up into her hairline and turned her head toward him. "Do you?" he asked, his voice wistful. "God knows I like you."

Her heart did a little jig. "Now I know, too."

"We are neither of us very clever."

"But honest."

"Lily," he said her name, a plea more breath than sound. "Lily, darling. Shall we be more than honest?"

"Oh, Julian." In the dim light, she could make out the fire in his beguiling eyes. To wait any longer to taste him would be a waste. Casting caution to the wind, she swung totally into his embrace and pushed up on her toes. She slid her arms around his shoulders, the towel falling to the floor, and with only hot urgency between them, she said, "Yes, let's be."

He'd be damned for this tomorrow. But tonight, she wanted him and he had this ravenous need to possess her before she decided she was wrong.

He crushed her against him. Never had he wanted any woman's lips on his more than hers. Never had he hungered for any one with more thoughtless urgency. And against his chest, he felt the wealth of her breasts. Unbound as surely they were, her bosom flattened against him. Her nipples went rigid and he forced back a groan. She'd come to him very freely. Natural. Trusting.

Was he as trustworthy as she presumed? With any other woman, that answer would have been no. With any other woman, he would have been greedy, opportunistic. With any other woman—any woman whom he would meet in the dark for an illicit rendezvous—he would not hesitate to capitalize on her lack of virtue. With this one, he would not dare to offend her. More, he couldn't disappoint her—or himself.

He cupped her cheek. He brushed her lips with his own. He held her tenderly and then he took her. All she offered. All she was.

Her lips. Plush, soft and needy. Answering him with a new kiss. This one more urgent, desperate.

He fell backward against the wall, bracing himself to hold her and not let her go. He needed one kiss, gentle, beseeching. And another, that turned fierce, then raw.

He caught her up to pull her with him to a chair. He had to sit before his knees gave way. How he found one, he'd no idea. He only knew she was in his lap and he had his hands full of her, her sculpted back, her slim shoulders, her firm breasts. Her bountiful breasts that he knew for certain stood tall and plump without aid of any corset. Against the wet cloth, he thumbed her pinpoint nipples. She let her head loll back and he bent, mad to please her, and suck one taut areola, soft cloth and fragrant flesh, into his mouth. With a cry, she dug her nails into his shoulders as he bit her nipple and moved to lave the other.

She had come to him so freely and he was a cad to ravish her so. But his hunger was painful and her surrender too compelling to refuse.

She wiggled, kissing him eagerly. Her bottom pressed

down against his. He groaned, certain she had no idea how she lured him on. He couldn't stop to tell her. More fool he.

He arched her up so that he could take more of her marvelous breast into his mouth. With an avid tongue, he stroked her. She undulated, her nails now talons in his skin. With his teeth, he nipped her. She shuddered and he quaked, recognizing her feminine plea for more of this. More of him. He'd be an idiot not to give it. He'd be a devil to enjoy it. But he had to stop.

Stop now.

She deserved a bed. And he would do her justice only in a broad one.

He shut his eyes. Curled her against him. Her taut, ready body, pliant in his arms. He shouldn't want her. But the rage to take her ran through him like molten lead. He couldn't have her another time. Another night. Not unless he—*of course*—married her.

Could I?

He stared at her. She was wide-eyed, as stunned by their passion as he was.

She was his beauty, his lovely Lily, and he meant to seduce her, ravish her, enjoy her. Lily, Lily, she was his flower. Fresh, wild, charming. Lily.

He knew what had thrilled her. His taste of her had destroyed all her own reason along with his. "Darling, that should—"

She slanted a finger across his lips.

"I need more," she whispered and thrust her hand in his hair, kissing his eyes, his cheeks and mouth with furtive need.

He stilled her, a thumb at the corner of her mouth, his tongue sliding inside to seduce hers. She was a willing partner, that rare woman who could match him in appetite. Virgin that she most assuredly was, she had more enthusiasm for the sport than most. He welcomed the chance to teach her more about the pleasures of love than she anticipated.

Moaning, she pushed away. Put a hand to her mouth. "I'm sorry," she murmured and shot from his lap.

He caught her by her wrist. "Don't go. Please."

She stood, kneading her fingers, her eyes flicking from him to the door, a trapped animal. "That was— You must not tell."

"I won't."

"Papa would skin me."

"No, never."

She nodded, frightened. "Yes. It's our bargain, you see."

He gave a shake of his head. "I don't understand."

"If I'm ever caught out being improper, he'd demand I wed immediately. To one he names."

"I do doubt that." Killian Hanniford would not throw away this lovely flower on anyone. Julian tugged her into his arms and cradled her head against his throat. He squeezed his eyes shut, trying to control his desire for her but loving the pride of protecting her. With a shaking hand, he petted her hair. "Sweet girl, you're fine. You're safe. Don't quake. I won't hurt you. Wouldn't. I promised you."

She sniffed, her face in his jacket, her words muffled. "But I didn't."

Confusion filled his feverish mind. "Didn't what?"

She lifted her face and his heart dropped. She had tears in her eyes. "I didn't promise to be good. And now look what I've done. I'm a reprobate."

Oh, her torture tore at him. He put his palm to her cheek. "Lily, you've only kissed me."

She shot to her feet, pivoted away and rolled a shoulder. "I've mauled you."

"Darling, no," he said with compassion for her embarrassment and pulled her lithe body nearer. "That fault is mine."

She blushed so wildly he saw her face redden in the dim light of the kitchen.

He caught her chin and tipped her face up toward his. "I owe you the apology, Lily. And I am sorry. I should not have—"

"Please don't. Don't take it back."

God, he loved her pluck. "I must. A gentleman does and I was rash."

An impish light shone in her eyes. "The two of us, rash together?"

He ran his hand up her arm, wrapped his other arm about her waist and positioned himself flush against her. Whether from embarrassment or distress or damp clothes, she shivered. He put his lips to the crown of her head. "I enjoyed every second of our kisses."

She groaned and shook her head, burying her face in his riding jacket. "More than."

So much more. And worth every transgression. Even if now he must decide what those very acts implied. He planted his lips in her fragrant hair. "Dear Lily. You've done nothing more than I and I wouldn't call myself a reprobate."

She snorted.

He wished he could see her face, but he didn't want to push his luck here. Not when he had a point to make. He resumed stroking her hair down her back. "I've wanted to kiss you, Lily, ever since I first saw you in bright sunlight in the Rue de la Paix. I concluded that my desire to do that was a whim, a bit of lust. I told myself my need would die if I no longer saw you, was nowhere near you to be tempted. But I've learned where you go, whom you visit. And I could not resist the lure. I've seen you. I've come near you, Lily, I've talked with you, laughed with you, ridden with you in the moonlight and my need to kiss you hasn't died."

She stopped shaking.

He cuddled her closer. "It's become stronger. A living, breathing beast of a thing."

She raised her face and her lips parted. He'd dare to say she was awed.

He'd awe her more if he could. "To know that you want me, too, was more than gratifying. It was exciting. I won't tell anyone. We'll return to the party and all day tomorrow, this will be our secret. Eh? What do you say?"

"You'd do that?"

"I tell you there's no benefit in me telling anyone." *When I want you for myself.*

She tried to laugh. "You're not such a roué after all if you don't want the world to know you ruined me."

He sucked in air. "Well, first of all, I'm shocked I'm put at the level of a roué. My life has not been unblemished but still, my pastimes go more to cards than ruining American ladies who've done nothing more than kiss me."

"I did more than that. I climbed into your lap and —and—"

Thrilled me. "Met me kiss for kiss."

"Oh, don't."

He wrapped her closer, his arms tight about her. "Don't worry, darling. We're fine. You are. And no one will know. Not tonight or ever after. And that means that tomorrow night, we can ride again." He pulled away, gazing down at her as if he were merely a long-lost friend. "You want to ride again properly tomorrow night, don't you?"

She straightened up, nodding and smiling. "Oh, you know how to talk me around, don't you?"

"I do hope so." *Might you agree with me on all matters?*

She tipped her head. "Listen. The rain has stopped."

"See that? The world is right again. You and I will run back to Carbury's. No one will be the wiser."

~

"I'll take your riding clothes to warm in the sun, Miss Hanniford." Her maid was a prune-faced English woman whom her father had hired four weeks ago. She had an eagle eye and the disposition of a fox. Lily didn't trust her entirely, but hoped to earn her loyalty. The woman flung Lily's damp garments over her arm. Her brown eyes held no expression, but the way she peered at Lily told her she wanted an explanation. For any confidence, the maid would have to wait a few weeks.

"Thank you, Nora." Lily rose from her dressing table, every hair in place, ready to face those in the breakfast room. Even Julian. Especially Julian.

"And I'll clean your boots, too, shall I?"

"Please do," she said nonchalantly.

The woman knit her bushy brows. "Will you be needing them this afternoon?"

In too good a mood to be cowed, Lily grinned at her. "I doubt that, Nora. Do dry them out well, will you?"

"Yes, miss." She ambled toward the door and when she opened it, there stood Marianne.

Lily waved her in. "Good morning."

Marianne noted the items in Nora's arms and waited until the servant closed the bedroom door. "Is there something wrong with your riding clothes?"

Preserve me from coincidences that give me away. "No."

Marianne wrinkled her nose. "Wet wool smells."

"Hmm. Yes. Perhaps it does." She stood and straightened the belt at her waist.

"You're being glib." Marianne put her hands on her hips.

"Am I? I don't know why."

"I wish I did."

No, you don't. "Let's have breakfast, shall we?"

"Where were you last night?"

"Here." *Tossing and turning, reliving kisses.* "Sleeping."

"You were not." Marianne shook her head at her. "I was here. I *know.*"

Lily huffed. "Caught. Wonderful. Very well, I went out. Riding. And I had a marvelous time, too."

"With whom?"

Lily pursed her lips. "No one."

Her cousin hooted.

Lily felt her cheeks flame. She'd have to get better at subterfuge. Certainly to get out tonight, she'd need to. "You mustn't let on. It was innocent fun."

"And you got caught in the rain."

"Yes. Yes, I did. I was cold. I was freezing. And the whole incident was glorious. So do not yell at me."

Marianne's face glowed in delight. "Why would I do that?"

Lily was flummoxed. It was her turn to put her hands on her hips and stare at her cousin. "Aren't chaperones supposed to be dastardly?"

"And spoil your fun? I suppose. But if you like him—"

"I do."

"I thought you didn't. Not at first."

Lily lifted her shoulders. "I was more afraid of—I don't know—marriage, marrying the wrong man, being courted for Papa's money."

"And now you've given in?"

"No. I see other possibilities." She walked to the window and looked out over the garden toward the stable block. In the brilliant sunlight, all she envisioned was immaculate dark masculine creature who'd held her in his arms and kissed her as if she were precious. "I like him for himself. We get on together. It was his idea to take me riding last night. And I loved the freedom of it."

"As long as he's a gentleman about it, I suppose, no harm can come of it."

"None did."

Marianne strode around to face her and her smile was rueful. "You have a look about you that says there was more to the evening than rain and riding."

Lily wiggled a brow and headed for the door. "Perhaps there was. But I'm not telling."

"So there's no need for Uncle Killian to load his shotgun?"

Lily broke into laughter. "None."

"Well, then, let's have our breakfast." Marianne scurried to catch up with her. "One question, though."

"Of course. What?"

"Did Nora help you remove your corset last night?"

"She did."

"So the one I saw on your bed was the one she helped you remove?"

"That's two questions," Lily noted.

Marianne rolled her eyes. "Which means that when you went out last night—?"

"I didn't wear one."

Her cousin's mouth fell open.

"I assure you without it, I wasn't cold." Lily patted her arm as they descended the stairs.

Marianne stumbled, nearly missing a step, but laughing in spite of herself.

In the breakfast room, Carbury and Julian lingered over coffee and their newspapers. When Lily and Marianne appeared in the doorway, both men rose. Carbury looked beyond them, searching for Lady Elanna, Lily surmised. And

Julian appeared strained. Lily hoped whatever distressed him was not anything about last night's midnight ride.

Carbury regained his seat while one footman attended to Marianne's chair.

Julian came round to hold Lily's and as he scooted it under her, one finger touched her shoulder. A caress brief and light as an angel's wing.

"Did you sleep well?" Julian asked the ladies, his gaze drifting to Lily.

Marianne and she agreed as the footman hovered to offer them tea or coffee.

Julian, who had a chair to Carbury's right, regained his seat and quickly folded away his newspaper.

"What news this morning?" Lily asked him while the footman poured her coffee. Julian was not a man to move rapidly, but purposely and his readiness to put it aside concerned her. "Anything we should know of?"

"The usual." Carbury shook his head. "The government debates a trade bill."

"We should have fine weather today," Julian offered with a twinkle in his eye. "Not a cloud in the sky."

"The rain we had last night," Marianne said, "cleared things up, wouldn't you say?"

Lily gave her a kick under the table.

Julian sat quietly, his notice drawn by their interplay. "I agree. So then. Croquet, perhaps, on the lawn?"

"No cards?" Lily teased.

One of his dark brows dipped low. "So early in the day, Miss Hanniford?"

"No gambling before noon?" She was into the joke now and tsked. "In Texas, any time of day is good."

Carbury scowled. "You can't be serious."

Marianne put down her cup, quirking a brow at their

host. "Survival demands you amuse yourself through an Indian raid or a tornado."

Lily nodded her head at Julian as if to say, *So there*.

Julian looked incredulous. "Tell me you haven't done that."

"Played poker during a tornado? Yes, I have. You've never shaken so hard in your boots until you've heard a whirlwind rip through your town and lift up barns and cattle and throw them down hundreds of feet away."

Julian stared at her. "I say, you've been through the worst circumstances."

Carbury shook his head as if he didn't believe her. "Incredible."

"And Indian raids?" Julian asked her.

"Most of our Indians—Apaches they were—fled west before the war, so playing poker during a raid is a tall tale old cowboys tell. And Marianne, too." She winked at her cousin.

Marianne chuckled and paid attention to her coffee.

"But both of us play to win." Lily twitched a brow at him. "Still want to give us a turn?"

He laughed heartily. "I look forward to learning new tricks."

"After breakfast, then?"

"It'll be my pleasure," he said.

"Say that after you've lost to Lily, my lord," said Marianne. "I think I'll examine the side board. You?" she asked Lily with a bat of her lashes.

"You make me sound like a cardshark."

Rising to her feet, Marianne nodded to Julian as if they were conspirators. "She is. Never doubt. And you, dear sir, are in for it. Do not take your purse."

"She's that good?"

Marianne closed one eye. "Better."

He chuckled. "I love a challenge!"

"Oh, good morning!" Carbury shot to his feet, wiping his mouth, perky as an eager swain as Julian's mother and sister walked in. "Your Grace. Lady Elanna. Delighted to have you. Delighted."

Julian followed with greetings to his mother and sister. The two were seated at the table, with Elanna invited to sit to one side of Lord Carbury.

As Lily followed Marianne to the breakfast service on the sideboard, she could not mistake Elanna's thin smile to the older man. Their banter was hollow. Elanna's responses lacked emotion.

If theirs was to be a marriage, Elanna would be less than half a partner. Carbury might even think he had desire enough for both of them, but Lily doubted that was a proper match. Did Julian see it? She looked around and her gaze met his. He had seen, he did note and he did not like it.

Good. Still, Julian could not save Elanna from Carbury's quest. Not for long.

Meanwhile, the Duchess of Seton stared at her daughter, willing her with glittering eyes to mend her ways.

Elanna sniffed, lifted a shoulder, and put an ounce more enthusiasm into her conversation with Carbury.

Lily returned to her chair, sat and put her fork and knife to good use. On Carbury's orders, Elanna and her mother were served their breakfast by the footman. The ladies remained in their seats, as Carbury rattled on about God knew what.

Lily ate her breakfast with silent dedication. Aware of Julian's eyes on her, she listened to a polite discussion between Elanna and her suitor. They did not agree on politics or horses, flowers or colors best to complement her complexion. He liked Bach. She preferred Chopin. He liked *Ivanhoe*. She loved *Frankenstein*. It was as if they dueled and bloodying the other was the only way to survive the morning meal.

Lily had seen arguments between her parents, but nothing as contrary as this. Elanna meant to wound him. Carbury meant to dominate her.

Julian frowned at the discourse. "I wonder, Elanna, if you'd like to learn how to play poker?"

"Poker?" She looked as startled as if he'd saved her from drowning. "Why?"

He leveled an appraising eye at her. "Miss Hanniford is about to teach me. I thought you'd enjoy it. After you finish your eggs. What do you say?"

"I was hoping," Lord Carbury said to Julian, "Lady Elanna would consent to talk with me in the salon."

"Oh, I see. Well, Elanna, your choice." Julian emphasized that last.

The duchess cleared her throat.

But Elanna snapped her gaze from her mother to her brother. With a flutter of gratitude, she shook her head. "Thank you. Another time, perhaps. I thought I'd go talk with Lord Carbury, you understand."

"I do," Julian said with some grace and much disappointment in his voice.

"A fine choice," said the duchess as she picked at the bits on her plate.

The butler appeared in the doorway. "Pardon me, my lord, but the Duke of Seton has arrived."

Carbury absolutely beamed, put down his napkin and got to his feet. "Delightful! Please tell him I wish to speak with him. Say, an hour."

"I will, my lord. Please know too we have another visitor who has arrived in his own carriage. Mister Killian Hanniford."

"Show him to his room," said Carbury.

"Yes, sir." The butler turned to Julian. "Lord Chelton, your father, His Grace, asks to see you in the library."

Julian frowned. Bad timing and a foretaste of ill omens whenever his father appeared at a country party. "Really? But very well. Excuse me, won't you? And Miss Hanniford, I'm afraid our card party will have to wait."

Lily took the news of her father's arrival with pleasure. But something about the Duke of Seton's appearance disturbed Julian.

"I'll take a walk in the garden instead," she said. "Perhaps this afternoon will be a better time to play."

Julian gave her a compassionate smile. "It will."

CHAPTER 9

"*Y*ou arrive and immediately demand to see me?" Julian confronted his father as he crossed the threshold of Carbury's library. "Rude, to say the least. What is the matter?"

The Duke of Seton was a man who loved his precedence in society, his noble name too. Once he had loved his wealth, but that was gone and so the other powers were ones he used often. Even at a gathering like this one which he had always detested for the forced intimacy of strangers. "I've had a meeting of some importance to our future."

Julian stepped forward into the musty library. He disliked this room, dark and dusty, needing a good swipe with vinegar and soap. The rest of the house seemed bright and spanking clean, so this dingy room was out of character. He often wondered why. "Tell me what it is."

"Hanniford has made a better offer for the shipping company."

"How wonderful. Did you take it?"

"No."

"I see." Julian swung himself down into a high-backed

Chippendale chair and examined his nails. "Well then. Since you have taken over the negotiations, why tell me?"

"I need your help."

Julian glanced up. "How so?"

"I want you to argue him higher."

"I withdrew my presence from this discussion. It is yours now."

Seton flared his nostrils. "Absurd!"

"No." In the past few years, Julian often had refused his father's demands. It had come more easily each time. As their fortunes declined, he'd done what he could to soften the financial blows. He'd curtailed his own spending, even cut back on gambling playing only against those from whom he knew he could win. Too bad his winnings from those friends were meager. To boot, he'd ended his relationship with his mistress. He'd cut staff to four at his own residence here in Kent. He'd also advised his father on how to trim staff at Broadmore, but of course, the old man had rejected his advice. Julian had learned to keep his own council and do for himself.

Now he had reason to do more. Since last night, Julian had pondered what his future might hold. His fascination with Lily was a living breathing being, far more vital than any dalliance he'd ever fancied with another woman. Their midnight ride and their enchanting entanglement had aroused more in him than he ever anticipated. He wished to protect her. From himself. But he also wished to possess her. For himself alone. That meant more kisses and more caresses. Her compliance, her need of him too, meant he could not walk away from her.

Furthermore, he would not hurt her feelings or her reputation. Nor would he collude with his father to persuade hers to do anything even remotely concerning their business dealings. He wanted Lily Hanniford. Efficiently. Totally unconnected to her father, his own and any business dealings they might or might not conclude.

He meant to pursue her, too. Learn if her lust for him—for that was what last night was—might be the kernel of a more tender emotion. Learn if his own was irrational longing, some idealized imagining of her as charming and daring, wild and carefree.

He'd not meddle in his father's affairs.

He had too much interest in settling his own.

"I say, boy, you refuse me this?"

Julian stood. "Yes, sir. I do."

"Even at the cost of Elanna's future—"

How dare you. "You gave her until June." His father was a right bastard. Especially since the estate began to lose thousands of pounds at the turn of the decade. "I expect you to honor that."

"Or what?"

"I'll help Elanna run away."

"Don't be foolish, boy."

"Don't be unprincipled, father."

Seton flared his nostrils. "We are at an impasse."

Julian nodded and headed for the door. "Right you are."

Worried about Elanna, he headed straight for the main salon. But the doors were open and no one was inside. Whatever the conversation was that Carbury had intended with her, they had finished.

Julian turned for the stairs and strode to his sister's bedroom door. He knocked—and knocked again. With his hand to the knob, he was ready to enter, when the door fell open. Facing him was Elanna's maid, her tiny eyes circled white with fright.

"What's the matter, Bess? Where is—?" But he saw Elanna in silhouette beyond her sitting room, standing before the window in her bedroom. She stood deathly still, her hands clasped before her but her posture sagged, so unlike his elegant little sister.

"Go away, Julian." Her voice was a rasp.

"I wish to talk with you."

"I don't wish it. Please leave."

He checked Bess' stance. The servant assumed the posture of an animal on guard, terrified.

"What's happened?" he asked Bess.

But the gray-haired woman bit her lip.

"Elanna?"

She stiffened, defiance in every line of her body. "Go away, Julian."

"Let me help you."

"You can't. I love that you've tried. But you must let me go now."

What does that mean? "Did something happen in the salon? Tell me."

"No. Meet Miss Hanniford in the garden."

"I must know—"

"No, you will not. Seize happiness for yourself, Julian. Do it. For me." And then she turned to one side and walked out of his vision.

Roiled, defeated, exhausted, he made his way downstairs and out to Carbury's orangery.

When Julian caught sight of Lily again, she was bent over a camellia bush in the huge glass house filled with sunlight and plants of every size and shape and fragrance. The sun shone on her hair, turning her dark tresses to glistening midnight.

And when she raised her face to welcome him, her countenance was aglow with an emotion so tender, he wished he had a portrait of her as she was in that moment when he knew—yes, he knew—he must have her as his wife.

But she searched his expression. "What's wrong?"

He took her hands.

"Tell me if you wish. I won't pry."

He led her away from the door of the glass edifice where tall evergreens obscured the view from the house and anyone who might look out upon the splendid wealth of the gardens. At a white wrought iron bench, he urged her down.

Still holding her hands, he smiled briefly, painfully. "I worry about Elanna."

"She wasn't happy to talk with Lord Carbury."

"You can see she doesn't care for him."

"Yes." Lily nodded. "And that he is—well, not as charming a suitor as one might hope for."

Julian lifted her hands, turned them over and kissed each one in the center of her palm. "How sweet you are."

At his touch, she gave a little frisson. "I am honest, as we said we would be."

He pulled her hands so that she circled his waist. So close, she smelled of lilacs. So near, she gazed up at him with admiration that he hoped one day to merit.

He wrapped his arms around her and brushed his lips on hers. "What should I do if I find myself addicted to your kisses and you are not near me?"

Her blue eyes veiled with sadness. "Don't kiss another."

"Never." He sent the tip of his tongue along the fullness of her lower lip. "I must have you or no one." He seized her mouth, the power to claim her going to his head. She came fully against him, trusting and eager, her lips opening to his beseeching tongue. She inched closer, a small moan marking her desire to match him.

He broke away, his hand to her cheek. The need to have her here on this bench was a violent fire that spread to his blood. "I must stop. Tonight, you'll meet me?"

"At the stable doors?" The rapture he saw on her face told

him she would come to him anywhere, any time. How wonderful. How dangerous. "Yes."

He stood, pushing her hands to her lap. "After dinner. When all are abed."

"I'll teach you how to play poker some other day then?" Hope and disappointment mingled in her features.

"Many other days. I promise. Forgive me, but I must leave you."

"Propriety calls, does it?" she teased him.

"That," he said with a sad smile, "and I have urgent family matters."

Dinner was a nightmare. Carbury was an animated host, his attention on Elanna nigh unto oppressive. Julian's father was either surly or pleasant beyond bearing. His mother seemed radiant. Elanna who had once more refused to see Julian that afternoon played the part of a featherbrained debutante and flirted with the three eligible men. The two eligible women cast disapproving eyes at her, to no avail. The three men appeared to love the attention. Killian Hanniford and his niece Marianne Roland attempted their part with lively introductions of subjects, which fell to Lily and him to take up. Meanwhile, Carbury's older female guests chatted on, filling in the numerous holes of the conversation.

Julian frowned down into his soup.

His plans for the day had become mincemeat. No talk with Elanna about Carbury or any other matter. A warning that Father was getting itchy. Hours pondering his own finances to divine if he might afford...yes, a wife. A wife. *This* wife for himself.

He sat back, his appetite gone.

He knew the answer. Of course he did. He didn't have to

put ink to paper. He'd examined his ledgers over and over again. He'd already cut staff at Willowreach. Months ago, he'd reined in his spending on tailors and wines. He'd given up his small house in Paris last autumn, the need for it gone along with the dismissal of his kind but suddenly unexciting French mistress. With frugality, and even without acquiring any dowry from Lily, he could afford to feed her. But clothe her? Hire a maid for her? Allow her parties and at homes? No. There would be no cash for any of that. And he loathed the idea that she'd do without all those niceties she so obviously enjoyed.

How could he ask her to marry him and do without the comforts she richly deserved?

He'd be a cad. Perhaps not as bad as Randolph Churchill, the duke of Marlborough's younger son, who had quickly proposed marriage to the American heiress Jenny Jerome, only to find that her small dowry of two thousand pounds per year would be all he'd have to live on. The difference between Churchill and him was that he wished not to take any of Killian Hanniford's money. None at all. He would not be beholden to him. And not so connected that Hanniford might wish to use him as a negotiator with his father, the duke. Certainly Lily's father would grant her a dowry. Any father of title or wealth had done so in England for centuries. But poor and needy as he was, it belittled Julian to take it. If he married an English girl, she'd come with money. Chances were she'd come with even less than Lily, but before he'd ever set eyes on Lily, he'd intended no marriage for many years anyway. Not until he'd improved his lot, shored up his pride with some achievement and solvency. And he'd never expected a woman to fund his life either. He'd expected her to provide an heir and organization of his house, period.

He simply wanted Lily. Unencumbered with her wealth

or her father's influence. Only one matter stood like a wall between them.

He did not wish to be purchased. Not by her. Not by her father. He'd lived his whole life holding his head above the crowd because his parents were notorious gamblers and libertines, caught in their cups more than once.

He'd told himself he'd never allow himself to become a laughing stock, too. There was deplorable behavior among his parents, but he'd remained discreet. Not a drinker or a known gambler or a debaucher, he'd been an unremarkable aristo. But married to a wealthy American girl who'd come lugging her dollars in a carpetbag? 'The Dollar Girls', the scandal sheets called them. Could he bear the slurs without cringing?

Still he had to reconcile his fear with his need and his desire. His conundrum simply was that he wanted her more than he despised what she represented.

Across the expanse of the table, she caught his gaze and solace warmed in her clear blue eyes. Was her sweet regard not worth more than money or scandal or shame?

"I have a toast to make," his father said and raised his wineglass. "It is with pride that I announce the engagement of my daughter, Elanna to our good friend and neighbor, Lord Carbury."

Gasps of suitable delight went up from the assembled guests. Congratulations followed with much consumption of wine. Carbury beamed as he grasped Elanna's hand and squeezed it so tightly her blood drained the skin white.

What in hell?

"Elanna accepted him this afternoon," the duchess declared.

This is why Elanna had avoided him earlier. The earl had proposed and she, trapped by time and looming poverty, had accepted.

She'd been sold.

He fisted his hands. That would destroy any woman or man's composure. The worst had happened to her. She'd taken a man she did not want.

He shot a look at Lily. But she was offering up her own blessings to the match and drank with the others to health and welfare of the new couple.

Fear stabbed Julian like a knife.

Would Hanniford sell his daughter to a man she did not want? The American had no reason to. But when a man was ruthless, it was possible. Would she agree?

Julian doubted it.

But then, he could not take the chance.

The moon glowed brightly as Julian stood before the stable doors, the two horses already saddled. Across the yard, he examined the path from the house. Anyone who gazed out of the windows at the right time and the right place could see her cross.

He patted the noses of the restless animals. "She'll arrive soon. Be assured."

A flash in the dark caught his eye. He spied her dashing toward him. His survey of the windows showed him no need for alarm. No one stood there.

"Hello." She ran right up to him, breathless. Tonight she wore her riding jacket and her usual hip-hugging man's pants, but no hat. Her hair curled over her shoulders in rich dark waves. "Have you waited long?"

Eternities. "I occupied myself and prepared the horses. No need to call Colin tonight, I thought. Come. Mount up." He wished to be alone with her. Away from here and the turmoils of the day. He helped her up on the mare. "Those trousers of yours are certainly an aid to riding."

"Not good for a lady's reputation, however." She watched him climb up and directed her horse toward the far lane and the woods where they'd gone last night.

"I won't tell."

"I know you won't." She narrowed her gaze into the road ahead. "Others would. Many would rejoice to ridicule me or Marianne and especially my father."

"For profit, yes, I know." *All too well.*

"So much of your society is built on propriety and yet so many hide their foibles. Even your Prince of Wales carries on with women at house parties."

Julian sighed. His horse kept pace with hers. "Those parties are arranged by many who wish to curry his favor. It's disgraceful on everyone's part."

"You wouldn't ever do that," she said with conviction.

"No. I wouldn't. I cultivate other aspirations. Some new, others older and not so well accomplished."

"I like a man with ambitions. Tell me about them."

"I'd improve the yield of our farms on the estates. Though I'm no farmer. I'd like to see my tenants better fed and healthier. Though I'm no expert on diseases."

She dropped her jaw and the look on her face stopped his breath. "Truly noble. Unlike some I've met."

What other men had caught her fancy or merited her disdain? "For example?"

"I'd be impolitic to reveal them."

"Do. For me." When she demurred, he said, "I won't tell."

"Let's say of the three other men who visit with us this week, I like only Lord Pinkhurst."

"Pinkie?" Why did that man pique her interest? "He's a good fellow. In want of a wife." *With two thousand a year. Not much. Barely enough to put a lady into his bed.*

"He's pleasant. Funny. Kind. But—"

"But what?"

"If I tell you, that gives you too much information."

"To do what?"

"Make fun of me."

"I may be cold, solitary, even sour, but I doubt anyone has ever said I was critical of others."

She cast her eyes away, her shoulders flexing in discomfort.

"Please don't think me capable of ridiculing you. Far from it."

"Why would you ask about my feelings for Lord Pinkhurst then?"

"I'm curious because—" *Oh, hell.* "I want to learn what kind of man does appeal to you."

She stiffened in her saddle, as if she girded for battle. "That's very personal."

"Of course it is. It gives me an advantage."

"Do you need one?" she threw back at him.

"Do I?" he persisted, undiplomatic as that was.

Her eyes locked to his, she considered that a long moment. "He's asked for my hand once."

Julian stiffened, alarm winging through his blood. "I would assume because you're here with me that you refused him."

She sniffed. "I did not."

No? "What then?"

"I told him I was not considering any proposals until June."

"Why?" he blurted, in frustration and fear.

She rolled a shoulder. "I want to take my time to consider such a momentous decision."

"I'm pleased."

"Are you?" She faced him, her brilliant gaze locking on his

146

and searching for truth.

I wish to God I had Pinkie's income. That sum could commend me, if only a little. But he couldn't tell her that, lest she link his finances to his desire for her hand. "Very pleased."

She said nothing but only nodded and rode onward.

He sought to bridge the gap. "I'd like to show you the house. It's old, filled with treasures and totally mine."

"Wonderful." She followed his lead.

At the kitchen entrance, he dismounted and reached to help her down. Looping the horses's reins over the iron rail, he opened the door, took her hand and led her inside. He'd spent most of the afternoon rehearsing a speech about marriage and money and a future they might build together. But as he escorted her through the scullery and up the servants' back stairs to the first floor and the pink marble foyer, he felt lost. His mind went blank.

"Oh, my," she exclaimed as she turned in a circle to view his ancestors whose portraits hung in the massive hall. "My relatives are not so many."

"And not so dour, I'd bet." He hurried to the butler's closet, found two candles in holders and lit them with a flint.

She lifted her taper to illuminate one painting and pointed toward one male peacock in vermilion velvet doublet and black codpiece. "Who is this gentleman?"

"Ah, Randy Roderick Ash. No gentleman at all. A courtier to Her Majesty Queen Elizabeth. A spy for the Crown. A seducer of many women. Father of too many children, all illegitimate but one."

"Good for the family," she said with humor. "And who is this lady?"

"The fourth marchioness, Lady Ann Ash. A terror they say. Ruled her husband with an iron hand, saved the estate from the clutches of Oliver Cromwell and bore her husband ten children."

"A lioness. Was she never Duchess of Seton?"

"The marquessate was given as a land grant separate from the duchy. The estate has remained in the family as the support of the marquess, run separately."

"So this house is really yours?" She seemed surprised.

"It has always belonged to the next marquess of Chelton upon his twenty-first birthday. Along with the sixteen thousand acres of rich farmland. Half as grand as many in this county, but good soil."

"Does that mean you are self-supporting?"

Good God. The things she asked. Thank heaven he had answers. Sound ones. "Slightly. We have hopes for a good harvest this season. But bad weather has taken its toll." He paused.

She tipped her head. "And what else has?"

"Over the past few years, I've poured most of my winnings at the tables into new plows, younger horses and new seed. But I'm not as skillful a gambler as I thought. What I've contributed has meant some improvement." *But it needs more. And damned if I want to marry and use my wife's money to make it so.*

"Pinkie tells me his own estate fails to produce what it did even last year. You are not alone in your predicament."

He stared at her. *Pinkie would want her dowry to shore up his failing income. The bugger.*

She caught sight of something in the parlor. "Might we go in there?"

He nodded, pleased she diverted the conversation, while he searched for a way to move the conversation to his main goal.

"Whose is that?" she asked when she stood beneath the massive silver sword crossed with a straight saber.

"My grandfather's sword on the left. He fought with Wellington and took the saber on the right from a French

Cuirassier whom he relieved of his life. He insisted my father become expert at fencing and so my father bade me learn the same value of a good thrust and parry."

"I'm glad you need not use it."

He put a hand to his heart, pained. "But if you should, I am prepared."

"I'm impressed. My relatives are an even more ragtag bunch. My father comes from the wharves of Dublin. My mother was born to poor farmers in Baltimore. The fights they fought were to eat and stay alive."

"And done very well, I'd say."

"My father has. I've no claim to ingenuity." She waved a dismissive hand and walked toward a landscape painting of courtiers at the hunt. "Do you track game?"

"Shooting parties. Yes, we do. Have you gone to any since you're here in England?"

She shook her head. "I'd love to be invited."

"Really?" That stunned him.

"Quite." She looked up at him over her shoulder. Her abundant hair curled over her ears in enticing tendrils and her mouth was open, ripe with humor. "I'm a very good shot."

"A good horsewoman and an excellent marksman. I must remember that."

"But you'd hunt with me? Even if I bagged more grouse?"

Her teasing had him laughing. He put his own candle down on the table behind her and took hers from her to set aside as well. When he returned to her, she melted against him. Her lips parted. Her breasts bore into him. She was all warmth and sensual woman. He enveloped her, the wealth of her a raw temptation to his desire to remain a gentleman.

She went up on her toes and brushed her lips on his. "Say you'd hunt with me."

"Not for years and years," he heard himself saying as his

lips sizzled with the lure of her own on his. "I'd have better things to do with you."

Horrid man that he was, he scooped her up and found the settee, his legs weak as a baby's from wanting her. He sent his hands into her hair, the heavy silk alluring to his fingertips. She wiggled, her efforts to sink into him spiking his cock to ribald heights.

She placed her mouth on his, a full kiss, mad in its appeal.

He bent over her, smoothing her hair back over her ear, admiring the beauty in his arms and warning himself...*warning himself* to remain in control.

She gasped, clutching him closer and rubbing her breasts against him. "Show me."

"What?"

"The better things."

He crushed her to him. "You're too adventurous for your own good—or mine."

She arched an elegant brow. "Say it's our secret."

He swirled her beneath him to the cushions. "A witch."

She chuckled.

But her laughter was caught short by his assault on her mouth. His tongue laved the seam of her lips and she let him inside. He stroked the wet cavern of her with a demanding glide and she undulated under him, willing and wanton. The fires inside him exploded in flames of glory. She was his. Would be.

He needed more of her. His lips branding her skin, laying claim to all she was. He lifted the hem of her white blouse, his suspicion that, like last night, she wore no corset or chemise a correct one. And in his fury to have more and quickly, he tore the thin cambric straight up the center. She was bare to him, her bounteous breasts pale and glowing in the rays of the moon.

"Darling," he said as he cupped one breast and admired

the large round nipple that hardened as he gazed at it. "I have never seen such perfection."

And then he took her areola in his mouth and sucked her high and hard into him.

She bucked, her nails digging into his jacket, her legs restless.

He caught one of her thighs and hooked it up around his hips. The new position made him growl for now his cock was nestled in the hollow of her loins. He caressed her hip and sent his hand further along the line of her cleft. Dear God. Had she nothing but those sweet damn trousers between his hand and her finest treasures? Finding the waist of her trousers, he slid his hand inside and down. Her skin was silk. Her folds were heavy, flowing with need of him. She was so ready for him, he pressed his forehead to her chest. And madman that he was, he sent his fingers along her juicy cleft and up inside, deep into her hot flowing core. She wanted him, in all ways. Of that, there was no doubt. Virgin and minx, innocent and wanton, if she wanted him, he'd give her all he could.

He captured her mouth and sank his fingers higher inside her. She groaned and shifted to give him better access to her core. It was then he turned gentle and heathen and found her nub. Satin hard, her bud stood in invitation and he circled her, tapped her, rubbed her over and over as she writhed and let him take her up to a rough ecstasy where she clung to him, suspended in her own passion and cried out, drifting down to him and his fierce embrace.

He cuddled her close, the aftermath for her so vital to his suit. She shuddered and nestled near to him.

"Julian," she murmured.

He kissed her time and again.

With one hand, she cupped his cheek. "That was marvelous."

He grinned at her, the rogue in him coming out. "For me, too."

She wrinkled her forehead. "I daresay not as much."

"You know the mechanics of this business, do you?"

"I grew up on a ranch. I've seen horses and cattle in their throes. But—" She licked her lips. "Never imagined it was this...thrilling."

He pinched her nose and pulled the two sides of fabric of her ruined blouse together. Then he slipped off his jacket, urged her to put it on and pushed himself away from her.

He rose, strode to the fireplace and back. His cock raged to have her. But his code of honor told him he mustn't have more than he'd taken already. "I promised you and myself I'd never hurt you."

"I believe you."

"You shouldn't."

She startled, her lashes fluttering in confusion. Presently, she clutched the garment to her chest. "Why not?"

He jerked around. For all his days, he'd never get over how direct she was. "I want you. Badly. Want to offer you more and yet I..."

"Don't stop," she urged him.

"I want to say..."

"Please tell me, Julian." The light in the room did not reach her. But he could see her heart in her beguiling blue eyes. She was too precious to toy with or avoid her appeal.

"Lily, I have nothing. Soon, less than nothing. We Setons are on the verge of ruin."

She blinked. "I am not enamored of money."

"How wonderful of you to say."

Standing, she clutched his jacket more tightly about her. "I don't say what I don't mean, Julian."

He had to be as forthright. "You come with stipulations."

Her eyes darkened. Her mouth thinned. "Not I. My father's, you mean."

"No—"

"It's the shipping company. You object to…to what? American money?" She grew angry.

He winced. "I object to being bought!"

She sucked in a breath. Insult had frozen her. "And I to being sold."

"We are two people who want someone whose circumstances offend their pride. What if," he asked with bated breath, "we were neither sellers or buyers, but simply two people who were meant for each other?"

Shock limned her features. "Are you asking me to marry you, Julian?"

Could he ask for her hand in all good faith?

Her face fell. She whirled away toward the door.

He caught her by the wrist. "Don't go. Look at me. I'm asking if—"

"Shouldn't you first seek *my* permission to marry, my boy?"

With a gasp, Lily spun, whirling back against Julian and facing their intruder.

Julian braced her. Outrage burned through him. "Why are you here, Father?"

The duke strolled toward them and Lily shrank backward into Julian's embrace. The look on the older man's face was no less than a sneer.

Her blood froze. Ashamed of her dishabille, shocked at the man's hauteur in the presence of his son, Lily steeled herself for whatever confrontation the duke so obviously intended.

He removed his hat, casually ran a hand through his

wind-blown silver hair and focused with lascivious brown eyes on her hold of Julian's coat at her breast. "I told you, Julian, I wouldn't approve of this match."

"*What?*" Julian spat. "You did no such thing,"

The duke wiggled a finger, indicating Lily's bodice. "Here's proof why such a union is unsavory."

"You lying basta—"

"He's wanted you from the start." The Duke of Seton was pleased with himself, cutting her with his disdain, strutting as he paced the room. "Did you know?"

She straightened, drawing away from Julian's comforting body. Julian had been attracted to her, and she'd believed him in spirit and truth.

"Ah. I see you did not. He knows what you're worth, girl. He needs your dollars."

She couldn't move.

"Come with me, Lily. Don't listen to this creature." Julian turned her wooden body toward him, his mouth a taut line of anger as he tucked his riding jacket around her more securely. "I'll escort you back."

"You need to tell her what we agreed to, boy."

Her heart fell to her feet. "Julian?"

If looks could kill, Julian would have struck his sire dead. "We had no agreement."

The duke laughed and walked forward so that he could capture Lily's gaze. He seared her with his menace. "He lies."

"I don't believe you," she got out. Could Julian have struck a bargain with his father about courting her? She'd become enchanted with him. But did he care for her, truly? "He couldn't..." *Wouldn't seduce me.*

"But he has no money." The duke extended an arm toward the appointments in the room and hall. "Not enough to support a wife. With his titles and his looks, he could have any woman. Why would he choose a gauche American? The daughter of a dockside brawler and a thief."

Much she could bear, but insult to her father was not one. She broke from Julian's grasp, headed for the hall and the servants' stairs.

"Wait! Lily!" Julian tracked her.

She scrambled down the steps and reached for the kitchen door, a way out of this horror.

Julian caught her around the waist, pressed his body flush to hers, his lips in her hair. "Darling, don't believe him. You mustn't."

"Let me go."

"Why he plays this game, I can only guess."

"I won't." She rested her forehead to the wooden door. Despair drained her of strength.

"Lily, please. Let me tell you what he really wanted from me and you."

"He'll say," said the duke from the head of the stairs, "that he forbade his son marry a woman of loose morals."

That slur gave her new vigor. She wrenched out of Julian's hold and managed to pry the door open.

But she had one foot out and came smack up against the Duchess of Seton.

The woman wore a smirk. "See here," she said and stepped aside to reveal a giant of a man, "your daughter, sir, is truly in an unacceptable condition."

"Papa," Lily said as she beheld the forbidding countenance of her father. Trapped in a maze of conflicting people and emotions, she stood her ground. But her hope to escape withered.

The duchess folded her hands before her, self-satisfaction in every line of her form. "I'm sure your father is outraged."

"Madam," said he to the lady, "I'll have none of your interference. Lily, what goes on here?"

"I came riding with Jul— Lord Chelton. He showed me his home."

Her father lifted his eyes to Julian. No good will greeted that man. "Why take her out in the middle of the night?"

"Sir, I acknowledge it was foolish. This is my fault because I—"

Julian should not take the blame. "He was being kind, Papa. I wanted to ride—"

The duke snorted. "Oh, aye! In more ways than one."

Killian Hanniford was at his most ferocious when countered by one who wished to take him down in scurrilous ways. He set his jaw, his black eyes flamed.

Inside, Lily cringed.

"Your Grace," her father said with spite in every enunciated syllable, "my daughter is as fragile a flower as yours. Today, you gave yours to a brute of a man."

"I say, Hanniford!"

"No bluster, man! I see who you are. I am not blind nor as loose of principle. As for my own daughter, I take pride in her every move. If she wished to ride at night, she has the ability, if not the proper sense to take a maid and a footman instead of your son as her escort." He offered his arm to her and with a shaking hand, she took it. "I also see by my girl's attire that there was more to this night than riding and visiting a house."

"Mr. Hanniford." Julian stepped up to them. "I would not hurt her."

"Is that so?" he asked with disbelief in his tone. "A hideous way to prove it."

"Papa, please." Lily squeezed her father's forearm. "Don't argue. Take me back. I wish to return to London."

"No, Lily," Julian objected. "You can't."

"But—"

"Sir, hear me out," Julian pleaded. "I wish to marry Lily."

She met Julian's gaze, her heart bleeding. "No, he doesn't."
Not for love or money.

Her father huffed. "How good of you, Lord Chelton."

"I was proposing to her before my father arrived and interfered."

Wasn't it more a litany of reasons why he wouldn't ever marry her?

Her father stared down at her. Resignation stood in his eyes. "You'll marry him."

"No!" She stepped backward. "This is outrageous."

"I agree," her father said. "This is proper—"

"You can't make me."

"It's best, my dear." He looked older, defeated. "The circumstances are such."

She'd never seen him without a swagger. "How can you say that, Papa? You agreed to let me choose my own husband."

"By your actions here tonight, Lily, you have chosen."

She shook her head vehemently. "I—"

"I forbid the marriage," said the duke.

Julian confronted him. "Are you mad?"

The duke gave his son a sardonic smile. "I warned you."

Julian glared at his father, then turned to hers with wildness that cast his features in stone. "He's scheming, trying to manipulate us all. I won't let him."

"Intriguing. How so?" asked her father.

"He wants a higher price for the shipping company. Wanted me to negotiate again with you to persuade you. I refused. He's angry at the loss. Angry that I'd court Lily in my own way. Angry that he's penniless, by his own folly."

Her father pursed his lips and studied the duke. "So you'll not give your consent to their marriage unless…what? I offer a higher price on stock?"

The duke lifted on his toes, preening like a fool. "I'd say you have the right of it."

Her father shot a look at Julian. "You must be of age."

"I will be thirty-one June first, sir."

"Do you own stock in the shipping company?"

"No, sir."

"Splendid. Send your lawyer to me for transfer of Lily's dowry."

Lily gasped.

Julian went white as a sheet. "I will, yes."

"Well, then, Seton." Her father seemed without joy as he looked at the duke. "We have a wedding to plan."

Julian beamed at her father. "Thank you, sir."

Lily shrank away from them. "You cannot sell me."

Her father glared at her. "You consented to too much tonight. I do not sell you, dearest, as ensure you will live without disgrace."

The duke lurched forward, his face ruby red. "You need my approval!"

"He's right," proclaimed the duchess with overweening pride. "Society will expect it. If Julian were to marry her, the chit would need my *entre* to the *ton*. And then there is the unfortunate possibility that this instance of riding at midnight and the seduction in my son's parlor would get out."

Julian seethed. "You wouldn't dare put that abroad."

She tut-tutted him. "Don't be naïve, dear one. Servants talk, you know it."

Julian cursed broadly. "I thought you were a hellcat, but I'd no idea how unscrupulous you were. You'd do this for money? Renounce decency?"

Lily could bear no more. She'd heard of families who starved because they drank away their wages or gambled the gold from their teeth. But the hypocrisy of the duke and duchess cut her like a knife. Did the son fall far from this tree —or could she trust Julian in spite of what was said and done here? "I don't want anything from any of you. Not acceptance, not titles, not money—and not marriage."

Julian caught her hands. "That's not true. I want you."

"Listen to him, Lily," her father urged. "This rejection does you no good."

She yanked away. "No."

"I'll not have scandal on my doorstep, Lily. I told you that before. I warned you. This is as much your doing as Lord Chelton's. Fix it."

"No, no," The duke persisted. "I won't approve of it."

"Quiet, Seton. You'll have your price for the sale." Her father patted her hand and led her more snuggly by his side. "I'll have my daughter wed with all due respect. You will approve. And you, Your Grace," he said to the duchess with a murderous look over the rims of his glasses, "will put no rumors of this night out to anyone. Understood?"

With an indignant lift of her chin, the woman demurred. "As you wish."

He looked at Julian. "How soon is a wedding possible without feeding the gossips?"

"The banns should be read in church for three Sundays."

"See it done. That makes the wedding the first week in June. Our house. I will post the engagement announcement in the newspaper. Also, Lord Chelton, be sure to find some exquisite family bauble that your mother has not yet sold to pay her nefarious debts. It will become an engagement gift for your fiancé. Send it round to the house Monday. We'll host a ball two nights before the wedding. Meanwhile, Lily goes to Paris for fittings for her trousseau."

She opened her mouth to object.

But he quashed her efforts with a shake of his head. "Do not disappoint me. None of you."

CHAPTER 10

$\mathcal{T}$hree weeks later, Lily walked to the head of the grand staircase in their home and steeled herself for the day ahead. Behind her, she trailed a three-foot ecru veil to match the satin and tulle of her wedding dress. Ahead of her walked her younger sister Ada in a Corinthian green who'd arrived only yesterday with their older brother Pierce. Beside Lily was Marianne, resplendent in a raspberry confection, who had assured her innumerable times that marrying Julian was the most wonderful thing that had happened to her.

But it terrified her. She'd lain awake most of the night, anticipating with delight what might happen in his arms…or dreading what might not happen if he did not come to her.

Early this morning, Marianne had swept into her bedroom, taken one look at her and thrown back her bed linens. "Up! Up! To your bath, woman. He cares for you. Weren't you sure of that when you went riding with him?"

With a heavy heart, Lily doubted it. "That was before that hideous scene with his father."

"And after, Julian didn't walk away from you, did he? No.

So, there you are." From behind her back, Marianne had revealed a bottle of brandy. "I keep it in my room for a nip now and then. A bit of Dutch courage is the answer. You'll have one shot. Maybe two!"

Lily had drunk three.

"How's my breath?" she whispered to Marianne as they rounded the first landing.

"Chewing the mint leaves worked."

"They'd better." Lily could imagine what the *ton* would say if the bride were discovered to be tipsy for the nuptials. Two scandal sheets had already speculated "If the American Girl L —H— had urgent reasons to accept the proposal of a certain marquess of C—. She skips her presentation at court to marry. What can compel her?"

My father. That's who.

He stood at the bottom of the stairs, resplendent in his formal cutaway, his jet-black hair glistening in the morning sunshine streaming through the front glass. "You're stunning, my darling Lily."

She took the last few steps down in the comfort of his smile. "I hope this service is short."

He patted her hand and looped her arm through his. "Chelton assures me it is."

She gazed down the hall toward the ballroom. Two footmen stood aside the closed doors. The guests there totaled two-hundred and ten. The prospect of greeting each of them made her stomach quake. She'd requested an intimate affair, but her father had insisted that only a large one, a lavish one, would hush any of the tattlers. Lily had succumbed to his intentions, wishing no arguments.

"Lily's the most glorious bride, isn't she, Papa?" Ada, at eighteen and fresh to London, was atwitter with excitement for the day and every aspect of her own future. With her curly cinnamon hair and grass-green eyes, she was a bubbly creature whom everyone adored.

"I'm proud of her," he answered Ada, but his attention went to Lily. "Never forget that."

I won't. She lifted her chin.

Pierce at twenty-seven was the younger version of their father, strapping and virile. He tugged at his gloves and bent to kiss her cheek. "Give 'em hell, Lil. They don't deserve you."

Ada hugged her and turned to take Pierce's arm. Her father nodded to the footmen that they were ready to begin. The servants opened the doors and her two siblings disappeared into the huge golden room where the crystal chandeliers were ablaze at ten in the morning for the much-heralded 'wedding of the season'.

Marianne squeezed her hand. "You'll be happy."

Lily caught her breath. *I'll work to make it so.*

"Come, Lily." Her father tipped his head. "I detect Chelton's a good man. But if he's not, you know I'm here for you."

"I do, Papa. Thank you."

They stood at the threshold a moment until the assembled guests rose to their feet. Her father had ordered hundreds of yards of green garlands to adorn the chairs. And in the aisles stood twenty-five-foot-tall vases of white lilies. The fragrance washed through her with a sweetness she hadn't prepared for. At the end of the center aisle stood another sight she hadn't anticipated. Julian Ash, Marquess of Chelton, tall and crisply elegant as ever in his bridegroom's finery—gazed at her with apology in his beautiful dark eyes.

The possibility that he might be fearful of her reaction to this marriage had never occurred to her. They had not been alone with each other since that hideous night at Willowreach. Her father had forbidden it and in fact, had allowed Julian to visit here only three times. Each time was for tea or dinner and the two of them were in the company of her father and Marianne or, like last night, a few business acquaintances of her father's as well as Ada and Pierce. Lily and Julian hadn't conversed together about any matter, let alone addressed the delicate issues of their relationship. So this apology from him was novel—and welcome.

But no sooner had she registered his emotion than he blinked, stiffened his spine and donned an expression that she swore signaled his indifference. *Is it such a catastrophe to wed me?*

She halted.

Her father clamped her arm to his side.

Can I run?

Julian blanched.

Does she hate me so much she'd leave me at the altar?

She seemed frozen, staring right through him. But then Killian whispered to her. She inclined her head to listen.

And she walked forward.

He let go his breath.

She was so heartbreakingly lovely in that froth of white tulle and satin—and she should be his. Not simply because he'd debauched her that night in his home. But because she cared for him. Cared enough to allow him to touch her. Certainly, she wouldn't marry him without affection for him. Affection? Or was it lust?

He had enough of that for both of them. God, he'd been so besotted, so heinous to maul her. But he was willing to pay the price. A sweet one it was, too. To have her. All of her. Forever more.

Damn the circumstances of how or why he must take her to wife. Yet he welcomed the timing. Three weeks had gone by like three eternities. He'd been busy preparing for her. In London, he'd registered the banns with the parish church. In Willowreach, he'd had his suite refurbished. He'd met with her father, too. Signed the papers. Agreed to take his money. Enough to swell his bank account. Enough to pay last year's debts on Willowreach and put him afloat to run the household. Better even that Pinkie's two thousand a year. Although he hated to admit it to his estate manager, Lily's dowry would permit him to hold his head up for the coming year. He'd pay off two new reapers for his tenants. In addition, he'd agreed to Killian Hanniford's stipulation that none of her dowry be used to pay off any of the Broadmore mortgage debts incurred by his father. That last was an easy promise to make. One his father, when Julian told him of it, raged against.

But his father's objections were hollow arguments.

Julian cared for none of them.

He wanted Lily. Just Lily. In his arms and tonight in his bed.

He frowned as he saw her take her measured steps down the aisle. Doubts riddled him. He hadn't had a private conversation with her since their tempestuous embraces at Willowreach. He'd wanted to ask her if she'd rued the time she'd spent kissing such a craven creature as he. Without that chance, he was left to hope that as her husband, he'd be allowed to do more than kiss her. More than what he'd done that night in his parlor—

And would she let him?

She and Killian stepped right before him and Killian put his daughter's hand in his. Lily's flesh was cold as ice. The older man locked his gaze on Julian's, a warning of unearthly magnitude in the American's black eyes.

With a tiny hope Lily might one day care for him more than she did today, Julian took her arm to direct her toward the clergyman. The man began a litany of which Julian heard none. At the appropriate times, he spoke, his voice tempered, his words rote.

In unmarked moments, she was his. He was hers. And their future was before them, a set of promises to each other.

He trusted her to keep hers. Yet their shared past and his family's imperfections meant he would have to work mightily to prove to her he would keep his own.

With polite farewells to her father and the rest of her family, Julian led her from the arms of her father and helped her up into his town coach. His hands were cool. His expression unreadable.

Is he happy?

Can he be? Forced to marry her, he must question his motives that night in his parlor. Lily sought her own. But her answers lay wrapped in the emotions he'd roused in her—and not just that one night, but all the other occasions when she'd enjoyed his company.

Enjoyed, the operative word.

A word too grand for today's events.

To distract herself, to look busy, she fished in her little reticule for heaven knew what.

She heard the coachman snap the reins. The vehicle lurched forward and the two horses clip-clopped their way along the streets. Jostled in body and spirit, she clamped her hands together.

Julian and she hadn't exchanged more than ten words since the ceremony this morning and the air was tight with anxiety. Lily smoothed the blue wool skirt of her carriage dress, at odds and ends what to say to her new husband now that they were alone. For many minutes, she busied herself with unbuttoning her pelisse and removing her bonnet. But she finally had to fall back to the cushions, unable to fiddle all the way south to Julian's country house. He'd think her a nervous ninny. Which of course, she was.

She pressed her lips together, frustrated at her awkwardness.

"I hope you'll be comfortable in this to go to Willowreach." He removed his gloves and crossed one leg over the other.

Was he trying to appear nonchalant? "I'm certain I will be."

"I sold my traveling carriage a year ago. I didn't need so big a conveyance for only me. Sold the four horses, too. This was less costly to maintain."

"It's perfectly fine," she said truthfully, more at ease in the purple velvet squabs now that he attempted to make conversation. "How fast does it go?"

"We should be home before supper." He cleared his throat and pushed aside the edge of the curtain. "Good weather for us. The coachman should make good time."

Three hours what what it had taken to go from London to Lord Carbury's house weeks ago. Willowreach was so close to Carbury's that she knew she had that time left until she and Julian would be doing more than talking. Before they went to his bed, she hoped they could bridge the gap between them in some ways. "Does he live at Willowreach?"

"Who?"

"The coachman. I thought you had only the one stable boy at the house."

"I do. But this man, Goodrich, is my father's man from Broadmore. I had him come down to London just to take us to Willowreach."

"Thank you. That was thoughtful."

Julian shifted. Tapped his palm on his knee. "I thought the wedding very well done."

"I'm glad it met with your approval. We tried to meet your mother's expectations. Elanna was a help, too. She sent me lots of letters with answers to my questions."

"She prepares for her own wedding in three weeks. Or I should say, my mother does."

"When will we go up to London?"

He blinked, his gaze soft and searching. "You aren't looking forward to it, are you?"

"I'll go, of course. But I thought— I wondered if we'll stay with your parents in their London house." Her relationship with Julian's parents had not begun well. To be in their company so soon after her own wedding presented a fresh challenge she must prepare to meet.

"We should. But you don't want to, do you?"

She considered her hands. "I'd rather stay with my family."

"Of course you would. I understand. Ada and Pierce have just arrived and you've had little time with them."

It was the best possible reason to offer to avoid the Setons. "Would you mind if we did stay in Piccadilly?"

"Not really." He inhaled. "It's a very good plan. I worry about Elanna though. I'll need to visit with her before the wedding."

"Do go. She'll want to see you."

"Hmmm," he said with knitted brow and lifted the edge of the curtain again. With a shake of his head, he let it drop. "I hope to God she can be happy."

Lily had to change the subject to one less foreboding. "One person who was happy today was Remy."

"And another was Marianne," he added with a sly smile.

"They spent so much time together even Ada remarked on it—and Ada is notoriously unobservant. Did you know that when we were in Paris, Marianne went to see an exhibit of Remy's works?"

"Is that so? I wonder if he knows that."

"Would that be important?"

"That he thought Marianne interested in him?" Julian crossed his arms and bent over with chuckles. "Essential, I'd say, to his well-being."

"He likes her," Lily said with a grin.

"He does." Julian smiled at her. "Almost as much as I like you."

His declaration was not all a bride could hope for but it helped to salve the wound of being forced to marry him. "Do you?"

"Very much."

She tipped her head, wistful and hopeful.

"You have to know that."

Her hand went to her throat where she wore his engagement gift. The four-foot long rope of flawless pearls had to be priceless. As she'd taken them from their red velvet box last week, her father had gasped with approval. Marianne had stared, her mouth open. "I'm delighted with these. Thank you."

"I was pleased you wore them with your gown. And now, too. They're not and never have been my mother's."

That had her beaming at him. She slid her fingertips over the perfect satin of one gem.

"They belonged to my Great-Aunt Priscilla, her own engagement gift from her fiancé who died at Waterloo. She was a bluestocking with a stinging wit and I loved her with a small boy's fascination for saucy women. Before she died, she gave them to me. 'A gift for someone you care for.'" He patted the seat beside him. "Come sit with me and we can talk more of it."

She cast him a sideways glance. "I hate to ride backward. You come sit with me. Here." She patted her cushions.

"It's dangerous you realize."

Her eyes went wide. "In your *carriage*? What can you do?"

He threw back his head to laugh. "Anything."

"You're serious?"

"Quite." He searched her expression.

"But…but you wouldn't. Would you?"

"No."

Her jaw fell. "Oh."

With a wry look, he rose from his seat and positioned himself next to her. Close but not too close, he took one of her hands and put it on his knee. "Let's be friends, shall we, and talk as we used to?"

She licked her lips, her eyes on their entwined hands. "I want to."

"So then. Anything is possible in a carriage. Anything between a man and a woman is possible standing up or in a chair. On the floor."

"Oh, you are making fun of me now."

"Never."

"And the reason we don't do it in a carriage? Or…um…in this carriage?"

"Too damn uncomfortable."

Her cheeks flamed. "I see."

"Now. Tell me something else."

"As long as we're not talking about *that*."

"We won't."

"What would you like to discuss?" she asked with some trepidation.

"Were you drinking alcohol before the ceremony?"

She clamped a hand over her mouth.

He took it away and he was grinning at her. "You were, weren't you?"

"I had a few glasses of brandy."

"Good for you. I had a few myself. Scotch."

She made a face. "I like gin."

He hooted. "Wonderful."

"Now you think I have no taste."

"Why? Because you like gin?" He lifted her chin with a finger. "That's ridiculous."

"A coal miner's drink?"

He rubbed his thumb along her cheek. "It doesn't matter, Lily. You like what you like. Like who you like."

She liked him this way. Kind and affectionate. "You're not ashamed of me. That I'm American and my father is—"

He slanted a finger across her lips. "I'm proud to call you Lady Chelton."

"I worried," she admitted with trepidation in her mellow voice.

"You mustn't."

He gazed away, paused in doubts. For him to admit that was equal to a confession for him. And a change of mind and heart. It had been a revelation to him only in the past few weeks.

Like the dawning of a new sun over his all-too-barren landscape, he'd risen each morning welcoming more and more the day he'd marry this young woman. And his pride was not so much assaulted by the prospect of calling her his wife, as it had been when listening to his father stipulate the terms that Seton demanded of Hanniford for its promulgation.

Julian had stood before his father in the house on Green Park and gaped at the duke's audacity.

"I told Hanniford I want ninety thousand pounds for the majority stock in the company." His father had practically preened as he said it.

"What?" Julian had been astonished.

His father grinned. " Over and above any marriage settlement."

Julian scoffed. "You're quite out of your mind."

"He's got the funds. And then some."

"It's no reason to rob him."

"He needs a husband for his wayward chick," his father said, rocking back on his heels, his hands over the swell of his belly.

"I'll marry her without him buying control in the company," Julian threatened.

His father had flushed an unnatural red. Lately, even the whites of his eyes were bloodshot. "Do that and your mother and I will not attend."

"I'll take Lily to Scotland."

"Marry her over an anvil? Ha! Hanniford would set the dogs on you. Never forget he wants her accepted. Shame her with a hasty marriage and tongues will cut her dead."

"That would change with time."

"But Hanniford is not the patient kind, my boy. Ninety thousand. It's mine and Hanniford has not objected. I have him by the short ones. So you negotiate whatever you want from him to live off."

Disgusted with his father's demands of the American tycoon, Julian had wanted a quick and bloodless marriage settlement with Killian. Taking no part in the discussions, he ordered his lawyer to negotiate with Lily's father. Last week, Julian's lawyer had sent him the final marriage contract. He'd opened the envelope with a heavy heart. He'd never indicated to the lawyer any desired sum. Her dowry, he'd said, whatever it was, would be satisfactory with him.

But when he'd read the first page, he had to sit down to cope with the shock. He re-read it twice. Lily Hanniford would come to him with sixty thousand dollars in settlement.

That was fifty more thousand than he'd had his hands on at any one time in years. The astonishing sum would be paid in full to his London bank on the day of the wedding. It was to be invested in transportation stocks, spinning off enough income for them both to live on handsomely. One quarter of that was to be Lily's pin money to do with as she wished. Her father had made only one stipulation on use of the money. None was ever to be used to service debt on the estate of Broadmore. In other words, Julian's father and mother would never see benefit from Black Hanniford's wealth.

All of which was just fine with Julian.

He had never intended to marry for money. Abhorred the very idea. That he had torn himself apart, liking her, wanting her, desiring her in spite of his endeavor to remain free of financial obligation, was all for naught. But he'd learned a valuable lesson.

He'd thought the barrage of American millionaires and their darling daughters an assault on British pride. Instead, he'd discovered his pride was remarkably intact. So was his integrity. He was doing the right thing by Lily to marry her, after nigh unto debauching her in his stables. But he was also doing right by himself, because he cared for her. More than he'd ever intended to care for a woman.

He turned to her, smiling at him as he held her, and squeezed her hand. "I'm proud to call you my wife. Who you are has less to do with where you were born or to whom and more to do with what you say and what you do."

"I want you to be proud of me."

"And you of me," he said with solemnity at this new endeavor to please her.

"I am. I have no reason not to."

He caressed her soft cheek. "I am not as accomplished as your father."

"I would bet you have as many sterling qualities. Perhaps more," she said with a sparkle in her blue eyes.

"I cannot count them."

"Should I?"

He gave a laugh, shook his head and settled her more securely in his arms. "A vain effort."

She rolled her eyes. "You've sold the traveling coach to save money."

"A trifle."

"Not so. You sold four horses, too. I bet they were fine stock, and you let them go for less than their value."

He blew out a gust of air. "I did."

"You love your sister and question if she can be happy with her intended."

"That's familial responsibility," he explained.

"And love." She smiled at him. "And then there's the matter of me."

"Ah, yes." He liked this topic and cradled her closer. She was a fine woman to take home to fill his house and his life. And his bed. Most especially tonight, she'd fill his bed. And his loins quickened at the expectation that she'd prove to be more than a fascination in his life. "My American with the beguiling blue eyes."

She seemed to shiver at his compliment. But her eyes were warm with need. "And a distaste for riding side-saddle."

"A penchant, too," he teased, "for riding at night."

"Creating a scandal," she said and the joy drained from her face, "so that you have to marry her."

He cupped her jaw. "I wanted to marry you. Was about to ask when all of them intruded upon us. I hate that they spoiled that for us. For you."

"You would have asked?" She seemed in awe.

"It's what I wanted then. What I wanted for the past three weeks. What I want now— I hope I can make you happy."

"Happy? I hope so too. But I'm aware this is your duty, that you had to do this to save me—"

He thumbed her lower lip, temptation rising in him to kiss away her every fear. "This is more than duty."

Tears welled in her eyes.

He hated that he could cause her so much anguish. Her pride was at stake. But so was their future.

"Tell me," he whispered as he urged her even closer, "if this tastes like duty."

He put his lips to hers and she melted against him, giving as much as she got.

Breathless, he broke away. "Is it?"

"What?" She stared at him, her eyes half-lidded and dreamy.

"Duty?"

She focused on his mouth but ran one hand up into his hair and held on. "Kiss me again and I'll know."

With pleasure. He chuckled. Her mouth this time was open and he darted inside, his tongue savoring the silken cavern. She met him with fervor. A violent need to possess his wife exploded in him. He'd waited so long, months, half a year, to claim what he increasingly knew he could not live without. She was all naivete to him, all sensuous ingenue, a blithe spirit and he, rogue that he was, burned to put his hands all over her and capture all those essences he'd long forgotten in himself. She was soft and wholesome, yet yielding and oh so tantalizing.

She pulled away with a gasp of delight. "That's the sweetest thing I've ever done."

Dear lord. What madness do I have license for now? Go slowly, man. Slowly. On a groan, he secured himself into the corner of the coach and brought her with him over his lap. With deft fingers, he plucked hair pins here and there from her coiffure and undid the top button of her blouse. Her hair fell around her shoulders and he captured a handful to bring it to his nose and inhale her fragrance. He brushed his full palm over her cheek and led her to rest her mouth on his as he whispered. "I should do this as a man who's come to call on his intended. You missed that necessary step in courtship."

"Are there a lot of steps?" She sounded spellbound and a little dismayed.

Darling minx. "A few."

"Then do it." She snapped shut her eyes and puckered her lips.

She was a rare woman. Lovely. Tempting. And funny. "My dear wife, you look like a governess sucking on a peppermint stick."

She opened one eye. "Are you putting off kissing me? If this is the way it's going to b—"

He slammed his lips on hers, muffling her cries and kissing her in a thousand small pecks to catch his breath. She'd undo him. All his resolve to be a gentleman, take her prudently and ensure she enjoyed her deflowering as much as he.

"I like that," she said between his sips of her mouth.

"And this?" he asked before he took possession of her lower lip and bit her gently.

"Yesss," she breathed and wiggled so decidedly that he longed to be naked with her.

His hands found the other buttons of her cambric blouse and worked at them. Her breasts had tormented him for too long. He remembered their firmness, their fullness, her large rosy nipples and he could taste them now again if he wanted.

And he wanted.

She batted his hands away and worked at her own buttons. She had no more than three undone when he slid his hand inside along her satin skin. Her corset was a rigid, cutting thing. "I'm going to forbid you to wear stays for the next forty years."

She let out a laugh. "I'll be a scandal."

"No, you won't," he promised as he took her lips over and over again. "No one will know. They'll never see you. You're not leaving our bed for at least that long."

He left a trail of kisses down her long, graceful throat. She arched up against him, her hands clutching his lapels. "Could you find me that fascinating for that long?"

He snorted. Cupped one round breast and stroked her nipple. "At least."

She sent her tongue along her lower lip and writhed as he stroked her to a hard point. "Yes, um. Yes. I think you're right."

"God, why do we bind women up in these contraptions," he muttered as he turned her around. "Let's loosen your stays."

She lifted her hair, her breathing hard. "Oh, let's."

He pulled her blouse up, found her stays and the bows, tugged at them and had her free of the monster with his hands sliding around her, inside the cups to treasure her glorious breasts. He let his eyes fall closed, the wealth of her in his hands making his cock stand like a warrior ready to take her.

But she turned in his arms. She stroked his cheeks and kissed him as if she were enthralled by him. "I've wanted this. More of you than I had that night in the stables."

Adrift in her spell, he opened his eyes to see her as he would wish her to be evermore. Wistful and passionate, besotted with him, her blue eyes spoke of a future of bliss. Could he give it?

He looked down, her breasts free of the garments, the cotton and stays arrayed around her in her lap. He caught up one fabulous orb and put his mouth to her gossamer flesh. He sucked at her nipple, warm, firm and ready.

She groaned, giving him all she was.

He covered her nipple with one palm and lifted the other to receive the benediction of his lips and tongue and teeth.

She whimpered, hanging on to him with straining hands, her hair, waist length, hanging over her half naked body, as she reveled in his touch. If this is what she lived for, he'd take her every chance he got and never let her out of his sight. The prospect consumed him like an inferno.

He rucked up her skirts. Led her to straddle him. He couldn't take her. Wouldn't. That would be crude, ugly, but oh, he needed to give her something more to fill the urge she begged him for.

"Come here, just here," he urged her, his voice a rasp of violent desire. He knew it might be too much to ask the gods for her to have worn no drawers and if she wore the horrid version with a flap in the back, he'd be stymied for certain in his quest to satisfy her. He slid his hands along her knees and she trembled, her gaze hot and fearful. "Shh. I won't hurt you. But let me see what you've got here that we might dispense with."

As his fingers caressed her thighs, she stilled. He pressed further and oh, yes, yes. She'd acquired—or someone with intelligence had persuaded her to buy the lingerie that had a long slit between the legs. He could touch her, tend her, massage her and pleasure her.

He slid a finger along her hot, wet passage. Her folds were heavy with desire and silky with need of him. He stroked along her seam easily, lightly. She moaned, her head falling forward to his shoulder. By her sighs, he understood he could claim this essential part of her as his own. "Darling Lily," he gruffed as he caressed her back and forth over her plump lips, "you are so wonderfully made."

She moved her hips, offering up her essence into the fullness of his palm.

"Sweet woman." He swallowed, trying desperately to quell his heartbeat and summon an expertise he suddenly feared had abandoned him. "Let me show you how it can be."

With one finger, he stroked higher into her core. Flowing with fragrant juices, her body opened for him. He stopped breathing.

"And then there is this," he whispered and kissed her cheek as he found her delicate nub, pinched it and made her buck. But she stilled and then sank over his fingers, surrendering to more. He kissed her ear, her throat. "Darling Lily, this is what awaits us both."

And in seconds, she undulated, digging her nails into his shoulders, her body in an arc of sexual triumph while she throbbed around his fingers. This woman, *his* woman, was that rare beauty who could love and give and feel and never regret a moment's loss of power.

As she calmed, she sank to him and nestled into the crook of his shoulder. He smoothed her skirts and helped her curl her legs over his lap. He held her, sated but ravenous for her. If he could tame his madness to unbutton his trousers, if he could persuade his cock to wait a few hours for his own fulfillment, he might make it home without becoming a lecherous fool.

Sighing, she stroked the edge of his jaw. "Lord Chelton, I think you lied to me."

Alarmed he examined her. Had he hurt her? "About what?"

Her dark hair wild around her shoulders, her eyes filled with sensual dark fire, her magnificent breasts bare to him and glowing in the coach lamplight, she teased him, all mischief. "You said doing anything risqué in a coach would be uncomfortable."

He hugged her tightly to his chest. Relief swam through him. "So, Lady Chelton, what is your assessment of making love in a coach?"

"Oh," she said, met his gaze with seduction in her look and pressed her thighs together, "I must have another go at it. With you, of course."

He hooted.

"That sample was splendid but brief."

"I promise you more, darling," he said with an urgent kiss to her succulent lips. "Much more."

"And soon?"

"Very."

CHAPTER 11

*T*he sun was setting as the coach pulled up to the main portico of Willowreach and idled. Julian secured Lily's coat around her shoulders, her undergarments ordered, but still in a wrinkled, jumbled state. At least, she was modestly covered...and still tingling from their intimacy.

"Follow the butler straight away upstairs to your suite, Lily," he told her. "By now, I'm sure your maid is settled in. Change and come to the dining room when you wish. Last week, I ordered a light supper for us."

"A formal service?"

"Not at all. Don your nightclothes and a wrapper, if you wish. Be comfortable."

Comfortable. The word had her smiling, hopeful he and she could resume the very gratifying explorations they'd begun in his coach. "I will. What of the servants?" she asked him as Foster swung open the cabin door.

"Only my butler and a footman in attendance. Your attire will be appropriate."

Dizzy with the prospect of such ease between them, she

tried to cover it with a mundane duty. "Elanna said I should ask to receive the staff first thing."

Julian brushed his palm over her cheek, his touch tender and surprisingly tremulous. Against his chest, her nipples beaded. She wanted his mouth on her again to quench this new thirst she had for his affections.

"Tomorrow," he told her, then left his seat and offered his hand to help her out. "No need to rush. You'll be here forever."

She liked the sound of that. Out in the brisk breezes of evening, she rose on toes and, servants or not, she put her lips to Julian's cheek. "Thank you."

"For what?" he asked quietly, footmen around them to gather their luggage.

"Being you. Kind, most of all."

His features stilled, his gaze flowing over her face as if he'd drink her in, eat her up.

Her insides, where he'd caressed her, clenched and she caught a breath, wanting his fingers daringly tormenting her again.

He swallowed loudly and hard. He glanced around, waiting until they were alone. "We'll go in quickly or we'll scandalize everyone as we climb back into the coach and make it rock."

She burst out laughing, discovering that fun with him was becoming a charming habit. "Never fear. I'm off!"

That night weeks ago when Julian had shown her the salon, Lily had barely registered the entry hall and appointments. Now she caught her breath at the beauty of the mansion before her. Ivory and gold-veined marble on the floor, green porphyry columns that rose to three stories high next to the stairs. The cupola in the glass dome above her let in the cerulean shades of sunset. The butler bowed and led her up the main stairs, a wide expanse so grand Lily was certain an entire coach could glide down the steps with ease.

"The marchioness's suite of rooms adjoins the marquess's," the servant told her. "His lordship had your suite redone with new draperies and rugs, madam. But he left much for you to do as you wish. I hope you're comfortable but should you need anything, madam, do not hesitate to ask."

"I won't. Thank you."

He thrust open the door for her. Lily smiled at her maid who bobbed. Nora, who'd traveled ahead early this morning from London down to the house, greeted her with a nod and congratulations.

"Thank you. Have you settled in?"

"Upstairs, yes, my lady."

Lily shrugged out of her coat.

"Oh, my!" The maid fluttered about her, regarding her mussed clothing with horror in her eyes. "Ma'am, are you —well?"

"Very, Nora." Lily had not thought how her disarray might affect her maid. The woman was in her forties and from her references, she'd worked for an elderly baroness before coming to Piccadilly to tend her. Lily had assumed she was experienced in all matters vital to proper service. "I expect your discretion."

The woman cast her eyes to the floor. "Of course, my lady."

"Take this away." Lily held out her coat. "And repair my blouse, if you can. If not, so be it. Take it to the rag bin."

"I put out your dinner gown, madam."

Lily'd been trussed up like a Christmas turkey all day, except for her journey here, and she welcomed the idea of wearing next to nothing to dine with Julian. 'No stays for years,' he'd said in the carriage and her body flushed at the memory. "I'll wear one of my new silk negligees. The pink one. And the cranberry brocade wrapper."

"But, ma'am, for supper?"

Nora was not used to a woman who did not dress to the hilt for every occasion. Why had Lily not noticed that before? Because it had not been an issue until tonight.

"Yes. And I'll have a bath now, too."

"Of course," Lily said and turned to the six-foot cheval mirror, which reflected her, head to toe. She was indeed, a mess. 'Ravished' was the word that came to mind and curved her lips.

She spun toward Nora. "Help me off with all of this."

I have a husband to please. And myself.

The ormolu clock on her sitting room mantle struck eight o'clock when Lily left her bedroom and stood upon the land-ing. She fingered the one embroidered frog closing her wrapper. The garment flowed around her, the swish of the soft brocade against her silk nightgown a sensuous tease to her overheated body and her erotic aspirations for the evening to come.

Although it was not considered appropriate for a lady to leave her bedroom in such meager attire, this was her home. Her new home. She wanted to live in it as she and her husband saw fit, not as nameless others might dictate. She'd spent most of her life adapting to others' rules, others' wishes. If she were honest with herself—and she wished to be—then even her marriage to Julian was conformity with society's rules. Albeit, one that held promise of more than a suitable arrangement. His desire for her was evidence. And hers for him was a lure to passion greater than that she'd found so often in his arms. She must trust herself to risk losing her heart to him.

She descended the stairs, taking in the marvelous decor of the house. Its stately magnificence sent ripples of excitement up her spine. She was chatelaine here.

She grinned.

And stopped.

Julian stood at the bottom of the staircase, one foot to the first step, an elbow to the banister. He wore an onyx velvet smoking jacket and gray trousers, a soft white shirt open to his throat. With a finger across his lips, he stared up at her with glowing dark eyes. A marvelous specimen of manhood. And he was hers.

"You make this old house sparkle."

She resumed the stairs down, an imp in her emerging to play. "You must be careful not to compliment me too much."

"Will you grow proud and dismissive of me?" he asked, his question half joking, half serious.

"I don't know how I could."

His face froze.

"What did I say?" She paused again, anxiety eroding the romantic aura she'd felt ever since they'd kissed this afternoon.

"Come down," he said, waggling his fingers at her and trying to be debonair. "I was obtuse."

She stood a step above him, their eyes level. "I doubt it. What struck a wrong chord in you? Should I be proud and haughty? If that's what you want—"

He sank both his hands in her hair and kissed her mightily. Her lips stung with his ardor. "I don't want that. I want you as you are."

She steadied herself with one hand on the banister and one around his waist. She searched his gaze and in his words, she heard truth. But only a portion of it.

"You're perfect." He winked at her, put a finger to the embroidered frog and offered his arm. "Come to the dining room. Do not look at the butler or the footman. They will be admiring the new mistress of the house. And then they'll disappear."

"Wonderful." She inhaled, relieved that his plans focused only on her comfort. "Will you show me the house tonight?"

He patted her hand. "If you wish."

"I want to absorb it all," she said as they strolled by Chinese porcelains, two giant medieval tapestries and a huge landscape painting of a hunting party, "But my goodness. Such a tour may take days."

"Indeed."

"Do you have a catalogue?" He led her past a small red salon where two card tables sat beneath a portrait of the Tudor Queen Elizabeth.

"A list?" He seemed incredulous.

"Yes. You should. I mean, do look at all of this." She waved a hand at the gold goblets on the table beside trencher plates made of Sèvres china. "Do you know where each piece came from? Country? Year? Purchaser?"

"No." He led her to the dining table where only two places were elaborately set. "But I'm certain my estate agent must have an idea."

The footman held out her chair and she sat.

"You may leave us." Julian told his two servants. "I'll serve Lady Chelton."

The butler placed her napkin across her lap and bowed his way toward the far doors. Then he closed them.

"Will you drink?" Julian lifted a crystal decanter filled with red wine.

"I will. Thank you." While he poured, she inhaled the aromas of the dishes on the sideboard. "I will compliment the cook when I meet her tomorrow. What do we have this evening?"

"Curried chicken. Young potatoes and squashes." He recited the menu, nonchalant as she'd never seen him before. The charm of it suited him.

"Superb. I'll have some of each."

"A hearty appetite," he said as he made his way over and picked up a china plate.

"Are you afraid I'll become well-padded?"

"That's up to you." He heaped slices of ham over potatoes and ladled a sauce over it.

She craned her neck. "If you keep adding to that plate, I may not fit into any of my trousseau."

As he marched over to her, he murmured something and deposited her supper before her.

"What did you say?"

He turned his back to fill up his own plate. But she heard him clearly. "Perhaps you might not need clothes for a while."

She sputtered in laughter, her hands flying to her hot cheeks. "That ends my life as a debutante. Not only will I now waddle everywhere, but I will blush until Christmas."

He shook with glee, his broad back in the exquisite jacket an alluring sight. He piled his own plate in silence punctuated by occasional outbursts of chuckles. Then he turned, his eyes dancing. "You are a treasure, my lady. Eat your dinner. Then I shall attempt to do the house justice with a decent description of its wares."

His tour was quickly done, his excuses for not knowing the provenances of his possessions numerous and apologetic. "I'll have a list drawn up for you, ancestors included," he said and led her into the salon where weeks ago he had kissed her and sealed both their fates.

"I'll like that. But oh," she enthused as she glanced around the room, rays of gaslight shining on the rich deep purple finish of the walls. In these glorious shadows, Julian took on a deliciously dangerous complexion. The rogue in his element, the aristocrat commanding all in his reach. "I love this."

"The Violet Saloon. Designed by my great-grandmother to conceal the effects of her bout with smallpox." He directed her to a large Chippendale chair before the fire. The subtle flames complemented his complexion and form. In the warm hues, his black eyes and hair were in handsome counterpoint. He was so suave, so devastating to her composure. Always had been. And soon he would see just how deeply he affected her. She'd surrender much to him tonight. Innocence. Loyalty. Some of her independence.

"Would you care for a brandy?" He raised a bottle from a glass cart. "Very good. French. And old."

"That means strong, doesn't it?"

"It does."

She lifted her chin, adventure always appealing to her. "I'd like to taste it. What I drank this morning was, I think, watered down."

"Become a connessieur, would you?"

"Certainly." She relaxed in her chair. "A lady must have unique qualities to recommend her. Plus if we finish that, then I'd need to buy more. I should purchase what I think is best for us and our guests."

His grin was beguiling as he poured two small glasses and gave her one, only to leave her to walk to the other side of the room. He swirled his brandy in silence while he stared into the fire, legs splayed, a hand on his hip, his profile stern.

"What bothers you?" she asked him, thinking it ironic that he should be the one to be troubled on their wedding night.

"The marriage settlement. Did your father tell you what he offered?"

That topic could lead her to alcohol and so she took a hearty draught. "He did. Generous, it was. What did you think of it?"

"Bountiful is the word that springs to mind."

"Ah." She took another sip.

"I never wanted to marry for money."

"So you said."

"Did I?" He ran his hand over his mouth, his look bleak.

Had he forgotten their conversation? Or he wished to make a point of his position? Whatever it was, it irritated her. "I didn't want to pay for a husband. That makes us equal."

"Did he tell you about his purchase of the shipping line stock from my father?"

Now she grew angry. "He did. I know it all, Julian. I'm not proud of it."

"You're not?"

"I wanted to be wanted for myself." She drained her glass and stood. "Might I have another?"

His gaze locked on hers. "I want you for yourself."

Words stuck in her throat. But important ones rose. "And I for you."

The tension fell from his face and he came to stand before her, then take her glass. "I can pour you another or we can go upstairs. It's your choice."

He wanted to undo that elaborate looking frog at her breasts. Open it. Reveal all that was beneath. Sweep every layer aside that divided them.

And here he was at sixes and sevens. Nerves eating at him. Asking her preference on their wedding night, of all damn things.

At thirty-one years of age, with a few mistresses to his credit, he should possess enough finesse to enchant his new wife. But she was a virgin, a novel entity for his jaded soul to deal with. Willing as she was, he perceived her anxiety—and too, her dislike to discuss money. He'd been an ass to bring it up. He rued his folly. His experience, however copious, did not bear the patience nor skill that was now demanded of him.

"I'd like to go to our rooms," she said and handed over her empty glass.

She did want to be his wife, in deed as well as law. Even in spirit. That he was happy about, but it was yet another reason to take her with caution and with care.

Commanding his wildly beating heart to slow, he found a smile and led her up the stairs.

He opened the door to his suite for her. The footman had turned the gas lamps to low earlier when Julian had gone down to supper. The rooms shone to soft perfection.

Lily swept inside, the train of her wrapper softly scoring the Aubusson carpet, raising his pulse once more.

"I had my rooms redecorated after our engagement was announced," he explained as he followed her into his sitting room, the glow of the lamps lighting the way toward his bedroom beyond. "I'd done with the place as it was for ten years, not wishing to spend the money on it nor having a need. The last time it had a re-fitting was more than fifty years ago when my grandfather welcomed his own bride here."

She walked around, touching the blue settee, the backs of the sapphire brocaded arm chairs and the cream-colored chaise longue. The black lacquered chest caught her eye and she paused to admire it.

"Most of the furnishings here date from the period when the family traded in the Orient. That Chinese chest is more than a hundred years old. The chairs are from an Indian maharajah, a gift to my father. Only the upholstery is new. And the wallpaper."

She continued around the walls, stopping here and there before a framed work. "This man is who?"

"My paternal grandfather. That lady there?" He indicated the portrait on the opposite side of the mantel. "That's his wife. My grandmother."

Lily put her hand to the pearls that she still wore around her throat. "Do you have a portrait of your great-aunt?"

"I do. Or rather, you do. She's in your dressing room."

Lily beamed at him. "I hoped that might be she. I saw her when I went in to change for supper. She was pretty, wasn't she?"

"Very."

"A pity she lived alone."

"She didn't want to marry for less than love," he said and at once wished he hadn't. That was what he and Lily had just done. And he wasn't feeling particularly secure about it.

"Do you know if she regretted never marrying?" Lily asked, walking toward the entry to his bedroom.

"That she never said. Instead she wanted me to understand the importance of choosing a mate wisely."

"I hope you have."

"I think I have," he admitted and held out his hand. "Come with me."

She shook her head, refusing to take it. "I have to know…"

He took pity on her and stepped to her. "What?"

"Do you think we'll be happy together?"

"I want to be."

But she stepped back.

"Lily, if you don't wish to proceed, we can wait. We have years and years together."

"This should happen before that!"

She was so dear. "It will. Don't worry. I'll show you to your rooms. We have a connecting door." He gestured toward it. "You can return whenever you wish."

"All right." She walked forward.

Trailing him, she said nothing. So much for his hope to unhook that pretty little frog.

He turned the knob of the door and pulled it open.

She walked through but halted on the threshold—and whirled to face him. "I'm being childish, aren't I?"

"Be you." *He had to be noble about her reluctance, didn't he?* "Good night."

Smiling at her, he began to close the door.

But she put a hand to the wood. "I really don't want to wait. I liked what we did today. In the coach. Can we do more of that, please?"

He hauled her close. She was spontaneous, natural, the qualities that lit his heart and had him taking her in his arms, smoothing her hair from her temples and burying his lips in her fragrant hair. She came to him trusting him, and he detected that beneath the wrapper, she wore next to nothing.

He stroked her collarbone down to her cleavage and that tempting red frog.

Undoing the closure of her robe, he pushed aside the fabric. Cool night air met her skin and she shivered in his arms. She fell back against the wall.

He cupped her jaw, smiled at her with raw desire and put his lips to her cheek. "We can go slowly."

"I don't want to," she confessed. "You'll think I'm unwilling."

"I don't."

She let her forehead fall to his shoulder. Her hands gripped the lapels of his robe. So often she'd seen horses mate. Cattle, too. And her herding dogs. Their cries, all harsh. The event over very soon.

"Your fears are groundless, my dear." He tipped up her chin. "Let me kiss you."

And so he did. With gentle lips, he pressed his mouth to hers. He went slowly, tasting her soft mouth and arching her up against him in a crush. She clutched his shoulder as he trailed his tongue down the cord of her throat and nuzzled aside her wrapper. With a tug, he brushed it to the floor.

She clamped her thighs together, hot and wanting, needing so much more.

He swept her up in his arms and strode to the oversize chair beside his bed. He curled her on his lap, and rested her in his embrace. He sent one large hand over the swell of her breast, warm and commanding over the silk of her gown.

She gasped in pleasure, her eyes drifting closed while a violent urge grew molten in her core. She recalled his hands on her in the coach, the thundering sensation he elicited from her and she starved to have it again from him. Surrendering to that storm inside her, she looped an arm around his shoulders and rose to claim his mouth in a torrid kiss. He responded, spark for flame, groaning.

She couldn't bear any more and pushed away, then jumped from his arms.

"Don't go," he pleaded, confusion lining his brow, bereft.

She shook her head. "No, that's not what I want."

He frowned. "What then?"

The silk negligee she'd chosen was nigh unto transparent.

She knew it. Had chosen it for that very reason. Brazen. He'd call her that.

"Dear heart," he whispered as he stared at her, his eyes hot, magnetically drawn down her body and back up to her face. "You are exquisite."

She swallowed harshly.

"And if you stand like that any longer, darling, you'll catch your death of cold."

Her lower lip trembled. "I always have cold feet and hands in winter."

He couldn't seem to keep his eyes on her face. "I could warm you if you like."

"I like." She affirmed that with a nod.

He narrowed his eyes at her and the seduction she saw there robbed her of breath. "Come here."

She couldn't bear to wait any longer. All this talk was reassuring, but only so far. And then she was left hungry, ravenous for his hands on her and his lips and his teeth...

She crossed her arms and in one swift move, reached down, grabbed the silken stuff into her hands and whipped it over her head. She let it slip from her fingertips to pool upon the floor.

The expression on Julian's face became a blend of reverence and salacious delight that she swore she must imprint on her mind for the day she died.

"Lily," he breathed and got to his feet to catch in his arms and stride to his bed. There, tenderly, he laid her down and slid beside her. "I'm amazed at you."

Her eyes stung with embarrassment. But the rest of her wanted whatever he had to give. "Pleased too I hope?"

He put the flat of his palm to the bare skin of her stomach and caressed her, back and forth. "Very much so. I think too it's time I pleased you."

He cupped one of her breasts, his gaze voracious as he studied her and circled her nipple with two deft fingers.

"Ohhh," she moaned, coiling.

"You're very responsive, darling. I touch you and you melt." He shaped her areola into a turgid point and she squeezed shut her eyes.

She writhed and he hooked one leg over hers, pinning her to the soft linens. Grabbing his hair, she looked into his eyes. "There's more you did weeks ago in the salon."

"Ah, yes. This?" He sucked her nipple into his mouth.

And she whimpered.

"This too." He trailed his hand down her torso to stroke her thighs and cup her there. Gently, he pressed one finger inside to caress her deeply. Then he added another. His strokes were sure and slow.

She flailed her head against the sheets.

"I know," he whispered, ragged, and shifted to take her other breast into his mouth and lave her to a throbbing torment. "You're superb, darling," he reassured her and slid lower on the bed.

"No!" She clutched at him. "Don't go."

"Never." On his haunches, he winked at her and crawled between her legs. Then he sank between them, put two fingers to her fiery flesh and opened her wide.

She twisted, the urge to run and hide or scream thrown to the wind in delicious surrender as he spoke to her in firm and soothing words.

"I want to taste you. Let me." And he lowered his mouth to her and lavished her with ardent little kisses along her secret folds.

She keened in delight, grabbing the sheets and arching, pausing in mid-air, full of the sultry wet strokes of his tongue. She hovered in space, expectant, rabid to have more, more and more again.

He gave it. Spreading her lips wide, he found that same spot he'd discovered in his coach, but this time, his fingers gave way to the glories of his tongue. He sampled her sweetly with a kiss. Slowly with a long tender suck and then he massaged her with the hard flicks of his tongue.

She lost her breath, panting. "Julian, Julian," she cried over again as he spun her higher and tighter into a tornado of wild delight. She couldn't think, move, wanting only this madness he gave with abandon and moans of pleasure. "Oh, Julian," she groaned as she launched herself over a new and spectacular cliff to land, pulsing in his arms.

Languid, she locked her gaze on his. He smiled, briefly, and combed back her hair. "Shall you have more?"

She caught him close. "Yes, yes!"

He turned to one side, divested himself of his silk trousers and came back to her, crawling up between her legs. Hooking his arms under her knees, he grinned at her and moved so near she resisted his searing flesh on hers. And then the probe, slow and sure, of the tip of his cock. Next the fullness of him, a wider girth and hotter. At last, the entire length of him, so large, so hard, her mouth fell open.

He caressed her cheek and asked if he was hurting her.

She shook her head in wonder. Not like the animals at all was this joining. "No. I love you inside me."

"Oh, Lily, I love it too."

And with swift strokes, he surged into her once and then again. He was sure and deliberate in his strokes. Until she caught his tempor and went with him, soaring up into sweet oblivion. He took her up to that precipice, rocked them there with kisses and cries. Then they sailed down. So that, at last, she was his wife. He was her husband.

Of bliss, she could name only one missing piece. Did she love him? He her? Or were they a good bargain for each other? The marquess and the heiress. The one bought, the other sold. Could they find love somewhere in between?

She could. At the realization, tears sprang to her eyes.

He noticed, thumbed them away and cradled her close.

Yet she wondered if for those who were bought and sold, was love a commodity that was durable?

CHAPTER 12

$\mathcal{N}$ora drew back the blue damask draperies and white sheer curtains, the rays of the sun warming Lily in bed and making her turn toward the space where Julian had lain last night. Gone now, he couldn't have left too long ago as the sheets were still warm.

"Would you like your breakfast on a tray, my lady?" Nora turned toward her, all efficiency this morning and not meeting her gaze.

"No, thank you, Nora. I'll go down. Draw a bath for me quickly, will you?" She fingered the pearls at her neck. Amazed they had suffered no harm in the evening's festivities, Lily smiled to herself and rolled over to hide her grin in the pillows.

The maid puttered about so much that Lily emerged from her pillows to sit up and witness her activities. "You can put out a morning dress for me, Nora. But I'll have my breakfast first, then return up here to dress for the day."

"But, ma'am, that is not done," the maid said, her brows high.

"I will, Nora. I'll have my velvet dressing gown now." Lily

preferred to dress herself and feeling so deliciously decadent from her husband's ardor, she abhorred the idea of whale-bone and constriction.

Less than an hour later, she sailed down the staircase to enter the dining room. There at the far end of the table sat her new husband, barbered, well dressed for the day in a tweed jacket and twill waistcoat. He read a newspaper, but at her entry, he glanced up. This look on his face—dare she call it reverence or awe?—was another one she wished to commit to memory for her dotage.

"Come sit with me, my lady." Julian beckoned her and with his fingers, made a motion to the footman to serve her and leave.

She came to sit at his right hand and allowed the footman his duty of seating her. Beneath the table, Julian pressed his knee to hers. She undulated in her chair, her inner core molten and pulsing at his seduction. At her uncontrollable needs, she caught her breath. But her body defied her as her breasts beaded and her mind bent to the thrilling memories of the erotic ways Julian had excited her last night. And in the meantime, the footman took for blasted ever to serve her coffee and a plate of eggs and toast and bacon.

When he closed the door and the latch clicked shut, she exhaled.

Julian's hand covered hers and pulled her up. He whirled his chair around and yanked her into his lap. "I've waited hours to have you again."

She marveled at him, ecstatic that he could be hungry for her. "Me, too."

His hand to her nape, he kissed her, devouring her lips and thrusting his tongue inside to trace the cavern of her mouth. She cupped his cheek and kissed him back.

But his other hand was already traveling her thighs and parting her legs. "Darling," he said as his mouth sucked on hers and he sent two fingers up inside her very needy core. "You are very wet."

"Could you help me with that?" she offered and moved to allow him greater access.

He barked in laughter and brushed aside her skirts. "I could. Good woman, you are, to have worn no pantaloons."

"I wanted you," she said as she kissed him and rocked against his fingers.

"Stand up," he ordered her. And when she did, he led her to the far end of the dining room table and laid her back upon the bare expanse.

"Can we do this?" she asked in wonder while he opened his flies and his large hard cock popped out. "Don't you have...um...other things to do?"

She shivered, eager, her mouth watering to have his long firm member inside her.

"You are my only occupation at the moment. Besides, the table is old. Solid. And you—" He breathed through flared nostrils as he surveyed her flesh naked from the waist to the tips of her toes. "You are beautiful. And mine."

Swallowing loudly, she spread her legs, eager, wanton, discarding old lessons about virtue and timidity. "Be quick and then let me— Ohhh."

He slid inside her, his eyes closed, his face up, his cock solid and searing, consuming her to the hilt. He seemed mesmerized, transported. His long dark lashes fluttered and he opened his eyes to caress her with hot intent. In a fluid motion, he began to pump inside her, filling her with frenzied need. All the while, he pinched and circled that special point inside her folds. And he drove her mad.

Sinking down into the black comfort of his possession, she lolled her head upon the hard wood of the table. Her breasts ached for his teeth. Her hips bucked, urging him closer, faster, tighter.

"Is this what you had in mind for breakfast?" he asked as he slid in and out of her.

"Better than."

"Me, too."

She laughed and whimpered as he began a regular plumbing of her depths in a smooth and fascinating rhythm. "Wives don't bare themselves on the dining room table this early in the morning?"

"Most don't."

"Do you mind that I do?"

He shot up inside her and held. "Do you?"

She bit her lips. "Oh, no. I love this."

He slid out and in again, rock hard against the limits of both their bodies. "I want more of you than this."

Tears burned her eyes. Whatever remained to give him was a mystery. But his desire was all she needed to know. "Have me."

He grabbed her at her nape, leaned over her and ground his lips on hers. His heat, his ardor, was frightening and beautiful. How had she created that emotion in this man? Or was that what every mating came to? This ferocity? This bliss.

He slammed into her, her body arching up, her cries loud and pleading with him to take all of her.

He growled, coming into her at the same moment that she broke apart, trembling, pulsing. Her culmination was more violent, more satisfying than those the night before. He withdrew his cock from her and arched over her, his forehead to her stomach, his lips to her mound. "You are sensual and generous. As unique as those pearls you wear." He raised his head and branded her with the delight in his eyes. "You and I will do very well together."

"If we start each day like this," she told him with a wicked grin, "I'd agree."

He threw back his head to laugh. "Come, my dear. You need sustenance for these games."

She brushed down her garment, accepted his hand and tossed him a wink. "Patience is a virtue, I'm told. But I'm very inclined to play."

He pointed to the table. "I will not see you waste away. Sit and eat first. Afterward, we can adjourn to the bedroom."

"You'd humor me?" she asked with a whisper full of bright intentions.

He cupped her cheek and kissed her deeply. "In that, as in much else. Yes. Always."

Minutes later, she finished eating and Julian lead her up to their bedroom.

He had taught her to crave him.

She followed him, grinning with satisfaction.

They would indeed do well together. In bed. For as long as that fascination lasted.

Would they do as well together out of bed? They could make each other laugh and they could talk about serious matters, like money.

That was a sound beginning.

"I apologize for my delay, Chelton." The family lawyer, Phillip Leland, strode across the carpet and gave Julian a small bow. With his offices in the City, Willowreach was a long journey for him. But Julian had sent him a letter the day before his wedding to request his help and he'd come. "I had to spend the night in Ashford. But the rain is hideous. Many roads flooded."

"Sorry to bring you down to me in the downpour." Julian offered him the chair before his desk.

With a shock of bright gold hair and large eyes, Leland

was a long, lean drink of water. He was a dedicated man, working more hours than he should for their impoverished family. Once in an altercation with a man who'd insulted his sister, he'd suffered a saber cut to his left cheek and a leg injury. Limping, he headed toward the chair and sank into it. "It never ends. Terrible prognosis for your crops."

"Just as bad for your wounds."

"I do feel it in my bones."

"A few of my tenants are down with hacking coughs. A few children too."

"A shame. Unnaturally cold for mid-June." Leland, though Julian's age, seemed to shiver.

"Tea will be here soon. But something stronger in the meantime?"

"Stronger would be welcome."

Julian went to his sideboard, unstoppered a bottle of Italian brandy and poured two bountiful portions. "Here you go. Drink up."

Leland downed a goodly portion. "Thank you."

"I hated to ask you to come south in this mess," he said and wandered back to his desk.

"And so soon after your wedding, too."

Julian couldn't suppress the smile that spread upon his lips. He'd been wedded to Lily all of six days and each new morning, he felt lighter. Dare he say, giddy. Foolish, perhaps even childish, but true. Serious matters overtook his delight and he shook his head at Leland. "My haste is necessary."

"A problem with your wife's marriage settlement?"

"Not at all. I'm very pleased with the funds. Far more than I expected." *More than I deserve what with my dim view of marriage in general.* "I wish to discuss a few financial matters. First, we own two parcels of land in Ireland I'd like to sell and quickly, too. Hopefully you can find a buyer."

Leland looked dubious. "Your father has approved the sale?"

"No, but he will. Must."

Leland stared at thim. "You know that few here in England have cash for that."

"Sell it to Americans, if you must. Not Killian Hanniford. I have far too much of his money to go begging for more. But anyone else is acceptable."

"Very well. Which lands?"

"The one you could most likely sell first would be the profitable one outside Tipperary."

"That's a well-appointed estate. But the tenants will not be happy to hear you're selling."

Julian could not see another way to make a substantial sum of money. "We can hope the new owner is a kind soul and they grow to like him. See to the sale. "

"I will," Leland said. "And your second reason to call me here?"

"I wish to discuss Elanna's marriage settlement for Lord Carbury."

"I progress with that for your father, the duke." He placed his empty glass upon the nearby deal table.

Julian applauded the man's discretion. Leland would say nothing about Elanna's projected sum, lest he give away confidential information. "I'm sure you do. What I have to say is not known to my father. Not in specifics. But he is aware of my feelings about my sister's marriage."

Leland folded his hands in his lap, his countenance blank of all emotion. "I understand. How then may I be of service?"

"They marry in a few weeks. I need this done quickly." Julian had to save his sister from some disaster if he could. He knew a few of the stipulations of her settlement, but he would not inquire for all of them. "I have funds which I would like to apply to Elanna's dressmakers and milliners' bills. All she incurred since January."

"That is most generous of you."

"There's more. I have five thousand I wish you to invest in her name at Rothschild's. Railroads, steamships, tea, I care not where or how, nor do I wish to know. Furthermore, Carbury is never to learn of it and frankly, neither is she."

"That is most…unusual." Leland tipped his head, puzzled.

"It is. I know it. But I wish it done."

"Still, I am confused. Why invest it if she never knows of its existence? Why not simply—"

"Give it to her?" Julian smacked his lips. *How to say this?* "I will be quite frank, Leland. I trust her."

With a pointed look at his friend, Julian allowed the silence to imply that he did not trust Carbury.

Leland arched a golden brow.

"However, I do not give this marriage much of a chance of happiness."

"I see."

Julian inhaled deeply. "I fear for the future. I also predict that if Carbury knew of the money, he could by law take it for himself. And should my sister ever need funds to remove herself from his presence, I want her to have independent means. If I am not nearby, if she suffers, if no one believes her—" *And she must escape him.*

Leland held his gaze for a long minute. The gravity of what he'd heard pulled his eyes wide. "How then is she to learn of these funds?"

"You will tell her if and when it becomes vital. For now, you will become her friend, her confidant. I've add three hundred a year to your Willowreach fees to visit her once a month every month. Choose a certain day and time. All so that you incur no suspicion to your actions. And so that she never suspects your reason."

"But how do I impress upon her that I am the one she must come to if she's in trouble?"

"Find a way. You like her." *She knows it.* Julian had seen how the man regarded Elanna whenever she appeared in the same room. Such longing was borne of boyish yearnings. It was not kind of Julian to use them to his own ends, but he hoped that Leland might forgive him if it ever came to sadness.

"I do." Leland considered his hands, his jaw flexing as he thought of what to say. "Might she not be persuaded to break the engagement with Carbury?"

"You know why she cannot."

"We are each creatures of our class," Leland said with a bitterness that had them both silent.

"At last." Julian said as the butler laid a tray before the small table near the fireplace. "Here is tea. Let us talk of sunnier subjects, shall we? And spend the night, will you? We'll dine and make a party of it. I'll not have you riding back to Ashford tonight in this foul weather."

Lily hoisted her umbrella in one hand, her skirts in another and hurried from the kitchen, down the path to the stables. She hadn't been here since she'd become Julian's wife and she thought it an appropriate time to visit the groomsmen and the horses. She longed to ride. But the rain was not cooperating. Plus Julian had asked her to remain indoors.

"The rain is so heavy, I've reports from my men upstream that a dam we built last summer may not hold. The lanes aren't safe."

She'd been indoors all this past week. Although making love to Julian was a deliciously proper past time for a new bride, she'd been inordinately lazy, lolling about their suite, becoming accustomed to her own private sitting room and dressing room. This morning, he was busy meeting with the Ash family lawyer. He'd called the man down from London and worried about his safety when he hadn't shown up yesterday. A few minutes ago, Mister Leland had arrived and Julian had hurried downstairs to greet him.

As she came upon the stable, the doors were ajar. When she pushed one open to step inside, she saw the stableboy who'd helped her that first night she and Julian had gone riding at midnight.

"Good afternoon Colin. Pardon me," she said smiling to the boy and his companion, a gnarled and grizzled white-haired man. The two of them were debating the looks of an old horse's hoof. "I didn't intend to interrupt you."

The stableboy stood straight, dragging off his cap and pulling his forelock. "Pardon, m'lady."

"How do you do, sir?" she nodded at the older man.

He grinned at her. "Aye. Good to make yer acquaintance, m'lady. Richards, I am."

"Wonderful to meet you, Richards." She peered over at the horse's hoof. "Threw a shoe, eh?"

"A while ago, I'd say," said Richards.

"Me, too."

"Second one, he's thrown in a week," Richards added.

"A shame. Can you give him a new one quickly?"

"Lamb's our farrier. Sick, 'e is, though."

"Oh. That's not good." This morning, she'd heard Julian discuss with the butler and housekeeper that a number of farmers in the village were ill. He'd asked them to scour the house for extra blankets to send to the village. "What's wrong with him?"

Richards patted his chest. "Cough. Deep. Loud."

"Bronchitis?" she asked.

"He's not the only one, either. My sister's got it. And she be increasin' too."

Pregnant and sick with a debilitating cough. In this weather? That was disaster.

"In the village, is there a chemist?" she asked them.

"Among us?" Richards asked like she might be hallucinating.

"No," said the boy.

"Where is the nearest?"

"Ashford," said Richards.

"Far away, is it?" she asked.

"Two hours ride," Richards told her.

"Not bad. Well, you see, I've nursed many sick people before. I'd like to help."

The two men stared at her as if she had two heads.

She might be the new marchioness and a new bride, but she was not without skills or brains. Or persistence. "Could you take me to the cottages? Please?"

Richards was more than skeptical. He scratched his shaggy hair above his ear. "In the rain?"

"You walked here. So can I."

He shot his bushy brows together. "'Is lordship may not like it."

"To give help to his tenants who are ill? Of course he will like it. Tell me where they are. You needn't come with me, if you don't like. I take my own responsibility."

He pulled a doubting face.

"I do. Always," she assured him.

Phillip Leland was a handsome frog, what with his overly large green eyes and brilliant hair, the color of old gold. Tall and thin, he had an aristocratic bearing that told her he must have come from a very good family who lived beneath their station. When Julian had told her that the two of them were second cousins through his father's family, she understood how the two men, so divergent in class and occupation, got on so well together. He was a relative.

He had told her his father had earned a living at writing novels in installments much like Charles Dickens had done. "At first, he wrote novels suited for social commentary. But when he did not become as popular as other authors, he began a series of books for children. He created a character who was a mouse in the house of a duke," he said as the three of them sat in the purple salon after their dinner.

"The mouse stole cheese from the larder and books from the library," Julian said with a chuckle.

"And raised his sons to become barristers and his daughters to become physicians," Leland added.

Overjoyed, she clapped her hands together. "Disregarding class and gender?"

"True revolutionaries," Leland said with a rueful grin.

"In America we would applaud that," she said.

"Here," he said, "we take our revolutions a bit more slowly."

"And how did you decide on the law? Was it your father's stories of his little mouse that inspired you?"

"I confess it's true. But what I'd really like to do is write a novel. I've penned a few shorter stories that a London publisher considers."

"That's wonderful," she said. "I like to see people engaged in what delights them. My cousin Marianne takes comfort in drawing and painting."

"Is that right?" Julian asked as he took a chair opposite her. "I had no idea she did that."

"Has she shown her work?" Leland asked.

"She does it only for her own enjoyment, claiming she'd

never match a professional's expertise. But her subjects are unique." Lily finished her glass of brandy and put it aside. "She paints women and children. Quite charming."

"Do you also draw and paint?" Leland asked her.

"Oh, no. I'm afraid my talents are totally lacking. I draw lovely little stick men."

Both men gave a laugh.

"I wish I could contribute something to the world like that. But I think my skills are in nursing."

"Nursing?" Leland was clearly shocked, his bright eyes even bigger than before.

"Yes." She glanced at her husband whom she'd not seen all afternoon until he'd appeared in his dressing room to change for dinner. "Now is a good time to tell you, Julian, that I went to the tenants' cottages today to check on those who are ill. I fear three have bronchitis. I saw a few children. Two have croup. Those blankets you ordered sent down to them are useful to make tents for bronchitis kettles. But they have only two in the whole village."

"Steamers?" Leland asked her. "What do you mean?"

"Breathing in steam is very useful to keep the lungs clear. The best way to do that is to make a tent, then force in air with kettles specifically made for the purpose. They have a wide base so they don't tip over and a very long spout."

"I'm glad you went," said Julian, his brown eyes heavy with concern, "but you may also now fall ill."

"You mustn't worry," she told him. "I've been near people who have much worse maladies and never been sick a day in my life."

"Still—"

"It gives me great joy to be of real use to someone." *I can't spend my life ordering about servants and then not care for them when they are in need.* "I'd like to purchase more equipment. Help them regularly."

"I wouldn't dream of refusing you joy, my dear. But that could endanger your health. Though I am sad to say it, the farmers do not have benefit of the best food and warm fires. I'd like to improve that, but struggle with the means. This rain doesn't help. The crops will be spare…" He narrowed his gaze on his glass, disturbed.

She tipped her head, aware she must not shame her husband in front of his friend. "If by small favors, I can improve their health, I want to. In fact, I'd like to buy more copper kettles for them. Nelson inhalers too. A special type, you see. But I'd need the name of the local doctor."

"As you wish." Julian raised his glass to sip, his deep brown gaze delving into hers with what was appreciation. "I'll see to it in the morning."

"I'd like to find the local chemist's shop too to order a balsam compound of aromatics for the kettles."

"You and I will do that, too," Julian said with a smile spreading on his lips. "They will be most grateful."

She nodded, thrilled and a bit embarrassed by Julian's seeming wonder at her suggestions. She wished to change the topic. "So. Tell us, Mister Leland, do you return to London tomorrow?"

"I am called to Ashford, my lady. Your husband and I have a mutual cousin who gives an annual ball. He insists I join him. In fact, it might be useful if I approached him about your Irish project, Chelton." Leland looked at Julian with intent. "What do you think?"

"A fine idea. He might be interested. He just might." Julian nodded. "Ask him."

"What is your Irish project?" she turned to Julian.

"I wish to persuade my father to sell an estate near Tipperary."

"I thought none of you could sell your land." Entailed property was bound by inheritance laws.

"This land can be sold," Julian said. "It's free of the entail. Good fertile acreage, too. Someone will like it."

"Wouldn't it be best to keep it?" she asked.

"I would if we could afford to, my dear. But my father has not and cannot supervise it as he should and another owner would do very well for the tenants. And I know my father would welcome the cash."

"I see," she said. "Of course. And you think your cousin might buy it?"

Julian nodded. "He has the money. And he has a penchant for Irish race horses. This would be good investment for him."

"Have I met this cousin?" she asked Julian. "At our wedding, perhaps? Forgive me, I may have forgotten him in the rush." She feared she may have committed a *faux pas* to ask this, considering that Leland had not attended their wedding either.

"No, he was unable to attend," Julian told her. "Lord Burnett journeys every year to France on the anniversary of his sister's death to plant flowers at her gravesite."

"Dedicated to her, he was," Leland offered. "I would think you both would have been sent an invitation to Burnett's ball."

"We have been," said Julian.

"Have you accepted for us?" she asked, hopeful of meeting such a thoughtful man.

"If you wish to go, we can," Julian told her with a sparkle in his eye. "I at first declined thinking you might not wish to attend a public function so soon after our wedding. Then too it is five days before we leave for Elanna's wedding."

"Oh, but I do love to dance," she said wistful. "Might we still attend? Or is it impolitic to invite ourselves so late?"

"I like Mister Leland very much." Lily entered Julian's master chamber. Her cerulean-blue silk and white lace peignoir swirled around her like a cloud. Her black hair was down, brushed to a high shine, her long waves curling over the full rise of her breasts. She was a sensuous angel, supple beneath the flowing fabric dotted with the innocence of the French lace. As so often these past weeks, to look at her was a feast.

He opened his arms to her. She dazzled him. "I'm pleased you like him. He is a family treasure." He explained the distant relationship to her.

"Why then was he not at our wedding?"

"Ah." He stroked her hair, her silken strands twining through his fingers like an angel's breaths. His body hardened with need of her, a desire that grew more fierce each hour he spent with her. "Too far down the order, you see, for my parents. My father demands those in his service receive only their wages, not much else from him. But even invited, Leland would not accept."

"Why not? He is your cousin." Her blue eyes were upon him as if he were her only treasure.

"Twice removed, but there is more. He has a certain affection for Elanna. He stays away." *He can never hope to have her. Not as I have you.*

"That's very sad."

"We won't be sad tonight." He raised one of her hands and kissed the palm.

"No." She shook off her frown. "You'll tell me about the masked ball we're going to and your cousin."

"Valentine is charming." He cocked a wicked brow. "He'll fascinate you."

She lifted a shoulder, then ran her fingertip along the outline of his mouth. "Not as much as you do."

He nipped her finger. "Do I?"

She shivered. "Mmm. Especially since you don't object to me nursing."

He crushed her close, serious at once. "If you become ill, you'll stop. Promise me."

"I do." She ran a hand up over his cheek. "As long as you promise me one thing."

He inhaled and gazed with consideration at the ceiling. If she wanted money or jewels, a carriage… He had no means for any of those. "Tell me."

"At Valentine's? His party?"

Was that all? "What would you like, my darling?"

At his endearment, she giggled and reached up on her toes to peck him on the cheek. "You'll waltz with me. We haven't, you realize. We've done ever so much else. Ridden at midnight. Made love in your carriage."

"And you liked them both."

"Oh, I did!" She blushed. "You tease me."

"No." *I adore you.* "I applaud you."

"So we'll dance? You won't be one of those gentlemen who does it out of duty or…or hates it really? Tell me you aren't like that."

He stepped back a bit, wrapped one arm around her waist and took her other hand high. Then he led her slowly into the steps. "I'm not." *Not with you.*

She beamed at him. "You like this?"

"With you I do." He waltzed her around the floor, away from the Axminster carpet so they could glide along the polished wooden floor. "You're very good, too."

She flung back her head to grin. "And you are expert. How many women have you charmed, dear sir, dancing with them in ballrooms and gardens?"

In her question, he heard the implications of another, more serious. "I've waltzed with others, many others."

"And did you—?" She bit her lip, missed a step and paused. "I'm sorry."

"Don't be. You can know. I once considered marrying a young woman. We were both quite young. She married another."

Lily hung her head. "I see."

He put two fingers to her chin. "Look at me."

When she lifted her face, her eyes held trepidation.

"I was twenty years of age and thought I loved her. I declared for her and she for me, but we were not to be."

Lily waited, searching his face for more.

"She had another offer and she took it." *Miserable in her bargain, too, say the gossips.* "I'm glad she did."

Hope blended with curiosity in Lily's large gorgeous eyes.

He cupped her cheeks, his thumbs stroking the exquisite arch of her bones. "She hated to dance. Did not ride astride. And would never have made love in my carriage."

"She's a proper lady."

"Proper?" He thought of Margaret Sheffield in many other terms. Voluptuous, opportunistic, greedy. "Very much so."

"And you're not ashamed that I'm not...like that?"

He crushed her to him. "That you're kind and thoughtful? That you'd go to our tenants in the driving rain to nurse them? That you'd want to dance with me?"

"Often?"

"Until you wear out my shoes."

She vibrated with glee. Narrowed her eyes. And asked, "In the moonlight?"

He nodded, a silly grin on his face. "I do believe Valentine has a garden off his ballroom terrace."

She hugged him. "And you'll make love to me—"

My greatest pleasure. "Anywhere you like."

"Oh? Really? Dear sir, be careful what you say."

"Where, madam, would you like?"

"In his garden?"

He hooted in laughter. Scooping her up in his arms, he took her to their bed and placed her down upon the sheets. Then he bent over her. "Wherever you wish. Whenever you wish."

"You are so kind," she said.

And more in love with you than I can say.

CHAPTER 13

"*T*hank you for allowing us to attend your party. And to arrive late. Your home is lovely."

Julian smiled at Lily as she praised Burnett Castle with all the buoyant enthusiasm she naturally bestowed on those people, places and things she admired. The medieval castle, transformed to an Elizabethan house and a Regency show-case was a mélange of architecture only a lover of oddities could find appealing. "Julian has told me about it. How you've adapted it over the centuries."

"My wife likes to soak in the history of a place," Julian boasted to his cousin as they stood in the baron's entrance to his ancient keep. Her exuberance for the trip and her delight in meeting Valentine tickled him. "She enjoys the appointments of Willowreach and plans a master list of all the portraits and porcelains."

"You are welcome here, my lady," said Valentine Arden. "Do come catalogue all of my treasures. Alas, I have no wife. Not yet. And now that I see how well my cousin has done in his selection, I fear I shall of necessity take longer to find a suitable candidate for the job."

She removed her gloves. "I hope you do not mind that we are a day late."

"No matter." Valentine was gracious as ever. But he looked weary.

Julian worried about him whenever he went to France for his sister's remembrance. Val had hated the man and the means of her death. He seemed not to recover from the despair it invoked.

"The rest of our party," Val continued, "is in the courtyard conservatory imbibing what little sunshine streams in today. It's warmer there too. Perhaps after you've changed from your journey, you'd like to join us there."

Julian thanked him. "We will."

"I'll have tea sent up to you in your rooms. I say, Chelton, would you mind if I had a word before you went up?"

"No, of course not." Julian looked at Lily. "I'll be along, my dear."

Valentine motioned to his butler. "Please take Lady Chelton to their suite."

Julian followed Val down the hall to a small sitting room. "Good of you to have us on short notice, Val. I didn't think Lily would welcome the thought of leaving Willowreach so soon after our wedding."

"I'd say," Val said and arched a long blond brow, "from the looks of your American beauty, it is you who wasn't interested in leaving your home."

Julian took the chair Val indicated and smiled. "May you be as happy when you decide to marry."

"Thank you. That gives me hope of a smashing success."

"How was your trip to Paris?"

Val folded his huge frame into the large Rococco chair opposite Julian. He pursed his lips. "Never happy. However, one fine evening, I was invited to a dinner party at the Duc de Remy's house. A good gathering. Included your new extended family."

"The Hannifords are excellent company."

"To say the least. Your father-in-law is a cyclone."

Julian laughed. "And what did you think of the others?"

"A charming bunch. Ada, the youngest. Irrepressible."

"Like her older sister," Julian added with pride.

"And Pierce, the brother. He'll make his mark in business quickly."

"And indelibly, I'd add."

"The cousin, the widow, Marianne Roland was there. A beauty."

"She is," Julian said with a nod.

"The Duc de Remy is quite infatuated with her, isn't he?"

"Very much so. Since the first day he met her." Julian recalled the accident in the Rue de la Paix and how he, too, had become enchanted that day.

"I'd give him a run for her if it weren't so obvious she finds him irresistible as well."

"Does she? Good. Or I think it's good." *So busy with my own affair, I hadn't gauged another's.* "What was it that you wanted to discuss? Not Marianne and Remy, I'd wager."

"No." Val smoothed the wool of his trousers. "I wanted to give you fair warning. Wish I didn't have to. But she invited herself at the last minute."

Val's tone froze him. That anyone would invite herself to a country house party was novel, rarely done, accepted only among family relationships built on blood or proximity. Ominous to hear that a woman had done this. A female whom Val knew and knew well enough that she would presume upon his good graces.

"Margaret," he breathed.

"In all her glory. Arrived yesterday. Told me bold as brass that she'd come to examine the new Marchioness of

Chelton. When I told her you had declined, she was crestfallen."

"But remained nonetheless." Julian's mind rang with warning bells. Margaret, once an *ingenue* imbued with a certain *noblesse oblige*, had grown older, more worldly. One thing his wife was not.

"She did. I'm sad to say, too, she came alone."

Julian's mind raced. Meg Sheffield, in solo performance could obscure the sun and the moon. Her husband of eight years was the only one who could restrain her, threatening to tighten her purse strings. "Norfield did not accompany her?"

Val shook his head. "He does not approve of my Puritan rules for my country parties."

Julian tsked. "Against bed-hopping? Poor fellow."

"He sent his regrets and stayed in London. He claimed his duties in Parliament detain him."

"I bet they do," Julian scoffed. "All two of them."

Val looked like he eaten a sour drop. "One blonde, the other brunette."

"Thank you for the warning." Spurred by an urge to embrace his wife, Julian shot to his feet.

Val rose too. "I'll be your right hand in this."

As host, Val was one of the most acclaimed bachelors to entertain well.

"Thank you."

Julian left, up the stairs, along the hall, following the butler to their suite. He found Lily in their adjoining dressing room being buttoned into a tea gown. The welcoming smile on her face faded as she looked at him.

"Are you well?" she asked him.

"Nora? Leave us for a few minutes please."

The maid, normally dour-faced, did not appreciate his interruption. "Aye, m'lord," she said but busied herself with folding undergarments.

"What's wrong?" Lily approached him and wrapped her arms around his waist. "Lord Burnett has bad news?"

"A few of his guests are..."

She tipped her head. "What?"

"New to you."

"Oh," she said and dismissed that with a shrug, "well. That's not a prob—"

"Some are jaded." He cupped her cheek and admired the happiness in her eyes. "Unkind."

"That's not a matter I care about."

"You should. You must."

"Why? I have you." She nestled close to him and kissed the tip of his nose.

"But—"

"Did you not once tell me that if anyone made fun of me you'd see they were...ah, what did you say? Put to the streets."

"Ah. The cartoonist. Yes, I did." The ice block in his heart melted a fraction.

"And never forget, if they are still not deterred, I could challenge them to a shooting match."

He chuckled. How she lit up his life. "Darling, I don't think—"

"Don't think that ladies here do that. I know." She rose up and kissed his lips. "I know. But I am not a lady from here. I am a woman from *there*. And in Texas we shoot varmints who attack us."

She was suddenly in earnest, absorbing that what he was imparting was more serious than her humorous responses implied. "That is what you're trying to tell me, yes?"

He drew her close, the supple warmth of her person suffusing him and diminishing his fears. "Please don't shoot anyone, my darling. It's not in season. And furthermore, they'd take you away from me."

"No one could do that, Julian," she said with devotion shining in her clear blue eyes. "No one."

Of the twenty-five others assembled down this long medieval banquet table, Lily had identified fourteen she'd met previously in London or Paris. All were pleasant, polite. They were lords and their ladies down from London for the delights which Baron Burnett bestowed on them. Four more were of higher status, an earl, a viscount and their wives. Lily had not met them before and if Julian asked her, she'd tell him she enjoyed their company. Two were American heiresses whom she'd met often. Hilda Berghoff and Priscilla Van De Putte. Hilda still sought a husband and so did her mama who eyed the bachelors present like a coyote prowling for the kill. Priscilla, however, had found her match.

Shocking but true, Lord Pinkhurst had proposed to her. Priscilla's mama, the American girl told Lily earlier this afternoon, had happily approved his offer. And as for Pinkie, he seemed subdued even as he had greeted Lily with his old fondness for her.

Among the weekend party, there remained two men, in addition to Burnett, who were bachelors. Lily had met neither of them prior to today.

Two ladies were without their spouses. One was a viscountess whose husband suffered from a cough brought on by the unseasonal rains. Though he recovered, he had not ventured from his home.

The other lady who was unattended by her husband was the Duchess of Norfield. A few years older than Lily, Her Grace Margaret Sheffield, was the doyenne of this gathering as many deferred to her in conversation. Petite, dark blonde with a classical profile, the lady had a serenity that could intimidate. Her voice was a whisper that made one lean in to listen. Her words were polite, gracious to a fault. This, Lily knew at once, was a person she must monitor. At worst, this woman was the one about whom Julian had warned her.

Her Grace had been seated far down the table, so far down that the turning of the table for conversation allowed Lily to observe her with impunity. As one who'd been groomed to the finer points of social graces, Lily felt the eyes of the duchess focus upon her. Uncaring what the woman saw, she bent her attention to a viscount on her right and to Pinkie on her left.

"How are you settling in to Willowreach?" he inquired.

"Very well. Chelton has been very helpful. His staff as well." She'd congratulated Pinkie on his engagement earlier this afternoon when first they greeted each other in the conservatory. "I like Willowreach."

Pinkie's gaze lingered on her. Sorrow etched the corners of his eyes. "As you should. It's a lovely estate."

His platitudes disturbed her. She liked him, always had. Even if she didn't love him, never could. The need for honesty between them washed over her. "Are you happy?"

He stared straight ahead. "I hope to be."

Wincing at her rash behavior, she lifted her wineglass. "I apologize."

"Don't," he whispered. "We marry for many reasons. Great unions can come from different motivations, can't they?"

"I believe so."

Along the table, four down, she caught Julian's eye and nodded at him with assurance. She was happy. He was too.

Wasn't he?

∾

Julian led Lily into the ballroom. The beamed ceilings, the oak paneling, the little wooden figures—the eavesdroppers—in the rafters, gave the room a glow reminiscent of Tudor times. Many from surrounding estates had joined the house guests for tonight's ball and the room pulsed with laughter and the sounds of the twenty-piece orchestra. The huge gaslights lit the expanse in a golden aura that complemented his wife's flawless complexion and her stunning smile.

"This is wonderful. I'm so glad we came." She squeezed his arm. "You are very good to me."

"I merely return the favor, darling." He was proud of her. This, her first social event as his wife, was one she was thoroughly enjoying. Better yet, she was liked in return. She'd thrown herself into meeting everyone. She devoted herself to learning about others and refrained from discussing herself unless asked. She was an unqualified success.

"An American with poise and charm," he'd overheard one matron tell another.

"When might we join the dancing?" she asked, her eyes wide with glee.

Valentine had led out the oldest lady in attendance, the Viscountess Dorn. They swept the floor in graceful arcs and as the musicians began the roundelay, other couples joined.

"I think this is our chance." He led her to the chalked floorboards, put his arm around her slender waist, took her other hand and grinned at her. "Madam."

He took them out in small steps. Their first few were awkward, two people learning the other's rhythm and form in this new dance of love. Their bodies adjusted, melded. At once she became fluid in his arms, the wind at his command, a dream to hold. She leaned back and flowed with him, the joy on her face an exquisite display that rivaled her expression when she came apart in her delight in his bed. He'd been so right to desire her, so fortunate to marry her. She was quite perfect for him.

Filled with such ebullience, he danced her toward the open doors and onto the terrace. At the kiss of the night air on her skin, she gasped.

"Are you cold?" he asked as he swirled her along the terrace, the sound of the German waltz muffled by the breeze through the treetops.

She shook her head. "You didn't forget."

"I promised you this."

"So you did." And she began to hum with the music.

At the edge of the terrace, far from the French doors, he slowed their tempo until they merely swayed together. *I love you.*

The thought sprang up so quickly, his jaw dropped.

"What's wrong?" she asked, alarm on her face.

"Nothing." He stepped toward her and embraced her, the supple curves of her body a sensuous fit to his. "I have to taste you."

She circled her arms around his waist and closed her eyes as he pressed her near and took her lips with his own. Her mouth was warm, the flavors of champagne and mint a subtle aphrodisiac to his muddled mind. He sent his tongue into the cavern and claimed her, defined her. She moaned and crushed him closer. This woman was intoxicating and best of all, she was his.

His.

He broke away and grabbed her wrist. He'd visited here before, often. He knew the boxwood maze well and so he led her along the far path. Left, right, and straight. He recalled a folly, small, secluded, hidden by roses that he hoped to God were in bloom.

"Where are we—? Oh!" She halted as she surveyed the marble and wood structure before them.

He urged her up the steps and whirled her into his arms. "You are becoming necessary to me."

"Am I?" she said, breathless as he lifted her skirts and caressed her wet feminine folds.

She gasped but didn't object.

He sank down, careless of his trousers. He needed her and it was here he wanted her. He parted her fragrant lips, and touched his tongue to her sensitive spot.

She dug her fingernails into his coat. "Oh, Julian. Can we not lie down?"

He shot to his feet, glanced around. There. *There.*

He took her to the wooden seats around the circumference, dotted tonight with cushions. Julian grinned. His host, not so Puritan after all, had the foresight to provide for the lovers who would need an interlude during the ball. He urged his wife to lay down along the pillows, making mental note to thank Val tomorrow for his foresight.

With her skirts up around her waist, her pale eyes twinkling like stars above, his wife was an erotic portrait of bold desire. She opened her arms to him and he went to her and kissed her madly. His hands busy seeking out the treasures of her body, he noted how succulent she was. How ready. How willing. How loving.

That word again.

Love.

He licked her and she bucked.

He sucked her and she held her breath. His two fingers deep inside her, he imitated the act of love he longed to show her and she whimpered. Then she broke apart.

His beauty. His wife.

The woman he loved despite his best intentions.

Julian had debated simply skipping the rest of the festivities and spending the night making love to his wife in the big broad bed provided by his cousin.

But Lily had been appalled and demanded they return to the ballroom.

"If we retired, we'd be a scandal," she said as they hurried around their suite attempting to repair the damage done in the garden.

He had changed his trousers, the knees of his first pair woefully grass-stained.

She had giggled and clamped a hand to her mouth. "I should call for Nora to iron my skirts."

"You look fine," he told her, tracing the line of her naked shoulder with his lips, his hands covering her breasts. "You were magnificent."

She hooted and twirled in his arms. "As I recall you were the one who was magnificent. I was your passive partner in crime."

He pecked her on the nose. "Not so passive, my darling."

She tossed him a narrowed-eye challenge. "You should congratulate me that I didn't howl like a cat. They would have thought that scene delicious fodder."

He was reminded how Lily had hated the cartoons of her in the London broadsheets. This tale would be quite different. He arched a brow. "Shocking that a man and wife could actually find pleasure in each other."

"For years to come," she joked.

They'd laughed like children and headed back to the ball.

No sooner there, than George Pinkhurst approached with his fiancée, Priscilla Van de Putte. Julian put aside his hope to waltz once more with his wife.

"May I have this dance, Lady Chelton?" Pinklehurst asked Lily.

It was only polite for Julian to offer his hand to Priscilla in turn. He wasn't fond of her. She'd been the one to stalk him so bluntly last season that he'd sworn off Americans and heiresses.

Julian laughed to himself. That was what he'd thought then. Now? He was a changed man. A happy one. A ridiculously giddy one. Eager for his wife at her smallest smile.

But not just yet. He could bear to take Priscilla out for a few circles of the floor.

"How is your wife getting on with running your household, my lord?"

Dear God, the woman was forward. His Lily was not so brash. "She does well. Very well."

They took another round and Priscilla beamed at him, her tiny crooked teeth putting him in mind of Josephine Bonaparte whom histories said never fully smiled at anyone because her teeth were uneven and black. Lily's teeth were white and straight. Her smile was far more beautiful than anyone's.

"I hope I can adjust to living in the country," Priscilla said, making a moue, petulant as ever. "I've always lived in the city."

"There is much to keep you busy on an estate. Lord Pinkhurst, I'm sure, will help you with the duties."

"I've never run servants. My mother always did."

Must I listen to this? One did not *run* servants. "Staff know their duties. A good housekeeper can be your best ally."

She thought about that for a few seconds. Tipping her blonde head, she dismissed the idea with a wrinkle of her nose. "All of that is so boring."

Why was this woman telling him this? Sympathy was not one of his strong suits. Not for a spoiled girl who complained so readily to a mere acquaintance.

"Is your wife agreeable?"

How forward can this woman be? "I'm sorry."

"Oh, I beg your pardon. I mean, does she please you?"

His eyes sought the vision in jade-green organza who laughed as she swayed in Pinkhurst's arms. *Does she please me?*

More than. She was, always had been, effervescent, irresistible.

"I hope she does. She's beautiful," Priscilla rattled on. "And you deserve a woman you like. Love. I would have married you, you realize."

"I do," he managed to say amid his shock at this girl's outrageous conversation.

"But you were caught with her."

"What?" Would she dare to cite a dastardly tidbit? One that few knew. How could she know?

"Caught. In your stables, wasn't it?"

No. "How did you learn that?" He was tempted to stop, call her out over this. But if he did, he'd make a scene. That was the last thing he needed.

"It's in the London broadsheets." Priscilla looked surprised. "Didn't you know?"

Why would he? He didn't take them.

"When?" He diminished their progress in the orderly procession of couples round the floor.

She glanced from one set of dancers to another. "We're not in step, my lord."

"No, we're not. And won't be. Tell me."

"A few times. I don't know. The past few weeks. They've put in cartoons too."

Anger roared through him. His Lily, attacked. Again. "What do they say?"

"Well, I…"

"Priscilla, you initiated this. Don't stop now."

"They say that you married her out of obligation. Did you?"

"No." He led her off the floor.

"You're hurting my wrist, my lord."

"I am sorry." He loosened his grip on her. She was frightened of him. Shame tempered his ire. He was not a brute. "What else?"

"That her father paid you to marry her. That you—um —well—"

"*What*, for godssakes?"

"Ruined her."

He set his jaw. A thousand curses on whoever printed this —and millions more on whoever gave the rags these hideous distortions of the truth. "That is not true. I count on you to say that to any and all whom you meet."

"Yes, yes. Of course, I will." She rubbed her wrist. "I apologize, my lord."

"Accepted. Naturally."

"I think I'd like to adjourn to the ladies retiring room, if you don't mind." She looked hopeful and nervous.

"I can escort you." He offered his arm and led her to the far side of the ballroom. And once there, she gave him a small curtsy and escaped him, scurrying away.

"My, my, what did you say to her, Chelton?"

He pivoted toward the dulcet sounds of Margaret Sheffield. Gazing down into her dark green eyes, he was transported back to his youth and his desire to possess her. No one would argue, the woman was lovely. Polished. More than the American who had just escaped him. More than the young woman who had become his wife. He'd yearned for this one. But that desire had been different from his craving for Lily, hadn't it? Urgent. Demanding. An animal's impulse to mate and dominate.

He saw her now through the perspective of experience— and he congratulated himself that so far this weekend, he had side-stepped long conversations with her. "Nothing much."

"Enough to send her running. You must be kinder to those less hardy than yourself, Chelton." Her grass-green eyes challenged him.

"She told me tales that disturbed me."

"Oh?" Margaret snapped open her fan and fluttered it near her abundant and perfectly rounded décolleté. "So you took the stuffing out of her? Shame on you, darling."

"I was surprised."

"Not an excuse."

"No." He admired his wife as she enjoyed herself on the floor with Pinkie. He wanted her back. When she was near him, he felt whole. "I hope you don't wish to dance."

"No, I don't. But that's beside the point. You should ask me."

"It would be polite, I concede. But you did not approach me, Meg, in the hope of waltzing."

She sighed. "Truth. It is a fine weapon. So tell me a truth, Chelton. Are you avoiding me?"

"We've spoken, Meg."

"Pleasantries. Only. Pleasantries."

"We have little in common."

"Oh, my dear man. We have the past in common."

He pursed his lips. She was a dog with a bone. "Our past is more than eight years old. To some, that's ancient history."

She inhaled slowly, her gaze going around the room. "I remember it all very well."

"I don't."

She scoffed. "Has marriage made you crusty, Chelton?"

"On the contrary." *It's made me appreciate my wife.* He searched the ballroom. In the crush, he'd lost sight of Lily.

"Tamed you, I suppose? Interesting."

Julian followed Meg's line of sight. Lily twirled even more gracefully than before in the arms of Pinkhurst. He could be jealous. Could be…if he didn't know in his soul that Lily came to him each night naked and willing and *yes*, more in love with him than he deserved.

"And you're enchanted with her." Meg's words were an accusation.

He took them for a declaration. One that surprised him. One he could easily make aloud to her. "I am."

"It will erode."

He shook his head, though she'd named his greatest fear. He couldn't let her see how her prediction gutted him. "I doubt it."

"All enchantments disappear." She waved her fan in a flourish. "A genie appears who dissolves the magic."

That wouldn't happen with Lily.

"Don't look so stricken. All is not lost. When your days become humdrum, darling, do send for me."

"Why?" *What could you give me that I cannot find with Lily?*

Sparks of resentment flashed in her eyes. "You still hate me for rejecting you."

When she'd accepted Norfield's proposal, Julian had proof how easily passion turned to ashes. As if he hadn't had enough evidence with the poison of his parents' marriage. Or most of society's. "Your rejection reaffirmed what I knew from years of observing others. Love is rare and must be carefully cultivated."

"Ah, yes. I see your point. But do see mine, darling."

"Pardon me." He put a foot out to step away.

On a click, she shut her fan and pressed the tip to his chest. "You married her, but you'll never love her."

That seared him.

"I know you, Julian. You need a woman for your title, to get your heir. You need a woman for your very healthy appetites. One for your boundless pride. And word of mouth has it, you took this one because you were forced to. A trade to save her reputation, and you your finances."

He'd kill whoever spread these rumors. "Idle talk."

"Whatever the cause, darling. You'll want a woman who

understands you. Who puts your need for independence higher than her need for your commitment."

"You're wrong."

"Am I? What odds shall I wager that you haven't told her you love her?"

"Gamble all you have, Meg." But it was a bluff. He locked his gaze on hers, the barrier to his soul stalwart and impenetrable.

She glided away with a small huff of satisfaction.

As Nora, Lily's maid, and his valet, Pendley finally closed the bedroom doors behind them, Julian poured two glasses of port into the crystal glasses on their sideboard in their sitting room. Since Lily had rejoined him after his conversation with Meg, Lily was unusually somber. It was in her nature to ask him what they'd discussed and he would not avoid her questions.

Lily sailed in, her ivory peignoir whispering behind her across the carpet. Her black hair was down, her face was bright and clean of all rouges and powders. Still, she was extraordinarily lovely to him. Lovelier than when she was dressed and perfumed, a gilding she would never require.

"Thank you," she said, took his proffered glass and sank to the rose silk chaise longue. Stretching out her elegant legs along the cushions, he noted that she had not taken a chair nor had she left any room for him to sit beside her. "Did you enjoy the evening?"

"I did. But you don't look as if you'd say the same," he said, inviting her opinion as he sank in the chair opposite her.

She took a sip of her port and put the glass aside on a small table. "I adored dancing in the garden. Of course."

He knew for her the thrill of their encounter in the folly was gone. "But?"

She turned the full power of her clear blue eyes upon him. As if she could see through him, she scoured his expression. "Tell me what she has meant to you."

Julian considered the liquor in his glass. Then put it aside. There was no need to ask of whom she spoke. He had watched Lily trace Meg's steps as she left him in the ballroom. Their eyes had met and he understood that his wife would ask him the details. She deserved to know.

"Years ago, I was infatuated with her. We were young. It was her coming out season and I was making my own mark on society, it being the first time I actively engaged in the social whirl. She was very popular and had many suitors. But at the end of the season, it was clear that she favored three of us. A Scottish earl with plenty of money from a printing business and another man who was at that time, the largest landowner in England. He was also quite wealthy. In wealth, size of estate and title, I could not compete."

"But you did."

His elbows to his knees, he leaned toward her. "In my mind, yes. In hers, too."

"What went wrong?"

"She played me against the other two."

"How?"

"She ran a child's game asking us to write poetry and take her out for buggy rides."

Lily's delicate dark brows inched high. "Unchaperoned?"

"No. Nothing like that. But it was a series of silly trials."

"She was testing each of you?" Lily asked with a certain disdain in her features.

"She was. It seemed funny, romantic. We were young. Well, I was twenty-three. And I'd never been—"

They stared at each other, across the abyss created by his abrupt silence.

Her eyes turned dark with worry. "Say it."

"I'd never been in love before."

She swallowed, her slender throat convulsing with the news. "Go on."

He licked his lower lip. "I took hope that she favored me. I—"

"Why?" Lily interrupted him.

"She allowed me liberties. And so I—"

"Made love to her?" she asked in such a flat tone, he thought he might've imagined her question.

"No. Never anything so enormous as that."

"But what?"

He got to his feet. "You can't expect me to tell you everything."

"Why not?"

"Because it occurred eight, nine years ago and for you to know it all is irrelevant."

"Is it?" she countered him, her pale face turned up to him.

"It is." He would not hurt his wife unnecessarily.

"What happened?"

"That June, each of us proposed to her." He laughed that the memory had surprisingly faded, the sorrow was hollowed of its old aching sense of loss. "On the same day, as it turns out. She chose the man she is married to. Has been these many years."

"And he is young?"

"The same age as I am."

"And healthy?" she persisted.

"He is."

"And why is he not here with her?"

Julian shrugged. The salacious pastimes of the Duke of

Norfield were nothing his wife would ever understand, nor wish to. "I didn't ask her."

"What did she want to discuss with you tonight?"

Ah, well. That was easy to say. After all, he'd come this far. "My marriage to you."

Lily nodded, her expression blank. "She's curious. I saw that. And I suppose that's natural. Given that she'd like to resume her...her friendship with you."

"We are not friends."

She shot him a hard look of reproof. "Any woman who approaches a man with sorrow in her eyes and hope on her lips wants more than simple conversation, Julian."

He might as well admit it. "I agree."

His wife sat straighter in her seat. "Will she get what she wants?"

He strode to her, raised her face with gentle fingers and shook his head. "No. I've no need of her."

"You'll tell me, won't you, if you change your mind?" She looked so valiant it broke his heart.

"I won't change it, Lily."

"Good to know," she said and got to her feet. Then she walked toward her dressing room. "Thank you. I appreciate your candor."

"Lily." He wanted to explain but what more was there to say?

She tipped her head toward the other room. "I think I'll sleep in here this evening. Good night, Julian."

He was left to stare at the empty doorway, wishing he could have found words to dispel her fears. Wishing he could dispel his own.

CHAPTER 14

*D*odging the heavy rainfall, Julian climbed up into his carriage and sat beside his pretty wife. In her fetching spring green traveling suit, he would admire her and forbid himself to touch the perfection. In the past week since their return to Willowreach from Burnett House, he'd paid inordinate attention to her. Claiming they were still in their honeymoon period, he had romanced her and she'd returned to his bed with her old enthusiasm for sensual play. Keeping her busy making love, he'd discovered how unrestrained she was in how she loved, how she laughed, how she gave of herself. And not just to him.

Each day for the past four, she'd gone to the village to check on the tenants' health. Especially for the children, she was concerned. Julian had gone with her yesterday. In fact, from Ashford, he'd ordered a few supplies she requested. Powders and cough syrups, a catarrh she favored. When she noted that one of the tenant's wives was very great with child, she'd said how she'd like to purchase a stethoscope.

"I had a collection of instruments in Corpus Christi but I

left them in America. I want to purchase a new set. They'd come in handy here."

He'd agreed to buy a complete array of whatever she wanted. "I'll send to London. You shall have them very soon."

She'd hugged him tightly and exclaimed over and over again how pleased she was he'd let her nurse his people.

Why wouldn't he? It brought her joy. It brought his people health. It inspired pride in her.

And she came to him again that night and this morning exuberant and loving. Though he hadn't thought to buy her her instruments to lure her into bed, he relished his reward.

And he took delight in sending away her maid, even before dinner last night, and removing slowly, deliberately, every item of clothing she wore. She hadn't objected. And it hadn't decreased his appetite for her. Hours later, here he sat, eager as a boy to sample every tasty bit of her body.

And they were to spend hours in this damn coach. He snorted.

She was the beauty. And he was certainly an unruly beast.

His cock lengthened in awareness of her charms. Her lustrous black hair swept high into a soft coiffure, she wore a bonnet with an ostrich plume to match her outfit. Her eyes twinkled at him and he arched a brow at her, expecting a warning that he keep his hands to himself on this journey. He grinned at her and and shifted painfully against the squabs. He wasn't used to denying himself the pleasure of her delectable body.

But he perked to the sound of a man yelling at his coachman.

"Wait, milord, wait!"

"Someone calls for you, Julian." Lily had parted the curtain on the window. "An older man. Running in the rain."

He glanced out his own window but in the deluge could

make out no one. It had been raining ever since they'd arrived home, the thunder rampant. But in his bedroom, he and Lily had not minded so much. Out in the village, his servants told him the crops were submerged in puddles that threatened the saplings.

"Milord?" The coachman jerked open the carriage door, sheets of water dripping from his hat. "Tom Henry from Willow Bend's here. Quick, he says. Must see you."

"Bring him inside."

"Sir?"

"I'll talk to him. He can't stand in the rain, man."

Henry didn't come to him for any but serious matters. One of the Bend's village elders, he took his rank with prudence. Sixty years old, if not more, he tended the south fields of Willowreach as had his father and that man's before him. He was bent, grizzled but with a kind demeanor that the village children loved. They called him Saint Nicholas at Christmas time.

"Milord," Henry appealed to him, hustled inside by his coachman. He gave a small bow, pulling his forelock and shuffling his wool cap in two hands. "Milady. Fergive me, sir."

"Yes, Tom. What is it?"

"I didn't wish to bother ye, sir, but I thought ye should know. We've had two more go poorly with coughs last night."

"Did you get Doctor Winslow up from Ashford?" Julian noted the man's bleary eyes and slack demeanor.

"Aye, this morn, me wife did."

"And has he arrived?"

"He did, milord. He's says four lads 'ave bronchitis and maybe more to come because two 'ave fierce coughs."

"Does Winslow suggest a cure?"

"He made us build tents from our blankets, milord, and pipe in steam."

"Balsam mist is best," Lily interjected.

"It is." Julian turned, smiling at her. He recalled his own childhood malady, the racking pain of inflamed lungs and the aromatic relief of breathing in the moist air. "Did Winslow offer up Balsam mist?"

"He did, milord. But we 'ave only one copper kettle and we need more."

"At least one for each patient," Lily said, frowning at Julian. "Do you have any at the house?"

"One. My governess used it for me when I'd take ill. Henry, go into the house and tell the housekeeper. You need the inhaler kettle and the Nelson inhalers, too."

"How many of those do you have?" Lily asked.

"Two, three. I can't recall." Julian focused on Henry again. "Get your son to run to Ashford and tell Winslow I'll buy two more copper kettles and three marble Nelson jars. Use them."

"Thank you, milord. I will."

"If more become ill, buy as many as you need. I'll pay for them."

The farmer bowed in thanks, the coachman closed the door upon them and in minutes, they were off down the road to London.

"That's serious." To have so many ill at once suggested a contagion.

"It's the weather." Lily shivered. "I've never seen so much rain."

"Unusual and cold for end of June," he said. "I'd forgotten about the mist. Thank you."

"You were kind to have them buy more copper kettles and inhalers."

"Bronchitis is no minor malady. I remember what it's like to cough your lungs out."

"Were you sick often with it?"

"Twice. Three times, perhaps." He shook his head. "I can't

recall. My governess was a wizard, knew exactly what to do and I recovered quickly."

"Perhaps we should cut short our visit in London and return home the day after the wedding."

Lily's generosity always gratified him. She thought of others. So different from most other women he'd known. Her family had recently returned to London from Paris to attend Elanna's wedding. "Don't you want to stay in town and visit after the wedding with Ada and Pierce?"

"Your tenants' health is more important than my need to talk with my brother and sister. Besides, couldn't we invite them to stay with us for a few days?"

Julian did not welcome the idea of sharing Lily with her family so soon since their wedding. He'd had quite enough of company at Val's house party. But to prohibit Lily would be mean and ungracious of him. "If you'd like that, then do invite them all to Willowreach. Few like to stay in London as the summer approaches."

She pursed her lips and glanced out the window, her cheeks red.

He took hope from her embarrassment. "Why are you blushing, my dear?"

She clamped her legs together. The sensuous move was like spark to tinder.

"Lily?" He put two fingers to her chin and led her to look up at him. He ducked to avoid getting poked by the feather in her bonnet. What he saw in her eyes was molten blue desire. "Shall I dispense with your hat, my darling?"

"You shouldn't." She sighed, forlorn, her mouth turned down.

Resigned, he put his lips to her cheek. *Of course not.*

"I'll arrive a mess." She put a hand to his thigh and squeezed.

He shuddered.

Her eyes drifted closed. A frisson shook her. "But you want me."

"I do." Frustration assaulted him. He'd be a cad to pull up to her father's house and show that man how he'd mistreated his daughter.

She faced him, her expression stark with hunger for him. "Isn't there a way?"

Growling, he lifted her under her arms and led her to straddle him.

"Exactly," she breathed as she kissed him deeply, her lips parting from his ever so slowly.

He brushed her skirts and petticoats high up her shapely naked thighs. At the sight of her tight little bush, he swallowed hard. His cock strained against his trousers. He cupped her soft tight curls and sent one finger up inside her juicy channel. Barely biting back a whimper, she coiled over his chest and worked diligently at opening the buttons to his flies. In a second, she had his member out in her hand. She stroked him with sure intent.

He could have her. Give her pleasure. In his private carriage. Satisfy them both.

"Come sink over me." He heard himself, insistent, gruff.

Eager, she went up on her toes and inched forward. With her hand on him, she guided him to her entrance as she drifted down over his flesh. When she settled and he could go no farther, she flung her head back, mouth open. He'd never seen her more beautiful. With reverence, he rocked into her. She was all sweet hot heaven and he fought like a savage to keep his patience and give her as good as he got.

But she lowered her face and locked her gaze on his. All tempestuous siren, she rode him in swift, smooth rhythm. He lost his breath along with his mind and drove into her with a long moan. She was his and a glorious possession she was. She deserved all of him and he had every reason on earth to fuck her and fuck her well.

She came with a cry.

He followed, giving up his all to loving her.

Panting, murmuring senseless words, she fell against him.

The coach rolled on, striking a hole in the road, jostling her in his embrace. She flexed her muscles to hug his cock and he grunted in pleasure.

The feather on her hat stuck him in the eye. Chuckling, he pushed it away and cuddled her close.

She laughed.

"What's funny?" he asked, pushing errant strands of hair from her temple.

"I wonder what my father would say if we arrived like this in Piccadilly."

"He'd shoot me."

She nuzzled her nose against his throat. "I'd like to stay like this."

His cock was already shrinking. "You'd have to give me time to catch my breath."

She rolled her eyes. "We should, you realize. Go again."

He glanced down, both brows high. "And why is that?"

"You promised me an education."

He threw her a pained look.

"You said such things were possible anywhere." She ran a fingertip along the edge of his lower lip. "And to date, I count only our bed, the dining room table—"

"Don't forget Val's garden."

"I remember," she said with a shiver. "There's a stable left. A hay stack, to be precise."

"The floor," he added.

"And standing up."

His cock jumped at that idea. Stroking her inner thigh, he

parted her wider. "We'll perfect this position first. Hmm? What do you say?"

She wriggled in glee, her feminine folds yielding to the quest of his fingers. "Lead on."

"Right you are." And he continued his seduction of his willing, wanton wife.

"Lady Elanna is definitely not a happy bride."

Lily wished she didn't agree with her younger sister, Ada. The eighteen-year-old, along with her father, brother Pierce, and Marianne had also been invited to this pre-wedding ball given by the Duke and Duchess of Seton and they'd returned from Paris for the occasion.

"Doesn't her family see this?" Ada waved her fan, anxious for Elanna.

"They know." Lily watched Julian's sister in the far corner talking with her intended husband, Lord Carbury. *Are they arguing? Here?* "They approve of him."

"Even though she doesn't love him?"

Pierce, the younger, slimmer version of their tall, brusque, Black Irish father, gazed at the bride with a cool detachment. In his formal attire, the black and white highlighting his sharp bone structure, he was devastatingly handsome. Like their father, he moved quickly, decisively. He appeared a brash American who could enthrall or repel with one glance. "She's quite luscious. A perfect China doll. I see why the man wants her. Who wouldn't?"

Ada sniffed. "I think it's slavery."

Lily bristled, leary that a few guests who stood close by might overhear. "Do be discreet, my dears. This is my family now. Yours too."

Ada inched nearer Lily. "I know but this is terrible for her to have to marry him. To see them together is torture. We attended a dinner here last night, Lily. If you could have seen them. Horrid. He smothers her. She avoids him. Ignores him."

"Hates him," Pierce added and turned his back on the sight. Instead, he focused on Lily. "Tell me. I must learn. How are you, Lady Chelton? Well, I hope." His blue gaze, a shade lighter than her own, pinned her with ribald interest.

She took a sip of her champagne. "I am, thank you, quite well."

He narrowed his eyes on her. "You're sure? No discomforts? Irritations? Lack for anything, do you?"

"Nothing." She understood Pierce's concern—and his probe. After all, he hadn't met Julian until the day before their wedding and as her older brother, protector as he'd always thought himself to be, Pierce needed reassurance. Particularly now that he so obviously was appalled at Elanna's situation.

Pierce twitched his nose. "My new brother-in-law is kind?"

"Very. A gentleman. You will see."

"He has enough of our money to make him a gentleman, if not king of England."

"Please, Pierce." She hated that he was so put out. But he was used to stating his mind. "You're here to make an impression. Win friends. Make money. Gather your manners."

"I will when I see you are safe."

"I am." *I question to what degree if I am only desired.* She donned an assured face and arched a brow at her brother.

"I've no reason to trust any of them. Stuffed prigs, the lot of them." He placed his empty flute down on a passing footman's tray and took another full one. "Our groom-to-be there," he said with a withering look at Carbury, "grabs her arm with a longshoreman's grip. What kind of father permits *that* to marry his daughter?"

A poor one. "This is not our choice."

"Not what we would do," Pierce said.

Ada nodded. "I won't buy a husband I can't stand."

Lily shook her head. "Papa would not ask you to, Ada."

The girl tipped her head, considering Lily. "You're sure?"

"I am. Stop this, the two of you. There are finer things to do this evening than complain about others. Ada, you have a few admirers here. If you stop pouting, I think after Lady Elanna and Lord Carbury lead the first dance, you'll have worshipers at your feet."

"Oh, yes!" Ada sighed and clasped her fan to her chest, "I long to waltz. Do you think the orchestra will play that?"

"We shall see. Pierce, I'm certain Papa expects you to appear social, ask a lady or two to dance and wipe that scowl off your face."

"Ha, ha, sis," he said, casting off his gloom with a grin. "I want to see the new Marchioness of Chelton take the floor. Hope you haven't forgotten how to waltz."

"We both will show you," said Julian as he appeared at her side and took her hand, "how that's done."

"I'm so glad you're here," she told him as he led her toward the edge of the ballroom floor. The servants had chalked the slippery wood so that dancers could hold their forms. As soon as the engaged couple took to the floor and danced a few bars, the duke and duchess and Julian and she would join them. "I needed rescuing."

Julian shot a dark glance over his shoulder. "From Pierce and Ada?"

"They need to get to know you."

"Don't trust me with you, do they?" His voice was low, his expression as seductive.

"But they will."

"Invite them to Willowreach."

She demurred. "I rather like us as we are, for now."

He put his gloved hand to her waist and drew her seductively close. He brought her hand to his mouth. "Oh, my darling, you are a jewel."

The compliment raced through her like a waterfall. At moments like these, she could believe he loved her. What stopped him from saying it was the puzzle she could not put together.

At that moment, the orchestra struck up a Viennese waltz. The guests parted for Carbury as he led Elanna to the center of the floor. He beamed, a wreath of pride on his chubby face. She tried. Dear heaven, she tried to smile, but the look she gave her future husband was tremulous at best. And when he took her in his arms, she stiffened. *And did she flinch at the contact?*

Lily winced.

Julian gave some unearthly sound in the back of his throat.

Lily took a furtive glance at those assembled on the opposite side of the ballroom. A few narrowed their gazes on the bride. One older man frowned. Marianne, who stood beside Remy, caught Lily's eye and gave one slight shake of her head. She'd noticed. Remy however focused on Julian. Whatever passed between them had Julian pursing his lips.

At long last, Julian's parents took the floor.

At their own turn, Julian led Lily out and off they went. In long sweeping circles, Julian commanded her around the floor and she grinned at him.

"You're very accomplished, my darling," he said.

"We are a perfect match."

"Expert at this and so much else," he told her with a wink and they finished the dance with ease.

The delight in it drained from him.

"What's wrong?"

He inhaled and scanned the room. "My father."

"What did he want?" What had he said that so disturbed Julian?

"He's his usual self." The duke had asked to talk privately with him soon after she and Julian had arrived at their home that night. "Demanding."

She didn't want to know more. Seton's business was his own. And Julian's.

"Shall we have another champagne?" he asked her.

"I think we should."

"Let's. I've a mind to show you the garden and kiss you among the roses."

"Is there perhaps a folly, too?"

He snorted, then led her through the double doors and into the moonlit night. There he strode toward the tall maze and swirled her against a cool patrician statue. His lips on hers were insistent, demanding a fierce response. She accepted them, but wondered at the cause.

She assumed he'd tell her all later. For now, his kisses were enough to occupy her mind and her body.

Outside his parents' house, Julian waited while Ada and Lily climbed up into the Hanniford town carriage. Pierce and Killian gestured for him to join the ladies and the two men followed him into the coach. The three men sat together facing the ladies.

"Remy brings Marianne home," Killian informed the party as he settled into his corner. "I told her I don't like it, but she insists."

As a widow, Lily's cousin had a bit of leeway to stay in the company of a man without a chaperone.

"Can she do that without hurting her reputation?" Pierce inquired of Julian. Acting like Cerberus at the gate, Pierce enjoyed his role and Julian sensed he would not give it up easily or soon.

"To a small extent, yes. She should come right home to us and not linger in his carriage." Although the way his friend paid the blonde American beauty such respects that he'd danced with her four times this evening, Julian could wager the Frenchman wished to do more than simply see her to the door.

"She'll create a stir," Ada confided, a sheepish look at their father.

"Marianne knows her own mind, Ada," Lily said. "She likes the duke. They've known each other as long as Julian and I. And she wouldn't do anything to hurt us."

Killian grumbled. "To hell with us. I'm concerned with her. The Duc de Remy has a notorious reputation for keeping mistresses. I simply demand he treat her honorably."

Julian took that as a blow. Remy was not unprincipled. He loved women, lots of them. Usually one at a time. But he'd never loved one long enough or well enough to marry any. The extraordinary aspect of Remy's regard for Marianne Roland was that it had lasted this long—and as far as Julian could tell, without culminating in any physical intimacy. He'd have a talk with Remy about his enchantment with the comely lady. Tomorrow at the wedding breakfast.

Killian pursed his lips, rubbed his fingers together and stared at him. "I understand, Julian, that you and your father talked this evening before the ball. Did he tell you about the purchase of the company stock?"

Anger rose to clog his throat. Outrageous that Killian

would even ask about a private conversation, he found a polite response. "He did. He told me it's almost complete."

"He threw a wrench in the works, too." Killian grew red with irritation.

His father was angry, resented that Julian had taken Killian Hanniford's money, insulted that his only son had taken the American buccaneer's oldest daughter as his wife. Worse, he was insanely proud that Elanna was about to sell herself to take the Earl of Carbury into her bed. Certainly, the Duke of Seton had quite a few misplaced values. To say nothing of poor ethics and worse morals. It's what had made him the man he was today. Or less than. "Whatever that obstacle is—and I do not wish to know—it is none of my business."

Across from him, Lily went quite still and stared at Julian with wide eyes. Did she expect an argument?

Julian would not give it. Nor would he yield ground.

Killian waved a hand. "Does he want you to negotiate with me?"

"No, sir. He didn't ask that of me."

Killian cocked a brow at him as if to ask what was discussed.

Julian inclined his head but glanced away. The worse thing he wanted to reveal was the topic of that conversation. He'd been trying to forget it, in fact.

The Duke of Seton sought funds. Money. Lots of it.

But his father could die before Julian ever considered giving him a farthing. He could then squander it in hell.

Elanna and Carbury's wedding at St. George's in Hanover Square had gone flawlessly. Although Elanna appeared angelic in her finery of cream Bruges lace and Italian raw satin, she'd looked like a ghost. Her cheeks were wan and her eyes glassy as she walked down the aisle toward her groom. Carbury appeared as he always had when near his bride—proud. Triumphant.

His attitude was a bit galling, actually. Lily took her eyes from the earl, haughty as he fawned over his bride of two hours. His meaty hand on her shoulder. In fact, too far down her shoulder to be prudent in polite society during his wedding breakfast.

Standing beside her and Ada in the Seton house dining room, Julian saw it, too. He winced, emptying his glass. "Excuse me, please, my dear. Ada. I'm must talk with Remy." Marching off, Julian looked as if he were going to a firing squad.

Since last night at the Setons' ball, he'd been silent, brooding. Lily had attempted to draw him out, teasing him with risqué temptations if he'd communicate with her. He'd declined with kind apologies, even as he made love to her with a brooding intensity that set her pulse pounding. She'd been left to speculate what had turned him sour during his discussion with his father. She'd asked but Julian had declined to answer.

Ada leaned close to Lily, fighting a devilish grin. "Did you know that Marianne did not come home until after two o'clock?"

Lily had suspected as much when Marianne had not answered her bedroom door this morning when Lily knocked.

"Papa doesn't know," Ada added. "But I'd bet he suspects."

Lily trained her gaze on her father who stood, champagne flute in hand, focusing down on a tall, elegant woman in a whimsical, blue feathered hat. Lily couldn't see her face, but odds were she was beyond stunning. Papa didn't countenance any but that. Yet by the cut of her blue moire gown and the abundance of sapphires at her throat, she was a lady of means. By her posture, she was a person at ease in this posh gathering of wedding guests. But by the way she spoke to Black Irish Hanniford, she imparted some fantastic tale with hand gestures that spoke of birds and trees and maybe even monkeys. While he…

Lily bit her lip, quelling her laughter.

Her father focused on the lady's mouth as if he'd nibble her for breakfast.

"Papa thinks she's fabulous," Ada said on a giggle.

"It's about time he thought that of a lady, wouldn't you say?"

"Wouldn't you mind if he married again?" Ada asked as if she'd never thought he'd do such a thing.

"At the moment, he's interested only in talking to the lady, Ada."

"Well, since Mama died, he's been so alone."

Not quite alone. Ada, away at boarding school and sheltered from the realities of their father's day-to-day existence, had no means to know of their sire's mistresses. With one in Baltimore and one in Corpus Christi, he was always well occupied and had seemed content with his arrangements. Never complaining. Never talking about finding a wife.

"It's been thirteen years now," Ada mused. "He must want companionship, wouldn't you say?"

Lily had always predicted her father's type of companionship would be a buxom widow who knew how to laugh, preferably in bed. Naked. Marianne added that the lady better know a few Irish pub songs and be able to drink like a sailor.

"He should find a woman who amuses him." *This one looks eligible and…eminently beddable.*

"I say," Marianne approached them, worry lining her

brow. "Do *not* look over now. Too many are. But we have unhappy lovebirds."

"Oh, no." Lily feared an argument between them. Had done since the dreadful announcement of their engagement. Horrible that today their pot would boil over and in public. But there was no mistaking Elanna's raised voice and Carbury's rebuke. Elanna's fists were clenched and Carbury's eyes bulged from his head. This looked like war.

Where was Julian?

Lily panicked, glanced about and saw him in deep conversation with Remy. Julian could stop this.

"I will not, I tell you!" Elanna yelled at Carbury. "You cannot force me."

"But I will, my dear," Carbury said with a sneer.

Elanna yanked free of him, her fists clenched, triumph in her posture as she marched away from her groom.

Julian and Remy darted forward.

Elanna sailed past Lily, tears cascading down her cheeks.

"Bastard." Pierce came abreast of Lily. "I could kill him."

"Stop!" She caught his arm. "Dear God, don't move."

Everyone in the room froze.

Carbury's eyes bulged from his head as he whirled on Pierce. One gentleman took a step toward him.

Julian stepped in front of the earl and waylaid him.

The Duchess of Seton fluttered among them, her lips quivering with restrained anger and chagrin. "Nerves, nerves. Nothing more. Do play on," she encouraged the cellist who had been giving forth some Bach or Beethoven ditty.

Carbury glared at Julian. Straightening his waistcoat, he reddened. "I'll see to my bride."

The duke hastened behind Carbury, muttering to himself.

Alarm spread across Julian's face. His brows shot together

as he swung toward the exit where his sister and Carbury had disappeared. Then he hurried after them.

Marianne groaned. "This marriage was never going to work."

Ada glanced from her cousin to Lily. "What? They never liked each other?"

"Like?" Pierce gave a joyless laugh. "She loathes him."

With a flick of her eyes, Lily warned her brother and sister to say no more.

"Should you go?" Marianne asked Lily as they watched the duchess scurry from the ballroom.

"Do not." Remy stood beside them, his attention riveted on the vacant doorway.

Down the marbled corridor from some far room, voices rose and rushed toward the reception in echoes of hate. Male, female, high-pitched, accusatory.

"I'll get the butler," murmured Remy to the assembled group. "I know him well. He must close all the doors. Excuse me."

Lily could scarcely catch her breath. Ada and Marianne blanched. Pierce focused on the doorway to the hall, and began to pace like a leopard in a cage.

Remy reappeared, the butler and two footmen behind him. Down the hall, the sounds of slammed doors reverberated into the ballroom.

But closed doors did not silence the sounds of bitter arguments.

A crash of china and a woman's scream rent the air.

The guests were mesmerized.

Julian rushed into the ballroom ,shouting at Remy to 'Come, come quickly!".

Remy ran after him.

No one spoke. Lily stared at Marianne, undone by the chaos.

Within a minute, Remy charged into the room. His face bright red, he rushed to Marianne and Lily. "Come quickly. They need you."

Lily thrust her flute into Ada's hands. Marianne did too.

Pierce headed toward the doors, but Remy grabbed his arms and hauled him backward. "Don't."

"What's happened?" Pierce demanded of him.

"The duke has had a stroke."

CHAPTER 15

"**Y**our breakfast, Your Grace, as you wish here." The Seton butler gave small bow to Lily, his scowl a storm upon his brow. He wasn't pleased that the new young duchess did not stay in bed to break her fast as the lady of the manor should. He was inconvenienced to the nth degree, the intrusion to his day putting her in mind of a bothered scorpion. Silent, stealthy, stinging her with a subtle lash of his rectitude, he'd sneak up on her anywhere in this eerie carcass they called Broadmore House. Like the insects who lived in the southern Texas plains, he'd better learn how to scurry away from any retaliatory strikes. For as sure as the sun rose and set, one day she'd rebel and dress him down like the duchess she'd become.

After three weeks here at Broadmore, being stung by him and hobbled by the Dowager Duchess of Seton, alone save for Julian's arms circling round her at night, Lily was in no mood to tolerate much more nastiness.

"Wonderful, Perkins. You and the footman may leave me to dine alone." Lily spoke to the under servant, embarrassed to ask the question which she had asked of him yesterday. "Forgive me, what is your name?"

But it was the butler who cleared his throat in a most reproachful manner and answered her. "Finch, Your Grace."

"Thank you." She brought herself up short. Orders from Julian's mother were she was not to acknowledge staff. In any way. "I shall remember it next time."

The footman hastened to pull out her chair for her, then pour her tea.

"Put the pot there, Finch. I will serve myself."

Perkins glared at her. That, she was certain, was not what butlers were allowed to do. The dowager duchess influencing his attitudes, perhaps? She gave him the arch of a brow.

He demurred, unhappily so, but nonetheless. He puttered about after the exit of the younger man and finally, he closed the double doors upon her.

She was blessedly alone. *Again.* In the dining room. With the grim countenance of one of the forbearers of the Ash family staring down upon her. He—name as yet unknown to her—loomed over her, six feet tall with lace cuffs dripping down to his ruby-laden fingertips. In his ornate vermilion velvet suit *a la* one of Charles the Second's cavaliers, he looked so fancy, he might have been a woman going to a ball.

Lily snorted and consoled herself with a satisfying drink of her tea. Her toast stood in a little silver contraption they called a caddy. She picked up one triangle. And dropped it. Cold. *Again.*

Is there nothing warm in this entire mansion? Not toast. Not portraits. Not rooms. Not husband.

Not even my husband. Not as he was during their first few weeks together. Attentive, madly passionate but silent as he took her in his arms each night, he made love to her like a man possessed by demons. She had pressed him for causes.

He had not shared them. So be it. She did not question him further for the cares that lined his forehead as deeply as the Broadmore butler's.

She might understand Julian's troubles, his added responsibilities now as the new Duke of Seton, but she did like his withdrawal. She vowed to approach the matter, but looked for an suitable opportunity. One bit of news that would brighten his days was her purchase of the Irish lands he'd wanted his father to sell through Leland.

Phillip had arrived yesterday to prepare for the reading of the will tomorrow. Early this morning, he had sent her a note via the butler through her maid Nora that the sale had completed. She was now the proud owner of eight-thousand acres of prime farmland near Tipperary.

That news would lift her husband's spirits.

She scraped back her chair and headed for the sideboard. The silver salvers had better have kept the heat in the eggs and bacon or she would scream.

The door squeaked open. Angry that Perkins would disturb her, she whirled around.

Her mother-in-law stood upon the threshold.

Well, that put an end to any hope of a peaceful meal.

"*What* are you doing?" The woman virtually seethed the words.

Obvious, isn't it?

Her plate full, Lily resumed her chair. She would not be bated.

"I asked you a question."

"Have you had your breakfast yet, madam?" Lily had not been invited to call her anything else, nor would she ask for any moniker more informal for a long time.

After the woman had heard her husband pronounced dead in the parlor in London, she'd fainted at her departed husband's feet. Lily and Marianne had run into the room to see the duke upon the carpet. Julian had caught up his mother and put smelling salts to her nostrils. The duchess struggled up from the floor. Then in a manner Lily understood most staid ladies of the upper crust would eschew as the lowest form of crassness, she wailed as Julian pronounced her husband's death.

Like a dervish, she'd ordered the service in the Broadmore family chapel and burial in the family mausoleum. She'd moaned, dabbed her cheeks, and told tales of how happy she and her husband had been. "Until…" she said with malice, mystery and a dab of melancholy. "Until he ruined us…"

On, she'd ranted and raved as if she'd lost a cherished partner. To have torn at her hair like ancient mourners might even have been in character for the woman, had she indeed cared for the man. But Lily had seen no devotion between them. For the greater realm of the duke's and duchess's social circle, the woman's drama may have convinced them of her anguish. To Lily however, the lady's actions were a play. A tragedy. A lie.

Nor had she stopped. One day after the duke's demise, the woman had led a procession of the family up to Broadmore with the body of the duke leading the way in a black bunting-draped caisson. The dowager rode with Julian and Lily in the Broadmore coach. Elanna and Carbury, their honeymoon cut by the death, followed in Carbury's carriage. Those two had stayed only two days and at Carbury's insistence, had departed for the coast of France. If Lily thought that Elanna might be pleased to have some solitude with her groom, she might have envied the young bride's escape. But that was not the case. As the couple left for Dieppe, Lily witnessed a new resentment take hold of the dowager. Indeed, the woman added another note to her repertoire.

Suddenly, she concentrated less on mourning and more on making Lily's life miserable.

Lily was to do her correspondence in a room upstairs. Tiny, airless and without a fireplace, the room had once been —Lily was certain—a closet. Plus the only chair was wooden, minus upholstery. Extremely uncomfortable.

Lily's lady's maid Nora, whom she'd brought with her after her marriage, was to take on other household chores. None of them was usual for Nora's stated position.

Furthermore, Lily was not to plan the meals. That was the dowager duchess's job. Always had been.

Nor would Lily help plan for tomorrow's reading of the late duke's will in the library. The dowager had claimed that duty as solely her own. Elanna and Carbury were to arrive today. So too Julian's cousin Valentine Arden, Lord Burnett. And all the servants of Broadmore. Lily had suggested tea for everyone, but she'd been vetoed because of the expense of feeding the staff tea and cakes. If the dowager pinched any more pennies, they'd all be eating gruel three times a day.

"Of course, I've eaten." The woman marched toward Lily, her presence more forbidding than the man on the wall who peered over them. "It is most unbecoming for the mistress of Broadmore to take her breakfast anywhere else but in her bed."

I take my husband in my bed, not my meals.

"I prefer to dine here." She tucked into her eggs.

"It's most, *most* unladylike. What will the staff think of you? I forbid it." She took hold of the bell pull, ready to summon a servant.

Lily froze her with a glare. "As I see it, madame, you can forbid me nothing. If I wish to eat here, I harm no one."

"You know nothing of harm. Nothing of procedures or traditions."

Lily put down her fork and knife. "I know that if I dine here, I relieve the staff of work they need not do."

The lady clasped her hands together so tightly, her knuckles went white. "Servants are here to work. They are paid. They have their keep. That is sufficient."

Lily had no idea what each person earned, nor what their keep cost the estate—and she'd correct that lack. However, she did know that the reason she'd seen so little of her husband lately was his worry over money. For the past ten days or so, Julian had spent long hours with the estate manager to examine the records. He'd told her no financial details. Each day, he worked and each day, he became more vexed, his temper short, his attention wandering, his passion for her dulled. What little time he did take to talk with her was riddled with concern over the incessant rain, the drowning crops and the disgruntled tenants. His preoccupations with the welfare of those on Broadmore, as well as reports of more tenants at Willowreach down with croup and bronchitis, had pushed her aside. She disliked Julian's aloofness. Feared it might erode what intimacy they'd begun to build. Money, which she'd always taken for granted, might buy comfort and splendor, but it did not contribute to contentment.

"You must finish your meal quickly." The dowager waved a hand at her.

"This is my house, madam."

"No, it is mine." The woman preened, her thin nose reminding Lily of a bird of prey.

Lily itched to be so crass as to remind this lady of precisely what she owed her. Or rather her father. "You will not chase me off, madam."

"I am chatelaine here, you presumptuous chit. You come to England to throw your father's money at us. You are an

American spawn of a pirate, spreading your legs for Chelton so that he—"

Lily set her jaw, determined to maintain her dignity. "*He,* madame, is referred to as '*His Grace,*' and I detest the insult to my father and myself."

"As do I, Mother."

In the entrance to the dining room stood Julian. He looked the very devil, his hair plastered to his skull, wet from the rain, his dark eyes heavy with fatigue.

"This is unseemly, Mother." He approached her and she sniffed, uncowed. "I thought better of you."

Lily frowned over that. *She* hadn't thought better of the dowager. She'd been given no reason to think highly of her. If Julian and his mother were to have a confrontation, Lily was determined to witness it.

But the woman did not give in easily. "I will not have your wife creating havoc in this house, Chelton."

Lily's stomach knotted. How could the woman be so insulting to her son? Was she determined to ignore her husband's death? Why? Honoring the man now did nothing to redeem herself for the way she'd traded her husband when he was alive.

Julian raked his hands through his disheveled hair. "For Lily to take her breakfast where she pleases does not inspire havoc."

"The servants will take advantage of her."

You take advantage of me.

"I doubt that, Mother. She's had servants."

"Not ours."

"Well, I tell you now, madam," he bit off his words, "she may dine here."

And soon, I'll do the menus. Consult with the cook. And the housekeeper.

"You make a mistake to allow it," the dowager warned him.

Lily put down her napkin and rose. She'd take her power into her own hands. "I must begin my correspondence. You may find me, Julian, in the pink parlor."

"No!" Her mother-in-law shook in her vehemence.

Giving a small curtsy to both, Lily sailed past them.

"Let her go, Mother, and stop this arguing. She is my wife."

I am. And always will be.

One look out the window of the salon and Lily put down her pen. Had the rain finally stopped?

In a rush, she finished her letter to her father. The day the Setons and she had left London for Broadmore, her family had once more departed for Paris. Her father and Pierce had meetings with bankers in Paris and Ada had appointments with Worth and French lingerie designers.

Her father had bid her goodbye on the steps of their house on Piccadilly. Julian left her to her privacy and spoke with the coachman as she bid adieu to her father.

With a kiss to her cheek, her father whispered, "Enjoy your new husband. He'll recover from this loss in time and be yours again soon. And I like him."

She hugged him. "Me, too."

"I noticed that."

"Write to me of Paris. How Ada and Pierce get on. And Marianne."

"Ah, well." He raised a wicked black brow. "That one will have no troubles. Remy will be upon us, I'm sure, with all due haste."

"Do you object?" she asked while the coachman cooled his heels holding open the door for her.

"I'm not sure yet. Climb in. Off you go." He'd handed her up into the carriage. The coachman climbed to his box and slapped the reins.

She'd left her family to come to this one, this house, these conflicts with her mother-in-law. She was not quite as happy with her husband as she had been at the start of their marriage, but perhaps that was a normal change. She was not happy with much else, especially here at Broadmore. And the rains only exemplified her dour mood.

But since the sun was shining…

And it was gloriously so. She sealed her letter to her father, and gathered her others to Ada and Marianne. Hoisting her skirts, she raced from the salon, up the staircase to her rooms. Hopes to escape the house and its troubles burst like bubbles in her brain.

In minutes, she'd changed her black gown to her riding outfit. This new one, fine red serge and part of her trousseau, had a skirt she loathed, but it was normal attire—and God forbid, her mother-in-law see her in pants. She hated to think of it. Down the back stairs and out the kitchen doors, she hurried along the shady lane toward the stables. She hadn't yet visited. Not in the torrential rain. But this was a perfect time.

Briefly, she'd been introduced to the stable hands the day after they'd arrived from London. The master groom, Docker, was a burly, balding man who had kindly brown eyes and a big smile for her. His two stable boys were sturdy chaps who resembled him. Introduced by only their given names, they were most likely his sons.

The stable block was a long red-brick structure half a mile from the main house. She'd glimpsed it from her bedroom, just through the evergreens. The doors were open and she walked in, expecting to see one of the hands. No one was about. All the horses were gone, out to pasture, probably.

The sliver of sunshine that pierced the heavy clouds must have inspired everyone to get out and about.

Well, she wasn't going back to the house, that was certain. She wanted to walk, clear her mind.

She turned for the lane south. This was a perfect time to introduce herself to the tenants. As with so much else, the dowager had her own dictums about how Lily must comport herself with these people. At all costs, she had ordered her to stay away from the village.

'They live in squalor and you mustn't go near.' She'd told Lily that night before last during dinner when Julian had brought up the tenants' maladies. Three of the tenants' wives were bed-ridden with coughs. Many of the children, most of them very young at three and four, were down too.

Lily had sighed. *'But if they are incapacitated, I can help.'*

Her mother-in-law had not heard of it. *'You are strong. Stay that way.'*

'But I was a nurse in a hospital in—'

'Julian!' With a clatter, the woman had dropped her fork to her plate. *'For the love of heaven, forbid her this, will you?'*

'No. He cannot.'

He had put up a hand to stop their argument. *'Mother, Lily, please—'*

The woman had stared at Lily. *'Your job is to remain strong. Bear an heir. A spare. You are not to go traipsing off and become ill yourself. You might already be increasing.'*

Lily had considered her hands in her lap. She would not give her mother-in-law any insight into the passion that bound Julian and her together more than once every night.

She had lifted her face and met the lady's gaze. *'I hear your rationale.'*

'Good. That's settled then.'

She had let the woman think what she wished.

She would anyway.

~

Hours later, Lily trudged her way back to the stables. The walk to the village had been longer than she expected. The work to nurse the sick there had been more than she'd expected, but rewarding. She needed another medical kit filled with instruments. She'd order it tomorrow and keep one kit here, one at Willowreach. Today, she'd learned how necessary such items could be. She'd taught two women how to build croup tents and tend kettles for constant hot steam. Tomorrow, she'd return to them. But when she did, she'd ride.

Inside the stable block, Lily saw no one. At four in the afternoon, they should have been heading back. But then she wasn't familiar with English farming ways. Perhaps they let their animals out for more of the day. The searing Texas heat demanded ranchers send their animals out at dawn and bring them in by noon or one before the sun fried them to a crisp.

Resigned to returning to the house, she took a step. And stopped.

Someone was here. She heard them. Two men with bass voices. In the far stall.

Her feet fell on tampered earth and scattered hay so she made no sound as she strode toward them.

But she stopped.

She cocked her head to listen.

One of the men was Julian.

"The sale of that land in Tipperary was profitable."

She smiled to herself. *I know it was.*

"Indeed," Phillip Leland agreed.

Discreet about it too. As I asked him to be.

"A stroke of luck, I'd say, to find a buyer so quickly."

Not very.

"I'd like to thank them for their purchase," Julian said.

"Not a good idea, Chelton. Anonymity is what they asked for."

"That's the one bit of good news I've had in weeks, Leland. But I must press upon you that tomorrow, I don't want the will read aloud. I wish to heaven you could change this. Overlook it."

"I'm bound by ethics as His Late Grace's executor. I must do as instructed in the written will."

"Why *do* that? To read these clauses aloud will only irritate my mother."

Lily stopped breathing. More trouble from her mother-in-law? Was she not causing enough already?

Leland remained silent.

"I see. Of course." Julian again, frustrated. "Precisely what he wished. Even after death, they never stop impaling one another!"

She shrank backward.

"Are we certain everyone will attend? I understand you have contagion in the village."

"We do and yes, they have agreed to come. My estate manager is quite ill. But he will make the effort and arrive to hear the final terms."

"Lady Carbury, too?"

"Oh, yes," Julian said, weariness in his words. "My sister brings along the earl. As if he'd let her out of his sight."

"She's very unhappy," Leland said. "I scarcely knew her when I visited last week. She is beside herself. A different person."

"Yes. From the night he decided to court her, Elanna turned. At the Paris Opera, we were." Julian cursed beneath his breath. "I wish she hadn't agreed to wed him. Nothing for it now."

"Carbury required no dowry. Shocking that."

"Ugh. Not really, Leland. Carbury wanted only her in his bed."

"That much desire is not healthy when it's one-sided."

Julian sighed. "The crux of their problem."

"One good thing about tomorrow. Lord Burnett agreed to attend."

"Ah, my cousin Valentine will be ecstatic if my father has given him that painting of his mother. He's been after us for years for that. With more money than a choir of angels, he needs only those things he desires. He'll be over the moon with the gift."

"And what of the gratuities to the servants?" Leland's voice was low and troubled. "Can you pay them?"

"I can."

Julian had not shared with her any of the conditions of his father's will. Awards of money to the staff was a noble gesture of the late duke whom she never would have thought capable of such kindness.

"Should I ask how you got it?"

Lily would bet it was her marriage settlement.

Julian scoffed. "I didn't win it at the tables, if that's what you're after."

"Your wife's dowry then?"

"No."

No?

"Your Grace, to settle the questions in the City of your finances, I need to know how you got the cash. I daresay it's not a new mortgage. I would have had to officiate at that."

"The Irish sale was a boon. But I also had those winnings at cards from the last time I was in Paris. That's where the money came from to pay Elanna's debts. And that other money I told you to put aside for her."

Julian put aside money for Elanna?

"Kind of you to offer her that means of escape," Leland said with sorrow.

"She took Carbury's offer too quickly."

"Yes," Leland said. "She had to marry, sooner or later. At least she does not bear your financial burden."

"We'll weather this," Julian said with a steely will and a bit of bravado. "I will."

"Your determination is welcome, Your Grace. But we are in desperate straits. I've done the tally. Our mortgage payments equal now more than half our income."

Lily's mouth dropped open. Her father always said that one did not accumulate debt greater than a tenth of one's income. Julian's was more than half?

"Lack of money," Julian said with a weary sigh. "It rules estates, marriage, even the question of love."

The question? Was there a question of Julian's love for her?

Lily's head reeled. She stepped backward, her palms to the rough wood of the stall to steady her. How much of Julian's statement was true? She had believed he had married her at the very least because he valued her. Liked her. Even desired her.

She had thought that as their marriage progressed, that he and she had a relationship built of respect and passion which could blossom into love.

Could she have deluded herself?

Julian was pacing, his footsteps crunching dried hay. "I had approximately eight thousand pounds left. I used half to spruce up Willowreach before my wedding. So I have the cash for the servants, Leland. I'm happy to pay it. It's the one request my father made of me that makes me proud of him."

Lily put her hand to her throat. Tears blurred her vision. That her husband would use his money to save his sister from a disastrous marriage was valiant. That he'd use it to refurbish his home for her was sweet.

But if he loved her wealth more than her, what value did he place on their marriage?

"Are you concerned about the reading of the will tomorrow?" She ventured to ask Julian in their bedroom that night, hoping to draw him out and have him confide in her.

"My mother will wail," he said, shrugging out of his robe and kicking off his slippers to climb into bed naked. "She always expects more than she gets. Nothing new there. An embarrassment. As for Elanna? She appears to be without emotions."

"I worry about her." Lily walked around to Julian and sat beside him. "I hate to think how much she dislikes him."

"Dislike? Hardly," he said, wincing. But he took her by the wrist and planted a seductive kiss in her palm. "Don't think of it. Come here."

Happy to do that, she bent closer.

His lips on hers were a brand.

"I miss you," she whispered.

"I'm here." His eyes cleared, registering her complaint. But he chose to turn it aside and sank to nibble at her shoulder. "Always have been."

She didn't want to argue, but she pushed away. His large dark eyes swept over her, desire for her sending her into a frisson of need. She trailed one hand over his muscular chest to his lean hip and groin. "After the will is read, we'll put our lives in order, won't we? And get back to adventures in hay stacks and carriages?"

He threw back his head to laugh and grabbed her to him for a stunning kiss. "We'll do them all, Your Grace. But first —" He wiggled his brows, happy for the moment. "Why don't you perfect how well you ride?"

He was too disarming. "Haven't I proven that?"

"With my horses, darling. Not with me." He led her to spread her legs and sink over him, large and hard as he was.

Her mouth fell open. Her body swelled to take him inside. And she was lost, found, swept up, his arms around her.

As his fingers pushed up her negligee, she surrendered conscious thought. As he bared her to him, she gave up to his every caress. When he sucked her nipples into diamonds, Lily arched up into that lusty realm where he made her soar and tremble. As he rocked her to a throbbing height, she joined him in the rapture she craved. Later, mindless, she crashed into his solid embrace.

Reality returned with a piercing thought. In the midst of enjoying him, she'd forgotten that new torment that he might not love her. The lack cut her like a knife. The wound, salved by his caresses, went deep. No sutures bound it up.

Searching for remedies, she laid awake for hours while Julian slept on. The only one was simple—and superficial. She could seduce him to remain in bed with her for endless days where she might have physical proof of his devotion.

But that was foolish.

A young girl's daydream.

In reality, she was a woman whose husband had married her for her money.

A woman who loved her husband—and had no idea if he might ever return the affection.

Lily entered the salon on Julian's arm and took her place in one of the two large Sheratons by the window. He sat in the other and nodded to Phillip Leland, the lawyer, that he could begin.

Lily had never been to a reading of a will. It seemed morbid. She'd even thought it unnecessary but Julian had told her that while his father's title and entailed lands automatically became his on his father's death, any other gifts granted were outside that. According to his father's wishes, they were to be announced and were to be given only when all named in the will were present.

Lily gazed upon the assembled guests in the crowded salon while Leland adjusted his glasses. Julian looked wooden, drained. The dowager staid, safely shielded from observation by her black veil with velvet chenille drops. Elanna? Elanna was more of a mystery.

She wore no veil, carried no handkerchief. Effecting a haughty demeanor as Lady Carbury, she'd pulled taut her lustrous rosewood hair into a severe braid curled like a half-crown at her nape. In a move utterly *de trop* for the occasion, she'd rouged her cheeks and her lips. Her black serge gown was as plain as a serving girl's, her lack of fashionable bustle a reason—in addition to the rouge—for her mother to take her aside minutes ago and scold her for it. But the new Countess of Carbury had considered her mother with a detachment that set the older lady sputtering. Elanna was done, it appeared, with pleasing others. Even her husband was a recipient of her daunting *sang froid*.

Among the others in the room, Lily saw no sobbing. No tears. No grief so much as impatience and among the servants, hope.

Money did that to people. Whether its possession or its lack, money made them hungry. Or covetous. Angry or resentful. Happy for a moment.

Which does Julian feel for the acquisition of my money?

She fidgeted in her chair.

"Are you well?" Julian leaned toward her, his anxious face turned from the guests.

"Yes. Yes, quite."

"Your cheeks are flushed. You seem distressed."

Unwilling to lie to him, she told him what she could. "I wish this were over."

His mouth quirked up at one corner. "You are not alone."

She licked her lips and focused on Leland. He began his reading.

Julian Quentin Ash, only son of Quentin Fernshaw Ash, was to claim his father's personal effects, including jewelry, robes of state, private carriage and personal property of twenty thousand acres of land in Ireland and ten thousand in Australia.

Charlotte Deirdre Anne Ash, wife, was to claim the dower house at the Broadmore Gate, along with one phaeton and the services of two staff for the remainder of her days. She was to have what jewels her husband had made expressly for her and they were enumerated. All other items were to remain in the family vaults for use by future mistresses of the house.

Elanna Corinne Ash, daughter, was to receive the pair of blue and white Chinese Ming vases from her dressing room.

Valentine Jasper Arden, Lord Burnett and the duke's nephew, was to receive the portrait of his mother, Louise Caroline Ash, by Frederick Winterhalter.

"And for the servants of Broadmore—" Leland began the bequests the late duke made to each of the household staff from Perkins the butler down to the scullery maid, the groom Docker and his two stable boys, the head gardener and his men. Even the game keeper received a sum of money for service to his master. These particular monies would be paid each servant tomorrow morning at nine o'clock.

The servants filed out. Perkins followed and closed the doors behind him.

Lily allowed herself a sigh of relief. This ordeal was nearly over. Tomorrow morning, Elanna, her husband, Leland and Lord Burnett, would depart. Lily would have then only the dowager to contend with. And she'd find the right opportunity—and the right words—to deepen her relationship with Julian.

Her mother-in-law shot to her feet. Her face was red, her hands clenched.

Everyone turned to her.

"The dower house is mine to use, but with only a maid and a butler. Are you quite mad?" she asked, her gaze skewering Leland, then pinning Julian.

"That is the stipulation, Mother." Julian did not move, sans all emotion.

Lily could feel the winds of a storm brew, the roar of it whipping through the rooms of the mansion.

"I will not go."

Julian clasped his hands together. "We can discuss this after all have left us."

"No."

Her belligerence sent Lily backward in her chair. All others in the room, save Julian, got to their feet, intent on the doors.

"What is my portion?" the dowager persisted, her inquiry of Phillip Leland.

"Tell her. She might as well know all." Julian rose.

She sneered at him and fixed her gaze on Leland once more. "My portion? You read no amounts."

Leland stood with an apologetic glance at Julian. "His Grace, your husband, did not wish the sums to be known publicly, Your Grace."

She grumbled. "But I must know."

"Three thousand a year."

She winced. "Absurd. When I married it was be ten."

Leland inclined his head. "It was. But conditions have changed and three is what the estate can afford you."

She faced Julian. "I demand more."

"There is no more to give you. Father did not invest your jointure in stocks that bore sufficient interest. Even three thousand a year is a huge amount to divest from the family assets."

Her mother-in-law cast her gaze about the salon, her dark eyes a venomous snap. Beneath her black veil, she indicated her sorrow with a quivering chin and an appropriately crushed handkerchief in one hand. "I cannot live on three. I will not."

"I'm sorry." With a polite incline of his head and finality to his tone, Leland let that be the end of this topic.

"The servants' stipend?" The dowager duchess would not let go her ire, pinning the lawyer to his spot. "Where did that money come from?"

Leland barely breathed. "Your son, the duke gave it to the estate."

"Really?" She spun toward Julian with violence in her gaze. "From where?"

Lily could bear this woman no longer. Her bitterness, her false dignity, her sense of entitlement were appalling. Lily could not wait for the day she moved to the dower house.

"Where?" the woman insisted with a stomp of her foot. "Ah. The American's dowry."

One brow arching high, Julian considered her with a disparaging eye. "No."

"Where then?"

"You are being unruly, madam," Julian warned her.

"I insist."

"Do it all you like," he said and made for the doors. "I will not remain to listen."

"I am your mother."

He whirled to face her. "Yes. And I wish, only once, you might have acted like it. But for more years than I care to recall, I have seen you teach me by word and example, that more than my mother, you have become a selfish, rude, ruthless creature."

Lily stood, she knew not how. Never had she heard anyone in her family have such an exchange. Never had she deemed it possible. But suddenly, she saw clearly one reason why Julian might never love her. Might not even be capable.

He'd been nurtured by people who knew not how to care for others. Not selflessly. Not completely.

One glance at Elanna told Lily she was horribly right.

The young woman was smiling, the expression triumphant. Sardonic.

Marriage had transformed Elanna. How, why, what Carbury and she did together, how they got on, would never be fully known to Lily. Nor did she wish to learn.

But to look at Elanna told her one more fact very clearly. Elanna had withdrawn from her husband along with all others in her family. Her reasons were her own. She'd had examples set before her of parents who tormented each other. If her own marriage was not happy, she could think that the norm.

Did her brother bear the same tendencies?

Could Julian turn on Lily the way his mother had turned on his father? Would he love? Or did he only lust?

CHAPTER 16

*I*n their dressing room, her husband reclined in the huge porcelain bathtub which barely contained his long, strong form. His head back along the rim, he had closed his eyes. His sensual mouth formed a slash, grim. And as Lily watched his facial muscles move from frown to scowl, she guessed he relived the reading of the will earlier this afternoon.

He'd dismissed his valet, and she had waved off Nora. They could retire for the evening. The guests in the house were invited to partake of a cold buffet in the dining room at their leisure. Lily had suggested that and her mother-in-law had not, for once, countermanded her order. Breathing a sigh of relief, Lily had closed the door upon their two personal servants. She wished to be alone with Julian to draw him out on the day's troubles.

"Would you like me to wash your back?"

At her words, he peeped open one eye. "The best suggestion I've heard today."

"Is the water warm enough?"

"I hate to overtax the plumbing system."

"You are the owner of this plumbing, dear sir, and if it doesn't suit you, who will it please?" She strode to the cistern and put a hand to the heater. Warm. She turned the spigot. The water gurgled through the pipe and emerged in a solid stream to Julian's tub. "How's that?"

He tested the flow. "Excellent."

She got a wash cloth from the linen cupboard and got down to her knees. She dunked the cloth in his water. "Lean forward."

He complied.

She began a slow circular massage of his broad back. "I think Phillip did a marvelous job today."

Julian made a sound that he agreed.

"Val was happy with his mother's portrait," Lily said recalling the way the man admired the painting of the striking blonde woman.

"She was lovely. And Winterhalter did her justice. I remember her."

"She was your father's sister?"

"She was. Ran away with Val's father. Supposed to be a scamp, but a rich one. Still my father and his did not approve. She was cut from the family inheritance, even her portrait had to remain here. Did her well, it seems, not to be in touch with us. She was, you see, very happy with her husband. Unlike those of us in this family."

It chilled Lily to hear him include himself in the family curse. Swallowing back any negativity, Lily ran her hand down Julian's spine, the nap of the cloth tingling the skin of her palms. "She was very lovely."

He raised his head and wiped the drops of water from his jaw. "We're not a bad looking family." He turned his head to gaze at her and let his eyes caress her features. "You make us look even better."

She winked at him and went back to her task of washing

him. He was so masculine. Muscular and fit, he was a handsome creature. *Her husband. Hers.* And not hers completely. She tried to be valiant. "Elanna resembles your aunt."

"She does. In looks." His last words held an ominous note. "I'm glad she and Carbury go home tomorrow. I cannot bear their animosity."

"How can she be so indifferent to him?" Lily asked and hated that she'd let slip such honesty.

"I gather he merits it. Though I'm not certain why."

Her worst fear of the Carburys' relationship was almost outlandish. "Does he mistreat her?"

Julian snorted. "Ha! You mean like my father 'mistreated' my mother?"

"Well, I—"

"You can say it." He leaned over, bunching up his knees and circling his arms around them. "You did not see much of it."

She paused. "Enough. I saw enough."

"They never stopped punishing each other."

"For what?" she whispered. *Oh, that was bold.* She bit her lip.

He pivoted and looked her straight in the eyes. "They loved each other when they first married, but in turn, each one took another to bed."

"That," she said with tears in her throat, "is very sad. Why would they?"

"Why would they?" Julian winced and lifted his face to the ceiling. "Because it was possible. Because he was a duke. She was a duchess. Men and women coveted the chance to say they'd bedded them. Because he was obsessed with his title and his pride. And she was obsessed with…"

What? Her reputation? Her title? Her—

"Revenge."

"How   how do you know?"

He shrugged. "Bits and pieces of the resentments came out in their arguments over the years. They were reputed to be a unique couple, renowned lovers, fated mates, envied. But others sought to ruin the perfection. For their own amusement, I gathered. Society can do that. Indulge in such cruelty. And the two of them were silly enough—weak enough—to allow it."

She sought to put distance or perspective between his parents' tragic marriage and what could happen to her own. She stopped her ministrations, the cloth dropping to the water with a splash. "Elanna is not full of vengeance."

"No. She's full of hatred."

"But—"

He raked a hand through his wet black hair. "It doesn't matter. Her marriage appears to be a disaster as well."

"I don't want ours to be."

He spun to look at her. The frown that creased his brows alarmed her.

She shrank away.

He grabbed her hand. "Neither do I."

She began to smile when he shook his head.

"I fear I don't know how to be a proper husband."

Tell me you love me. That would make you a perfect husband.

He rose from the tub, grabbed a towel from the rim and anchored it around him. Stepping out, he reached for her and drew her to him.

He lifted her face and kissed her with a ferocity she hadn't known from him. As if he were not thinking, only feeling, he led her to their bed, removed and then tossed her peignoir and her negligee to the carpet and put her to the edge of the mattress. There, he cupped his hands behind her knees and brought her legs around his hips. The towel had fallen and she embraced him, wet and full and ready for him.

In a second, he sank inside her. Her eyes fluttered shut as

he filled her and satisfied them both with breathless passion. But what they built together out of this lust for each other left her wondering, wanting more that she feared he might not ever be able to give her.

"I'll bid them all goodbye," he told Lily the next morning. He bent to place a kiss on her mouth, her lips beautifully swollen from their love play last night. She'd been pliant in their first coupling, then turned ravenous in their second. He was a fortunate man to have a wife who loved her bed sport. He could not have planned for a better mate. And yet, he was ashamed to say, he denied her what she needed to make it perfect.

Denied her the declaration that teased his lips every time he kissed her and pushed inside her wet and giving walls. If he said he loved her, would he—like others he knew—lose his pride, his very self in the process? Could he give himself away so completely?

If he did, she'd have such power over him. Such terrifying power.

He lifted her hand and kissed her palm. *Escape was easier.*

"Have your breakfast here, will you?"

"I don't like to." She fingered the buttons on his coat, fixing it so that he was dressed to perfection to greet his guests downstairs over breakfast.

"I know, but you needn't endure them." The sheet over her breasts slipped, her large rosy nipples a ripe temptation. He'd bitten one last night in his madness for her and his teeth had marked her. Tempted once again to join her in bed, he compensated by bending to lick her luscious skin and suck one hard point into his mouth. His cock jumped.

She undulated and clamped shut her eyes.

Be a gentleman, not a beast. Drawing away, he grinned at her. "You did your part yesterday, darling, and they made you sad. I want you happy. I'll tell Nora to bring you a tray."

She pulled at the sheet and he winked at her as he turned away.

In the dining room, his mother and Leland were already seated. Shocked that his mother deigned to eat here rather than in her own bedroom from a tray, he bid her good morning with a half smile. To Phillip Leland he gave a broader one.

"I've been talking with Mister Leland," said his mother, "about my allowance."

"I see." Julian sat quietly as Perkins the butler and a footman hurried around him with pots of tea and coffee. "And? What of it?"

"I tell you, Julian. I need more money."

He ground his teeth. In front of Phillip who was a very distant relation, she might have addressed him as simply Seton. But she had this persistent reluctance to recognizing that, indeed, he was now the duke and she must in public call him by any number of honorifics. His given name was not permitted. Her failures in addressing him correctly were her attempt to show she superseded him. She did not. And he would not allow it.

Furthermore for this dressing-down, he would not dismiss his servants. This was his house, his domain, his money and his debts. And he would be master here.

"Madam," he said in the frostiest tone he had ever used with anyone, "there is no more money."

She glared at the butler and the footman in turn. "They must leave."

Both men froze in their tracks.

Julian locked his eyes on hers. "They will remain."

"You had money for them," she accused him. "If you have it for them—"

"No. I do not have more for you."

"I understand you sold that Irish land you wanted your father to sell. There's money from that."

Julian felt Leland's eyes upon him, but he would not meet them. He knew the man would be apologetic for divulging that, but it was no secret that he'd asked him to sell the land.

"The proceeds from that sale go to our debts, Mother."

"They can be serviced." She waved a hand.

"They *are* serviced. By this sum." He sat straight as a pin while Perkins placed a plate of eggs and bacon before him.

She shook her head, fuming. "I understand you used money to refurbish Willowreach before your marriage."

Where in hell had she gotten that information? He'd ferret that out, by God. He picked up his fork. Stabbing a portion of food, he suppressed his desire to rage at her. "That is my business."

"She needs no comforts."

She needed every comfort.

"And I refuse to live like a pauper."

"Then perhaps, Madam, you should find employment."

Silence reigned.

"You have money for doctor's implements. For chemist's potions. Then you have money for me."

Leland stared at his plate.

Julian was aghast. The woman knew no bounds. Why did he not foresee this? Was he blind? Or just too trusting?

Or was it that living with a woman who was not vindictive, not manipulative, not unprincipled had changed him? Made him whole.

"My wife wishes to care for our tenants and servants. I welcome that."

His mother growled. "She buys anything she wants."

He stood with such force, his chair toppled backward.

"Perkins," he addressed the butler. "See to it that my mother leaves the house today. You will have her maid and two of the upstairs maids ready her trunks. Two footmen go to the dower house immediately to open it and clean it as best they can. Two more go tomorrow to finish the task."

His mother pushed back from the table and rose. "I will not go."

"You will go or I will throw you out. Choose."

White as a ghost, she groped for words. Her jaw worked but she was incapable of sound.

A very good thing, too. What else could be said that was more sordid than what they'd already uttered?

She marched out.

Perkins, wise man, shut the door swiftly behind her.

The footman replaced Julian's chair and Julian resumed his place.

Leland inhaled.

"I am sorry you had to witness that," Julian told him.

"Don't be."

Julian sipped at his coffee. His appetite however had fled.

Presently, Leland said, "I'm afraid I have more bad news."

Julian gave an outraged laugh. "Well, do tell me. It can't be worse than this."

"You asked me to look into certain rumors about you and the duchess in the London tabloids."

"You found the papers?"

"I did. I had my assistant combing the pages daily ever since you told me."

"Right after my father died."

"Yes."

"And what?"

"They are scurrilous. Astonishing in their content."

Julian could not believe it. "How so?"

"They allege that you and your wife engage in…" Leland was red with embarrassment.

"Come, Leland. We are men. Out with it."

"Risqué sport."

Julian swallowed his disgust. What went on his bed was his private purview. "I don't understand."

"They say you indulge in erotic play with chains and leather."

Julian shouted in laughter. "Fantasy."

But the hesitant look on Leland's face said there was more.

"Go on."

"That you married your wife after you compromised her in your stables and your home."

Foul rumor. What Meg Sheffield had told him he'd put down to fiendish minds not a ninnyhammer who told tales. But certainly only three others had first-hand knowledge of events in Willowreach.

"That you married her for her money."

Julian squeezed shut his eyes. This was true. Partially.

"That your wife—" Leland cleared his throat and took a drink of his coffee. "That she rides astride and without her corset."

"At midnight," Julian whispered.

"Yes."

"What else?"

Leland slumped in his chair. "That you took to your bed another duchess and—"

"*What?*"

"And that your wife on the same night took a viscount."

His mind whirled with impossible scenes. "The only time — Dear God. The only time we've ever been near a duchess and a viscount was at Burnett's house party."

"I know."

"So who—?"

Leland shook his head. "Someone who was there?"

Julian clenched his hands. He was beside himself. *Meg?* She would repeat such gossip, but she wouldn't shame herself by reaching so low as to perpetrate such rumors. Who else might have a reason to spread such lies? And who else knew about the midnight rides and lack of corsets and—

Julian shot from his chair, his gaze riveted to Leland. "You have a list of these publications?"

"I do."

"Give it to me."

"You wish me to speak with the publishers?"

"No. I will." He got up from his chair. "Join me please in my office in ten minutes, will you, Leland?"

He got to his feet. "Yes, my lord."

"Bring that list."

"I will."

"Perkins, tell my wife and my mother I want them in my study in ten minutes."

Lily stared at her bedroom ceiling, counting the acanthus filigree in the stucco frieze. Five, ten, fifteen, twenty white leaves in one ring. Twice as many in the next. They circled the expanse much as her thoughts did. Endless whirls. No beginning. No end. She loved him, her husband loved her not...enough.

She sat up, the linens crumpling around her naked body. Blushing at the memory of how Julian had kissed her minutes ago, she shivered and shook off the thrill of it. She responded to his ardent lovemaking so naturally, so freely.

But his actions weren't love, were they? Passionate, yes. Erotic, certainly.

Without the full ardor she gave him. Without the regard she wanted from him.

She rose from the bed to walk to the window. In the July sun, she soaked in the warmth. Her skin absorbed the heat, the glow baking into her bones. This was what she missed, the intensity of the earth in her soul. In south Texas, for ten months of the year, you couldn't escape the sun. It burned your skin, your blood, and if you were not smart and stayed too long outside, it could burn your brain. Your reason gone.

She'd been so cold here, especially here at Broadmore, that her brain hadn't melted, but frozen.

She could stay so long that her heart would, too. And what then would happen to her love for Julian…or any children they might bear? An icy fear gripped her. Could she turn as cold as his mother? As forbidding? As bitter?

Would he turn against her as his father had his mother?

She pushed back the draperies, the shock of her thoughts acid in her mouth.

She couldn't let that happen. Not when they'd begun together so well. It was the death of his father that had changed their lives so radically. Julian's new responsibilities and the virulence of his mother's attacks against her ate at her confidence.

She couldn't allow it any longer, lest she lose her own self-worth. But what could she do to change any of it?

She couldn't change the dowager. She was who and what she was.

She couldn't change Julian, nor did she care to. She loved him as he was. But she could help herself. The best she could do would be to accept the fact that he might not change. He might not ever love her. Not fully.

Tears welled behind her eyes. She forced them back. She would not cry. What good would it do?

He didn't love her. Not as she did him.

She had bargained that he would. That he would come to that easily. But it would take longer and she questioned if she had the patience to wait for it. Even now, as she did, she lost a bit of her own integrity day by day, night by passionate night.

She put a hand to her eyes and dug deep inside herself for courage. Whenever she'd been faced with a problem in the past, she had sought solitude. She'd ridden out on the ranch by herself. Society here proclaimed she needed a cursed maid or a groom or a footman ready to hand. She needed or wanted none of them. And because she had married into this strict society, she been compliant. Agreeable. Too much so.

But now she would not be.

She'd take what she wanted for herself. And what she wanted was time to think and time to rediscover the patience and fortitude she'd need to live with a man who wanted her for her money and her grace and her good humor and her body, but who might never reciprocate her deepest love.

She must accept that or live forever in the shadow of her own sorrow.

Turning, she spied her peignoir. Julian must have picked it up from the floor this morning and put it on her chaise longue.

She heard a rustle in her sitting room. Her lady's maid, most likely, had arrived with her breakfast tray.

"Nora?"

Something shattered to the floor.

Her maid stuck her head around the door jamb. A blush colored her cheeks at the sight of Lily naked. She seemed surprised, on edge. "Yes, ma'am. It's me."

Suddenly shy of the woman who examined her body too intently, Lily reached for the silk robe and pulled it on.

She picked up her hair brush, a prickle of unease running up her spine. "What broke?"

"Oh, your ring dish."

"I see." The maid was not usually clumsy.

"I'm sorry, ma'am. I'll pay for it from my wages."

"No matter. I'm sure we have others, don't we?"

"We do."

"I'd like a breakfast tray up here this morning, Nora." She'd like the servant to leave her so she might pack a small reticule with a few clothes. "Bacon, eggs, tomatoes, if we have them. Coffee and tea."

A knock came at the outer door.

"See who that is," she told the woman.

What would she take? Where would she go?

Nora and Perkins exchanged comments.

Presently, her maid reappeared. "His Grace wishes you to go to his study."

"Oh?" *What now?*

"Me, too. Immediately."

"Very well." She'd wash and dress quickly. That was best. The less time she had to think of it, the better she would be.

Lily entered Julian's study, the dark oak paneling casting shadows on those already assembled. He'd ordered the gas lamps turned up but the silence added to the somber atmosphere.

"Come sit here, Lily." Julian pointed to the Chippendale chair beside his desk.

She crossed the room, while Nora hung back near the door.

"Perkins," Julian said to his butler, "you may leave us."

Phillip Leland, the dowager duchess, Nora and she were the only ones in attendance. Why her own maid was here raised unusual questions of propriety.

The dowager regarded the servant with narrowed eyes. "Why is she here?"

Julian came round his desk to lean back against it and cross his arms. In one hand, he held a sheet of paper. "We shall learn."

The dowager shifted in her chair, her jaw set, her gaze upon the paper in Julian's hand.

"Mister Leland has been very kind to bring to my attention a matter that deeply concerns me. Since we've been here dealing with the death of my father, I have not had opportunity to give my attention to the London news. And now we must."

The dowager scoffed. "If we want to read the papers, Julian—"

He lifted his hand and rattled the paper. "I have here a listing of London scandal sheets. *The Tatler, The Flyer. The Red Parlor.* A penny a piece for hideous stories of degradation. Fit for no one of any refinement but nonetheless, popular."

The duchess lost all color to her face.

Nora sucked in her breath.

Lily examined the servant. Her wide eyes, her grim lips. What was wrong with her? What concern had a maid for London broadsheets?

Lily stiffened. *What has this to do with me?*

"A number of articles have appeared in the past few weeks in these gossip sheets," he went on, "and the contents are intriguing."

A premonition of the subject matter had Lily squirming in her chair.

"They recount stories that not only are malicious lies but family secrets."

Lily froze. *About me? Cartoons again? Oh, the shame of it. Why do this?*

"Only a few people could have ever collaborated to reveal

these items to the presses and I want to know now why you would do such a thing to shame us all." And he turned the full force of his rage on his mother and the servant who stood behind her, Nora.

"What have you to say for yourself, Mother?"

"You are quite insane if you think—"

"Do not deny this. The only others who might have knowledge of these things are Lily's father and my own. Hanniford would never disparage his own daughter and my father lies outside in his grave. So, you see, there is no reason to dance around this. You did this to damage me and my wife and you enlisted this maid to assist you in this dastardly business."

"I won't sit here and be accused of this."

"Don't sit. Get out."

She sprang up. "She is not worthy of us."

"Enough!"

What had the woman said about her? Lily put a hand to her brow. Did it matter what the dowager had told these papers? What others thought of her? It once had. Mightily. But now?

Julian straightened. "You, madam, are not worthy of her. Leave."

"I demand—"

"Nothing. You can demand of me nothing. Go. Now."

The dowager rushed from the room.

Julian skewered Nora with his anger. "You too will go."

The maid looked from Lily to Julian.

He pulled on the gold fob at his waistcoat pocket and glanced at his watch. "You have ten minutes or I throw you out."

Her face scarlet, Nora attempted to form words. But snapped her mouth shut and scurried away.

Phillip Leland watched her go, then faced Julian. "I will depart myself this morning." To Lily, he said, "I'm so sorry,

Your Grace. This was a nasty business and I hated to be the bearer of such bad tidings."

Whatever was in those broadsheets, Lily never wanted to know. "I would never ridicule you for bringing such a thing to light. Thank you."

He inclined his head and quickly left Julian and her alone.

Julian walked toward her and made to take her in his arms, but she side-stepped him.

"I will make this up to you."

Light-headed, Lily steadied herself by putting a hand to the back of a chair. "You needn't. It was not you who did this."

"No, but I would not have you hurt."

"So you've said."

He blinked, her words a mystery to him. "My mother will not hurt you again. Nor the maid."

And what of you? Will you hurt me? "Thank you. I must go."

She took a step and wobbly as she was, he was quick to take her arm.

"I'm well." She pulled away from him. "I need to think on this."

He swallowed. "I will speak with the publishers of these rags. Ruin them. I'll see to it they never run other pieces about anyone."

He was so dear to say it, but he was penniless and they, so he said, were popular. He could not buy them off. "You must not spend your money or your time on them. You have tenants to aid, estates to run."

He questioned her statement with a searching look on his face. "I promised you once I would call out anyone who ran such pieces about you."

"I know. But what good does it do? There will be others."

"I'll see to it there are none."

She put a hand to his cheek. "You're kind, Julian. Sweet. Devote yourself to your people, your livelihood."

"But you are my first concern."

Was she? "I need a rest from this turmoil. The arguing. The hatred. The sadness."

"Of course. I understand. Go upstairs. I'll get the house-keeper to assign you another maid."

"Thank you. One who is young and untried. And one I can take to Willowreach."

He stepped to her and took her in his arms. With gentle fingers, he lifted her face. His own was ravished. "You want to go to Willowreach?"

"I was happy there." *We both were.*

"I'll go with you."

She shook her head. "I must go alone. Let me, Julian. Let me. I need this."

He pressed her close, his hands urgent on her back, his lips in his hair. "Promise me you'll write to me when you want me once again."

She placed a kiss to his jaw. "I will."

Then she hurried away from him and all she'd hoped for but had not achieved.

CHAPTER 17

*J*ulian sat, watching his estate manager close the door to his study. He rose to walk to the window and look out on the kitchen garden. Lettuces and tomatoes bloomed. Cabbages were popping up their pale green heads through the thick loam. The oak trees swayed in the breeze. All nature went on, eager for the sun.

He had little joy of it.

Three weeks had passed since Lily had left Broadmore. The heat of late August was upon them and Julian was noted the stay from the incessant rain and damp. Some of the crops had improved. His financial affairs had as well, courtesy of the sale of the Irish estate Leland had sold for him. He experienced some peace that he no longer dealt with the virulence of his mother. He kept well away from the dower house where she was installed with the two servants he'd allotted her. She did not venture near him. Wise of her.

The maid Nora had left the house without a peep. Glad of that, he thought it fitting she should have no severance, only her wages to date, and certainly no reference.

Among those in the estate cottages, his tenants inquired

about Lily. Those especially eager to see her return were two who recovered from their bouts of bronchitis and parents of the children whom she'd help recover from croup and coughs. His stable master Docker and his two sons also asked after her. "She liked to ride, Your Grace."

Julian could see they missed her smiling face, as he did at his table, in his parlor, in his arms.

He sighed and glanced to his desk. From London, he'd received a package he'd ordered from a friend of his in London who was a surgeon. The mahogany case contained a complete set of ear, nose and throat examination instruments. Strange items that his friend had written could help one diagnose aural diseases and laryngeal diseases. He'd added a set of small surgical knives, three scissors and a dozen German suturing needles plus a pair of forceps. Two weeks ago, he'd ordered them, hoping to give them to Lily upon her return here.

But each day that passed, his hope of her return died a little more. His effort seemed pointless because he wrote to her each day at Willowreach but she did not reply.

He grimaced. He must face the possibility that his marriage was so torn that he might never mend it. Unless he could persuade her to return to him.

A new satchel of medical equipment might cause her to smile, but presents alone would not lure her back to him. He had to give her himself and if he waited much longer, nothing could induce her to come home.

He spun for the hallway, found a housemaid and told her to fetch his valet and Perkins to him immediately.

"Send round my carriage," he told the butler when the man stood before him. "I'm off to Willowreach and don't know when I'll return."

~

Five days later, Julian climbed down from his cab to take the steps to Killian Hanniford's house in the Rue Haussmann. He'd noticed that no letters from him or anyone in the family had arrived at Broadmore for his wife since her departure. They must know where she was.

His father-in-law remained in residence in Paris while he sent the rest of his family to a villa in the southwest of France. Julian knew of this because Lily had told him of their plans when first they wrote of them in June. Julian had asked her if she cared to join them, but she had refused, saying she didn't want to leave him.

But that was weeks before the fiasco with his mother, the maid and his discovery of their collusion with the broadsheets. Weeks before his wife had left him. How drastically things had changed.

The Hanniford butler opened the door to him. Julian recognized him as the same man who'd served in that capacity almost a year ago when first he'd met Lily and become enchanted with her.

"Wonderful to see you, Your Grace." Foster took his hat and gloves. "Mister Hanniford is with a visitor. A business associate. We did not expect you, Your Grace."

"I did not send a telegram for good reason. Please tell Mister Hanniford I'm here. It's urgent."

"At once, of course." Foster, clearly alarmed, stepped with speed.

Julian followed him into a large salon overlooking the boulevard.

"May I offer you a brandy, Your Grace? Or tea? Perhaps you're hungry from your journey?"

"No, Foster. I'm fine."

The servant left him to his own thoughts. He paced before the window. The afternoon sun died as shoppers lined the pavement, slanting golden rays across the summery colors of the ladies' gauzy dresses.

Where are you, Lily?

"Julian." Killian Hanniford filled the doorway, his booming voice commanding attention. "This is a surprise. Good to see you, although I must say, I'd rather see you with Lily than without. Where is she?"

Julian did not sit and he did not smile. "Do you mean to tell me she's not here?"

Killian tipped his head. His black eyes went to slits. "What did you say?"

"Where is she?"

The man extended an arm toward the settee. "I think you'd better sit."

"I have no time."

Hanniford strode to the table where a few bottles of cognac stood. He unstoppered one and poured two glasses. When he returned to stand before Julian he said, "Why don't you know where she is?"

He took a hefty drink. "More than three weeks ago, she told me she wanted to rest."

"Rest?"

"She—we had suffered a few revelations and afterward, she wanted to think, to be alone."

"That's different from *rest*, my man."

"She told me she was going to Willowreach. She went in my carriage, took a chamber maid, and according to my staff, arrived later that night."

Killian downed his own brandy. "How long did she stay?"

"Two days."

"And then?"

Julian drained his glass. He licked his lower lip. "She had the groom take her into Ashford where he says she caught the public coach to Canterbury. I've looked for her there.

Spoken with friends of mine. Asked at the local hotel, but there is no word. No one who has seen her. So I need to know, if she has come to you. I must see her."

"I don't like the idea of her traveling alone."

Julian smarted. "Neither do I, but now you must tell me where she is. She'd been away long enough and I need her back."

"Do you?"

Julian did not like the murderous look in Killian's eyes. He took the blame, yes. But he could change. Make amends. "I would expect she told you what happened. With the broadsheets and my mother and the maid."

Killlian shook his head. "I have no knowledge of any of this."

"Perhaps that's best all forgotten." Julian put aside his empty glass.

"You argued?"

"No. I failed hcr."

"I see. Is it important that I know how?"

Julian shook his head. "Only that I do, and that I correct the error."

"Or the lack."

"Yes. The lack." *Lack of declaring how very vital she is to my very life.* "I was a fool to let her go."

"I doubt you had a choice."

Julian was confused. "I don't know what you mean."

"You couldn't deter her." Killian picked up Julian's glass and went to pour them both another. When he returned, he pushed the brandy into his hand. "When her mother died, she ran away. She was all of eight years old. A charming minx, full of fire and charm. She could not bear it that her mother had gone from her. They had a special relationship. They made bread together, wrote stories together. Rode out, my wife on her horse and Lily on her pony. When I told

Pierce and Lily that their mother was gone, she shed not a tear, but ran to her room. That night, she snuck out of the house. We were beside ourselves with worry she'd been kidnapped, taken by one of the sailors who roamed the waterfront, chained upon a ship in the harbor. But I found her a day later in my warehouse on the Baltimore docks. She'd taken coins from her own little purse and bought herself oranges and a loaf of bread. She'd taken her old blanket from her bed, too. So she knew where she was going, what she was doing and why."

If that was meant to make Julian feel better, it didn't. Panic snaked through him. "If she's not here with you, where do you think she is?"

"I doubt she's with Pierce and Ada in Biarritz. They would have told me."

"Where is Marianne? In Biarritz? Here? She would know."

Killian stared at him. "Marianne is not here, either. And I assume you did not write to your friend, the Duc de Remy?"

"Why?" More bad news was coming. Julian could sense it in the man's cool black gaze.

"She lives with him. Against my wishes." Killian's disapproval drew out the Irish scrapper in him.

Julian had always hated opposing this man. "I have to find Lily. I'll visit them. Ask for her."

"Do that, but I was there last night. Unannounced. We had a row. Lily is not with them, I tell you. I would have seen her."

Killian was very protective of his charges. All loving, all encompassing. Julian was a pale comparison to the dedication of Lily's father. It stung him to admit.

"Lily's not with you. Not in Biarrtiz. Not with Marianne." He thought of one last terrible possibility. "Would she have returned to America?"

≈

Phillip Leland lived in a town house in Queen Square. His home, once his parents' abode, was a respectable red brick with neat white trim. Julian had never been here but as he looked at it now, it was a stately house for a bachelor of the legal profession. It stood on a quiet expanse of genteel respectability, except when a friend drove up in a traveling coach at five-thirty in the morning and banged upon the broad oak door like an escaped inmate from Bedlam.

A bespeckled man, most likely Leland's man of all work, yanked open the front door.

"Yes, sir? Yes, sir! May I 'elp you?"

"I'm here to see your master." Julian removed his hat and handed over his card. "Immediately."

The man adjusted his glasses to read it. "Sir? Oh, un. Your Grace. Yes, well, sir. Right away sir." And off he scrambled down the hall while Julian let himself in and closed the front door.

Upstairs, the servant created a commotion and within minutes, Phillip Leland descended the wooden stairs. He pulled tight the sash to his navy brocade dressing gown and ran a hand through his wild golden hair. "Your Grace? What are you doing here?"

"I need to talk to you. About Lily."

"Lily. Certainly. Lily." He blinked, still half asleep, having trouble making sense of Julian's words.

"My wife, Leland."

That spurred him to action. "Of course. Come with me. The parlor. Jenner?" He spoke to his man who stood in the shadows. "Get cook to make us coffee."

"Aye, sir." And off the man went.

"I've no time for coffee."

Leland took in Julian's attire. Yes, he must look a mess,

traveling like a banshee from Paris to Calais, bargaining for a spot on the next steamer packet to Dover. Arriving in the middle of the night and catching a public conveyance up to London. Unable to wait for the next train. Unable to bide his time when he had to find his wife.

"What can I help you with, Your Grace." Leland indicated the sofa.

Julian paced and refused the offer. "Lily. Tell me, Leland. What kind of money does she have?"

"Sir?"

"What I mean is, what funds might she have that she could buy passage to New York or Baltimore?

"She does have her own pin money, via the marriage settlement."

"Did she access it recently?"

Leland blanched.

"So she did." Julian breathed in relief. "How much did she take?"

"I don't think it appropriate that I tell you."

"Why not? Did she forbid you to do so?"

"No, sir. Not forbid me."

Now he was furious. "Well, what is wrong with telling me what she took the money for or how much?"

"Because, Your Grace, it was to be a surprise."

"A surprise?" *Was Leland insane?* "Hardly that, man."

"She said she'd tell you in her own time."

Julian did sit now. Puzzled, he sank to a chair. "Phillip, I'm at my wits end. I need to find my wife. She's gone too long and I fear if I don't find her soon, she'll be gone too far for me to ever get her back. She's not at Willowreach. She left there weeks ago. She's not in Paris or Biarritz. If she's returned to America, I must follow her. So do tell me. Did she ask you to give her enough money to buy passage home?"

"No, sir. She did not."

His last hope drained out of him. He'd lost all that kept him sane. He wanted to scream. "Might you have any idea where she might have gone?"

"I do, sir." The man attempted a small smile.

"Where?"

"Your Grace, have you ever been to Tipperary?

Traveling to Ireland had never been a journey Julian considered. The estate his grandfather had purchased more than five decades ago had been an afterthought to both that man and his son, Julian's father. To a great extent, for him also. As he rode from the port of Rosslare inland to Tipperary, he admired the beauty of the green land. Marveled at its potential and at his wife's bravery to come here alone to a strange country.

He'd hurried as quickly as possible from Paris back to London, then south to Willowreach and north to Broadmore. The materials he'd purchased in London would arrive by messenger this week. The improvements he'd ordered to Willowreach and Broadmore would be finished, he was assured by his tenants, by the time he returned with his wife. Or so he hoped.

He pressed his fingers to his temples, the stress of the past weeks causing a royal headache. Part of his problem was this blasted coach ride. The directions he'd given the driver were rough, but they were the ones Leland had given to Lily. She'd confirmed her arrival in a letter to the lawyer more than two weeks ago. So Julian trusted that the directions were useful. Would that his words were useful to get his wife back.

Showers beat upon the roof of the coach at erratic intervals. Such intermittent rains were a pleasant change from the downpours they'd suffered in England in the spring and early summer.

The house he saw from the road was a simple Georgian, whitewashed brick in need of a clearing of the brush in the yard. The stone lane to the house looked newly laid and raked, an improvement Julian credited to his wife.

He climbed down, waiting for the driver to deposit his valise and the other leather bag he carried. His valet Pendley he'd left in Waterford this morning. For this journey, he wished to go alone.

He strode up to the front door and knocked. No one answered. He tried again.

This time, a lady called from inside. And a woman pulled open the door to him.

It was the chambermaid whom he assigned to Lily when she left Broadmore weeks ago.

"Your Grace?" She bobbed a curtsy. "M'lord, we did not expect you."

"I am aware. May I?" He indicated that he had luggage and wished to enter.

She pulled the door wide. "Oh, yes, sir. M'lord. Sir. Come in."

He picked up his cases, stepped inside and put them down. The house smelled of beeswax and bleach. The wooden floors were clean if scuff-marked and dull. The paint upon the walls could use a new coat. But the house had the charm of the Regency era with soft green upholstery to the salon and white lace curtains floating against ivory draperies at the floor-length windows. His wife had been at work here.

He fingered his hat.

"I can take that, m'lord. Gloves, too. Ah, we 'ave no butler, sir. No footmen. Beggin' your pardon."

"No need of that. What is your name?"

"Lucille, sir." She bobbed again, nervous and glancing

backward to the far side of the huge foyer. "You want Her Grace, I'm sure."

"I do. Please announce me."

"Ah, well, sir. She's not 'ere."

No? Where has she gone? "Where might she be, Lucille?"

"Down at the cottages, sir. I mean, m'lord. She goes every afternoon. We've a lady at 'er time, sir."

It took him a moment to realize the Lucille told him a woman was in labor. "I see. How far away is this cottage? May I walk?"

He would not wait for Lily to return. He understood women could take days to deliver a baby.

"Oh, yes, sir. A short trek." She smiled, relieved to show him the way and not deal with him any longer. "I can show you."

"Please." He picked up the small leather satchel and followed her.

She led him to the back of the house, down the back servants' stairs and out the door to the kitchen garden.

"Down this lane, half a mile. All our tenants live there. You'll find her. Ask for her."

"Thank you. I will." And off he set, nerves jumping as he took the narrow lane round a bend and into a clearing. Five, six cottages, white with thick thached rooves stood together. And from one came the soft moan of a woman at her task of birthing her baby.

He paused outside the cottage, at once shy of intruding in a private matter.

The door was thin wood, bright blue. He gathered his gumption and knocked.

The door fell open and there she stood.

Her hair caught up in a pile upon her head, she was fresh-faced with pink cheeks and inquisitive clear blue eyes. She put a hand to her throat. "Julian."

She looked hollow-eyed, the only sign that she might have tended her patient all night long.

No matter her weariness, the sight of her refreshed him like a cool swim on a hot day.

But seeing him did not elicit any emotion in her save surprise. She examined his features, his clothes. "How did you come?"

"The steamer from Portsmouth. Coach from Rosslare."

She pivoted to look back into the dark interior of the cottage. "Give me a minute."

He nodded and she shut the door upon him.

He turned his face to the sun, hoping for guidance to utter the right words to make her return to him.

When he heard her open the door, he was astonished to see her lead a young girl by the hand. The child was two or three years old with a riot of strawberry-blonde curls and piercing gray eyes.

"This is Deirdre," she introduced the child. Her chubby cheeks were tear-stained and her eyes red. "Come outside for a bit, Deirdre. She needs to stay with me."

"Of course."

"Julian, I wonder if we shouldn't wait for a conversation until after Deirdre's mother gives birth. I don't want to leave her. She requires someone to soothe her. You understand." Her blue eyes widened meaningfully and he realized that at the moment, his needs were less important than the woman inside that cottage.

But he was also struck by how commanding his wife sounded. No ingenue stood before him. No young bride eager for her groom's approval. But a woman who took her own power. "I do. We don't have to talk right now. I'm here at a difficult time."

"If you return up to the house, I'm sure Lucille will see to your needs. Tea? Brandy? A luncheon, perhaps?"

"Thank you, yes."

"And there's a cistern in the ceiling above the master's dressing room. Do pull the lever and enjoy a bath, if you wish. The water might not be very warm, but the sun beats down through the window upon the tub and makes it enjoyable."

That Lily would offer him this in her own room was a kindness he savored. "I will. I brought this for you. Perhaps there's something in here that you'd need now."

He put the leather satchel into her arms.

"What's this?"

"A gift." He gave her a smile and to the child, a small wave. "Until later."

The hall clock chimed nine when Lily made her way through the house to the foyer. She was bone tired, the ordeal of the ten-hour long labor and breach birth of a boy sapping her of strength. Julian's leather case in one hand, she dropped it to the first step of the landing, not knowing what to do with such a marvelous collection of medical instruments and devices. He'd paid a lot of money for them. The very best, she could tell by the exquisite cut of the steel. Honored, humbled by his thoughtfulness, she was overwhelmed too by the fact that he'd found her.

And that he'd come to her.

That gratified her even as it made her question what he meant by appearing on her doorstep. The medical case was a superb gift but it could not compensate for what she truly wanted from him.

And she wondered if he even knew what it was her heart required of hm.

This time, she must tell him.

This time, he must tell her if he was capable of it.

"Is she safely delivered?" Julian's grave words enveloped her.

She turned.

He stood in the entrance to the salon. In a light blue waistcoat and white shirt, his dark hair tousled, he was a heart-warming sight.

"Yes. A healthy boy. He was breach. I had to turn him and it was not easy for her."

"I'm sure you were a help."

She noted how weary he looked, even in the faint moonlight streaming through the windows. "You waited for me."

"I could not sleep. I came to see you. Talk. There is no rest for me until I do."

She bit her lip. "I am so tired, Julian. I doubt I can do this tonight."

"Please hear me out. I have rehearsed this so often to myself that if I don't say it soon, I'll be quite mad. You needn't decide anything tonight. In fact, I wish you wouldn't. But listen to me. Will you?"

She nodded and walked around him into the salon she loved. In daylight, the room seemed a continuance of the lovely green of the countryside. Light and gay in sunshine, the room in moonlight had an ethereal quality that spoke of sighs and kisses. How often had she longed for Julian here to embrace her and tell her he adored her?

She sat in one of the sumptuous chairs by the fireplace. She looked up at him and waited.

He inhaled. "Do you like it here in Ireland?"

Happy for the reprieve not to delve into their conflict, she looked around the room. "I do. The house, the land, the tenants are—were a boon to me when I arrived. The house was a shambles. We cleaned it, though it needs more. The stove in the kitchen must be replaced. The floors could do with a proper buffing. As for the land it's rich, but we need to improve the farming methods. The tenants had an old pony that died. They couldn't plow. I bought a Connemara at the Tipperary fair a few weeks ago. She's a sweet bay two years old and we should see good results from her."

He stared at her, silent, unmoving. "I miss you."

His words filled the room. Deep bass sounds of despair and longing. She should be happy.

But she caught back a sob. "I missed you, too."

He went to his knees before her, his hands crushing hers. "Come back to England with me, please."

"Oh, Julian." She fought for her dignity and no tears. "I like being the lady of this manor."

His face, dearer to her than any other, went lax. "I made mistakes."

"Not many," she told him in all truth.

He frowned. "I failed you."

That she would not argue.

"Allow me the chance to show you I am changed. I am a better man. Your man."

This was not a declaration of love. But then, what would she have done if he had said it here and now? Words were no proof that he'd changed. Did she owe him the opportunity to do more?

He squeezed her hands. "Come to England with me. I've many things to show you."

"I wanted to show you that I was worthy of you. That I could be a wife, a marchioness, even a duchess to be proud of."

He raised her hands and kissed each one. "You did. I failed to show you I could be a husband you would love."

That was not true. She had loved him for many months. Unsolicited, she had given him her heart and trusted him with her devotion.

All she had ever wanted was to have it returned.

"You needn't promise me to remain," he said at last, his eyes cast downward at her hands. "Come for a month. Return here if you wish. Or go anywhere. A month. Then decide to stay or go. And if you want to leave, I won't stop you."

CHAPTER 18

*T*heir journey to England was a week in which Lily fought with herself minute by minute. In her small home in Tipperary, she'd been happy. Or perhaps satisfied was the more appropriate word. She enjoyed the people, hard-working, quiet and devoted to their families. If she brought them a new measure of prosperity with better seeds, the Connemara pony and medical care, they brought her a renewed contentment in the simpler life of a rural village. It was that she had missed of Texas. That she wanted to enjoy wherever she lived.

She took the staircase down to breakfast the morning after their arrival. She'd slept soundly and alone. Since Julian had appeared in front of her in Ireland, they'd not shared the same bed. He did not ask. She did not offer. There was much that must be said and done if they were ever again to be lovers.

She strolled into the dining room, the footman Finch fighting a smile at her appearance, the ancestor on the wall above him still stuffy and much too pretty for his own good. And at the head of the table sat her husband in his morning jacket and soft white shirt. The handsome devil she'd married made her heart jump with desire.

Julian stood, pushed back his chair and pulled out her own.

She hated the formality of it, but she understood his need to do it.

Finch poured her coffee and Julian regained his seat, then folded his morning paper.

"Did you sleep well?"

"I did." *Our big bed is the most wonderful furnishing in this house.* She grinned at her own thought.

"What? You must share."

She rolled her eyes at him and cast a sideways look at Finch. "Never."

"Would you like the paper?"

"Not today. Maybe not for a long time. I enjoyed being blissfully ignorant of politics while I was away."

"Finch, please give me a selection from the sideboard, would you?" She enjoyed simply sitting here, looking at the house through the prism of her Irish perspective.

She and Julian remained quiet while the footman served her.

"Thank you, Finch," Julian said. "I'll ring when we're finished."

On their journey, she had asked about the health of her own family. Julian had recounted his conversation with her father and she had written to him to assure him of her health and safety as well as her return to England with Julian. In that week, she not asked about his family. Now she felt ready to learn.

"How is Elanna? Have you seen her?" She sipped her coffee.

"Once a few weeks ago. She is the same."

"Unhappy."

"And resentful of her need to marry."

"We could hope Carbury changes."

Julian's mouth turned down. "He is not motivated."

As a topic too close to their own circumstances, Lily let that pass and put her attention to her eggs. "And your mother?"

"I have not seen her. Have not called upon her and she has not come here."

At another impasse, she let that subject slide. "And what of the tenants who were ill? With the warmer weather, I hope they've improved."

"They have. I thought after we finish eating, we'd go visit them. What do you say?"

Minutes later, they left the house to walk down the lane. Along the way, she saw Docker and his two sons working in the stable block.

"I'd like to say hello," she told Julian, took a few paces to the right and waved at the men. "Good morning, gentlemen. Nice to see you."

All three doffed their hats and welcomed her.

Docker cast Julian a sideways look and a question. He'd talked to his master groom last week, asking that he notify him at once when the item arrived that he'd ordered from the saddler in Ashford. The man had delivered it early this morning and Julian weighed when would be an appropriate time to reveal it to Lily.

She struck up a conversation with the three, her knowledge of horses apparent in her questions and comments.

"Shall we ride later?" she asked Julian when they had bid the men good day and continued down the lane.

"Yes."

"After sunset?"

He nodded. His gift waiting for her in the stables was not

as grand as the one he hoped she would like down in the village.

There, eleven of his tenants lined the lane to greet her. She'd won a place in their hearts when she'd nursed them and they hadn't ever had such assistance from his mother nor, he would guess, from any other Duchess of Seton. Lily greeted them by name, something he was learning to do.

"We're glad to see you, Your Grace. We missed you."

"We did," called another.

A girl of six or seven ran forward with wild flowers in her hands.

"Mabel," Lily said, "thank you. These are lovely. Did you pick them yourself?"

The child nodded, her long brown braids bouncing on her shoulders.

"And how is your mama, Mabel?" Lily winked at the lady who stood beside her. "Is she better?"

"She doesn't cough. Me not ever."

Lily giggled and took the flowers into the crook of her arm.

"Will you come inside, Your Grace?" the girl's mother asked Lily with a twinkle in her eye. Julian had planted the idea that it should be one the tenants who revealed his surprise. After all, the gift was theirs and Lily's more than his.

"Wasn't this a deserted cottage?" Lily looked at each of the women and then at Julian. "Isn't it?"

"Not any more, m'lady. Come along."

He remained outside. But he heard Lily gasp and laugh. The sound, melodic and bright, was music to him, a favored song revived from his memories of her.

He turned on his heel to stroll into the woods while his wife whooped with joy at her surroundings.

Heedless of his wanderings, he soon found himself back at the stables.

"My lord?" Docker called to him, a hand to his brow to shield from the sun. "Will you show her today?"

"Maybe. She's in the pretty cottage. They're with her. Laughing."

"As they should be, sir. It's fine thing you've done there."

"I think so. I'm back to the house. My wife and I will come down later for a ride after dinner." Nervous as a child called on the carpet, Julian left the stables.

Half way home, he heard her call to him.

"Julian! Julian?" Lily shouted to him and he turned to see her, her skirts in her hand, running up the lane like a child.

Her glossy black hair had fallen from her pins. Her cheeks were red. Her beautiful blue eyes danced, alight with glee. Before him, she glowed. She caught her breath, a hand to her chest. "Julian, what you did! It's marvelous."

"You like it? Think it's complete?"

"Oh, heavens, darling, it's the most fabulous canteen I've ever seen. You've thought of everything. Ether and iodine. Bandages and plaster. Needles."

"I'm sure you'll need more. More of everything."

"Eventually." She reached for his hand. "Thank you. How did you think of this?"

"That was easy. I tried to think as you do. About others. About what you can give them of yourself."

"You've spent a fortune."

"I'm shocked at how affordable it all was."

"After the medical kit for Tipperary, this is an extraordinary gift, Julian."

"There is another kit just like it in your bedroom for the infirmary here."

She sucked in her breath.

"And another at Willowreach, along with a duplicate of

this infirmary. I wanted you to have the best that was possible wherever you went. Wherever you go."

"I'm enormously grateful." Suddenly, she seemed sad and took her hand from him. "I know they are too."

"Their health is mine." *Your joy is mine. And your lack is my despair.* He had to walk away. He couldn't bear to remain and see her struggle for words.

He'd failed her.

Again.

"Julian, wait!"

He halted. Fresh misery washed over him. He had to stop hoping for her change of heart.

She took his arm and pulled him around. "I am truly overjoyed with your gift. I never expected such a superb facility."

"Don't go on, Lily. I can see it doesn't matter. It doesn't change anything."

"But it does." She sounded conciliatory.

He shook his head. "I wanted you to see how I welcome who you are. What you are. That whatever you want to do with your days is the way you should live your life. That I love you as you are. Not as I thought I wanted my wife to be. Not as others thought you should be. But you."

She seized his hand.

His heart cracked in two. "I loved you from the start. The day in the Rue de la Paix. The night at the opera. The house party at Carbury's. I couldn't stay away. I tried. God knows, I didn't want the shame of marrying you or anyone for their fortune. I told myself I was better than that. More noble. And I nursed my pride. But when it came to you, I loved you in spite of your wealth and your father and even the machinations of my own. I would have married you if the devil himself had warned me off." He sank a hand into the wealth of her silken hair and she flowed against him. "I love you, but if you cannot bear me and you wish to leave, do it."

"And if I would never leave you?" she asked on a thread of sound. Tears stood in her eyes.

"Wouldn't you?"

She rose on her toes to bless his lips with hers. "I love you, Julian. I've waited so long to tell you. Denied you my own declaration and it killed me. I needed you to love me and I couldn't bear that you might not."

He cupped her jaw and examined what truth he saw in her lovely blue eyes. "You'll stay?"

"You love me. Oh, Julian, how could I ever go?" She kissed him, once and again, and he scooped her up in his arms to kiss her back.

As he tasted her lips, his heart was sewn up with the balm of her own declaration. "You won't leave me again."

"Never. Wherever you are is where I must be."

DARING WIDOW, A NIBBLE OF
BOOK 2

September 11, 1877
Rue des Abbesses
Montmartre
Paris, France

*R*emy skimmed his hand across the page. With an arc here, a shadow there, his impression of the line of dancers blurred, sharpened. A rush to capture their expressions and exertions in graphite flitted through his imagination. All were impressions to develop later when he was alone tomorrow morning as he drank his coffee.

He cocked his head, stopping to consider his sketch. Not bad for midnight and a liter of wine. He liked the idea of painting a chorus line, the women laughing, hoping for a few men to seek them out backstage. Remy had made one of these women famous and sought after last spring when he debuted a portrait of her alone in the dressing rooms, her long red hair falling to her shoulders, her hand to her pert breast. Pretty thing, she'd retired from the cabaret line to one *comte's* love nest in the Rue Moncey.

Remy was a connoisseur of bodies. Their form. Their function. The supple flow of muscles beneath the obliging skin. The toned ones that showed dexterity. The thin ones that showed their poverty.

The fat ones, the gross ones, whose gluttony had induced an effluence of flesh. The crippled ones. The children, too pale, too pocked to have ever been a heavenly cherub. The deprivation that deformed the perfection of their birth and left a wreck prone to disease and catastrophe. All showing the disease that could kill and the charm that could enchant.

Remy folded his foolscap sketch pad and tucked his graphite into the special pocket in his waistcoat that he'd designed so it didn't mark his clothing. He hailed the *garçon* to deliver another flask of *vin rouge* for him and his friend.

"No, don't," said Julian Ash, the Marquess of Chelton. "I'm ready to leave. You appear to be too."

"You're right. I'm done for tonight." Andre Claude Marceau, Duc de Remy, Prince *du sang*, and the English marquess had been friends for years. Fellow *bon vivants* since their mothers had introduced them eight years ago, they traveled the city together whenever Julian's business brought him to Paris. Though Julian was five years Andre's junior, they shared a view of the world that accommodated them as aristocrats with land and a greater desire than skill for administering it. That was why Julian applied his nighttime activities to gambling and Remy himself to the pleasures of molding bodies. In bronze or marble, graphite or pen, Remy called himself an artist. More than that, he styled himself a lover of bodies.

Human bodies. Strong or weak, lean or well-fed. A man, now and then. A child, less often. But women. Ah, the female of the species lured him as no other fascination. And tonight's bevy of women at this *cabaret* could appeal for perhaps another five minutes.

"I like Sabine there." Remy lifted his chin toward the woman who pranced onto the riser, her glossy cheap red satin skirts hoisted to her waist.

"Her charms are—" Julian choked on a laugh. "Abundant."

"*Certainly.*" Sabine, spicy dish that she was, loved to display her copious charms. In particular, she was adept at the new sensation in this northern arrondissement of Paris, the *cancan*. She drew an audience—and embellished her salacious reputation—by her acrobatic skill to kick high and yet keep time with the three musicians. More than that? Well, few could say her best offering was her long Gallic face. Nor her curvaceous legs. *Non.* What attracted attention to her was the thick curly black hair at the junction of her thighs.

Remy considered what it would be like to make love to Sabine. "She provides a good cushion for the romp, would you say?"

"I will pass, thank you." Julian downed his glass. "I bet you have too."

"You know me too well."

"Time to go to Tourelane's," Julian said.

"You've a desire to lose more money to the *marquis?*" Remy asked him. Julian was a gambler who had motivation to play, but not the persistent skills that could embellish his meager coffers.

Julian stood, straightening his white shirt collar and sapphire waistcoat. His dark good looks cut a fine figure in his black evening clothes. A few ladies cast their greedy glances down his elegant form. "A man must try."

Patrons were clapping in time to the raucous music, leering, laughing and pointing at Sabine and her distinguishing charm.

"Agreed. We can find better amusement."

Remy stood, waved their *garçon* over and pressed a few francs into his hand.

"*Monsieur le duc, merci,*" the waiter began. "You and *le Marquis* have not finished your wine."

"Take it for yourself, Henri. Tell the owner I said it is yours. With my regards." Remy put his top hat on his head, adjusting it to the wealth of tawny curls he could never seem to tame.

"Sabine will finish this number but we have a new dancer you may like better." Henri liked his money from Remy and wished to keep him here drinking.

"*Non,* Henri. *Le Marquis* and I have another engagement. *Excusez-moi !* We'll see you soon."

The man bowed with small deference. "*Merci, a bientôt. Merci.*"

"You overpay him," Julian remarked with a smirk. "Again."

"He's good. Knows what we like."

As Remy turned, an ostrich plume caught his eye. A flash of platinum hair followed. Pink lips. Skin of cream topped with cheeks that spoke of strawberries. The colors of her, the health of her, the wealth she wore were complements to the symmetry of her long winged blonde brows, the perfect oval of her face and the wide lush sweep of her mouth.

He paused. "Who is that, Henri?"

"*Pardon? Que?*" The waiter followed Remy's line of sight.

"The lady with the white feather in her hat?" Remy cursed the flickering gaslight that gave him nothing more of the champagne blonde with the expressive brows and kissable lips. "The one with the dark-haired woman in blue and the tall blond man? There."

"I'm certain I do not know, *Monsieur,* but I can inquire and—"

"*No, merci,* Henri. That—" That would be improper. And he'd learn who she was. Well dressed, expertly coiffed, she was graceful as she crossed the room and took a table with her escort and her companion. "That won't be necessary."

Julian had already made it to the door. Pushing aside the heavy red velvet drape covering the entrance, he raised his brows at Remy as if to ask what the delay was.

He'd just seen an angel.

But he'd find her again.

Watch her.

Memorize her.

Draw her.

He smiled. And if he were fortunate, he'd do more.

Buy DARING WIDOW now to continue the saga!

TRAVELS WITH CERISE

TALES FROM MY RESEARCH and TRAVELS WITH CERISE!

Dowries! How big could they be? How small?

As large as a father's generosity and prosperity or as tiny, a bride's dowry was a moveable feast. A few, such as that of the daughter of the Duke of Marlborough (c. 1719), could be as large as 6,000 pounds with a yearly jointure of 800 pounds. This plus property could signal quite an alliance that kept control of large swaths of land in the extended family.

A tiny dowry could mean the difference between life and death, providing food and clothing for an impoverished couple—and little for a daughter of that union.

Usually a father paid for the wedding, the party or breakfast if any, and the trousseau, if any. Wealthy fathers often gave their daughters ample new wardrobes and accoutrements for their new home. Less prosperous fathers gave little or nothing.

But the settlement of money and any other items such as land was negotiated by the bride's father with the groom's and perhaps the groom, himself.

After the wedding, the (hopefully happy) couple were to take a few days or weeks in a honeymoon. Afterward, they were to return and call upon certain others in town or in their social sphere.

Into the later decades of the Nineteenth Century, larger dowries became the mode and often a necessity for young aristocrats impoverished by mismanagement of their estates and by inflation. As the old century turns to the dawn if the twentieth, we see American girls with millions to offer their prospective grooms. Those marriages based on money were often very poor ones. With the advent of the Great War, much of this fell away. Young men wished to marry for compatibility. Young women did not wish to be sold into loveless marriages.

WHO IS CERISE DELAND?

Cerise DeLand

Cerise DeLand loves to write about dashing heroes and the sassy women they adore. Whether she's penning historical romances or contemporaries, she has received praise for her poetic elegance and accuracy of detail.

An award-winning author of more than 50 novels, she's been published since 1991 by Pocket Books, St. Martin's Press, Kensington and independent presses. Her books have been monthly selections of the Doubleday Book Club and the Mystery Guild. Plus she's won nominations and awards for Best Historical of the Year, Best Regency and scores of rave reviews from *Romantic Times, Affair de Coeur, Publisher's Weekly* and more.

To research, she's dived into the oldest texts and dustiest

library shelves. She's also traveled abroad, trusty notebook and pen in hand, to visit the chateaux and country homes she loves to people with her own imaginary characters.

And at home every day? She loves to cook, hates to dust, goes swimming at least once a week and tries (desperately) to grow vegetables in her arid backyard in south Texas!

Lady Fiona's Tall, Dark Folly, #1

Lady Mary's May Day Mischief, #2

Miss Harvey's Horribly Lovable Fiancé, #3

Lady Willa's Divinely Wicked Vicar, #4

Miss Weaver's Last Handsome Frolic, *#5*

Victorian Romances

Those Notorious Americans, Steamy Family Saga series:

Wild Lily, #1

Daring Widow, #2

Sweet Siren, #3

Scandalous Heiress, #4

Ravishing Camille #5

If You Were the Only Girl in the World, *#6, Winter 2022*

Let Me Call You Sweetheart, #7, *Summer 2022*

Naughty Ladies, Coming from Dragonblade Publishing to launch their new FLAME line of sexy romcoms!

Lady, Be Wanton, #1, *March 8, 2022*

Lady, Behave, #2, *May 3, 2022*

Lady No More, #3, *July 5, 2022*

Medieval erotic romances

Knights of Passion Series: Re-releasing soon!

At Her Service, #1

For Her Honor, #2

With Her Kiss, #3

Military Romances

You Were Always Mine, #1, 7 Brides for 7 SEALs

No Getting Over You, #2, 7 Brides for 7 SEALs

SEALs Going Hot, box set

Burning for Nero

Conquering Zeus

A Long Time Comin' (erotic romance)

Contemporaries

Is That a Gun in Your Pocket? (erotic comedic suspense)

Tall, Hard and Trouble, box set, romantic suspense

Santa, Cutie, Holiday Box set, December *2021!*

Always, A Collection of Romances, *Coming Soon!*

Sign up for Cerise's newsletter: <u>Cerise's Bon Bons</u>

And if you would like to read more by Cerise, she writes under her own name, Jo-Ann Power! Do sign up for her newsletter for tales of historical fiction and great mysteries!